"Treat yourself to some super reads
from a most talented writer."
—*Romance Reviews Today*

Praise for Anne Gracie's novels
To Catch a Bride

"Anne Gracie at her best, with a dark and irresistible hero,
a rare and winsome heroine, and a ravishing romance. Catch
a copy now! One of the best historical romances I've read
in ages." —Mary Jo Putney, *New York Times* bestselling author

"Swiftly moving . . . Appealing and unconventional . . . Will
captivate readers." —*Romantic Times*

"[An] action-rich, emotionally compelling story . . . It is
sure to entice readers." —*Library Journal* (starred review)

"There is so much I liked about this one, it's hard to find a
place to start." —*All About Romance*

"It was loveable and laugh-out-loud, full of heart and of
memorable and interesting characters."
—*Errant Dreams Reviews*

"A fascinating twist on the girl-in-disguise plot . . . With its
wildly romantic last chapter, this novel is a great antidote to
the end of the summer."
—Eloisa James, *New York Times* bestselling author

"One of the difficulties of reviewing a favorite author is
running out of superlatives. An Anne Gracie novel is guaranteed to have heart and soul, passion, action, and sprinkles
of humor and fun." —*Romance Reviews Today*

"A fabulous historical." —*Genre Go Round Reviews*

continued . . .

Praise for
His Captive Lady

"With tenderness, compassion, and a deep understanding of the era, Gracie touches readers on many levels with her remarkable characters and intense exploration of their deepest human needs. Gracie is a great storyteller."

—*Romantic Times*

"Once again, author Anne Gracie has proven what an exceptionally gifted author is all about . . . She gives life to unforgettable characters and brings her readers along for the ride in what has proven to be an exciting, fun, and heartfelt emotional journey. Absolutely one of the best romances I've read this year!" —*CK²S Kwips and Kritiques*

"Anne Gracie has created a deeply emotional, at times heart-wrenching, journey for these two people who must learn to trust one another with their deepest feelings and darkest fears." —*Romance Novel TV*

"Anne Gracie at her best, and her best is very good. She has a lyrical writing style reminiscent of Mary Balogh, and the talent to bring readers vibrant characters, potent plots, and sizzling sensuality . . . YUM!" —*Reader to Reader Reviews*

"A winner . . . A charming, witty, and magical romance . . . Anne Gracie is a treasure." —*Fresh Fiction*

Praise for
The Stolen Princess

"Gracie begins the Devil Riders series with a fast-paced and enticing tale . . . Captures both the inherent tension of the story and the era with her hallmark charm and graceful prose." —*Romantic Times* (4 stars)

"Anne Gracie's talent is as consistent as it is huge. I highly recommend *The Stolen Princess* and look forward to the rest of the series." —*Romance Reviews Today*

"Anne Gracie always delivers a charming, feel-good story with enchanting characters. I love all of Ms. Gracie's stories and *The Stolen Princess* is no exception. It stole my heart, as it will yours." —*Fresh Fiction*

More praise for Anne Gracie and her novels

"If you haven't already discovered the romances of Anne Gracie, search for them. You'll be so glad you did. She's a treasure." —*Fresh Fiction*

"A powerfully emotional, steal-your-heart story . . . This magical romance not only warms your heart, it raises your temperature, too. Brava!" —*Romantic Times* (Top Pick, 4½ stars)

"Have you ever found an author who makes you happy? Puts a smile on your face as soon as you enter her story world? Anne Gracie has done that for me ever since I read *Gallant Waif* and through every book thereafter." —*Romance Reviews Today*

"One of the best romances I have read in a long time . . . *The Perfect Waltz* is the book to share with a friend who has never read a romance novel—consider adding it to your conversion kit." —*All About Romance*

"One of those books that needs to be read from beginning to end in one sitting. Honestly, I couldn't put it down!" —*Romance Reader at Heart*

"Romance at its best . . . I was captivated by this story . . . Rush out and pick up this book—you won't be disappointed." —*Romance Junkies*

Berkley Sensation Titles by Anne Gracie

THE PERFECT RAKE
THE PERFECT WALTZ
THE PERFECT STRANGER
THE PERFECT KISS

THE STOLEN PRINCESS
HIS CAPTIVE LADY
TO CATCH A BRIDE
THE ACCIDENTAL WEDDING

The
Accidental
Wedding

Anne Gracie

BERKLEY SENSATION, NEW YORK

THE BERKLEY PUBLISHING GROUP
Published by the Penguin Group
Penguin Group (USA) Inc.
375 Hudson Street, New York, New York 10014, USA
Penguin Group (Canada), 90 Eglinton Avenue East, Suite 700, Toronto, Ontario M4P 2Y3, Canada
(a division of Pearson Penguin Canada Inc.)
Penguin Books Ltd., 80 Strand, London WC2R 0RL, England
Penguin Group Ireland, 25 St. Stephen's Green, Dublin 2, Ireland (a division of Penguin Books Ltd.)
Penguin Group (Australia), 250 Camberwell Road, Camberwell, Victoria 3124, Australia
(a division of Pearson Australia Group Pty. Ltd.)
Penguin Books India Pvt. Ltd., 11 Community Centre, Panchsheel Park, New Delhi—110 017, India
Penguin Group (NZ), 67 Apollo Drive, Rosedale, North Shore 0632, New Zealand
(a division of Pearson New Zealand Ltd.)
Penguin Books (South Africa) (Pty.) Ltd., 24 Sturdee Avenue, Rosebank, Johannesburg 2196,
South Africa

Penguin Books Ltd., Registered Offices: 80 Strand, London WC2R 0RL, England

This is a work of fiction. Names, characters, places, and incidents either are the product of the author's imagination or are used fictitiously, and any resemblance to actual persons, living or dead, business establishments, events, or locales is entirely coincidental. The publisher does not have any control over and does not assume any responsibility for author or third-party websites or their content.

THE ACCIDENTAL WEDDING

A Berkley Sensation Book / published by arrangement with the author

PRINTING HISTORY
Berkley Sensation mass-market edition / October 2010

ISBN: 978-0-425-23382-5

BERKLEY® SENSATION
Berkley Sensation Books are published by The Berkley Publishing Group,
a division of Penguin Group (USA) Inc.,
375 Hudson Street, New York, New York 10014.
BERKLEY® SENSATION and the "B" design are trademarks of Penguin Group (USA) Inc.

PRINTED IN THE UNITED STATES OF AMERICA

10   9   8   7   6   5   4   3   2   1

There are so many people to thank: at Berkley, my editor, Wendy McCurdy, for her patience; Judy York and George Long for the beautiful cover; and the Berkley copyediting team. Thanks too to my writing friends, Barbara S., Linda B., Kelly, and Trish, my Maytone friends for always being there, and Dave for disease and injuries, as usual.

In memory of my parents,
Jack and Betty Dunn,
who loved for a lifetime,
taught children,
and kept bees.

Prologue

Bath, England 1819

"*F*ind you a suitable wife?" The Honorable Nash Renfrew's aunt stared at him through her lorgnette. Maude, Lady Gosforth, enjoyed using her lorgnette. It magnified her gimlet eye horribly and usually made the recipient of the stare squirm.

Nash never squirmed. "If you would be so good, Aunt Maude."

She sniffed. "From all I've heard, you have no difficulty finding women. Even in St. Petersburg."

Nash didn't blink an eyelid. How the deuce had she learned of his activities in St. Petersburg when her principal residence was in Bath? But her contacts were legendary. It was why he'd asked for her help.

He said coolly, "It's not the same."

His aunt snorted. "No, it's not. And you also want me to arrange a ball for four weeks' time? A ball—at the beginning of the season?"

"If it's not too fatiguing a task, dear Aunt."

"Fatiguing? Of course it is! I'm too old to give parties anymore!" she said with an attempt to look feeble.

"I'm sorry, Aunt Maude. I didn't realize. You're in such blooming looks, you see . . . Never mind, I'll hire some-one—"

"*Hire* someone? You'll do no such thing. Events organized by *hirelings*"—she spoke the word with loathing—"cannot be anything but vulgar. I will try, somehow, to find the energy to arrange something—and to find you a suitable gel—but I warn you, Nash, with such short notice and at the beginning of the season with all the invitations already gone out, it will be the paltriest, most insipid affair."

"I know. I'm sorry." Nash had no fear it would be anything but magnificent. He added casually, "Can I prevail on you to send an invitation to the Czar of Russia's aunt, the Grand Duchess Anna Petrovna Romanova."

The lorgnette dropped. "The Czar of Russia's aunt?"

"She'll arrive in London a few days before the ball. She knows nobody in London and has requested my assistance. She won't mind a small affair." The grand duchess was as gregarious as his aunt and adored a grand fuss.

"A grand duchess?" Aunt Maude sat up, her eyes sparkling with ambition. She achieved a weary sigh. "How you do run me ragged, boy."

"I know." He assumed a penitent expression. With a Russian grand duchess, this ball would be the event of the season and his aunt knew it.

Nash had applied for leave to return to England for two reasons: to take possession of an inheritance, and to find a wife. The ambassador, knowing how difficult the elderly grand duchess could be, had granted leave on condition that Nash dance attendance on the old lady in London.

Nash, the ambassador said, had a way with autocratic and difficult old ladies. It came, Nash informed him, from a life-time of dealing with eccentric and autocratic aunts and great-aunts. One of whom was currently peering beadily at him through her lorgnette.

"So on top of balls and grand duchesses, you expect me to conjure up a wife out of thin air?"

"Not just any wife. The right sort of wife. I wish to make an excellent marriage."

One well-plucked brow rose. "Naturally, you are a Renfrew,

after all. It is what we do. But what, pray, is your definition of an excellent marriage?"

Nash had given the matter a great deal of thought.

Apart from birth, breeding, education, and intelligence, his bride needed to be not just well born, but well connected. She should have some understanding of politics but be dispassionate about "causes." She should be well trained in the management of large social occasions and have a certain degree of charm. Above all, she should be discreet, refrain from gossip, and be tolerant of other people's eccentricities.

As for children, he had no need of heirs and no interest in children. If his wife wanted one, he supposed he wouldn't mind.

"And I suppose you expect this paragon to be beautiful and an heiress, as well," Aunt Maude said caustically when he finished.

Nash gave her his most brilliant smile. "That would be delightful, best of aunts."

She softened visibly. "Pshaw! Younger sons!" Then she'd eyed him thoughtfully, with the gimlet look that all her nephews were familiar with. "Not interested in marrying for love, then?"

Nash raised an incredulous eyebrow. "Marry for love?"

"Your brothers did and they're both very happy."

"Gabriel and Harry weren't raised at Alverleigh with the daily example of my parents' great love before them," Nash pointed out. "If they had, they'd be bachelors still, like Marcus and myself."

"Gabriel and Harry were raised by your spinster great-aunt on whose pantheon of life men ranked below dogs and horses, and slightly above cockroaches," his aunt pointed out affably. "She did, of course, revere Renfrew blood, which balanced things slightly."

Nash shrugged. "My point is, they've never seen how destructive love matches can be. My marriage will be a carefully planned alliance based on shared ambitions, not on the murky byways of passion."

She snorted again. "A bloodless arrangement."

"That will suit me perfectly."

"But to go through life without love or passion—"

"Passion?" Nash cut her off. "According to both my parents, theirs was the passion of a lifetime. And when they weren't ripping each other—and our family—apart with their jealous quarrels, they were circling each other like randy dogs." Nash repressed a shudder. "I would rather dwell in . . . in the middle of an ice field than live like that."

"You're wrong, dear boy, but I won't try to change your mind. You have the legendary hard head of the Renfrew male, after all. I'll find you your paragon, but don't blame me if you expire of boredom after six months."

He shrugged indifferently. "Marriage isn't meant to be entertaining."

She viewed him with dismay. "But, dear boy, it is. Marriage should be a continuous adventure."

"My work gives me all the adventure I want. But in your terms, perhaps what I want is a bad marriage."

Aunt Maude shuddered. "Never joke about such things," she ordered him. "Never!"

One

The horseman appeared on the ridge, a dark silhouette etched against a seething bank of leaden silver clouds. He remained motionless for a second or two, surveying the scene below, then he commenced the descent of the hill in a slow, controlled canter. As he moved, lightning rippled across the sky in a sheet.

"How very apocalyptic," Maddy Woodford commented from the front stoop of her cottage. "Whoever he is, he knows how to make an entrance."

Lizzie Brown followed her gaze. "Gentleman," she pronounced, buttoning her coat.

Maddy laughed. "How can you tell? Farmers and merchants can ride fine horses, too. Do you know him?"

Lizzie grinned and shook her head. "Never seen him before, but he's cutting across country, in't he? And it's private land." She shrugged and rolled her eyes. "Only a gentleman would do that. Us ordinary folks don't take trespassing lightly. People get transported for less."

"I suppose."

"Bound for Fonthill or Whitethorn Manor, I reckon." Lizzie

added with a grin, "Mebbe he'll pass right by you. You could stand in his way, miss. A gentleman would have to stop. You never know, you might catch yourself a fine, rich husband."

Maddy snorted. "With my luck he'd be the sort who'd ride straight over me without even looking, and there I'd be—"

"In a right pile of muck!" Lizzie finished, and both girls laughed. "No, he'd stop, for sure, specially with you looking so pretty with your hair all fancy." Lizzie gave Maddy's hair a critical look. "I did a good job on that, I reckon."

Maddy put a hand to her newly coiffed hair. Lizzie was using her to practice. "You did a beautiful job, Lizzie. You'll make a wonderful lady's maid."

"I hope so, Miss Maddy. I'm sick to death of milking cows. And you'd make some gentleman a lovely wife, I reckon."

"As long as they don't find out I haven't a bean to my name." Maddy laughed. "Besides, I'm not convinced a husband is worth the trouble."

The laughter died from Lizzie's face. "You're right there."

Maddy shot her a guilty look. "Oh, Lizzie, I'm sorry. I didn't mean—" She'd spoken without thought. Lizzie had been married just four months when her husband went to town with all their savings and never came back.

Lizzie wrapped a scarf around her head and said in a hard voice, "Don't mind me; you're right. A pig in a poke, that's what marriage is. You never know what you got till it's too late. Trouble is what men are, all right, but rich trouble, well, that's easier to live with."

Maddy nodded in perfunctory agreement. She didn't agree. Rich trouble was the very worst sort. And avoiding it was why Maddy was here, living in a run-down cottage. But Lizzie didn't know that.

Nobody did. Maddy didn't dare tell a soul.

"I'm off," Lizzie said. "That storm'll be here in a few minutes. Hope I make it home without getting drownded. Thanks again, Miss Maddy. Dunno what I would'a done without you and your lessons. Uncle Bill is grateful an' all." She winked. "I'm the worst dairymaid he's ever had, but you can't sack family, can you? He reckons if you can teach me enough to get me off his hands, he'll keep you in milk and butter and cream and cheese for the rest of your life."

Maddy laughed. "I might just hold him to that. And don't call me Miss M—" But Lizzie was already running along the lane.

Maddy shook her head. She'd lost track of the number of times she'd told Lizzie to call her Maddy, but Lizzie never would, even though they were the same age, twenty-two.

You're a lady born, and I'm just an ignorant farm girl. Besides, if I'm going to be a lady's maid, I'd best get in the habit of showin' respect, Lizzie would say.

Maddy shivered. The storm was closing in fast and she had seedlings to save.

In the last few days, the weather had suddenly turned freezing. Spring buds had frozen on the branch, early daffodils had turned to ice, and worst of all, the bitter frosts had killed off more than a third of her tender spring greens.

She fetched some sacking from beside the woodpile at the back door and began covering her precious seedlings, laying it over a trellis of support sticks, protecting the tender shoots beneath.

She'd planted her first seeds at the age of nine. It was a delightful novelty then, but those lettuces, nourished to maturity and presented with pride to her grandmother, taught her enough to make the difference between starvation and survival.

Maddy didn't dream about vegetables then. It was all handsome princes and balls and pretty dresses and love . . .

Slowly the handsome princes of her dreams had become merely handsome gentlemen, and balls, well, they were impossible, too, for even if some unknown person sent her an invitation, she didn't have a pretty dress and there was no money for anything new.

These days she would settle for a decent man. A farmer or a tradesman, it didn't matter, as long as she could like and respect him, and he respect her. She wasn't a child any longer and life was not the stuff of dreams, but a constant battle.

She straightened, arching her back as she checked the protection over the tender plants. The seedlings would survive. They had to. Her little family depended on it. They would survive, too. It was just a matter of working hard and being frugal.

And luck. She looked at the dark, seething clouds.

The thunder of hooves told her the horseman was right outside her cottage. He was indeed a gentleman. Everything about him declared it, from his magnificent thoroughbred to his elegant, many-caped buff greatcoat, high boots, and stylish beaver hat. He rode easily, as if born to a horse.

Who was he visiting? Sir Jasper Brownrigg, who owned Whitethorn Manor, had died three months ago, and apart from the vicar, the only other gentlemen in the district was the squire, and he was more gentlemanlike than gentleman born—a fine distinction, but one she knew her father would have insisted on. A frightful snob, her late papa.

And look where your airs and graces have led us, Papa, she mused bitterly. *To a situation where a few old sacks, some seedlings, and a milkmaid with ambition are all that stand between your children and hunger.*

And between Maddy and Fyfield Place.

The horse took a wide ditch in its stride, then headed for the long, low, drystone wall. The wall stretched for miles, rising and falling with the rise and dip of the land, an unbroken gray border snaking across the landscape.

The estate maintenance had grown slack since Sir Jasper Brownrigg had grown old and infirm, and stones had been knocked off and not replaced. The horseman veered slightly, angling his horse toward a section of the wall where some of the coping stones had been knocked off. At first glance, it looked like the perfect place to jump, but—

"No, not there!" she shouted. "The boys' mud slide—"

Her words were blown away by the wind.

Under her horrified gaze, the horse hit the slick surface of the mud slide just as its powerful hindquarters muscles bunched to make the leap over the wall.

It skidded. Its hooves scrabbled frantically for purchase, and failed. The horse fell. Its rider flew through the air and smashed into the wall.

In the sudden shocked silence that followed, the world seemed to stand still. Then the horse scrambled to its feet, snorted, shook itself, and trotted away, seemingly unhurt.

The dark huddle at the foot of the wall didn't move.

Maddy was off and running before she knew it, wrenching open the stiff old gate with the ease of urgency.

The stranger lay in the mud, half curled against the hard stone surface of the wall. His head was at an awkward angle. So was one leg. He lay ominously still.

Maddy slipped two fingers inside the collar of his coat, between the fine fabric of his shirt and his warm skin. She closed her eyes, concentrating every sense on the tip of those two fingers.

Nothing. No beat, no movement.

She recalled her flippant comment about the horseman of the apocalypse.

No! He couldn't be dead. Please God.

She smoothed the tumbled dark hair back from his alabaster pale forehead, and . . . felt nothing.

Of course! The intense, damp cold had driven all feeling out of her fingers. She rubbed her frozen fingers until they burned, then slipped them back inside his shirt, praying for a pulse.

And breathed again.

Blood gushed from his head, spilling over her fingers in a warm sticky flow. She would not watch another person die . . .

"You're not going to die," Maddy told the man fiercely. "Do you hear me? I won't have it!"

He pushed at her hands, moving his head and legs restlessly. It was a good sign. He couldn't have moved like that with a broken spine.

She folded her apron into a pad, clean side out, slipped it under his head, and used the apron strings to tie it on. She checked his body for injuries and found a muddy imprint of a horseshoe on the glossy surface of his high black boots: the horse had trodden on his ankle.

Something stung her cheek. Sleet. "We need to get you indoors," Maddy told him, as if he could hear. But how?

She hooked her arms under the man's armpits. "One, two, three." She heaved.

With all that mud, he should have slipped along nicely, but he was a big man, lean but tall, and heavier than she'd expected. And his clothing was soaked and getting heavier by the minute. After several minutes of heaving, she'd moved him a few inches at most. "It's hopeless," she told him. "You're too heavy.

"The wheelbarrow," she said on a sudden inspiration and ran to fetch it. It was old, heavy, with a drunken front wheel, but it worked and that was all that mattered.

How to get him into it? She tried lifting him, but no matter how she tried—shoulders first, legs first, heaving and struggling—he was simply too heavy.

"Blast!" she said as her last attempt left them both in the mud with the wheelbarrow tipped over. Icy needles stung her skin. An idea formed. She pushed him into the wheelbarrow, side down in the mud, fetched some rope, and lashed his comatose body to the barrow.

Using the prop pole from the clothesline and a large rock, she levered the barrow upward, shoving with all her might. With a lurch, the barrow thumped upright, the man safely aboard.

Her muscles were burning by the time she wheeled him through the cottage doorway, barrow and all. She was beyond worrying about clean floors and tracking mud. The cottage was tiny; the ground floor just one big room, with a fireplace and table, and in the corner, a large bed built into an alcove, built at some time in the past for an invalid grandmother. It was Maddy's bed now, and her first instinct was to tip the man straight onto it. But he was sopping wet, bleeding, and covered in mud.

She pulled back the bedclothes and lined the nearest half of the bed with an old oilskin cloak. It would protect her bedding.

She wheeled him closer to the bed, untied him, linked her arms under his armpits, and heaved. The barrow tipped and she ended up sprawled on the bed in a flurry of mud and wet limbs, the stranger's head cradled against her breast.

"There, safe now out of the rain, at least," she murmured, smoothing back the thick, dark hair from his alabaster forehead. As still and beautiful as a statue of an archangel, she could barely tell he was breathing. Alive but cold, too cold.

"We'll soon warm you up," she told him. She wriggled out from beneath him and lowered his head gently. She piled fuel on the fire, pushed the kettle over the flames, and set bricks to heat. With a clean cloth and some hot water, she wiped his face clean. And stared.

Beneath the spattering of mud and blood, his face was elegant. Austere. A hard-edged, wholly masculine beauty. Dark lashes fanned over the pale skin. His mouth had been chiseled by a master, his chin firm and squared and dark with unshaven bristles.

She shouldn't be staring. His beauty would be no use to anyone if he died, she reminded herself.

"Now to get those sopping clothes off you."

She pulled off his fine leather gloves. His hands were long fingered and elegant, the nails clean and well cared for. Definitely the hands of a gentleman, she thought with a rueful glance at her own work-roughened paws.

She stripped off his waistcoat, then his shirt and undershirt. There were fresh bruises on his torso, but nothing serious.

Her mouth dried as she reached for a towel to dry him. The male form had few mysteries for her, not since Papa's accident and being left with two small boys to bathe and dress, but this was different. Very different.

Papa had been old and his flesh was flaccid and loose, his muscles withered, and the boys were like little skinned rabbits wriggling in the bath, skinny but still soft with the bloom of childhood.

This was a man, young and strong and in his prime.

Papa had smelled of sour old-man flesh, talcum powder, and the pungent ointment she used to rub into his back and legs for the pain. The boys smelled of . . . little boys and soap. The man in her bed smelled faintly of shaving soap and cologne water, and horse, and wet wool and . . . something else. She breathed it in but could not identify it—some kind of dark, musky man-smell. It should have repelled her. Instead she found it . . . enticing.

She breathed him in again as she dried his broad chest and firm-skinned, hard-muscled body, rubbing briskly with a rough-textured towel to get his blood moving. The scent of him settled deep in her awareness. She pulled a blanket over and tucked it around him.

Now for the breeches and boots.

The boots were the biggest problem. If his leg or ankle was broken, tugging the boot off could worsen the injury immeasurably.

They'd cut Papa's boots off with a razor. She hadn't thought twice about it then. These days she was much more sharply aware of the cost of things, and these boots were very beautiful and very expensive.

"But it has to be done," she told him firmly as she fetched Papa's razor. She was glad she'd brought it with them. It was sharper than any knife.

Frowning in concentration, she cut the boot from him, eased it carefully off, and peeled away his woolen stocking. The ankle was swollen and already coloring up. She couldn't tell if it was broken or not. With that head wound, she'd have to fetch the doctor to him anyway. She hoped to God he had money to pay, for she certainly didn't.

"Now for those breeches," she told him. "And I'd appreciate it if you didn't choose this moment to wake up." She glanced at his still face. Not so much of a flicker?

She tried to be brisk and matter-of-fact as she undid the buttons that closed the fall of his breeches. She'd scrubbed the boys in the bath, so a full-grown naked male would not be very much different, surely.

Besides, though she wouldn't admit it to a living soul, she was curious to see what a man, a young man in his prime, really looked like.

That was the French side of her, she knew; the side of her that always got her into trouble. Papa and his side of the family were so much more modest and reserved than Mama and Grand-mère had ever been. Almost puritanical.

No matter how sick Papa got, he'd insisted his valet, Bates, performed the more intimate tasks. Poor Bates. He'd loathed the task, but Papa was not one to be gainsaid. No matter how feeble his body grew, his will remained strong.

The buckskin was cold and clammy and clung tightly to the stranger's body as she pulled the breeches down over his flat belly, taking with them the cotton drawers he wore underneath, following the line of dark hair that arrowed to his groin.

It was a struggle, but once past his hips, she was able to drag them all the way down. She dropped them on the floor, picked up the towel, and . . . stared.

She swallowed. He was a stranger. She ought to look away,

to respect the poor man's privacy while he was insensible and helpless.

She couldn't. Her first truly naked man.

What a curious thing his manhood was, lying there in its nest of dark curls, a dark pinkish color, and looking quite soft. Not at all living up to the descriptions she'd heard. Smaller than she expected, too. Men always exaggerated.

She glanced at his face and with a shock realized that his eyes were open and he was watching her. Watching her watching hi—

"You're awake!" she exclaimed, hastily tossing the towel over him. "How do you feel?" Her cheeks warmed, but she wasn't going to apologize. She'd had to strip his wet clothes off for his own good.

For a moment, he didn't respond. His eyes didn't waver. They were very blue. She didn't think she'd ever seen such blue eyes.

"You had a fall and hurt your head. Can you speak?"

He tried to say something, tried to sit up, but before she could reach to help him, he fell back with a moan against the makeshift pillow and his eyes closed again.

"Don't fall asleep. Who are you?" She shook him by the arm. He didn't respond.

He was alive, at least, and able to move. That was something.

She swiftly dried the rest of his body, trying not to think of how he'd caught her staring at his privates. She was embarrassed, yes, but not ashamed, she told herself. He was injured, she was supposed to look.

Yes, to make sure he hadn't broken his thing, a little voice inside her commented. She ignored it. She finished drying him, and not knowing what else to do about his ankle, straightened it and bound it lightly with strips of clean cloth. Then she carefully rolled him over onto the clean, dry half of the bed and tucked the bedclothes around him.

Using tongs, she pulled the hot bricks from the fire, wrapped them well, and placed them close against his body. It was important to keep his internal organs warm, and the bricks would stop him rolling out of bed.

She checked the apron still tied around his head wound. There was no sign of fresh blood.

Despite her proximity to the fire, she was shivering. She should change before tending to his head wound, otherwise she'd end up with a chill.

She glanced at her unconscious guest. There was no place to be private here. She should take her clothes upstairs and change, but it was freezing up there. The children dressed and undressed in front of the fire all the time and only went up to bed when she'd warmed their beds well with hot bricks.

She hesitated. His breathing was steady, his eyes didn't so much as flicker. She'd risk it.

Keeping her back to him as a token of modesty, she stripped her wet clothes off, toweled her chilly flesh dry, and dressed quickly in fresh, clean clothes.

As she turned, the stranger's eyes closed. An involuntary movement or had he been watching her? It was impossible to tell. Her own fault if he had. She could have changed upstairs.

Besides, she'd watched him, hadn't she? Sauce for the gander, she told herself. Still, her cheeks burned and she hoped she'd been mistaken.

Now for the head wound. "This isn't going to be easy," she told him. "It's in an awkward position."

She collected everything she thought she might need and arranged it on the bed. Then she climbed into the bed, dragged him into a sitting position, and slid in behind him. Supporting him between her knees, she let him sag sideways against her, until his cheek rested against her breasts.

"Immodest, I know," she murmured as she reached for the pot of honey, "but you don't know and I won't tell, and besides, it's the only way to tend to this nasty wound of yours."

His hair was clogged with mud and blood. She washed the worst of it off, then carefully cut away all the hair around the wound. It looked nasty and jagged and blood still oozed from it but she didn't think it needed stitches. Thank God, she hated seeing flesh pierced with a needle, let alone doing it herself.

She washed the wound well with hot salt water—as hot as she dared—doing her best to make sure nothing remained in the wound to cause it to fester.

If the doctor were here, he'd dust it with basilicum powder, but she had nothing like that. She'd heard cobwebs were good for stopping bleeding, but spiders made her flesh creep and there was not a cobweb in the house. All she had was honey. Honey was good for burns and small cuts, and it was the one thing she had plenty of. Gently she began to smear honey over the wound.

*I*t felt like a bosom.

His body was like ice. And like fire. He throbbed unbearably from his head to his heels. He tried to move.

"Don't move." Soft voice. Bossy. Female.

He tried to open his eyes. Pain splintered through him. Nausea.

"Hush now." Cool fingers pressed him against something warm and soft.

It was definitely a bosom. Whose?

A cool hand cupped his cheek, held him still against the bosom. "I need to tend to your head wound." Her voice was soft, gentle. Low.

An excellent thing in a woman, he finished the quote in his head. A spurt of ironic laughter racked him. He bit back on the pain. Fool. He tried again to move. Agony.

Head wound? Was he going to die?

If he was, this was the way to go, his face buried in the fragrant depths of a bosom, gentle fingers soothing him, a soft voice murmuring.

This bosom, these fingers, this voice.

Whoever they belonged to.

He felt her shifting. Pain speared through him, nausea, then . . . blackness . . .

Two

"Maddy, Maddy, we found a horse!" The cottage door flew open and her eight-year-old half brother Henry rushed in, followed by his brother, John, three years older.

"It's a magnificent thoroughbred, Maddy, a stallion," John told her. "A bay with the most powerful shoulders and hocks. I'll wager he can jump anything—"

"We caught him!" Henry interrupted excitedly.

"*I* caught him," John corrected.

"Yes, but I helped. You couldn't have done it without me, you know you couldn't!"

John turned back to Maddy. "I had an apple core in my pocket and he took it like a lamb."

"I fed him, too; I gave him some grass," Henry told her.

"And then I took him back to the vicar's—well, where could we keep a horse? And the vicar said he didn't mind. I'm sorry we're late, but the horse was wet and so I had to unsaddle him and dry him off—"

"We *both* dried him off," Henry said.

"Hush, hush, not so loud," she said, laughing. "And where are your sisters?"

"Coming," John said vaguely, looking self-conscious. "They were behind us when we left." As the man of the family, even if twelve-year-old Jane was his elder, he was supposed to escort his sisters. "But they're so slow, Maddy, and fussing about the muddy path and their shoes and I wanted to tell you about the horse."

Maddy's lips twitched. "I know, love, and they're deplorably uninterested in horses, too. Now I have a surprise, as well, but—ah, here are the girls." Jane, Susan, and Lucy entered.

"Sorry we're late, Maddy," Jane, the eldest said, unwrapping small Lucy's shawl as she spoke. "But the rain delayed us, and then the boys found a horse and they would have to catch it and then take it back to the vicar's and fuss over it, and then the path—"

"It's all right, Jane dear," Maddy assured her with a hug. Twelve-year-old Jane, as the oldest child, took her responsibilities very seriously. She'd been the most obviously affected by the change in their circumstances; with no other help, Maddy had no alternative but to rely on Jane for much more than she wanted to.

She hated doing it. She knew what it was like to have your childhood drowned by responsibility. She was desperate to let Jane become a carefree child again but she couldn't manage it. *Yet,* she reminded herself.

"The boys are not the only ones who've had a surprise today," she told the children. "They found the horse. I found the rider."

There was an instant babble of questions.

"Hush, hush, you must be quiet and not disturb him."

"But where is he?" asked Susan, looking around.

"In the bed over there. He was badly injured."

"Can we see?"

"Yes, but you must be very quiet. The poor man has hurt his head very badly and loud noises will give him pain."

The children solemnly tiptoed over to the bed, and Maddy drew back the faded red curtains that covered the alcove, screening the bed from view, as well as protecting the occupant from draughts.

"How did he hurt his head?" Jane whispered.

"It was an accident."

"Why is he in your bed, Maddy?" Lucy asked.

"Shh. We must all speak very quietly because he's very sick," Maddy told her. "And that's why he's in my bed."

"But where will you sleep?" Lucy persisted in a gruff little voice she imagined to be soft.

"We'll talk about that later," Maddy said, having wondered about that already.

"He looks nice," eight-year-old Susan said in a loud whisper.

"Is he a prince?" Lucy whispered hoarsely. "He looks like a prince."

"Are you sure it's his horse that we found?" John sounded disappointed. No doubt he'd entertained the fantasy that the horse would be finders keepers.

"Yes, I saw him fall and the horse run off."

"He fell off his horse?" John's lip curled slightly.

"Everyone falls at some time," she reminded him. "And the reason this man fell was because his horse skidded on an iced-up mud slide some boys had made."

"Oh." John and Henry exchanged guilty looks.

"Yes, 'oh' indeed, and now you're going to have to run to fetch the doctor."

"Now?" John brightened.

"Yes. You can have something to eat first. I've made some soup—"

"I've already eaten," John said.

"Me, too. Sausages and mashed potatoes! And pudding to follow!" added Henry with glee.

"Mrs. Matheson gave us all supper, Maddy," Jane said apologetically. She, alone of the children, sensed how Maddy felt about receiving the charity of her kindly neighbors. They were none of them well-off.

But Maddy didn't want to burden the children with her perceptions. "Sausages? How lovely," she said warmly. It might be charity, but Maddy also knew that were she ever-so-wealthy, the vicar's wife would still feed the children. She was a motherly soul with no children of her own.

Besides, Maddy didn't feel ungrateful, just uncomfortable at having to receive when she had so little to give in return.

"If you're all fed, I want you to run back to the vicar's and ask him to send for the doctor. No, it's too far for you to go to the doctor's, John. By the time you get there, it'll be dark. Just tell the vicar and he'll send someone in the gig."

"Jenkins," Henry said. "He'll send Jenkins."

"Yes, so give the vicar this note to give to the doctor and then come straight home."

John hesitated. "Can I take another apple for the horse? One of the really old wrinkly ones?"

Maddy rolled her eyes. "All right, but only one." She used the old wrinkly apples for pies.

"I want to go, too," Henry declared. He eyed her hopefully. "You always say two heads are better than one."

She grinned and ruffled his hair. "Go on then," she conceded. "But come straight home afterward."

S he put the children to bed early that night. They were fascinated by the stranger in the bed, and it was all she could do to keep them from checking on him every three minutes. They'd tiptoed round the cottage and spoken in hoarse, exaggerated whispers, but she wouldn't put it past any of them not to secretly try to wake him up.

The doctor had been, examined the man's head wound, and pronounced her treatment of it excellent. He applied basilicum powder but had no quibble with her use of honey as a healing salve.

"Been used for generations," he said. "As for that ankle, all swollen up like that, I can't tell if it's a minor break or a sprain. Leave it bound. We'll know more once he wakes up."

"He will wake up, then?" She'd been worried he might simply fade away. It happened, she knew.

The doctor shrugged. "Hard to tell with head wounds. At any rate he can't be moved until he does, and so I'll tell the vicar." He saw her look of surprise and explained. "The good reverend wasn't happy with him staying here. He didn't like the look of his luggage."

"His luggage?"

The doctor explained. "He examined the contents of the portmanteau that was strapped to the horse—in search of the identity of the owner, you understand. It contained everything of the finest quality, which suggests the young man is a gentleman, and

I concur. But there were no documents or any clue as to his identity. The reverend was, however, shocked by the lack of a certain item, which he claimed revealed the character of the man."

"In what way?" Maddy asked, fascinated. "What item was lacking?"

"A nightshirt," the doctor said drily. "According to Rev. Matheson, a young gentleman who travels without a nightshirt is a rake." The doctor snorted. "But I can see his point. An unmarried girl, such as yourself, should not have an unknown man billeted in her home, unchaperoned. However, it's my considered medical opinion that to move the fellow now would endanger his recovery. Best to wait until he's conscious and able to sit up under his own power."

"I'll be all right," Maddy assured him. "As for chaperones"—she gestured to the children—"I have five. Not that I worry about such things anymore."

The doctor nodded. "Didn't think you were the missish sort. You've done a fine job so far. If the fellow lives, he'll have you to thank for his life."

He closed his bag and moved toward the door. "If you wake in the night, could you check on him? I don't think you need to sit up with him, but keep an eye out for any change. If anything worries you, anything at all, send for me. He's not out of danger yet."

"What should I do if he wakes?"

"It depends. If he's calm, treat him as you would any individual. But if he's restless, fevered, troublesome, or in pain, give him this." He handed her a small vial of clear liquid. "A few drops in warm water. Keep it away from the children."

Maddy nodded.

The doctor paused at the door. "We'll make enquiries about him. With any luck someone will claim him and take him off your hands as soon as he's fit to go. Let me know as soon as he wakes."

Maddy had promised. She had no interest in keeping the stranger any longer than she had to. As it was, he was going to put her out of her bed. She'd have to sleep with the girls and it'd be a tight squeeze.

Now the children were asleep, and Maddy made one last

check on the stranger. He'd barely moved. She changed into her nightgown in front of the fire, then hurried upstairs.

Cold draughts lifted goose bumps on her skin as she stood beside the bed where her little sisters slept. Earlier, she'd thought it would be a squeeze, but possible. Now, she wasn't so sure.

Children didn't sleep in straight lines. They sprawled—Jane and Susan on the outside, little Lucy in the middle. There was very little room.

But with a strange man in her bed, there wasn't any choice. Maddy slipped in beside Susan, where there was the most space. She wriggled and pushed and the little girls grumbled in their sleep. She had one leg in when Jane woke, with a half scream.

"Jane, what is it?"

Jane, grasping the bedclothes in fright, said in sleepy confusion, "I don't know. I think I was about to fall out of bed. But I never fall out . . ."

"It's all right," Maddy assured her, getting out of the bed. "Go back to sleep." She tucked them back in, kissed Jane good night again, and tiptoed downstairs. The boys' bed was even smaller, there was no chance of her fitting in there. She'd have to sleep on the floor by the fire.

T wo hours later, Maddy was still wide awake and getting crosser by the minute. She was freezing.

All that was left of the fire were a few pale coals. Fuel was so hard to come by she couldn't afford to keep it burning all night. Besides, the woodpile was outside, and she'd freeze if she went out there. Flurries of sleet beat against the windows.

She'd made a bed of hessian sacks then wrapped herself in a patchwork quilt and two blankets. But the stone floor was icy and every draught in every crack in the old cottage seemed to find a way directly to her skin.

And all the time the steady, rhythmic breathing of the man in her bed taunted her. She could hear it in the lulls between the rain and wind. He was warm. She was half frozen. He was sleeping—it didn't matter why. Broken head or not, he wasn't lying awake, cold and tired and miserable and cross. She was.

He was unconscious, for goodness sake. Insensible. Oblivious. What harm could he do? She sat up, seized the patchwork quilt, rolled it into a thick snake, then stuffed it lengthways under the bedclothes of the bed, against the body of the sleeping stranger.

Her own little Hadrian's Wall, to keep her safe from the barbarian. The unconscious barbarian with his beautiful mouth and dark bristles and his clean, well-kept hands.

He didn't move or make a sound, just kept on breathing steadily. She smiled. Some barbarian.

She slid into the bed. Heaven. It was warm from his body. Nobody would ever know . . .

Maddy slept.

*I*n the bleakest hour of the night, the man in the bed woke. He lay in the unfamiliar surroundings, trying to make sense of his situation. He had no idea where he was, no idea *when* he was, for that matter, except that it was nighttime. But what day, and what place—it was a mystery. His mind was a blank.

Not a blank, he corrected himself, more like a swirling fog, with people and events half glimpsed and then vanishing. Taunting him.

His whole body ached. His head felt as though it had been split open. He lifted a hand to it and frowned as his questing fingers discovered the bandage. He'd been injured then. How? And by whom? And been bandaged by . . .

A woman. At the heart of all the swirling thoughts and fleeting images, he knew there was a woman. With gentle hands and a soft voice. And the smell of . . .

He turned on his side and breathed in. He could scent her. Like a hound, he could scent that she was close.

He wasn't alone.

Who was she that she shared his bed? He closed his eyes. So many questions. So few answers.

He didn't care. She was there and that was enough. He moved closer and found something else in the bed. A long lump of cloth. Why?

He pulled it out and tossed it aside, then returned to the woman. She lay curled on her side, facing away from him, warm

and soft. He slipped his arms around her and drew her close
against him, curling his body to fit the curve of hers.

Her foot brushed against his leg. It was cold. He tucked her
feet between his calves and felt them slowly warm.

The nape of her neck lay exposed on the pillow. He lowered
his face to the soft skin and breathed in her fragrance.

It felt right. His hold on her tightened. She was his anchor,
the one solid thing in a shifting sea of taunting ghosts. The questions hammering at the inside of his skull slowly faded.

He lay with his aching body curved against hers, his mouth
just touching the fragile skin at the nape of her neck, breathing
in the scent of her. Gradually the rhythm of his breathing slowed
until it matched hers, and he slept.

*M*orning dreams were the nicest. In morning dreams,
Maddy woke slowly, letting her deepest wishes run
riot, spinning fantasies . . .

Her fantasy lover . . . Warm, strong . . .

Skin to skin with nothing between them. The heat of his body,
the hard, relaxed power of it curled around her protectively . . .
possessively. The warm weight of his arm . . . Legs entwined, his
brawny, a little hairy, pressing her calves between his . . . His
breath, matching hers, in . . . out . . . in . . . out.

She lay entwined with him in a soft, soft bed, sharing
warmth, skin against skin, sharing dreams and plans for the
day, after a splendid night of making love . . .

That part of the morning dreams were always a bit vague.
She had only the haziest ideas of what making love entailed.
From barnyards, she knew the mechanics and it didn't appeal
in the least. It looked ugly and brutal.

Mama said for men it was a necessity; for women, a duty
to be endured and the pathway to endless, heartbreaking child-
bearing. Which was even less appealing.

But from Grand-mère she knew it was a source of joy.

Grand-mère had discovered it late in life. She'd been widowed for fifteen years, with no thought of taking a lover or a
husband until Raoul Dubois, a handsome peasant with broad
shoulders and strong hands, had set her in his sights.

Maddy was thirteen and had witnessed the whole thing with amazed fascination.

To Grand-mère's embarrassment, Raoul had pursued her relentlessly, undeterred by her lack of encouragement, their difference in station, or even the difference in ages—all of which Grand-mère used to try to drive him off.

Raoul would simply shrug those big broad shoulders of his. And Grand-mère would eye them, sigh, then renew her defense. Her increasingly halfhearted defense.

"*Non!* It's unthinkable! You are a woodcutter, and I—"

"There was a revolution, remember? In France now we are all equal." His grin was ironic; he knew, everyone knew, that the class differences were the same as they'd ever been.

"My father would roll in his grave."

Raoul shrugged. "Fathers roll. It is their fate."

"But I'm years older than you!" Grand-mère would argue. "It's inconceivable!"

Grand-mère was born in the same year as the poor, martyred queen, Marie Antoinette, of whom they must never speak. In '93, the queen had been cruelly guillotined. She'd been eight and thirty, which made Grand-mère well past fifty.

Raoul was a widower, a man in his prime, just turned forty. "What are years?" he would say with a smile. "You are a beautiful woman, and I, I am a man. That is all that matters. I ask for nothing, not marriage, not property, only you, *ma belle*." And he would smile that smile that had showed Maddy a side to her grandmother she'd never imagined, blushing like a girl and fluttering indecisively.

It took Raoul two years, but he wore her down.

After Raoul and Grand-mère became lovers, Maddy learned that sharing her life with a good man—the right man—made all the difference in the world to a woman who'd lost everything. Grand-mère was a new woman.

The anger and bitterness faded. With Raoul in her life, she was full of joy and laughter and . . . verve.

Maddy would wake sometimes in the night or the early morning and hear them making love. The sounds had alarmed her at first, but seeing her grandmother's shining eyes in the morning, she knew that the sounds were misleading, that it was something wondrous.

At other times she'd waken and hear them lying in bed, talking, the light murmur of Grand-mère's voice and the deep rumble of Raoul's. It sounded so peaceful, so cozy, and the lonely girl she was ached for the time when she, too, could lie in a bed, talking quietly in the night with her man.

Raoul and Grand-mère had five happy years, until a falling tree took Raoul's life, and the joy left Grand-mère's eyes forever. She died within a year of him.

But she'd left Maddy a precious legacy: the knowledge that with the right man there was joy to be had in the act of love.

Men and women always lie, cherie, *even in bed, but in the act itself, there is honesty,* Grand-mère had said. *And with the right man . . . ahhh, bliss.* And she would sigh.

Maddy would probably never marry—she was too poor and had too many dependents, but somewhere, she hoped, there would be a Raoul Dubois for her.

At the moment, he only appeared in her morning dreams, faceless, nameless, wanting nothing, only her . . .

Oh, to wake every day knowing that whatever the day brought, she would not be alone, that whatever troubles they face, it would be together. And that come nightfall, in this bed, they could find joy together.

She didn't need a prince or a rich man. Just a man and a cottage to share it with . . .

A cottage . . .

The rent. The thought crashed into her consciousness like a boulder into a tranquil pool. Morning dream number 5,061 in smithereens, she thought with sleepy irony. Another day to face.

She stretched, then stiffened as she realized that far from having someone to share her problems, one of them was in bed with her right now.

And that the stranger was holding her breast, gently but firmly. Possessively.

She froze. "What are you doing?" she whispered. Ridiculous question. It was perfectly obvious what he was doing. "Stop it."

He didn't respond. His hand didn't move. He just kept breathing, slowly and evenly as he had all night. He couldn't possibly be asleep . . . surely?

Carefully, she prized his hand off her breast and pushed his arm back where it belonged. Turning cautiously in the bed, she looked at him.

His face was slack with sleep, his eyes closed, his lashes twin dark crescents against his pallor. He moved restlessly and shifted toward her.

She stiffened as his hand curved over her hip and held her. "What are you doing?" His knees bumped against hers, and he slid one brawny leg between hers and sighed. And relaxed again.

She watched him, hardly breathing, but he didn't move.

He was asleep, truly asleep, she realized. He didn't know what he was doing, just seeking warmth and comfort.

As she had been. Unconsciously enjoying his warmth, the feel of his body, and taking comfort in dreams.

Dreams helped.

She lay quietly, watching him sleeping in the morning light. His hair was thick, brown like the skin of a chestnut, and tumbled across his brow. She smoothed it gently back. He sighed but didn't wake. She stroked his forehead, running a fingertip over a few faint worry lines.

His brows were thick and darker than his hair, his lashes unfairly long for a man. The skin of his eyelids was so fine and translucent she could see each vein and blood vessel. His eyes, beneath the closed lids, were moving. He was dreaming, twitching slightly, like a dog. A pleasant dream, for his lips curved in a faint half smile and she found herself smiling back.

At least he wasn't in pain.

Lines radiated from the corner of his eyes, and on either side of the mobile-looking mouth was a vertical crease that would deepen when he smiled. A man who smiled often, she decided.

She liked that. Life without laughter was like a month without sunshine; you could survive, but there was no joy in it.

His chin was firm and nicely squared at the end. She trailed her fingers down the line of his jaw, enjoying the light abrasion of his bristles. She placed her palm across the strong column of his neck and felt the steady pulse beating, *thud, thud, thud.*

Over and over, her gaze returned to his mouth like a moth to a flame.

It fascinated her. It was, quite simply, beautiful. She'd never thought of a man's mouth being beautiful, but his was. Yet there was nothing feminine about it.

His lips seemed carved by a master sculptor, they were so clearly defined, so perfectly formed. She touched his mouth gently, running her finger lightly over his parted lips, tracing the shallow groove that ran down from his nose. She lingered on a tiny, silvery scar at the left-hand corner of his mouth.

When had that happened? How?

He sighed again and moved his mouth against her fingers, closing over one and sucking, gently. She froze. A ripple of sensation trembled through her, and she carefully withdrew her finger, feeling strangely moved. After a minute he relaxed again into his dreams, his breath soft and regular.

She stroked a lock of hair behind his ear. *What are you dreaming of, beautiful man? Are you lonely, like me?*

She dismissed that thought immediately. This man would never be lonely. He was too beautiful, too elegantly dressed, and what about those laugh lines? No woman could resist him.

No, he wouldn't be lonely.

But just now, he was alone and in trouble. And while he was, he was hers.

She bent and kissed him lightly on the lips. His lips were smooth, warm, unresponsive.

"I'll take care of you," she whispered and kissed him again. "You're not alone."

He lay there, asleep, locked in his own world, oblivious.

It was time to shrug off the false enticement of the morning dream, to get on with her life. The stranger was hers to care for, but not to keep. It was foolish to spin dreams around him. The moment he woke, he'd be off, back to his friends and family, leaving her without a thought. Alone again.

She couldn't remember a time when she hadn't been lonely. All her life people had depended on her to take care of them. First Mama, then Grand-mère, then Papa, and now the children. She didn't mind that so much—she was perfectly capable.

But it was lonely, always being the one who had to face the trouble, find the solution, battle the odds. And always alone.

She climbed out of bed. Thank goodness the stranger hadn't woken. She would have been mortified if he'd opened his eyes and found her . . . touching him. He wasn't her Raoul Dubois. He didn't even know she was there.

Yet as she went though her morning routine—rebuilding the fire, heating water, washing, dressing, starting breakfast—part of her remained strangely desolate. It was always thus, she told herself, waking from a morning dream. Facing reality.

Dreams helped. But sometimes, some mornings, they only underlined her loneliness.

"*B*ut Sir Jasper promised!"

Her voice—worried? angry?—woke him from a deep sleep.

A man's voice rumbled in answer, harsh, threatening.

He tried to sit up. Had to help . . . protect . . . Nausea swamped him. He fell back.

Fragments of conversation came to him in drifts. "Check the records. Sir Jasper and I . . . an agreement . . . He *promised*."

He knew her voice . . . somehow, but the sense of it . . . He couldn't work it out. Couldn't—damn it—remember.

He pressed his hands against his temples, trying to stop the throbbing, and felt bandages. *Bandages?* He closed his eyes. The voices faded . . .

Three

~

"*H*e's a prince," Lucy insisted. "And he needs a princess to kiss him and then he'll wake up."

"That's Sleeping Beauty, silly," Susan told her.

"Same thing," Lucy declared stoutly.

"No, because Sleeping Beauty is a girl and he's a man." Henry joined in. "And a man can't be a beauty."

"Why not?"

"Because he can't," Henry said. "Only ladies can be beautiful."

Maddy smiled to herself. She disagreed. This man was wholly male, and beautiful.

"I don't care. He's been sleeping for nearly two days, and nobody sleeps that long, so a wicked witch must have put a spell on him. And witches only put spells like that on princes and princesses. So someone needs to kiss him and break the spell."

"A princess. Whoever kisses him would have to be a princess," John said with authority. "And we haven't got any princesses around here, so it will have to be a bucket of water."

"No!" The girls were horrified. "Don't you dare throw water on him, John Woodf—"

"Be quiet, all of you," Maddy intervened. "John, stop teasing your sisters. The man isn't a prince, Lucy, just a poor man with a sore head, which is no doubt the sorer for having a noisy bunch of children arguing over him. Now stay away from the bed, all of you—and for heaven's sake, keep your voices down."

With guilt-stricken looks at the sleeping man, they tiptoed away from the bed, continuing the argument in whispers. Maddy hid a smile. They had been, in fact, remarkably well behaved.

The doctor had visited again that morning and examined him. "As long as his sleep is peaceful and there's no fever, there's nothing much we can do. Let him sleep as much as he wants. If he wakens in pain, use the drops I gave you yesterday. If he shows signs of fever, cool him down and give him this." He handed her a paper of powders. "And willow-bark infusion—small quantities, no more than four cups in a day. You have willow bark, I assume?"

She'd nodded.

"If the fever is any worse than when young Henry got sick last autumn, send for me. But sleep is the best medicine."

So she let him sleep.

It was raining and it was hard for the children to stay cooped up and quiet after a long winter spent mostly indoors. They'd read and reread all their books a dozen times, they'd played every game they knew, and they'd worked on handcrafts all winter. Now, having had a taste of spring, those pursuits and pastimes no longer held any appeal.

Especially when there was a fascinating and mysterious stranger sleeping in Maddy's bed.

The children weren't the only ones who were fascinated. Maddy couldn't forget the sensation of having woken in a strange man's arms, pressed against the full length of him. The full naked length.

The warm intimacy of his embrace, the feeling of his long, hard body pressed against her, the almost protective way his arms held her, stirred up . . . feelings.

Feelings she didn't want to have. Shouldn't have, not for a stranger who was just passing by, a man who might have fallen from the sky. Her very own fallen angel.

She dried his clothes, brushed the mud off them, and washed his shirt and undergarments. Everything was of the finest quality. His waistcoat was embroidered in rich, subtle shades of silk thread and lined with silk. His coat was tailored from the finest merino wool and fastened with silver buttons— real silver buttons—any one of which could support herself and the children for a month.

Even his hands were from a different world. She glanced down at her own, ruefully noting the bramble scratches and the work-roughened skin.

A lady is known by her hands, Grand-mère used to say. Grand-mère's hands were always beautiful. But Grand-mère hadn't done the rough work in the cottage and garden—Maddy had.

Maddy still did. Her hands were clean and strong and supported a family. They were nothing to be ashamed of.

Nevertheless, when she saw her own hands beside the long, strong, elegant fingers of the sleeping stranger, she felt ashamed.

Yes, mixing the reality of him with her morning dreams was foolish in the extreme.

"Henry, weren't you and John going to make boats out of those walnut shells we've been saving? Girls, I think you should make a new book for Lucy," Maddy told them. "Lucy can tell the story, Jane can write it out, and Susan, you can draw the pictures—"

In the depths of winter, Maddy had hit on the idea of getting them to write and illustrate their own books. It kept them happy and occupied and the books were much beloved and reread often by them all, even John's, which were exclusively about horses. And though Lucy could not yet read, she knew her own three books by heart.

"A story about a sleeping prince," Lucy said immediately.

"Why not a frog prince?" John grinned as his sisters bridled. "If I threw water on him, the man might turn into a frog prince. Frogs love water."

"Oh, you are so—" Jane began.

"Don't encourage him, Jane," Maddy said briskly. "Of course John wouldn't throw water on a guest—"

"I might if they don't stop going on about princes and beauties," John interjected. "Besides, the man's so hot he'd probably enjoy it."

"What did you say?" Maddy turned to John. "He's hot?"

John nodded. "Yes, I touched his hand and it's really hot. But Maddy, I wouldn't really throw—"

But Maddy wasn't listening. She flew across the room and placed her palm on the man's forehead. He was burning up with fever.

She grabbed a cloth, dipped it into cold water, and began to wipe his body down. It evaporated almost immediately from the heat of his skin.

"Is he sick?" Jane stood just behind her.

Maddy hastily dragged the sheet over the stranger's private parts. "He has a fever. Fetch me vinegar and some more cloths."

The children clustered curiously around. "Stay away from the bed, all of you. You can help me best by keeping out of my way and playing quietly." Not that noise would disturb him in this state, but she could do without the distraction.

She sponged him down with vinegar. She spread cold, wet cloths over his hot body, and watched them dry. As she worked to cool him down, she could hear the children playing.

"There's a lot of shells. We could make a navy."

"Once upon a time there was a girl called . . . called Luciella . . ."

"Two navies and we'll have a battle."

"Luciella? There's no such name."

"It's my story and I can name her whatever I like."

"The Battle of the Nile! Bags, I be Nelson!"

"No, I'm the oldest, I should be Nelson. You can be Napoleon."

"It's not fair! Why do I always have to be Napoleon?"

"Because you're shorter." The boys hurried off, wrangling about who was to command the as-yet-unbuilt fleet.

"Keep some shells for babies' cradles," Susan shrieked after them.

"Hussshhh!" the others all hissed.

There was instant, guilty silence. And then a small voice, "Did we wake him, Maddy?"

"No." She wrung out another cloth and spread it over his firm chest.

"I told you," Lucy said in a loud whisper. "He won't wake up until he's got a kiss from a princess!"

Maddy couldn't help but smile at the little girl's persistence. She wouldn't give up on the stranger, either.

Fever could enter a body through a wound. If it had, there would be putrefaction. She unwrapped the bandages and carefully inspected his head injury. It looked all right—red but not inflamed looking or puffy. And she couldn't see any putrefaction.

She sprinkled more basilicum powder on it, just to be sure and put a clean bandage over it. She lifted his head with one hand to pass the bandage beneath it with the other, and felt something wet and oozy beneath her fingers.

Another injury, one both she and the doctor had missed. Festering untreated since the accident. Swiftly she cut the hair away. A tiny, insignificant-looking wound, but red and puffy and oozing. And beneath the darkness of the hair, she could see the telltale red striations, like tentacles emanating from the cut. Blood poisoning.

She sponged the injury clean with hot, salty water, then laid a hot compress on it to draw out the foulness, as hot as she could bear. She mixed the contents of the doctor's paper in a teapot and fed him the medicine through the spout. She boiled willow-bark shavings to make a decoction.

Outside, the wind whipped at the trees. Rain spattered the windows in gusts. The boys sat on the rug by the hearth, sorting through the bag of walnuts, tossing broken shells into the fire, keeping the perfect halves, and eating any nut meat they found as they fashioned sails and masts for their navies of tiny walnut boats.

The girls were intent on their literary creations.

Maddy sponged the stranger's skin with vinegar and water, replaced the hot compress on the infected head wound, and fed him small quantities of willow-bark tea sweetened with honey and ginger. And prayed.

* * *

The day wore on. Maddy fed the children quick, simple meals, just soup, cheese on toast, and scrambled eggs, and in between tended to the sick man in her bed. Night fell. She put the children to bed and came slowly downstairs. She was exhausted.

She checked on her stranger. He'd tossed off all his bedclothes again and sprawled naked and unaware, taking up almost the entire bed. She put her palm on his chest. His heart beat rapidly under her fingertips, and if anything, his skin felt hotter. Had none of her efforts helped?

She sponged him down again. She was inured to his nakedness now; she knew every inch of his body. She fed him some more of the willow-bark decoction and put a fresh poultice on the wound. He calmed under her treatment and she was able to cover him again.

In a weary daze, she went about preparing her bed on the floor. She'd made up her mind that morning that she would not risk waking again with a strange, naked man curled around her, his bare legs intimately entangled with hers, and his hand on her breast. It was too . . . unsettling.

She spread the bedding in front of the fire.

He could come to his senses at any time, the doctor had said. There was no telling how long or how short it would be. Of course, that was before he'd come down with fever . . .

The bed curtains were closed, there wasn't a sound from behind them. She changed into her nightgown and sat warming her toes at the fire.

What if the fever worsened? If she were on the floor, how would she know he needed her?

What if he threw off the bedclothes again and the fever broke and he was naked and sweating and helpless in the chill of the night? He could catch his death.

There was no choice.

She bundled up the quilt to make it into Hadrian's Wall— a sop to propriety, and yet what mattered propriety when she'd sponged almost every inch of his naked body? Nevertheless she shoved it in ahead of her and slipped between the sheets.

* * *

hrashing limbs and feverish muttering woke her in the night. "No," he mumbled. "No, no." His head rolled frantically, and clenched fists flailed at the air, beating off some invisible foe. "No, no . . . You can't . . ."

Keeping a wary eye on the wildly flying fists, Maddy felt his skin. Burning up, hotter than ever. She sponged him down, murmuring, "Hush, hush, I'm here now," as she smoothed his burning skin with the cool moist pad. "You're all right now . . . Nobody will harm you."

He turned his face toward her voice and opened his eyes, staring at her blindly, his expression anguished. But the big fists unclenched and the hands slowly dropped.

She kept on murmuring soothing words and slipped her arm under his head. "Drink this; it will make you feel better." She slipped the spout between his lips. He clenched his teeth in mute refusal. She tried again, but he jerked his mouth away, sending liquid everywhere. He thrashed his head around, muttering a string of words that didn't make sense to her.

"You have to drink this," she told him. "It will bring the fever down from within."

Again he looked at her with that blind, tortured stare.

Her voice. He was responding to her voice. She didn't know who he thought she was, but if it worked . . . Murmuring soothing phrases, she tried again to make him drink. He clenched his teeth and shoved her hand away.

She could think of only one thing to do. She took a mouthful of the bitter-sweet liquid and, stroking his face gently, she pressed her lips to his. His lips parted instantly and she let the liquid slowly dribble in. He swallowed without hesitation and grabbed her wrist, staring at her mutely.

She took another mouthful of medicine and fed it to him the same way, then another and another, until she thought he'd had enough.

That exchange, so desperate, so intimate, had awakened something in her. The struggle was now intensely personal. He was hers and she would not let him die.

She fed him water and medicine through the night, slow mouthful by slow mouthful, kisses of life. She didn't know

how long it took, she was beyond caring about anything except
the man in her bed, but finally, exhausted, he lay back against
the pillows.

She pressed her cheek against his chest to listen for his
heartbeat, but instead, exhausted, she slipped into sleep.

She woke some hours later, in the cold gray light just before
sunrise, shivering with cold, her cheek wet. Was she weeping
in her sleep?

Not tears. Sweat. The fever had broken, thank God, thank
God. She pulled the bedclothes up around him, tucking him in
one-handed so he wouldn't catch a chill.

Weak with relief, exhausted beyond caring, she fell asleep
pressed against his body, her imprisoned hand still tucked in
his loose but unbreakable grip.

S he woke with a naked man wrapped around her. Like the
previous morning only . . . more so. His hand cupped her
breast again, only this time there was no nightgown between
his hand and her skin. His questing hand had found the opening. He sighed, his hand moved, and her nipple hardened
against his palm with exquisite sensitivity. Her mouth dried.

She ought to pull away.

She couldn't make herself move.

His breathing was steady, rhythmic, undisturbed: he was
sound asleep. She lay quite still so as not to disturb him, eyes
closed, savoring the feel of his big, masculine body against
hers.

No morning dream, this. It was so much better . . .

Her warm, thick, respectable nightgown was bunched around
her waist, and her hips and thighs were naked, quite naked, and
plastered against his nakedness.

Intimately.

His bent knee lay between her thighs, clamped between her
thighs, nudging the cleft between her legs. With every breath he
took, his knee moved ever so slightly, rubbing lightly against
her in a slow, enticing friction.

Without conscious volition, she found herself pressing back
against him, arching her back, deepening the friction. It sent
shivers through her, delicious ripples of sensation that—

"Maddy, when are we having breakfast?" a voice called from upstairs.

Hurriedly, Maddy pulled away. She tugged her nightgown down, pulled a knitted shawl around her, and slipped from the bed. The icy floor doused her heated body with the chill of reality.

She flew about the cottage, putting the porridge on to cook as she hastily washed and dressed in the scullery. She'd been playing with fire. If he'd been awake, he would have pressed her further. Would she have resisted?

Embarrassment washed over her. She'd always thought of herself as a woman of strong character, but the truth was, she hadn't even been able to resist his unconscious touch; in fact, she'd increased it.

If morning dreams unsettled her, this . . . whatever it was, completely undermined her.

"It's our day for the vicar, did you forget?" Jane came downstairs with her sisters following.

"No, I just slept in and forgot the time."

"Is the man still sick?" Lucy asked.

Maddy smiled. "His fever broke in the night and he's sleeping peacefully now."

"Again?" Lucy declared. "He's never going to wake up, not unless—"

"Go and wash your face and hands." Maddy gave her a little push. "Breakfast will be ready in a trice."

"Maddy." John came downstairs, a leather satchel clasped to his chest, his face scrunched in an emotion Maddy was very familiar with.

She sighed. "What have you done now?"

He grimaced. "It's not what I've done, so much as what I haven't."

She glanced at the satchel. The vicar had given it to the boys for carrying his precious books to and from the vicarage. "Did you forget to do your reading?"

"No, but the vicar asked me to give you these, days ago, and I forgot."

He handed her a pile of white garments, neatly pressed and folded.

She removed them and shook the top one out.

"The vicar's own nightshirts," John explained. "For him." He jerked his head in the direction of the bed. "The thing is, Maddy, the vicar gave them to me on the first day, and told me I wasn't to take them out in front of the girls. He said Henry and me—"

"Henry and I."

"Henry and I should dress the man, or give them to the doctor to do it, but . . . I forgot. He said it was very important, a man's job, that I owed it to you as the man of the family."

"I see." And Maddy did see.

John bit his lip anxiously. "Do you have to tell him? The vicar, I mean?"

Tell the vicar she'd tended a man—stark naked—in her bed for several days? Not likely. If he got the slightest wind of it, he'd be down here demanding the stranger marry her. Conscious or not.

As if the vicar could force a fine, strange gentleman to marry an unknown woman with five young children to care for. It would be a storm in a teacup, upsetting everyone, and achieving nothing but fuss and embarrassment and resentment.

"I won't tell the vicar if you don't," she said. John's face split with a relieved grin and she ruffled his hair affectionately. "Now, eat your porridge and be off."

Four

"*L*ucy, come away from that bed."

The little girl pouted. "But Maddy, I was just going to—"

"I know what you were 'just going to' do and you know what I told you about that. Leave the man alone. Now, be a good girl and sort out these buttons for me." Maddy emptied a tin box of assorted odd buttons onto the hearthrug and soon Lucy was happily absorbed in the task, arranging the buttons by color or shape or size, according to her fancy. Maddy had played the same game, with some of the same buttons, when she was a child.

Lizzie Brown looked up from her writing task. Three times a week, in exchange for dairy products, Lizzie took lessons from Maddy in reading and writing and the skills needed by a lady's maid. She came while the older children were having their lessons at the vicarage, the boys in Latin and Greek and the girls in painting and the pianoforte.

"What was she planning to do?" Lizzie whispered as Maddy returned to the table.

Maddy rolled her eyes. "She's decided our invalid is a sleeping prince who's had a spell put on him by a wicked witch. He won't wake up unless he's been kissed by a princess."

Lizzie grinned. "Shame there's no princesses around here. But he's a fine looking man, so if you want a dairymaid-in-training-to-be-a-lady's-maid to have a go . . ."

Maddy laughed. "No princesses?" she said in mock outrage. She pushed a homemade book across the table. "Read this."

Lizzie's reading was slow and laborious, but she read the first few lines and looked up with a lively grin. "Luci*ella*?"

Maddy nodded. "Keep reading." It was the book the girls had made the day before. All about a poor, put-upon secret princess and a sleeping prince . . .

She sat back smiling as Lizzie concentrated, her mouth moving silently as she read the story. She was doing so well.

Abandoned by her husband, Lizzie was young and pretty but unable to remarry, and her options were limited. Her uncle had given her work as a dairymaid, but Lizzie liked pretty clothes and nice things. She didn't mind hard work, so she'd set her heart on becoming a lady's maid.

Maddy was so proud of her. In the year she'd known Lizzie, she'd worked so hard . . .

Lizzie finished the book and looked up, laughing. She glanced at the little girl arranging the buttons in long rows, and winked. "A princess, eh? I never knew."

"You read that book all by yourself," Maddy said quietly. "You didn't ask me for help with a single word."

Lizzie glanced at the book, surprised. "Neither I didn't," she breathed. "Glory be—I can read."

"And your handwriting is good, too."

"Not my spelling though."

"No, but many people have trouble with spelling. It just takes time and work and perseverance in memorizing the tricky words." Maddy touched the fresh arrangement of her hair. "And you have a real talent for dressing hair. This is so stylish, I could go to a grand London ball and not look out of place."

Lizzie looked her over and pursed her lips thoughtfully. "Hmm, I reckon that dress would stand out and all, patches no longer being all the rage."

They both laughed.

"Seriously, Lizzie, I think you could start applying for positions in a fine house."

"You truly think so, Miss Maddy?"

"I do. In fact, I'll write you a letter of recommendation this very minute."

"Now?" Lizzie looked dismayed.

Maddy was puzzled. It was as if Lizzie dreaded the idea of going into service. Yet in all the time Maddy had known her, she had spoken of nothing else.

Maddy put her hand over Lizzie's. "What is it? Have you changed your mind?"

Lizzie twisted uncertainly. "No, I do want to be a lady's maid—I hate milking cows, honest I do. It's just . . ."

"Just . . . ?" Maddy prompted her after a moment.

"I know it's stupid. I know he won't never come back to me. But if I go away . . . and he does . . . and I'm not here . . ." Lizzie made a defeated gesture.

Reuben. Of course. Lizzie's runaway husband. The love of Lizzie's life, or so she'd thought until he went to town one day with all their savings—supposedly to buy a fine breeding bull—and never came back. She'd never seen it coming and for months afterward had refused to believe that he'd left her willingly.

"How long has it been?" Maddy asked gently.

"More'n two years." Lizzie dashed a hand across her eyes, scrubbing tears away. "Stupid, ain't I, even thinking he might come back after all this time."

"Did you never hear where he went or what he did?"

Lizzie gave a bitter snort. "Half the village seen him on a wagon with a dozen others, din't they? Drunk and laughing, heading down the Bristol road—and there was no reason for him to go to Bristol, none! My quiet Reuben . . ." She shook her head. "I'd never seen him take a drink, ever."

Maddy gave Lizzie's arm a comforting squeeze. "If Reuben did come back, he'd ask at your uncle's farm, wouldn't he?"

Lizzie nodded. "Uncle Bill'd tell him where I've gone, all right, but first he'd give Reuben a good hiding. So he'd be mad to come back, wouldn't he? Even if he wanted. Which he don't." She blew her nose and sat up straight. "No, go ahead, write that letter, Miss Maddy. My Reuben ain't never coming back, and if he does, well, there's always Uncle Bill, as you say."

Her gaze sharpened at something behind Maddy, and her eyes suddenly lit with laughter. "Oh, would you look at that. It's true what you read in books."

Maddy whirled around, just in time to see Lucy climb onto her stool and disappear behind the bed curtains.

"Lucy!" She made a dive for the little girl and dragged her out. "You little wretch, I told you—"

"Too late," Lucy crowed. "I kissed him and now he'll wake up." Over Maddy's shoulder she looked expectantly at the man in the bed, but he didn't move.

"Soon," Lucy added.

A little later Lucy explained, "He probably needs a little rest first."

*I*t was early afternoon. Lizzie had gone home and Maddy had persuaded Lucy to take a nap upstairs. The children would return from their lessons at the vicarage in an hour or so.

She was about to go outside and do some work in the garden when she heard movement from the bed, and a sort of croaking sound. She hurried across the room.

He was awake, his eyes open. "Water," he croaked.

"Yes, of course." She ran to fetch water and grabbed the medicine the doctor had left with her.

He struggled to sit up but kept keeling over. The doctor had warned her he might have difficulty with his balance so she slipped her arm under him and levered him up, supporting him first with her body, then stuffing some pillows around him.

He leaned heavily against her and closed his eyes. He was pale, the skin under his eyes papery and bruised looking. Lines of tension bracketed his mouth, and his jaw was tight, gritted against pain. She gave him the water first. He swallowed it gratefully.

"And I need . . ." He scanned the room, then met her gaze with an agonized look.

"Ah," she said, understanding, and fetched him a large jar.

A few minutes later she poured some hot water into a cup and added the drops the doctor had left. "Now drink this."

He swallowed once then pulled a face and tried to push it away. "It's just medicine the doctor left," she told him. "It will help with the pain."

"S'vile!" he muttered.

"Of course it tastes vile, it's supposed to—it's medicine. So don't be a baby, just drink it."

He opened his eyes at that and gave her a look, but he drank it down with no further complaint.

His eyes were so blue.

He finished drinking and subsided heavily against her as if exhausted by the small effort of sitting up. He sagged slowly, his bristly jaw sliding down her body until it rested in the place between her shoulder and her breast.

She made to move away, to let him lie down again, but his arm came up and held her tight.

"Stay."

She had work to do, but he seemed so helpless, in such pain. She sat there quietly listening to the sound of his breathing and the twittering of the birds outside. Bird were always noisier after rain.

A lock of thick brown hair tumbled over his forehead. She smoothed it back with her free hand.

No sign of the fever remained; even his hair felt cool against her fingers. It was soft and thick, and unlike most men she knew, he used no pomade or scented oils. She found herself stroking his hair, like a cat, soothing him as he rested.

Poor, lost man. Whatever his destination had been, he was now several days overdue. There would be people worrying about him. Somewhere a wife, a sweetheart, a mother was fretting, imagining the worst. Or maybe a mistress.

A man like this would not be alone.

His face was graven, shuttered against the expression of pain, his jawline tense and his mouth tight and thin lipped and . . .

Beautiful.

She swallowed. How strange it felt to know nothing about him, yet know his body, his mouth so intimately. She knew the feel of it against her lips, had pressed her own lips against his to form a seamless bond, until he'd opened for her. She'd given him precious fluids. He'd left her with the taste of him on her lips, in her mouth.

She could taste him still.

Gradually his breathing evened out. Slowly the lines of pain eased. The medicine was working.

His eyes opened briefly and his gaze roamed the room, taking in the clothes hanging on the nails at the end of the bed, the faded red bed curtains, the window and the garden beyond. He frowned over each item, as if puzzled, then sighed and his eyelids fluttered and closed, as if it was all too much to work out.

"Can you tell me your name?" she asked. "Or where you were going? I can send a message to your loved ones."

He murmured something unintelligible and moved his head restlessly against her shoulder.

"It's all right," she soothed, stroking his hair. It was obviously too much for him to speak just yet.

He muttered something again and his hand brushed across her breast.

She jumped. He was half asleep, she was sure, and probably had no idea what he'd done. She settled back into the soothing motion of running her fingers through his hair. She wasn't sure who it soothed most, her or him.

"Mmm, nice," he mumbled and cupped her breast, stroking the nipple with a long, strong thumb. It sent a jolt of lightning through her body.

She jumped off the bed. "Stop that!" Half asleep or not, he shouldn't be doing such things.

She thought of the way she'd responded in bed this morning and flushed. It wasn't the same. He'd deliberately touched her.

And this morning she'd deliberately pressed back.

He'd fallen back, half buried in the pillows when she'd jumped off the bed. One intensely blue eye opened slowly. "Come back to bed."

"Absolutely not." Rev. Matheson was right; the man was a rake, after all. She felt oddly . . . disappointed.

He eyed her. "Wha's . . . wrong?"

Perhaps a rake needed to have it explained. "I don't like you touching me like that."

His eye lowered. "You liked it." The eye gleamed, then closed.

She folded her arms across her chest with its traitorous nipples and glared at the apparently sleeping rogue.

They hadn't even been *introduced*!

"Well, then, since you're awake enough for—um." She tried again, trying to sound calmer and more ladylike instead of someone who'd just been groped like a maidservant and wanted to hit him for the . . . the impersonality of it.

Not that anyone should treat a maidservant disrespectfully. But some men did. Rakes. "While you are awake, let us take the opportunity to make you decent."

The blue eye opened. "Not . . . beyond redemption, then?"

"I meant decently clad. I have the vicar's nightshirt here. Seeing you traveled with none of your own, he kindly donated some of his."

There was a faint muffled snort from the bed. "Been blessed, has it?" Even with his eyes closed and his face tight with pain, a faint half smile lurked on that wicked, beautiful mouth. Devilry shining through the pain. Irresistible. Devious.

She couldn't leave him naked under the bedclothes an instant longer. Dressed, he would be easier to manage.

Swaddled would be even better. Tightly, with his arms firmly bound to his sides.

Fallen angel? Devil, more like.

She hoped the vicar's nightshirt *had* been blessed!

She shook out the nightshirt and helped him into it. Into half of it, at any rate. It wasn't too much trouble to get his long powerful arms into it and carefully ease it over his bandaged head. She dragged it down to cover his broad shoulders and firm, flat chest, trying not to notice the small, flat masculine nipples as she did so.

Hers were hard and throbbing, which made it difficult not to compare.

She tugged the thick folds of white flannel down as far as his waist. He, of course, gave her no help whatsoever. She reached down to tug the garment farther and from the corner of her eye caught the gleam of white teeth.

"You might help," she told him

"Why? You're doing so well." How could he laugh when he was obviously in pain?

She left the nightshirt bunched at his waist. If he wanted to smooth it down over his hips and legs and . . . and other parts, he could do it himself. She briskly rearranged his pillows and straightened the bedclothes.

"What's your name?"

He didn't answer.

"Where were you headed? Is there anyone I can notify? A wife? Your family must be worried."

He gave her a strange look. His forehead furrowed, then slowly his eyes closed. His skin was ashen and the lines of pain around his eyes and mouth had deepened again. He really was exhausted.

She felt a little guilty at forcing him into the nightshirt, but she felt so much better knowing he was dressed, more or less. She couldn't leave him naked in her bed all day. Not with children in the house.

She wasn't cross with him, not really. He was what he was. It was her own fault she was feeling so disappointed and upset. She was the fool who'd let herself start to care, who'd begun to build fantasies around an unconscious man. Thinking morning dreams could come true.

Maddy didn't just need him decently clothed. She needed him out of her bed and out of her life as soon as possible.

*H*e wasn't sure how long it was before he woke again. He examined his surroundings with care, searching for some clue to where he was, apart from in a bed built into an alcove. He wriggled and the bed rustled. A straw mattress?

Half a dozen nails were set into a wall. Women's clothing hung from them: a couple of dresses, a pelisse, a faded green cloak. Only one nail with men's clothing: a coat, well-cut, doeskin breeches, and a fine linen shirt.

Nothing looked familiar.

He parted the curtains and found himself in a small, cramped cottage. The walls were rough-cast plaster, simply whitewashed, the floor made of uneven stone flags. The ceiling was low and blackened with smoke. The door was ancient and rough hewn, with a wooden latch to fasten it. Above the latch a heavy bolt gleamed new minted against the weathered wood. There was a fireplace with a fire burning and a kettle and a pot suspended over it.

His stomach rumbled. Something smelt good. Everything smelt good. Beneath the aroma of the food, there was a faint, all-pervasive scent of beeswax. Even the bedding smelt clean, of hay and sunshine and lavender.

Outside, children shouted at play. Whose children?

A woman moved into sight and he knew at once that this was she. She was familiar, yet not, slender, with a quick, graceful way of moving. Her dark auburn hair was coiled high on the crown of her head and he could see her pale, tender nape, kissed by a few fire-dark tendrils.

He knew what that skin smelt like, tasted like, felt like.

But he could not remember her name.

Her back was toward him. He admired the elegant line of her spine, the narrow waist and gentle swell of her hips accented by the strings of an apron. He liked the way her hips and her buttocks swayed when she moved around the cottage.

She returned to the table, this time facing him, and began chopping vegetables. She hadn't noticed him yet.

She frowned as she chopped, deep in thought. She was lovely. Not conventionally beautiful, but definitely appealing.

Her face was heart shaped, with creamy-silk skin, her broad forehead tapering to a small, decided chin. Her nose was tip-tilted and opinionated, her mouth was soft with full, pink lips that were, at the moment, pursed.

He couldn't tell from here what color her eyes were, and dammit, he couldn't remember. A man should at least remember that.

And her name. Dammit, what *was* her name?

Her chopping slowed, and slowly, as if she knew he was watching her, she raised her eyes.

"You're awake!" She dropped the knife and hurried across to him. "How do you feel this time?"

This time? He grimaced and touched the bandage gingerly. "My head . . ." The slightest movement set the hammers pounding at his skull, like blacksmiths around an anvil.

"Yes, you hit it when you fell."

"Fell?" That would explain the various aches and pains.

"Off your horse."

His brow furrowed more deeply. "*I* fell off a *horse*?" He might not be able to recall when he last fell off a horse, but he was certain it wasn't a common occurrence. He was offended by the very notion.

"Actually your horse slipped on an unexpected patch of very slippery mud and threw you. Don't you remember?"

He stared at her. *Don't you remember?* He started to shake his head, but stilled as the blacksmiths started hammering on his skull again. He tried to sit up, but his head swirled horribly and for a moment he feared he would throw up.

The nausea faded.

"You gave me a terrible fright, I can tell you. There was blood everywhere." She smiled. "But you've come through it now, and you're looking so much better than you have the past few days."

"Days?"

She nodded. "The accident happened two days ago."

Two days? He closed his eyes, willing the thumping on his skull to quiet. Nothing made sense.

"So if you will just tell me your name and your intended destination, or even your home address, I will send a message to your family. They will be very worried about you by now."

His family? He stared into her heart-shaped face with its sweetly troubled expression. Her eyes were deep golden brown, the color of brandy.

"My horse, was he badly hurt?"

She looked surprised. "No, it scrambled to its feet and trotted off—don't worry, the boys caught it. But—"

"And he's all right? Not injured at all?"

"He's perfectly hale and hearty," she assured him. "We stabled him at the vicar's, about a mile from here. We don't have anything big enough."

He nodded slowly and closed his eyes.

Maddy straightened the bedclothes, puzzled. He seemed more worried about his horse than he was about his relatives who would be worrying. Maybe he had no relatives? Maybe he was an orphan like herself and the children.

Or perhaps he didn't want her to know his name. He might be a wanted man. He didn't look like one, though.

"The vicar doesn't mind—he's the kindest man. And the

boys are horse mad, so it's a treat for them, really. They'd look after it even if it wasn't their responsibility. They tell me it's a beautiful animal. What's its name?"

"Name?" he repeated blankly.

"Yes, the boys have been wondering. The girls, too, for that matter." They'd all wondered about the stranger's name, too, but since he seemed reluctant to trust her with that . . .

"Girls, too," he repeated, bemused. "How many?"

"Three girls, and Lucy is only four, but she does like to name animals. They all do. It's a nuisance because it makes it very difficult to kill any of the chickens even if they don't lay anything, because you cannot sit down to a fricassee of Mabel or a meal of roast Dorothy, can you?"

She was talking too much, running on about nothing, but his silence was unsettling. That, and his frown and the way he was staring at her with those blue, blue eyes.

And the thought of what had passed between them earlier.

"Can I get you anything?" she asked him. "Are you thirsty? Hungry?"

"A jar?"

She brought it.

"*I*s he awake?" John glanced at the bed as he set down a pail of cool well water. His shadow, Henry, followed him in.

"He was," she said, "but he's fallen asleep again."

"Maybe his eyes are just closed. Can I look? He'll want to know about his horse."

"I told him his horse was all right."

"He asked about it?"

"He did," she assured him.

John and Henry exchanged looks and John gave a satisfied nod. The stranger was, it seemed, worthy of his mount.

"What's his name?" Henry asked.

"He didn't tell me." She forestalled the next question. "Neither his name, nor his horse's name."

The boys tiptoed over to the bed.

"Don't disturb him," Maddy warned them.

As she spoke, the man opened his eyes. He stared at the two boys, then subsided with a groan.

"He's in pain," she told them.

The girls had followed their brothers inside and joined them by the bed, staring at the stranger. "I can't see," Lucy whispered hoarsely.

Maddy brought the water. She slipped her arm under the man's head and raised him so he could drink. He drank the whole cup thirstily without opening his eyes. She held the cup out to Jane to refill.

After the second cup he sighed and opened his eyes again. He examined each small face lined up beside the bed. "Four children? *Four?*"

"Five," said Lucy, who'd fetched a stool to stand on.

"I told you there were five," Maddy said.

He stared. "Their resemblance to each other is extraordinary."

"Not me. Everyone says I look like Maddy," Lucy told him.

"Yes, but I didn't see you before," he told the little girl apologetically.

"I didn't see you, either. But I got a stool," she told him. "I'm standing on it now."

"An excellent strategy," he said. Lucy beamed with pride at the compliment.

"Do the others look like me?"

"Why would they look like you?" Maddy said blankly.

He gave her a thoughtful look but didn't respond.

"Are you hungry?" Maddy asked. "I made soup. You need to build up your strength."

"Is that what I can smell?" he asked. "It does smell good."

Taking that as a yes, she shooed the children back outside, sending John and Henry to take a message to the doctor that the stranger had woken and was in his senses.

She ladled some soup into a bowl, tucked a cloth around his neck, and sat on the edge of the bed to feed him.

"I can feed myself," he told her, reaching for the bowl, but it shook so badly in his hands she took it back.

"You've been badly injured. It's no weakness to accept help."

"I don't mind help from you," he told her, with a look that made her cheeks warm.

She concentrated on spooning soup into him, avoiding the

blue gaze that watched her so intently. She wished he would close his eyes, but then she wouldn't have been able to feed him.

The trouble was she had to focus on his mouth, his beautiful, masculine, perfectly chiseled mouth and all that did was to stir up other thoughts . . . feelings . . . from the morning.

"You never did tell me your horse's name," she said as she fed him. "The children will want to know."

He swallowed the soup thoughtfully. "It's very good soup," he said after a moment. "What's in it?"

He was still avoiding the question. Why?

"Nettles." His eyes widened and she chuckled. "They don't sting in soup and they're very good for you. The hardest part is picking them—you have to use gloves."

He allowed her to feed him another spoonful, making a show of tasting it properly this time. "Nettles taste like this?" It was a compliment.

"Not only nettles. There are other ingredients."

"What?" he asked suspiciously.

"Oh, just the usual, you know, eye of newt and toe of frog."

He smiled and she really wished he wouldn't. He was too charming for his own good. For her own good. "Well, that's me, done for. No, really, I'm interested."

He was, too, she saw. "Nothing dreadful, I assure you. Mainly potatoes, butter, cream, watercress, and a little parsley." In other words it was like most of their meals: made from ingredients she could grow, make, pick wild, or barter. Thank God Lizzie was a dairymaid.

"I could have sworn it tasted of chicken."

"The basic stock is made from a chicken carcass—"

"Not Mabel or Dorothy?" he asked in faux horror.

She laughed. "No, this one was Tommy, and Tommy, though very sweet as a fluffy chick, turned into a nasty aggressive cockerel who picked fights and even attacked the children. He thoroughly deserved his fate."

"Tommy has atoned for his sins. This is delicious." As she fed him, his color slowly returned. His gaze passed over her like a touch, caressingly. He was a stranger. She didn't even know his name.

She'd slept with him naked. Twice.

She'd saved his life, held him like a child.

He'd held her, not at all like a child.

"Please tell me your name," she said softly.

He gave her an enigmatic look, shook his head, then looked away.

She brought him a second bowl of soup but made no effort to speak as she fed him. His refusal to answer her question angered her. Who was he to withhold his name? A criminal of some sort? A wanted man as well as a rake?

He was thoughtful, distant, drinking the soup she fed him almost as if she weren't there.

She was very aware of him, his proximity, the lean masculinity of his body, the dark hair on his arms, the long-fingered, well-tended gentleman's hands. Those hands didn't belong here. She needed to send him on his way. Someone could send a coach for him.

"I am going to notify somebody," she told him as he wiped his mouth and handed her the cloth. "So, who should it be?"

"Notify?"

"Your family, or whoever you were on your way to visit when you had the accident. They'll be worried."

He sighed, but said nothing.

She stood and said in the kind of voice she used on the children when she was trying to exert her authority, "If you don't tell me, I'll have no choice but to inform the authorities. So who are you?"

There was a long silence before he said reluctantly, "I don't know."

Five

"What do you mean you don't—" She broke off. "You mean you don't remember who you are?" Was this another ploy to avoid telling her his name?

"No."

"You truly have no idea?"

"None at all. It's all a blank." His brow furrowed. "Are you saying you don't know me, either?"

"I never saw you until two days ago, when you fell off your horse outside my house."

His mouth twisted. "But I thought . . ."

"Thought what?"

He patted the bed. "You slept here, with me."

Her cheeks heated and she gathered up the things on the tray and jumped off the bed. "Only because you were unconscious— or so I thought—and because the alternative was freezing on the floor. And I put in Hadrian's Wall to keep us separated, but somebody"—she narrowed her eyes at him—"removed it. Both times."

"Hadrian's Wall?"

"It was a wall the Roman Emperor Hadrian built to keep out the wild Scot—"

"I know what Hadrian's Wall is. But how could you put it in our bed?"

"*My* bed," she said instantly. "And this is Hadrian's Wall." She gestured to the still rolled-up quilt, then blinked as she took in what he'd just revealed. "You know what Hadrian's Wall is? And yet you claim you can't remember your own name?"

"I don't *claim* it—it's true!" He made a frustrated gesture. "And don't ask me how I can remember a Roman emperor but not who I am or where I was going, because I can't explain it. I only know that it's true."

He sounded both angry and bewildered, and strange as it sounded, Maddy was inclined to believe him. "But I'm *certain* I know *you*," he finished.

"You don't. We've never met before."

"No. I recognized your scent in the night. Even in the darkness, I knew it was you."

She shook her head. "I don't wear scent."

"I know that. I'm not talking about something out of a bottle. It was *you* I recognized, your own womanly scent." The look he gave her scorched her.

She opened her mouth to say something, some withering remark that would put this too-familiar stranger back in his place, but no words would come. Her mouth was open with no sound coming out, like a baby bird whose cheep had dried up.

She turned away, her face—her whole body—burning. *Her own womanly scent.* How mortifying! She was scrupulous in her bathing habits, washing herself and the children every morning and night. But if he could smell her, well! She obviously needed to take a bath—immediately! With a different kind of soap.

That probably explained his overfamiliarity. He had a wife or a mistress who used the same kind of soap. Maddy made her own soap using beeswax and other ingredients. It would be expensive to buy, but not when you kept bees and could make it yourself.

"And now I've made you cross," he said.

She shot him a narrow glance. "Have you?"

He grinned. "Definitely cross."

She started washing dishes, hoping he would go back to sleep. She could feel his gaze on her the whole time.

"Can I ask you something?" he said when she'd finished washing and had started to dry.

"What?" she said warily.

"What is your name?"

"It's Woodford," she told him. "Miss Madeleine Woodford."

"*Miss* Woodford?" He tried to hide his surprise.

"Yes, miss," she said tersely. "Why?"

"It's just . . . all those children."

She laughed, suddenly realizing his train of thought. "You thought they were mine? All five of them? Jane, the oldest, is twelve. How old do you think I am?"

It was a rhetorical question, but he gave her a thoughtful, considering look, from head to toe, and she felt herself flushing under his gaze, instantly self-conscious. Wanting, absurdly, for him to like what he saw.

"I don't know," he said. "About . . . twenty-five?"

"Twenty-two," she said crisply. So she looked older than she was. Wonderful. Every woman's dream.

"The children are my brothers and sisters, half brothers and sisters, to be precise. They are my father's children by his second wife. They are—we are orphaned."

"I'm sorry." His voice was gentle.

"Thank you." She felt little grief for Papa. The children might, though it was her opinion they grieved more for the idea of Papa. And much more for the loss of their home. "Now, if that's all . . ."

"Are they my clothes?" He pointed to the hooks beside the bed, which were all she had as a wardrobe these days.

"Yes, but you're not well enough—"

"I want to check if there's any identification in them. I don't suppose you looked."

"The vicar checked. There is none."

"Didn't you look? Weren't you curious?"

She bit her lip. "I did look, yes, but—"

"But what?"

"I only checked to see if you had money."

He sank back against the pillow and just looked at her. "I see."

She felt her cheeks warming. "It's not what you think—well,

it is, but—" She was floundering. "I needed to know if you . . ." She trailed off, knowing how bad it sounded.

"Had money?"

The dry note in his voice flicked her on the raw. "Yes, because you were so badly injured I didn't think twice about sending for the doctor. Later I wondered how I could pay him—I have no money—so when the vicar sent the portmanteau, I wondered if . . . if you could pay."

"I see. And did I have money?" His voice was cool, dispassionate. Judging.

She nodded. "Plenty, thank goodness." A thick roll of crisp, new banknotes.

"And did you pay the doctor?"

"No, he didn't even mention money. He wasn't sure you'd live through the night. It's a very serious injury, you know. You were bleeding an awful lot. And then there was fever."

He put a hand to his head, feeling the bandage lightly. "So it's thanks to you I survived the night. Several nights." He gave her a look, as if he didn't know what to make of her.

As if he still thought she might be a thief. But there was nothing she could say to convince him, and if she continued to argue the point, it would only sound worse.

"The doctor will be back. I expect he'll send a bill when he's finished his treatment."

"I see."

"He also said he won't know if that ankle is broken or not— we brought the swelling down a bit, but you need to be conscious for him to know for sure. See if you can wiggle your toes. Things like that."

He shifted uncomfortably "I wondered about that. It aches like the very dev—a lot."

"Yes, your horse stood on it. But in the meantime, you're not to move or try to get out of bed."

She lifted his clothes from the nail, laid them on the bed, then pulled a small leather portmanteau out from under the bed. "The vicar sent this with the boys; it was strapped to your horse. Look through it yourself. Maybe something will jog your memory. And you can check the—" She stopped, realizing that if he couldn't remember who he was, he'd certainly not remember what was in his case. Or how much.

"It's all there," she said stiffly. "We may be poor, but I haven't touched a penny. I wouldn't."

"I know," he said gently. "I'm an ass. It's just—"

"That you don't know me. And I don't know you. Yes. Now, if you'll excuse me, I have work to do." She flicked the bed curtains closed and a moment later he heard the cottage door shut behind her.

Damn, he hadn't meant to upset her like that. He didn't know her—didn't know himself for that matter—and people robbed travelers all the time. But they didn't usually drag them in out of a storm and put them to bed in their own beds.

It was strange how he knew some things quite well but couldn't even remember his own blasted name.

But he knew she hadn't tried to steal or seduce money out of him; hadn't tried to seduce him at all, more's the pity. He would have been very happy to cooperate. She was lovely.

Not beautiful in the classic sense, but she was luscious, almost edible, with that silken creamy skin so soft and fragrant and inviting. He wanted to touch, taste, explore her from top to dainty, feminine toe.

Lord, he sounded like every bad love poem he'd ever read. Not that he could remember a single one at the moment. He gave a spurt of ironic laughter—and was instantly punished for it. He waited for the pounding of hammers in his head to subside, then reached for his things.

His coat pockets disgorged a handful of coins, a large roll of crisp, new banknotes, and a small piece of paper which had once had writing on it, perhaps an address. He unfolded it, but it was completely illegible, the ink having run.

His breeches contained a few more coins and a handkerchief embroidered with the initial R.

R: What could it stand for? A first name or a surname? Richard? Robert? Rupert? Rafe? He frowned. Rafe . . . There was an echo . . . but no. He felt no more like a Rafe than a Rupert or a Roger. Or even a Rollo.

A surname then? Roberts? Rogers? Reynolds? Richards? He ran through them, dredging up more and more possibilities. Robinson?

Rose? Russell? It was ridiculous. Raleigh? Rowe?

He went through his portmanteau. As she'd said, there were

no obvious means of identification. Apart from a small, businesslike pistol, loaded, but with only the maker's mark on it, and clothing—the bare minimum: a change of underwear, a spare shirt, a pair of stockings, a neckcloth—there was nothing else except toiletries and a razor.

The razor was a welcome sight. He ran a hand over his stubble. He had no liking for a rough beard and he was certain ladies didn't, either. He'd wash and shave later.

He sifted through his belongings a second time. Nothing caused a single bell in his beleaguered brain to ring.

He appeared to be a man of some means: his belongings were of the best quality. But there was no crest or even gold initials stamped on his portmanteau or toiletries case, so he was probably not from one of the better families.

And it was odd that he was, apparently, traveling alone, without a groom or valet, and on horseback, something few gentlemen did unless for a short, informal day trip. But nobody around here seemed to know him or notice his absence, so it seemed he was unknown in this locality.

Was he running away?

The complete lack of any form of identification, no papers, no letters, nothing except the large wad of banknotes—new notes—seemed odd. Peculiar. Even a little suspicious.

Was he, could he possibly be, some kind of shady character? He didn't feel shady, he didn't much like the idea, but then, he clearly wasn't in his usual mind.

Yet he was in her bed, and she'd shared it with him, stranger or no. That had to mean something.

Troubled by unanswerable questions and aching all over, he pushed his belongings aside, closed his eyes, and eventually, slept.

*D*r. Thompson inspected his head wounds with approving noises. "Outside seems to be healing well, but they tell me you can't even remember your own name, eh?"

"It's very frustrating. I can remember all sorts of odd things—facts and quotes and such—but nothing about myself or the events leading up to the accident."

"Fascinating." The doctor fixed him with shrewd gaze and

fired a string of questions at him: Who was the prime minister? When was the Battle of Waterloo? Where did he grow up? What was the sum of 241 and 398? What was his father's name? What were the Punic Wars? Who wrote *The Merchant of Venice*?

He answered them as best he could, answering some without even having to think twice and drawing a blank on others.

At the end of the inquisition, the doctor nodded. "Your brain seems working well enough, it's just your memory that's at fault."

He already knew that. "The question is, when will it return?"

"No telling," the doctor said cheerfully. "Man has circumnavigated the world hundreds of times, but we still have very little idea of what's in here." He tapped his temple lightly. "Or how it works. In some cases, the patient never recovers their memory. Or even their brain." Apparently oblivious of his patient's appalled expression, he added cheerfully, "Now, let's have a look at this ankle."

He unwrapped the injured ankle, probed and manipulated it, and eventually pronounced it a sprain. "Though it might be a cracked bone. I'll strap it up again on the off chance. Don't put any weight on it for at least a week. If it hurts, don't use it." He closed his bag. "Not unless you want to be a cripple for the rest of your life, ha-ha."

Cheery bloody bastard, he thought as the doctor left. The doctor's manipulations had left him exhausted. And frustrated.

"He's a very good doctor," Maddy said defensively. "He's not one to be groundlessly optimistic—"

"Oh, yes, I noticed his optimism. I'm to count myself lucky to have a brain at all, never mind if I never find out who I am. And if I move I'll be a cripple for life. And it's all so *fascinating*!"

She laughed. "It's good advice. You're looking rather gray around the gills, so why don't you have a sleep?"

There was nothing he wanted more, but he hated appearing so weak and helpless in front of her. "I'm perfectly all right—" he began, but she twitched the curtains shut and he was left alone.

"I'm not normally so feeble," he told the curtain. "I'm a fine, energetic figure of a man, actually."

She laughed and called back, "How would you know?" A moment later the outside door closed and he could hear her telling the children to play a little farther away from the cottage so the man could sleep.

How would he know, indeed?

"The man," that was his name. That or "you" or "sir," depending on who was speaking. It wasn't acceptable. He needed to think, needed to remember . . .

"Y ou're not supposed to go there, he's asleep!" A hoarse whisper woke him.

"But he's been sleeping for days!" Another loud whisper.

"That's because he hurt his head. And Maddy said we weren't to distu—John!"

The curtain was drawn back and the oldest boy peered in at him. "See, he is awake!" John exclaimed triumphantly. He lowered his voice and added in an unnaturally flat, calm voice, "Besides, I'm not *disturbing* him; I'm just talking to him. Very quietly. Aren't I, sir?"

"You woke him! And Maddy's going to be cross." The oldest girl looked in. "I'm so sorry, sir. I *told* John—"

"It's all right—Jane, is it?" She nodded and flushed with pleasure at him remembering her name. Other people's names were easy.

"I was awake," he lied. Keeping his head as steady as he could, he propped himself up on one elbow. "Now, John, how can I help you?"

"Well, it's your horse," the boy began.

"He's not injured, is he? I thought—"

"No, no, sir, he's perfectly splendid. It's just—"

"He hasn't got a name," declared a gruff little voice. There was a thumping and bumping as a stool was put in place, and Lucy's face appeared.

"You see, sir, we—"

"We being me and John," Henry joined in. "And we're the ones looking after him, so—"

"We want to call him Lightning, because he looks like a regular goer, and he has that blaze," John continued. "But the girls—"

"But it doesn't look like lightning! The blaze is a star, and so I think he should be called Star," Jane finished.

"Stella is prettier than Star," Susan declared, wiggling in between Jane and Henry. "And Stella means star."

"Stella's a girl's name and he's a stallion!" Henry said in disgust.

"And Star sounds girly, too, so we thought we'd ask you, sir," John finished. "Maddy said you've lost your memory, so we know it won't be his real name, but still, we have to call him something, so we thought we'd ask you to choose."

"I see." He looked at the five faces ranged along the side of the bed. "And do you have an opinion on what we should call my horse, Miss Lucy? Everyone else has shared theirs."

"Peggy," she said firmly.

They all laughed. "You can't call him Peggy, Lucy; he's a boy," Henry told her.

"I don't care," she insisted. "Peggy, after Pegasus."

"And he hasn't got wings—" Henry began but was hushed by his brother.

"Sir?" They all waited.

He rubbed his chin thoughtfully. "They're all very fine names." He was tempted to tell them his horse would respond equally to any name, but he could see that, to them, this was no small matter. Something was bubbling over the fire, something spicy and delicious. "Pepper," he said on a whim. "His name is Pepper."

"Did you remember it, sir?" John said, clearly pleased.

"I did," he lied. He didn't care what the horse had been called before; from now on it would be Pepper.

"And do you remember your own name, too?" Jane asked him.

"No, I'm sorry."

The children looked crestfallen.

"You have to have a name," Lucy told him worriedly. "Everybody has to have a name."

"Would you like to choose a name for me to use in the meantime?" he suggested. "I can't go on being 'sir' or 'hey you' or 'man,' can I?" He showed them the handkerchief. "Perhaps something beginning with R."

The children immediately went through the same litany of

names he'd been driving himself crazy with, and even hearing them in different voices, none rang a bell.

They settled on Robert. "But it's disrespectful to call an adult by his first name," Jane objected. "He needs a surname."

"He might have a title," John suggested. "And then we could call him by his title; Wellington, for instance."

"Rider," Lucy said. "Mr. Rider. Cause he rided here on his horse and then he fell off."

"Excellent," said the newly named Robert Rider, ignoring the "fell off" part. "Mr. Rider it is, then."

"Maddy's coming," Susan hissed. "And we weren't supposed to disturb the man."

"Not 'the man.' Mr. Rider," Jane corrected her as the children headed hastily for the back door.

Mr. Rider lay back on the bed and did his best to look undisturbed.

A moment later Maddy came flying into the cottage. She stuck her head between the bed curtains and said in an urgent voice, "No matter what you hear, or what is said, or done, do not wake up! Do you hear me? It is of the utmost importance that you appear to remain unconscious at all times. Don't move a muscle!" She twitched the bed curtains closed, and before he could ask what on earth was going on, he heard a knock at the door.

"Oh, Mr. Matheson, what a pleasant surprise," Maddy said in apparent surprise.

"My dear Miss Woodford." The speaker had a deep, fruity voice of the sort normally heard from pulpits. "I thought it incumbent that I call on you in your hour of need."

"My hour of need?"

The fruity voice lowered, retaining its dramatic flair. "Your Unwelcome Imposition."

"My unwe—oh, you mean the injured stranger. He's not really an imposition."

Little liar, the imposition thought.

"But of course he is," the Reverend Fruit-bowl declared. "An unmarried young lady, forced to give shelter to an Unknown Man! And a man—I may add, without sullying your Tender Ears—of Unsavory Habits!"

Unsavory habits? The imposition was tempted to demand an explanation, but aware of his hostess's instructions, lay indignantly feigning unconsciousness. What the devil did this prosy windbag know, to accuse him of unsavory habits?

"So you know him?" she asked calmly.

"Know him? I thank the Lord I do not. But I know of His Kind."

"What kind is that?"

"It would not be proper for me to explain, but suffice it to say—"

"You mean the kind that travels without a nightshirt?" There was a faint gobbling sound, but she went on undisturbed. "The doctor told me of your concerns, dear Mr. Matheson, but truly there is nothing to worry about. We managed to get him into the nightshirt you sent—"

"*We?*" the fruit-bowl declared ominously.

"The doctor and John, of course," she said smoothly.

Oh, she was good. The doctor and John had been nowhere in sight when she'd wrestled him into the blasted thing. No wonder the nightshirt swam on him. The Reverend Fruit-bowl was obviously as rounded as his vowels.

"I should hope so, too! And Miss Woodford, I beg of you, there is no further need for you to refer to an Intimate Masculine Garment. I realize it must be Distressing for a Lady."

And what would you think, good Rev. Windbag, if you knew she'd stripped me of every stitch of clothing and then put me in her bed, stark naked. And then joined me there, albeit chastely. He muffled a snort of laughter.

"What was that?" the windbag asked.

"Nothing," she said hurriedly. "And intimate masculine garments don't offend me in the least. I wash the boys' smalls each week. Now can I offer you a cup of tea? There is only peppermint tea with honey, I'm afraid, but—"

"No, no, I thank you. My good lady will have tea waiting when I return, but I'm sure I heard . . ."

"No doubt it was one of the children playing. They often

make the most ridiculous sounds, and oddly, it sounds quite clo—Rev. Matheson, I beg you, do not disturb—"

The faded red bed curtains were flung open.

There was a long silence as he feigned unconsciousness under the close stare of the vicar. He could hear the man breathing as he leaned over to scrutinize him closely. His breath smelt of port and caraway seeds.

He attempted to look pale and at death's door. How deeply did one breathe when unconscious? he wondered. And did one let one's mouth fall open or not? Not, he decided. It was not an attractive look, and he was sure she was standing by the vicar, watching him for any sign of awareness.

"A vicious-looking Ruffian," the vicar declared. "A Veritable Pirate."

"That's because of the bruises and bandage, and because he hasn't shaved for a few days."

So she thought he looked like a pirate, too, did she?

"He's like this most of the time," she told the vicar. "Day or night, he never moves, so you can see, I'm in no danger." She was defending him. Interesting.

The vicar huffed. "Dr. Thompson said he was conscious earlier today."

"He was, that's true, but he was so exhausted by the doctor's ministrations he lapsed back into unconsciousness almost immediately and hasn't moved a muscle since."

Without warning, a finger poked him sharply in the side, right on the site of one of his more tender injuries. He made an angry exclamation but managed to turn it into a groan. He hoped it was convincing. It hurt like the very devil.

"I don't like it, I don't like it at all," the vicar said.

And I don't like you poking me, he thought.

"He's harmless, Rev. Matheson, so please, come away. The doctor said his recovery will be quicker if he's not disturbed." She pulled the curtains closed and he was able to relax.

"I was going to offer to take him in at the vicarage. It's not right that a young, single lady be burdened with such a one as he."

"The doctor said he wasn't to be moved until his head injury shows sign of healing."

"He said the same to me," the vicar said testily. "But when will that be?"

"It's in God's hands," she said, and he had to stifle a laugh at the way she'd stolen the vicar's line.

"Then until this Happy Event takes place, perhaps my Good Lady should come and stay with you, as Chaperone."

She laughed, a sparkling sound. "Do not suggest such a thing, I beg you. Poor Mrs. Matheson. She would hate to be in such a small, stuffy cottage, shut in with five noisy children."

"She is very fond of children—"

"I know, and she's been more than kind to us. But there would be nowhere for her to sleep."

There was a short, tense pause.

"And where, may I ask, do you sleep, Miss Woodford? I happen to know there are but the two bedrooms upstairs, with two beds—"

"I made my bed the last two nights on the floor in front of the fire."

She's good, he thought. It was not, after all, a lie. She had made the bed on the floor. He'd seen her rolling it up in the morning. She'd simply left out the part where she'd slept with him. And the thing she called Hadrian's Wall.

"But—"

"And tonight I will do the same," she said with quiet assurance.

Not if I can help it, he thought.

"I don't like it—"

"It's very kind of you to worry about me, Mr. Matheson, but there's not the least need. I need no protection from this feeble, injured creature. And I am hardly a young ingenue, after all; I've been supporting myself and my brothers and sisters without assistance for some time now."

"Yes, but—"

"And with five little chaperones, I don't need another, so please, don't worry about me or the stranger. Most of the time he's unconscious and, when awake, he seems a very gentlemanly sort. Besides, I'm sure he'll recover his memory soon and be off."

He heard the front door being opened.

"But I don't like it," the vicar said unhappily. "Not one little bit."

A few minutes later she returned. "He's gone, you can relax now." She opened the curtains and looked in.

"Prosy old windbag," he said.

"He's a very kind man," she told him. "He and his wife have been more than good to the children and me, and I won't have you mock him. He's concerned for my reputation and safety, that's all."

"Then why on earth did you tell me to feign insensibility? I could have reassured him that I was a gentleman and—"

"And that would have been a disaster."

He frowned. "Why?"

She seemed about to say something, then stopped. "Take it from me, it just would."

"In what way?" he persisted.

"Very well, if you must know, I think that if he knew you were a gentleman and unmarried, he would attempt to force us to marry."

He laughed. "You cannot be serious. Nobody, vicar or otherwise, could force me into anything I did not want. Why would he even consider such a thing?"

She narrowed her eyes at him. "Because he thinks it a scandal that you're in my bed, that's why."

"Yes, but nothing's happened. And even if it had, I've been in dozens of—" he broke off, noticing her expression. "At least I'm sure I must have been . . . Probably."

"He was right to remind me that I don't know anything about you."

"I don't know anything about me, either," he reminded her. "But even I can tell that a marriage between us would be prepos—" He broke off.

"Yes?" she said with a sweetness that didn't deceive him in the least.

He tried to retrieve his position. "You don't want a marriage of that sort, either, or you wouldn't have gone out of your way to assure him I was—how did you put it?—oh, yes, 'this feeble, injured creature.'" It rankled. Injured, yes, but a feeble creature? As if he were of no account. "Why did you do that, eh? So that he wouldn't think me any danger to your reputation at all?"

"Exactly so!" she flashed. "I have no wish to be yoked in marriage to any man, let alone a man I know nothing about, who just happened to ride past one day and fall off his horse at my feet."

"I did not fall off, I was thrown when my horse slipped! And if you didn't want to be compromised, why didn't you accept his offer to take me to his house?"

"Because, you fool, despite growing evidence that you have the thickest skull in creation, the doctor said it could cause you serious damage to be moved!" And with that she snapped the bed curtains shut and stormed from the cottage, slamming the door with a bang.

Six

Maddy stomped into the garden. Wretched man. So the idea of marrying her was preposterous, was it? As if Mr. Nameless—who couldn't even sit up without getting dizzy, and needed to be fed like a baby—were some enormous catch, and she a person of no consequence!

She knew she wasn't any man's idea of a desirable bride, but did he have to laugh? She dashed an angry tear away.

She was probably better born than him anyway. Her mother's ancestors were of the *haute nobilite*—even if they had fallen from grace for a generation or two.

She glanced across to where the children were playing some sort of game over by the wall. Knights and maidens it looked like, with Susan and Lucy playing the maidens and Jane playing the dragon. Poor Jane. Never the glamorous role. Perhaps she should . . . No. Jane was enjoying herself, she saw, giving her brothers a very hard time as the dragon, roaring and hurling imaginary bolts of fire at them, and pretending to eat up their reed swords when they got too close.

The children were perfectly happy. She was fed up with

talking to children and impossible men. She needed to talk to the bees. She'd talked to the bees ever since she was a little girl. Grand-mère had taught her: *One must always talk to the bees, confide in them your thoughts, tell them the news, who has been born and who has died. Do this and the bees will never let you down.*

She wended her way through the densely packed vegetable beds, past the chicken house to the line of fruit trees parallel to the wall that they called the orchard.

Set into the wall were arched recesses, and in those recesses sat her pride and joy, her bee hives. The recesses had been constructed with the ancient wall, built specifically for bee hives. It pleased Maddy to be part of a continuing tradition.

The bad weather was in the past, she saw as she drew closer; the little creatures were busily flying to and fro. Bees were wonderful predictors of weather. Taking care to stay out of their direct flight path, she made her way to her favorite seat, a simple slab of thick slate set on top of two stones against the wall, with hives to the left and right of her.

A dozen bees buzzed around her curiously. She stayed calm, and deciding she was harmless, they flew off.

"Oh, bees, I'm so cross and out of sorts," she began. She told them all about her stranger with no memory, for you should always tell the bees about any newcomer.

"And as for being forced into marriage to avoid scandal, who in their right mind would want that? I can't imagine anything worse than to be tied in marriage to a man who'd resent you for the rest of his life. Don't you agree?"

They did, she could tell. Bees were sensible creatures.

Maddy knew what it was like to live with a resentful man. Papa had come to resent Mama, and theirs had begun as a love match—or so Mama said.

Maddy was not so sure it was love at all. Papa had been dazzled by Mama's beauty, her noble family, and her fortune. But his love cooled as he slowly realized Mama's family and fortune would never be returned, and Mama's beauty had faded as she failed, time and time again, to give Papa the heir he craved . . .

Poor Mama, grieving endlessly for her lost babies, blamed

so bitterly for what she could not help, for what tore her apart.

To live with such resentment . . . Maddy would wish that on no woman, least of all herself.

She went on to tell the bees of the more serious problem of Sir Jasper letting her down, and the problem of the rent on the cottage that was no longer payable in honey.

"I've insisted on an audience with this heir—when he gets back to England, if ever—and will try to oblige him to honor Sir Jasper's word, but I fear he will . . . No, you're right, it's not sensible to dwell on fears for the future. One must work and take care of the children and hope for the best, I know."

The bees buzzed back and forth. She knew they listened. Probably it was the queen who lived in the center of the hive who wanted the news, making babies her entire life and never getting out, poor thing. Like Mama.

Grand-mère was right. Talking to the bees always brought a sense of peace and comfort. Maddy felt better for getting her worries off her chest, and now there was weeding to be done.

She loved this garden, with its neat rows and ordered squares. She'd made it herself, wresting it, with the help of the children, from a tangle of weeds.

She knelt by a patch of yellowing leeks and began to pull them out. There were still potatoes and onions left, but she needed to get the summer vegetables planted. The period after winter and before the new growth was harvestable was the hungry time in the garden, the same as for the bees.

Ironic to reflect that she'd hated this garden at first, furious and resentful that she was forced to grow vegetables or let the children starve, furious that Papa had been such a careless spendthrift that his children were left with nothing—worse than nothing: there were debts.

Mr. Hulme had saved them from debtor's prison, at least.

And if she wasn't sufficiently grateful to repay him in the way he wanted, well, that was Papa's fault, too. He should never have put her in that position in the first place.

She hoed vigorously between the rows, taking satisfaction from the destruction of the new weeds poking their impudent noses through the soil, stealing the goodness from her tender new seedlings.

* * *

*H*e lay back against the pillows, pricked by guilt. He shouldn't have laughed. Of course she was upset. Nobody liked to be laughed at.

But the idea of the vicar forcing a marriage between himself and Miss Woodford had struck him as so unlikely. Even without knowing anything about himself, he could see at a glance that they came from very different backgrounds.

She lived in a laborer's cottage. He was pretty sure he'd never even been in a house so small and cramped. His fascination with it told him as much. So tiny and yet six people lived here. Seven, counting himself.

And so tidily organized, everything in its place and not a single thing that he could see that did not have some practical function. No items of beauty or culture, just workaday necessities.

There were anomalies, however—her accent, for one. And the children's. They spoke as he did, properly, without strong regional inflections.

Perhaps she was a gentleman's daughter, fallen on hard times. It made the question of marriage between them no less unlikely, but if she were gently born, he could understand why she'd been offended by his laughter.

When people of once-good family lost their position in society, it made them all the touchier about being shown respect. He would apologize when she returned to the cottage.

*H*e dozed for a while but woke when he heard her returning.

"Could I have some hot water, please?" he asked, struggling to sit up. He closed his eyes to stop the spinning, and when he opened them, she was standing beside the bed, framed by the faded red curtains, as lovely a sight as any he could imagine, her face flushed and a little rosy from her time outdoors.

She watched him gravely, a cup of steaming liquid in her hand.

"I'm sorry for what I said before," he began. "About it being prepo—"

"There's nothing to apologize for," she said quickly, with a look that indicated she had no intention of discussing it further. She held out the cup. "Here, take this."

He took it and caught a whiff that made him glance at the contents. It was some kind of browny liquid. He wrinkled his nose. "What is this?"

"Willow-bark tea. It will help with the headache. And ginger which will help with the nausea."

He handed it back to her untouched. "Thank you, but no. I want hot water for a shave." He ran a hand over his rough chin and gave her a rueful smile. "I have it on good authority that I look like a vicious ruffian, some kind of pirate."

She smiled. "You mustn't mind Rev. Matheson. His bark is worse than his bite. I'll get you some hot water, but first you need to drink this." She held the cup out again.

He made no move to take it. He didn't want any medicine. The last lot of stuff she gave him had given him lurid dreams. "No, thank you."

"I've been steeping it all night." She added in a coaxing voice, "And I've sweetened it with honey to help with the bitter taste."

How old did she think he was? "I don't care about the taste; I don't want it because the last medicine you gave me did strange things to my mind."

She tilted her head on one side, like a wary little bird. "Strange things?"

"Dreams, hallucinations, that sort of thing. And waking was like trying to rise from a bed of glue." He had no intention of telling her what sort of dreams—they were deeply erotic and involved her.

"It wasn't the medicine. You were delirious last night because you were burning up with fever."

"Fever? So that's why I've been feeling so dam—er— dashed weak."

She nodded. "You were very sick. The fever broke just before dawn but it will take a while before you get your strength back. Willow-bark tea is harmless and will help with your aches and pains—and don't tell me you have none, because I can read them in your face." She thrust the cup toward him again. "It's in my interests as well as yours to have you recover quickly," she reminded him.

"Oh, very well," he said, taking it and downing it on one big gulp. He shuddered and handed her the empty cup. "It tastes atrocious."

"It's worse without the honey. Now, I suppose you'll need this." She bent and pulled out his portmanteau, handing it to him before she went to fetch the hot water.

He took out his shaving kit and unrolled it, setting out his badger-hair shaving brush, soap, razor, strop, and a bottle of liquid that he unstoppered and sniffed. Eau de cologne, it smelled pleasant and familiar. He tested the razor. A perfect edge.

"Here." She returned with a tray on which sat a basin of water, a large cup, a hand mirror, and a towel. "Are you sure you can manage?"

"Of course."

She watched while he lathered up the brush with soap and hot water and vigorously applied it to his lower face.

"I'm perfectly all right," he told her.

She nodded but didn't move away.

He picked up the mirror in one hand and the razor in another. He frowned at the razor. It was shaking like a leaf. He gripped it tighter. It was still shaking. What was the matter with his blasted hand? He brought it toward his chin, but it was shaking so much he knew he'd be bloody at the first stroke. He muttered something under his breath.

"You've been injured and had a bad fever, and you haven't yet recovered," she said softly, taking the razor out of his hand. "I'll do it. I used to shave Papa when he was ill."

He wished he'd never thought of shaving, but it was too late to change his mind. She'd think he didn't trust her—and she'd be right.

Women shaving men? Insanity.

Particularly after he'd insulted her earlier. He devoutly hoped she really had forgiven him. One way or another, he was about to find out.

She ran a thoughtful glance over him. "I could either sit on your legs to do it or—" She caught his eye and broke off.

He tried to repress a smile, but really, she was too innocent for words. Sit on his legs indeed. It was all he could do to refrain from inviting her to do so, with his very good will.

A blush stole up her cheeks. In a brisk, no-nonsense tone, she said, "Swing around so you're sitting on the edge of the bed, please."

He obediently swung. He should *not* tease a woman with a deadly sharp razor in her hand.

But he could not seem to help himself. His legs dangled, bare and hairy, over the side of the bed. The vicar's nightshirt was not so very long. It reached just to his knees.

She pulled the sheet across and draped it primly over the offending limbs.

He wondered how long it would be before she realized what the only practical stance for her would be.

Her blush intensified. She'd realized it. Slowly, keeping his face as blank as he could, he spread his knees wide and waited.

She hesitated only a moment, then with head held high, she stepped between them. She did not meet his gaze. He was glad of it. If she could see into his heart, he'd fear for his skin.

Oh, he was very glad he'd wanted to shave.

In a calm, businesslike manner, she tilted his head to one side, refreshed the lather on his throat and chin, dipped the razor in the hot water, and placed it against his throat.

He braced himself, trying not to breathe or swallow as he felt the deadly instrument slowly glide up the curve of his throat to the jawbone.

No blood spurted in its wake. He breathed again.

She rinsed the razor in hot water and made the next stroke, smoothly and deftly, and gradually the tension in him loosened.

Another kind of tension took its place.

She shaved him with concentration, a tiny pucker between her slender winged brows, the tip of her tongue peeping out, curled against her top lip.

Her full attention was on the task in hand, and he was free to observe her as closely as he pleased.

Her skin was creamy, redhead-pale, and as fine grained as a rose petal. Across the bridge of her tip-tilted nose lay a scattering of tiny golden freckles. Most women regarded freckles as a flaw, but these were like cake crumbs sprinkled over whipped cream; they made his mouth water.

Her hips were braced lightly between his thighs, and from time to time her arms, and once her breasts, brushed lightly against him as she moved. It wasn't deliberate, he knew from the infinitesimal tightening of her mouth when it happened.

He tried not to look down. Her nipples were hard and thrusting beneath her drab gown.

She wasn't the only one aroused. He tugged more covers over his groin.

She turned his head to shave the other side, and all he could see were her ears, small and delicately made, caressed by a cluster of fine fiery tendrils. He longed to taste her there, to kiss the tender place just behind the ear, to nibble on her dainty lobes, to run his tongue around the intricate whorls and make her shiver and squirm with pleasure.

Without thinking, his thighs tightened around her hips and she jumped and nicked him.

"What do you think you're doing?" she said indignantly. "Look what you made me do!" She dipped a cloth in clean water and applied it to his cheek. It came away with a smear of red.

"It's nothing," he assured her. "Sorry I startled you."

"I'm sorry, too," she said, mollified. She dipped the razor in hot water again and resumed shaving him. "Your usual valet is no doubt a great deal faster and more efficient than I am. And I suppose all this sitting up is making you tired."

He didn't say anything. Tired wasn't the problem. Temptation was. Having this delicious armful of woman so close he could touch, smell, and almost taste her. Not to take her in his arms, roll backward onto the bed, slowly unpeel those drab clothes from her, and make slow, delicious love to her for the rest of the day was more than any red-blooded man should have to bear.

Why the devil wasn't she safely married? Or suitably widowed. A married woman or widow would know what he was about, would understand the pleasure that was there for the taking.

But she was an innocent.

And he might not know much about himself, but he was fairly certain he wasn't the kind of man who'd seduce innocents.

Unfortunately.

She finished shaving him and handed him a damp towel to wipe off the last of the lather while she took the tray away. He rubbed his face all over, then his neck and the back of his neck, and quickly, while her back was turned, gave his torso and armpits a quick rub.

Cologne water on his cheeks made a satisfying sting. "Thank you. I feel like a new man."

She smiled. "I'm not sure that you look any less piratical," she said slowly, her eyes running over his face, "but at least no one will think you a ruffian."

He captured her gaze and held it. "So, I'm a pirate, am I?" he said softly.

She swallowed but didn't look away. Her eyes were brandy gold and just as intoxicating. She moistened her lips and his mouth dried. He could feel his heart pounding.

He leaned toward her, intending to pull her down to him and kiss her senseless.

She swayed infinitesimally toward him, as if she might welcome it.

"Maddy," said a plaintive voice from the doorway. "Isn't it dinner time yet? I'm starving?"

Maddy blinked, and with a palpable effort, tore her gaze from him. "Ten minutes, John. Tell the others—and remember to wash your hands and face."

*H*e lay in bed, listening to the clatter of cutlery and low instructions as Maddy supervised the setting of the table by the girls.

"Will I take the tray to Mr. Rider?"

There was a low exchange that he couldn't catch and then the curtains parted and Maddy stood there with a tray. It pulled the fabric of her dress and apron tight over her breasts.

They were, he saw, aroused still, as he was.

Under his steady regard, her cheeks slowly warmed to a soft wild-rose blush, but her chin was held high. She met his gaze with a firm, direct look and said quietly, "Please do not flirt with me. I cannot afford . . . dalliance when I have the children to think of."

She wasn't asking for his cooperation, she was stating her terms: step out of line and she'd banish him to the vicarage.

He nodded and with an effort dragged his gaze away. There was also, he suspected, an unspoken admission that she was tempted. A gentleman would respect that. A rake would not. He wondered which he would prove to be.

The tray held a bowl of thick, savory stew sitting on a bed of mashed potato. A waft of fragrant steam rose from it. He willed his stomach not to rumble.

"Jane tells me your name is Mr. Rider. Mr. Robert Rider?" Her brows turned it into a question.

"I haven't remembered anything. It's just a name the children and I agreed on," he said, struggling into a sitting position. It was easier than before. His head only swirled a little, and once he was still again, the nausea vanished and hunger took its place.

"Miss Lucy was worried that I didn't have a name, so she suggested Rider since I'd 'rided' by."

She set the tray down next to him on the bed and pushed a pillow behind him. "And Robert?"

He shrugged. "We picked it—we picked both names—to go with the R on my handkerchief."

"*We* did, did we?" She gave him a rueful look. "I'm sorry, I did tell them not to disturb you."

"Oh, but they were very careful not to *disturb* me," he explained with a wry smile. "They just *talked* to me. *Very* quietly."

Her lips twitched. "That would be John, a born lawyer, able to wiggle his way around any rule. My father was just the same. I hope you like rabbit stew—and don't worry, it's quite legal. Sir Jasper gave the boys permission to—" She broke off, then added as if to herself, "I suppose that's also changed." She picked up the spoon.

"I can feed myself," he said firmly. "A spoon is not as dangerous as a razor, and this is not as runny as soup. Besides, I feel much better now." He added deliberately, "Since I shaved."

She gave him a sharp look.

He smiled innocently back.

The wild-rose blush deepened and she left him to it. The stew was simple but delicious. He ate slowly. Outside the curtains, he could hear them all eating and clattering and talking over the day's events. The children took it in turns to tell their tales of the day's events, and there was laughter and even a little friendly teasing. It was like no family dinner he'd ever experienced.

When he was a boy, he and Marcus took most of their meals in the nursery, supervised over the years by a series of severely starched individuals who all went by the name of Nanny, a different one each year.

Sooner or later Mama always found fault with the current Nanny, and a new one took her place, as strict and humorless as the last.

Mama did not like competition for her boys' affection.

Nursery meals were quiet affairs, attention being paid mostly to table manners. Talking was not allowed.

Even worse were the rare occasions when either or both boys were summoned to the family dinner table, there to have their table manners inspected while being grilled by their father. Unnerving affairs they were, mostly silent, punctuated by a question or criticism shot at them from the head of the table.

But here, outside this curtain, he could hear her asking each child about their day, and there was enthusiastic retelling of stories and contradictions and laughter. Laughter at the dinner table! Papa would have been—

He froze. With a clatter his spoon fell from nerveless fingers. *Papa? Mama? Marcus?*

His memory was coming back.

"Are you all right, Mr. Rider?" she called.

"Yes, thank you, just a little clumsy," he managed to respond.

He remembered . . . what? He closed his eyes and tried to think, tried to remember. Who was he? What was his name?

But the Swiss cheese holes in his mind remained. It was all there, he knew, dangling tantalizingly just out of reach, like something glimpsed in passing from the corner of your eye that disappeared the moment you turned to look directly at it.

But he *had* remembered something. People. His family. He had parents and a brother called Marcus.

What was Papa's name? And where was that nursery? He

could see it in his mind's eye, a long room, set high in a big gray house. On the western side, where in the afternoon you could stand at the window and watch the sun setting. Looking out over a park toward a forest. And beyond that, mountains.

Its name was on the tip of his tongue.

But he could not remember, dammit. Each time he thought he almost had it, it just . . . slipped away.

"Finished?" She stood there, framed by the faded red curtains, as lovely a sight as any he could imagine.

He glanced down. The dish was still half full.

"You look pale," she said. "Are you all right?"

"Yes, yes, I'm all right. But . . ." He didn't know what to tell her. His memory was coming back but he still knew nothing? Better to wait until he knew who he was.

But oh, the relief, that there really were memories there.

"Don't you like rabbit?"

"No, it's . . . it's delicious, but I'm full," he lied. Not full, just feeling a bit queasy. And that was nothing to do with the food and everything to do with the things he . . . almost remembered.

"Never mind." She took the tray. "It won't be wasted. John will eat whatever you leave. He's at that age where he can eat until you think he'll burst, and then ten minutes later he's hungry again."

He nodded, not really listening, and slid back down onto the bed. The relief was tinged faintly with dread. Who would he turn out to be?

He lay, worrying at it the way you worried at a sore tooth, fruitlessly. Elusive memories danced at the edge of his consciousness, slipping away as he tried to grasp them. Like catching moonbeams reflected in water.

He was only vaguely aware of the sounds of Maddy reading a story to the children, her voice low, the words indistinct but the sound musical and soothing. He listened to her getting the children washed and changed and put to bed and tried to conjure up memories of his own childhood, such as the ones that had come unbidden earlier.

But the harder he tried, the more they refused to come.

* * *

The cottage was quiet, the children were in bed. He could hear Maddy moving around, the sound of water being poured out and soft splashes, as if . . .

His attention was suddenly riveted. She was bathing.

In a cottage this size there would be no room for a bath, and any hot water she had would have to be heated over that fire. Which meant . . .

His mouth dried as he painted the image in his mind.

She'd have to stand in something like a basin. He swallowed, his ears straining for every sound, imagining her naked in front of the fire, the light of the flickering flames caressing each delicious curve and hollow as she stood in a small tin bath, washing herself.

He heard the trickle of water. In his mind's eye, she dipped her flannel in the water, then squeezed it out and soaped it up. He strained in the silence that followed, hearing the faintest sounds of soft movement as she rubbed the moist, soapy cloth over her creamy, naked skin.

What he wouldn't give to be wielding that cloth now. In Turkey once, he'd been given a bath by two young female slaves—it was a form of hospitality he'd never encountered before. The girls hadn't seemed unhappy in their servitude; in fact, they'd been a very jolly pair. They'd washed him all over with giggles and sly caresses and it had turned into a romp that lasted half the night. He had very fond memories of that style of—

Another memory! he thought with a surge of elation. And as before, it had come when he wasn't trying to think or remember. Not thinking about it was the key, then.

More splashing sounds distracted him. It sounded exactly as though she was pouring a large pitcher of water over her soapy body. He could almost see the rivulets trickling down her body.

If he took Miss Maddy to a Turkish bath, would she let him wash her? Would she wash him?

He was aching with desire.

There was just a faded red curtain between himself and her. A gentleman would not look. He was no Peeping Tom.

On the other hand, she hadn't warned him not to look.

It wasn't as if she didn't know he was there, or that he could open the curtains to look out—he'd done it several times before. Yet she'd said nothing. Maybe she wouldn't mind if he looked.

Perhaps she even wanted him to look.

What if she were trying to seduce him, standing naked by the fire and washing herself? He wouldn't want to be found wanting. Besides, she'd get cold.

Looking, he decided, was the polite thing to do.

His mouth was dry and his heart was pounding as he leaned forward, slowly, carefully drew back the curtain, and looked out.

The fire danced. A candle flickered. There was no naked, flame-lit siren waiting. The room was empty. There was no one there at all.

He could still hear the sound of water splashing.

"Are you there, Miss Woodford?" he called out.

"I'm in the scullery." She sounded startled, a little flustered. She might, he supposed, be bathing in the scullery, though it would be cold there.

"Are you all right?" she said after a moment. "Do you want something?"

He did. He wanted her. "What are you doing?" he asked.

She hesitated. "Just a bit of washing."

But which bits was she washing? "Can you come here a moment?"

"Is it urgent?"

"Yes." His voice croaked as he said it. He was rock hard and aching for her.

"Oh, very well." He heard the sound of dripping water, quite a lot of dripping water. He braced himself.

Would she come to him naked and wet? Or wrapped modestly in a large cloth that would cover her from top to toe, clinging most delightfully to where she was damp.

"What is it?" She came, wiping her hands on a cloth, dressed exactly as she had all day. Covered from top to toe in layers of clothing. Thick layers, dammit, all fastened and buttoned up.

She gave him an expectant, quizzical look. He'd told her it was urgent. He couldn't think of a thing to say. "Water," he said finally, like a great stupid. Luckily his voice still croaked.

She brought him a cup of water and he drank it as if thirsty. He was, but not for water. She smelt like beeswax and flowers, but then she usually did.

"Another?" she asked and he nodded.

She fetched another cup and waited, her head bent in thought as he drank it down. And that's when he noticed her hair. She usually wore it twisted into a knot on the top of her head, but at night she took it down, shook it out into a glorious mass, brushed it, then braided it into a loose, silky plait. Tonight the tips of the braid were unmistakably damp. His fingers itched to unbraid it, spread it across a pillow, and bury his face in it.

"Did you just take a bath?" he asked.

"I was washing the children's smalls," she said crisply, but her cheeks flushed rosily, and it wasn't the light of the fire or the glow of the candles. She took the cup and retreated without saying a word.

He lay back, quietly exultant. He hadn't been mistaken. She'd bathed. For him. Soon she'd come to bed, fresh and fragrant.

He couldn't wait.

Seven

She put the cup on the table and disappeared, returning in a matter of moments with a small bundle of twisted cloths. She shook each one out with a snap and hung them on a line strung above the hearth with a rather pointed air, silently emphasizing that she had indeed washed children's smalls.

His lips twitched. Didn't mean she hadn't bathed.

She dumped a pile of lace and feathers and ribbons onto the table. Then she took a hat and proceeded to destroy it.

"What are you doing?"

"Refurbishing a hat. Ladies in the village pay me to make over their old hats: it's a lot cheaper than a new hat, and I have a talent for it." Her nimble fingers worked quickly, ripping faded ribbons and squashed flowers from the dowdy headpiece.

"Wouldn't it be easier to do that in the daylight?"

"Yes, but I've been busy." She bent over the hat.

Firelight danced through her hair and candlelight gilded her skin as she bent over her task with a small frown of concentration. She never stopped working. He'd never seen her just sit and be. It was his fault she was behind with her work, and the thought made him angry.

She removed the last of the old trimmings from the hat then brushed it vigorously all over with a small wire brush.

"How did you come to be living like this?" he asked abruptly.

Her flying fingers stopped for a moment, then resumed their busy work. "Like what?"

"Living in a small laborer's cottage, apparently the sole support of five young children. From your accent, you weren't born to this."

"No." She took the sad-looking, denuded hat over to the kettle and held it over the steaming spout.

"So how did you come to be here?"

"My father died in debt." She pressed the hat onto an inverted bowl and smoothed it with her hands.

"Were there no relatives you could turn to?"

"None who wanted all the children. One distant, very rich cousin would have taken Susan. Just Susan by herself. No nasty, noisy boys or inconvenient toddlers, and certainly not Jane. She had the cheek to say to me, 'Just the pretty one.'"

She threaded a needle and began to stitch a ribbon to the hat, her stitches stabbing angrily through the fabric. "Pretty one indeed! Jane is a dear, loving child and just because she isn't as pretty as Susan . . ." Her needle stabbed into the hat with precise, angry movements. "She said she would consider Lucy when she was older, that she promised fair to be pretty, too."

"You would have given Lucy away?" he said, surprised.

She turned and gave him a long, considering look. "You think Lucy is my daughter, not my sister."

"No, not at all—" he began, though indeed he had wondered.

"She's not," she said in a matter-of-fact voice. "Yes, she's a lot younger than the others, and we're both redheads, but Lucy's eyes are blue, like her brothers and sisters, and mine are brown." She smoothed out several strips of colored net ribbon, selected a bronze one, and threaded her needle.

Her eyes weren't brown, they were the color of brandy or sherry, a luminous dark gold. Intoxicating.

"I apologize, it's no business of mine."

She shook her head. "I'm used to people saying it behind my back, so I rarely get the chance to explain. The truth is,

Lucy's mother died not long after giving birth to her. Lucy is the reason Papa sent for me."

"Sent for you? Why, where were you?" He did the sums. She would have been about eighteen or nineteen when Lucy was born. "In London, making your come-out?"

"No." She gathered the net onto her needle, forming a ruffle. "That's why I thought Papa had sent for me, to make my come-out at last. But his plans were . . . otherwise."

She held up the hat, turning it and examining it from all angles. "What do you think? Will the ruffle suit?"

He gave it a cursory glance. "Yes, very elegant. But you were telling me about your father's plans. Instead of you making your come-out, he wanted—what?"

She bit off the thread with her teeth. "He wanted me to take charge of the nursery."

"Where were you?"

"Living in . . . the country with my grandmother. My mother's mother." Her mouth twisted ironically. "Living much as I am now—growing vegetables and keeping bees. It's where I learned to refurbish hats. My grandmother had a flair for such things."

He glanced again at the hat. It looked surprisingly stylish. Had her grandmother been a milliner? If so, she was a good one. That hat looked almost French. No wonder the ladies of the village used her services.

It was apparent also that her father had married beneath him and wanted to disown the offspring. "Your father couldn't help?" Surely he could have afforded to support one young girl.

She shrugged. "Papa never did acknowledge anything that wasn't right in front of him. He was very good at avoiding uncomfortable realities. Besides, Papa never liked my grandmother. And she didn't like him."

She worked in silence for a while, the only sound the crackling of the fire in the grate.

He imagined her as a young girl, toiling away in the country, caring for her elderly grandmother, growing vegetables and learning the millinery trade. Then the excitement of being sent for, anticipating her come-out, only to serve as a nursery maid instead. She must have been crushed with disappointment.

She examined the hat with a critical air. "It needs something else. Perhaps some flowers. The fashion this year is for more ornate hats and Mrs. Richards does like to be *à la mode*."

Women were amazing. How could she know the latest modes, buried here? And that French accent was good. Someone had taught her well. "Did you ever make your come-out?"

She picked over the pile of bits and pieces, putting together a small posy of ribbons and fabric blooms. "No, never. Papa said there was no need. It was too expensive, he said, and he'd already made . . . an arrangement."

"An arrangement?"

"It did not please me." He could tell by the set of her firm little chin she wasn't going to explain any further. She stitched flowers onto the hat band.

"Could your grandmother not help with the children?"

She shook her head. "She died six months before Papa sent for me. I'd written to him of her death, of course, but he didn't send for me until after his second wife died and he had four young children and a newborn baby on his hand."

She sewed on the last flower, and added, quite as if it didn't matter, "Until then, I didn't even know I had any brothers or sisters. I knew, of course, he'd married again, but in the ten years he left me with my grandmother, he'd never once mentioned children."

Ten years! And then to find he had a whole other family, and herself the eldest of six.

The hurt, not to have been told . . .

Abruptly, a shard of memory pierced him. He had a brother he'd never been told about. Or was it two brothers? He wasn't sure. There were remembered sensations of anger. And . . . jealousy? Or hatred of the interlopers. But the details eluded him.

"When did your father die?"

"Two years ago. And all he left were debts and children, so . . ." She shrugged.

"Is there nobody else to help you?"

She held up the hat, turning it and examining it from all angles. "What do you think?" She put it on and turned toward him. He was astounded. How had that stylish-looking hat emerged from those odd bits and pieces. But he wasn't going to be distracted.

"Very pretty." So, she was left wholly responsible for children she barely knew, without support from anyone. Working every hour God sent. He watched her packing up her materials.

"You must resent it," he said quietly.

"Resent what?"

"Having the children foisted on you without—"

"*Foisted?*" she said in an astonished voice. "I don't resent the children in the least. I *love* them. They're my family, the most precious thing I have. That's why I refused to let that cousin take in Susan. As long as I can take care of the children, I won't let anyone split us apart."

"But—"

"If I do harbor any resentment—and I admit I do—it's toward Papa for his foolish, selfish, spendthrift ways that left us with nothing—less than nothing—with a pile of debts! But one thing I've learned in life is not to waste time in fruitless recrimination—it helps nobody and only embitters you. Now, I think it's time for bed." She smiled brightly and disappeared into the other room.

Her words and the dazzling smile that accompanied them caused a shudder of delicious arousal to pass through him.

He lay back and waited, his body thrumming pleasantly, already partially aroused.

She returned a few minutes later, clad in a thick flannel nightgown and a woolen shawl knotted in front, concealing the shape of her breasts. It was cold, he conceded, and flannel was a reasonable choice. But she didn't need it. He'd keep her warm.

She placed a screen in front of the fire, then hurried away, returning with a roll of bedding.

"What the devil is that?" He sat up abruptly, setting his head spinning. He could see perfectly well what it was.

She arched an eyebrow. "I beg your pardon?"

Damn his language, he thought. "What are you doing?"

She bent to pull the bedding straight and the nightgown drew tight over her hips. His body responded instantly. "I'm making my bed. And then, as the saying goes, I'm going to lie in it."

"You'll do no such thing!"

"This is my home, Mr. Rider, and I'll sleep where I please."

"You'll freeze on that stone floor."

She flipped back a quilt. "It's not nearly as cold as it's been the last two nights. I'll be all right."

"I won't allow it."

"Allow?" She gave him a cool look. "You forget yourself, sir."

"I forget many things, but I do not forget my obligations as a gentleman," he said grimly. He flipped back his bedclothes, all thought of seduction gone, and swung his legs over the side.

"What are you doing?"

"If you think I'm going to let a woman sleep on the cold, hard floor while I sleep in her bed, you've got another think coming." He touched his injured ankle to the floor and winced.

"Stop! The doctor said if you tried to use that ankle, you might cripple yourself!"

"It's entirely up to you," he told her. "If you persist in this nonsense about sleeping on the floor, then I have no choice but to sleep there instead." He made a move as if to stand.

"Stop!" She stared at him, frustrated.

He stared right back.

"You're so stubborn!" she said at last.

He could smell capitulation. "Pot calling the kettle black."

She clenched her hands. "I will be perfectly all right on the floor."

"Then so will I. In the meantime, that stone floor is freezing your toes."

The toes in question curled under his gaze and she stepped onto the rag rug nearby. "If they're cold, it's your fault for keeping me from my bed."

"I'm not keeping you from your bed," he said. He waved his hand. "Here it is, all toasty and warm, waiting for you."

"You must know I can't share a bed with you."

"Why not? You have the last couple of nights, and emerged quite unharmed. In fact, I'd suggest that you slept the better for having me in the bed. You were certainly warmer."

"How could you know that?"

He nodded toward her feet. "Your feet were half frozen that first night when you came to bed. You thawed them on my calves."

She flushed. "I did not."

He grinned. "That part of the past I do remember, very clearly. Like little blocks of ice, they were. Woke me up."

There was a long silence. She hovered, undecided.

He tried to sound as disinterested as possible. "You know it's the most sensible solution. What good would it do you or the children if you caught a chill?"

She bit her lip.

"Come on," he said in a coaxing voice. "I promise to be a gentleman. And you can bring Hadrian's Wall with you." He added ruefully, "Even if I wanted to seduce you, in the state I'm in you could easily fend me off. One biff on the head and I'll be out like a snuffed candle." And that, unfortunately, was true.

"Very well," she said, and he moved back to make room for her. "But nobody must ever find out. If they did . . ."

"How would anyone find out? I won't tell anyone, and if the vicar asks you, you will continue to lie to him, just as you did today."

"I did not lie to him," she said indignantly. "I told him I'd made up a bed on the floor, and I had."

"Yes, you merely left out the part about not sleeping in it. Perfectly unexceptional. And you've made up the bed on the floor tonight, as you said you would, so stop hopping about on the cold stone floor and get into bed."

She grabbed a quilt from the bed on the floor, rolled it into a Hadrian's Wall, stuffed it against him, and climbed in after it. She pulled the bedclothes over her, shivering.

"See, you're half frozen," he said, and put his arms around both her and Hadrian's Wall.

"Stop that," she said, but he could tell a halfhearted objection when he heard it.

"You can warm your feet against my legs if you like," he invited. The fresh, distinctive scent of her and her soap teased his nostrils.

She made a small huffing noise and didn't move. "You're pleased about this, aren't you? she said crossly.

"It's the only logical choice." He couldn't keep the satisfaction out of his voice. His gentlemanly promise had definitely slowed his plans for seduction. But so had his aching head, and there was more than one way to seduce a woman . . .

After a while she stopped shivering.

"I told you," he murmured. "All toasty and warm."

"Do your ribs hurt you at all?" she asked in a soft voice.

"No, not a bit—oof! What was that for?" She'd edged an arm under Hadrian's Wall and elbowed him in the ribs, hard.

"For being stubborn, manipulative, and impossible," she purred. "And for gloating. Good night, Mr. Rider. Sweet dreams."

Maddy smiled as she closed her eyes. He deserved it, she told herself. He'd blackmailed her into his bed. Her bed. And as she'd climbed into bed she'd caught a gleam, in the firelight, of a white, triumphant smile.

And as for his arms around her, pulling her against his long body, well, Hadrian's Wall was some protection, but not much. She'd tried to push him away, but she was so cold and he was so warm it was easier not to resist.

It wasn't just about the cold, she admitted to herself. Having his arms around her, sharing a bed, it felt . . . lovely. She felt warm, protected, and less alone than she'd felt for a very long time.

Her feet were still cold, but she was drifting off when she felt a stealthy movement in the bed. She feigned sleep, curious to see what he was up to, ready to repulse a rakish advance.

A large, warm foot burrowed beneath the rolled-up quilt that separated them. He hooked it around her feet and slowly drew them toward him. Drawn by the warmth generated by his body, she let her feet be taken and warmed between his calves.

She didn't know whether to laugh or cry. A wicked, rakish devil he was, to be sure, warming her feet in secret.

She fell asleep with a smile on her face.

*T*hump! *Thump!*
      Maddy's eyes flew open. A sick feeling curdled in her stomach. Not again.

Thump! Thump! The door rattled on its hinges but the new bolt held fast. A low moaning came from outside. Unearthly. Terrifying.

A shadow appeared at the window. Something scrabbled

against the glass, as though with claws. The hairs on the back of her neck lifted.

The moaning rose in pitch, louder and louder, until it ended on a deathly shriek. The horrid sound shivered through her.

The frenzied scrabbling continued. The glass couldn't take much more, she thought. Any instant it would shatter.

The man in her bed sat up. "What the devil is that infernal noise?"

"Nothing," she muttered. "Go back to sleep." He was an invalid. He couldn't help. She was shaking. With rage, she told herself. And sick, desperate fear.

She reached for the frying pan she kept under the mattress and began to slide out from beneath the covers. Iron fingers gripped her arm. "Nothing, my foot. Where are you going with that? What's the trouble?"

"It's nothing," she insisted. "Just someone trying to frighten me and the children." He might be an invalid, but oh, just having someone there with her was comforting.

"How do you know?"

"It's not the first time this has happened," she said tersely, watching where the sounds were coming from.

Another unearthly howl shattered the night, and the scratching at the window started again, a slow, teeth-shivering shriek. The glass panes creaked under the onslaught.

"Is it back, Maddy?" a small, quaking voice whispered from the stairs.

Oh, God, the children . . .

John and Jane were halfway down the stairs, pale as ghosts, their little faces pinched and terrified. Yet heartbreakingly resolute. Facing dragons—real ones this time. With shaking hands, John gripped the hunting knife his father had given him. Jane also shook like a leaf, but she grasped a rolling pin in businesslike fashion.

Behind them on the stairs, Susan squatted, her arms around Lucy, who was sobbing quietly. Henry stood with his arms protectively around his sisters. An eight-year-old, trying to be a man.

Rage drove out the worst of Maddy's fear. Children should not be driven to this. "Don't worry," she said in as firm a voice as she could manage. "He can't get in. He's just a nasty man trying to frighten us."

"What if he breaks the glass?" Jane whispered.

"Then I'll hit him over the head with this frying pan," Maddy said fiercely.

The first few times their tormentor had come in the night, she'd been too terrified to move. She'd huddled with the children, waiting for the creature to break in, braced for a fight.

This was the fourth nocturnal visit but he'd never broken in. She wasn't quite as frightened.

The window darkened and a face peered in. The children screamed. It was horrifying. He—or it—was faceless. The shambling figure wore a robe and hood, like a monk, but where his face should be was . . . nothing. Blank, white emptiness. It moaned, like something out of the grave, shrouded white fingers clawing at the glass on either side of the facelessness.

"It's a trick," Maddy said furiously. "He's trying to frighten us, wearing something like gauze or cheesecloth over his face and using a hidden lantern. John, you did the same thing once at Halloween, remember? He's not a ghost, just a beastly creature who thinks he can frighten us. Well, HE DOESN'T FRIGHTEN ME!" she shouted at the window. It was a lie. She was shaking like a leaf.

"There's a gun in my bag," Mr. Rider snapped. "Fetch it!"

She gave him a startled look. "A gun?"

"While he thinks you're alone and unprotected, with only rolling pins and frying pans to defend yourself, he won't be stopped. But if he thinks you have a gun . . ."

She ran to fetch the pistol.

"Take the children and wait upstairs," he told her.

"No, this is my problem." She wasn't going to run and hide and let a sick man—a stranger—defend her. This was her home.

"It might ricochet."

"Oh, I see." She hesitated as suddenly the possibility of killing a man loomed. "I don't mind if you wound him, but I don't want him killed."

"Why not?"

"Because I want to find out why he's doing this. And if you shatter the window, we will freeze."

He shrugged. "Very well. Now get those children out of the way."

She grabbed a blanket and gathered the children together. They crouched on the landing, huddled together under the blanket, watching breathlessly.

Again, the figure pressed his distorted gauzy face against the panes. Vile creature! Maddy's arms tightened around the small, shaking bodies.

Mr. Rider fired into the wood stacked beside the fireplace. The *bang!* was so loud Maddy nearly jumped out of her skin. There was a sudden silence, then the sound of running feet.

"Is he gone, Maddy?" Lucy sobbed. Maddy flew down the stairs and flung open the door, peering out into the darkness to see if she could recognize the fleeing man. But he was just a dark, robed shape, racing up the hill in the moonlight.

She closed the door and bolted it again.

The children crept downstairs, needing to make sure the terror was over. John and Henry searched the woodpile for the spent ball. Jane, Susan, and Lucy huddled in front of the fire in the blanket while Maddy warmed some milk. The man on the bed quietly cleaned his gun. Observing.

The children drank their milk, pelting Maddy with questions, but answers—real answers—eluded her. The children were satisfied enough with "a bad man"—the bogeyman of every childhood.

Maddy didn't believe in bogeymen. There had to be a reason.

"I can't imagine why," she told Mr. Rider as she climbed back into the bed. "He doesn't seem to want to break in. The first time he came there wasn't even a proper lock on the door, just a latch. One good shove and it would have flown right open. But he didn't even try."

He pulled the covers up around her shoulders. "He must want something."

"Yes, but what? We have no money and very few possessions. We don't even own the cottage. What can possibly be gained by frightening a lone woman and five small children?"

"Satisfaction?" he suggested. "There are bullies in this world who enjoy such things."

She considered it. "I haven't offended anyone that I can

think of." Except Mr. Harris, the estate manager, she thought suddenly, though all she'd done was argue about the rental agreement with Sir Jasper.

"How many times has this happened?"

"This is the fourth occasion in the last two weeks." And in the last two weeks, Mr. Harris had come around demanding an increased rent.

"There's nothing to be done about it now, so close your eyes and get some sleep," he said, pulling her back against him. "We'll work out what to do about it in the morning."

That "we" was very comforting, she thought as she slowly relaxed. As was the warmth of him spooned against her.

It was only as she was drifting off that she realized Hadrian's Wall was gone, but she was too tired and too sleepy to worry about it.

Eight

*T*he steady rhythm of her breathing altered. She was waking.

He'd woken a few minutes earlier, breathing in the fragrance of her, the scent of her skin where his mouth just touched the nape of her neck, the fragrance of her newly washed hair, soft against his cheek, smelling faintly of . . . something enticing.

Slowly he realized that the warm weight in his hand was her breast, that he was spooned around her, along the length of her spine, his knee cradled between her soft thighs, bare inches from her cleft.

His body was fully aroused. Aching with desire.

He ought to release her, turn away. He'd given her his word as a gentleman.

But their bodies had arranged themselves thus in sleep; it wasn't a deliberate attempt at seduction.

And he couldn't make himself move.

Besides, he wanted to see how she would react. Was she, like him, torn between temptation and good sense?

As far as he was concerned, propriety wasn't even a question. They'd shared a bed for three nights now. Or was it four? He couldn't tell; whole days and nights were lost to him.

But propriety was mostly about what other people thought. What they didn't know couldn't offend them.

Common sense was another matter.

Common sense dictated that neither of them took action that might have unwanted consequences. Common sense reminded him that he didn't know who he was. He could be married. He'd be a fool to act without knowing the risk.

And she—she would be foolish indeed to let herself be seduced by a nameless man. Reputation was one thing. To be pregnant and unwed, quite another.

There was no question of marriage. Cottage didn't marry castle. His memory might be in shreds but the few glimpses of "home" he'd recalled were of a large and impressive edifice—if not a castle, a very grand house indeed.

He was playing with fire but he couldn't stop.

He feigned sleep, anticipating the moment she became aware of where his hand was placed, where his knee rested, and what it was that was nudging insistently against her peach of a backside.

Would she shoot out of bed like scalded cat?

Or would she stay and snuggle?

With sleepy sensuousness she began to stretch, then froze with a jagged gasp. A period of cautious stillness followed.

He smiled. He could almost hear her mind ticking, working out just which body part was where.

And then he felt her response. His pulse kicked up a notch as her nipple hardened against the center of his palm. It took every bit of his willpower not to respond.

But she had to feel his erection pressing against her. He was rock hard and aching.

Her nightgown had ridden up to her hips. He could feel the exact point where smooth, soft feminine skin gave way to soft, well-washed flannel. He smiled to himself as she tried surreptitiously to tug it down, then suppressed a groan as the back of her hand brushed against his erection.

She froze. Her hand stayed where it was, unmoving.

Was it possible to get any harder? He doubted it.

It was hell, poised on the brink of paradise, unable to move, and concentrating on the rhythm of one's breathing. Should he "wake up" and put an end to this exquisite torture?

Every fiber of his body screamed to take her, seduce her while she was warm and sleepy and receptive.

But if he did, he'd never learn what she might do of her own volition. And he needed, quite desperately, to know.

She moved and he wanted to groan, but he kept his silence as she lifted away the arm that held her and turned in the bed to face him, raising the covers and settling his arm along his body.

He expected her to slide out of bed straight away, but she stayed, her face inches from his. He could sense her closeness. What was she doing? What was she looking at? He wanted to open his eyes and drink her in, but he wanted more to see what she would do.

There was a rustle of bedclothes and he nearly jumped from his skin as she smoothed away the hair below his bandage. Every inch of skin dying for her touch and she had to caress his forehead!

He kept his breathing regular, his lips slightly parted. She ran her finger over his mouth in the lightest of featherlight caresses, lingering on the scar at the corner of his mouth. She brushed her fingers along his jaw. Did he need another shave?

She eased the bedclothes down a little. *More,* he urged silently. He wore the vicar's nightshirt unbuttoned—he wished now he'd removed it in the night, dealing with it as he'd dealt with the thing she called Hadrian's Wall.

She raised the bedclothes a little higher and he felt a draft of cold air. He welcomed it. His body, or at least one part of it, was burning.

She was curious. *Higher,* he urged her silently, *higher. Take all the bedclothes off.*

It was foolish to be staring now, Maddy told herself. He could wake at any moment, and she'd be exposed, behaving like a . . . wanton.

She glanced at his face. The long thick lashes didn't even flutter. His chest rose and fell steadily, his breathing unchanged. He was sound asleep.

She was absurdly nervous.

Her gaze returned to the deep V in the neck of his nightshirt. He'd left every button undone and his solid, masculine chest, with its dusting of curly dark hair, fascinated her. Which was ridiculous.

She'd seen him stark naked numerous times, had dried every inch of him. His body should have no mystery left for her.

Yet she couldn't drag her eyes away.

As for what she'd felt when she tried to drag the hem of her nightgown to a more decent level . . . The hard, heated flesh that thrust against her . . .

It hadn't felt like any naked part of him she'd seen. And she was burning with curiosity.

She lifted the bedclothes higher . . . higher . . . The fabric of his nightshirt was tented, covering the place where she most wanted to look. She pinched a fold of the material between thumb and finger and tugged lightly. The nightshirt slid upward. She tugged again—

"Go ahead, lift it all the way," invited a deep voice laced with sleepy amusement.

She dropped the bedclothes. "I didn't. I wasn't." But she did. She was. Caught red-handed. Red-faced, more like. Her cheeks were burning.

He chuckled and it was like rich, warm chocolate. *Knowing* chocolate. "Go ahead, I don't mind."

She tried to think of something to say. "I was just checking . . ." She trailed off, unable to think of a single excuse.

He slanted a wicked grin at her. "And am I all right? Nothing broken? In need of attention?"

His head and his ankle were injured: she'd been looking right smack bang in between. Where she had no business to be looking. She squirmed with mortification.

"It doesn't matter," she mumbled.

"Actually I'm feeling a bit hot. And I'm sure there's a swelling. And it's aching. Are you sure you wouldn't like to check me?" His expression was pure, laughing devil.

"No, I—"

"Little liar." He reached out a lazy hand, cupped the back of her head, and kissed her.

It was a slow, soft kiss, warm as the morning sun, laced with the dark mystery of the night. Rich with promise.

A kiss that unraveled her defenses before she had time to put them in place. Not at all what she'd expected.

It was over almost before she knew it. He released her and drew back, leaving her slightly dazed. And wanting more.

She stared at his mouth, still moist from hers. Kissing him was not like she'd expected. Two nights ago she'd fed him willow-bark tea from her mouth and thought nothing could be so intimate.

She was wrong. Totally, utterly wrong.

She didn't know what to say. His blue eyes seared her, brighter than the morning sky, seeming to read her innermost thoughts. Her eyes dropped to the rumpled bedclothes and she blurted out the first thing that came into her head.

"You promised to be a gentleman." As if she'd been at all ladylike. A lady would never peek at a gentleman's . . . member. Particularly when he was asleep.

But how could he be asleep and also . . . aroused?

From the corner of her eyes she caught the glint of a smile.

"I *am* a gentleman." The way he said it, it might as well have been, "I am a wolf." More accurate, too.

"Nevertheless, you kissed me."

His eyes danced. "It was a very gentlemanly kiss." He leaned forward and murmured, "Would you like me to show you what an ungentlemanly kiss is like? Just so you know." The gleam deepened.

For a moment she forgot to respond, her imagination caught up with thoughts of what an ungentlemanly kiss might be like. Enticing thoughts. Probably quite reprehensible ones.

"Purely for educational purposes, you understand," he purred. Exactly like the cat who was about to get the cream.

"No," she said, firmly. "I'm not the least bit interested."

"Little liar." Again, he made it sound like an endearment.

"A gentleman wouldn't have kissed me at all," she said primly, rallying her stuffiest ancestors to the cause.

"Only if you took the 'man' out of gentleman."

She frowned, unsure of his meaning.

"No man could resist," he murmured, and before she realized his intention, he was kissing her again.

She'd liked the first kiss very much.

But the ungentlemanly kiss . . . sucked every . . . coherent . . . thought from her brain . . .

He kissed her open-mouthed, seeking, demanding, mastering. She tasted heat . . . dark masculinity . . . potent desire . . . as with mouth, tongue, and hands he claimed a response her body gave willingly, urgently.

She melted under the onslaught, pressing against him, writhing against him, all thoughts of modesty and propriety dissolved in the flood of sensation as she kissed him back, needing more, craving more.

Abruptly he released her. Maddy, her senses spinning, her limbs heavy and uncoordinated, nevertheless knew what she ought to do. She tried to climb out of the bed.

His hand shot out and held her by the wrist. "Don't go."

"What?" She was still a little dazed, her body still clinging to the effects of his kiss, her blood singing.

"We haven't finished."

Her body agreed with him, but, "We have." She tried to pull away from his grasp.

"There are things we need to discuss."

"What things?"

He held on to her, gently but firmly. "The things that went bump in the dark last night."

"Oh, that." She tried not to feel disappointed.

"Have you reported it?"

She sighed. "Of course, but it's done no good. The landlord's agent says I'm a foolish female frightened by shadows, the magistrate can do little without evidence of damage or a person to charge, and the vicar's solution was for us to move in with him and Mrs. Matheson. A few villagers I told suggested an exorcism." She saw his expression and explained, "They're convinced it's the Bloody Abbot walking again."

His brows rose. "The Bloody Abbot?"

"The ancient ghost of an abbot who was killed trying to prevent Henry the Eighth's men from destroying the religious carvings at the abbey. The village is very proud of him. But I don't believe it."

"You don't believe in ghosts?"

"This is definitely no ghost, just a man."

"Men can be as dangerous as ghosts, more so."

As if she didn't know that. But dangerous men didn't only bang on windows in the night. Some of them trapped you by other means, spooning their long, strong bodies around you in the night and dizzying you with long, sweet, addictive kisses.

He held her still, his long fingers imprisoning her wrist lightly, effortlessly. She tugged it for release. "I have to go." While her willpower lasted.

His gaze locked with hers as slowly he lifted her wrist to within a hairsbreadth of his mouth, so close she could feel the warmth of his breath on her skin. She couldn't look away, suddenly, absurdly breathless as, without breaking his gaze, he turned her hand over and kissed her slowly in the heart of her work-worn palm. The sensation shivered right through her. Without conscious volition, her fingers closed to cup his face.

"I'll find this false ghost of yours," he promised her, his voice husky, knight to maiden. "I'll get him, don't worry." He kissed her palm again, and again delicious shivers rippled through her body.

She ached to sink back into his embrace and lose herself in more of those deep, drugging, devouring kisses. She longed, just once, to forget about her problems and responsibilities and lose herself in sensation, letting a man, this man, make love to her.

Even if he was a rake, even if the love was counterfeit. She wanted, just once, to have the morning dream come true.

But if she did, she risked losing herself altogether.

She steeled herself to pull away from him and slid out of the bed. The sharp chill of the stone floor brought her to her senses.

Her blood might be singing with pleasure and excitement, and her foolish heart yearning after impossible dreams, but this was dangerous, too dangerous for a woman in such a precarious position.

She had to keep him at arm's length. Further. She could feel the imprint on his mouth against her palm still. Her fingers were closed protectively over it, as if they could keep and cradle his kiss forever.

If anyone in the village had the slightest idea of what had happened in the bed this morning . . .

Her good reputation was the fine slender thread that connected her in friendship to the villagers. And without their friendship—and their custom for honey, hats, and eggs—she and the children could not survive.

While the few people who knew thought him a helpless invalid, she was safe.

But he was no invalid now. She had to put a stop to it, before she allowed any further liberties.

"When my head is no longer a blacksmith's anvil, we'll try that again," he murmured with a faint, wry smile.

She turned and found him watching her, the way a cat watches a mouse it has already trapped, possessively, with leashed anticipation.

It was as if he'd dashed a bucket of cold water in her face. He knew nothing of her position, and from his expression, he didn't care. He was a rake.

And she was a stupid, dreamy fool.

"And will that be soon?" she asked.

He gave her a crooked, altogether wicked smile. "I certainly hope so."

"Good."

"Good?" His smile broadened.

"Yes, for as soon as your head is not a blacksmith's anvil," she said sweetly, "you will leave this house."

For an instant, it wiped the smug look from his face, then he rallied. "I can't. Where would I go? I have no memory, remember?" His piteous expression was patently feigned, his tone so ripe with confidence it enabled her to harden her heart.

"Where would you go?" she echoed. "To the place in the parish where any poor, lost soul is welcome, of course."

He blinked. "You'd never send me to the workhouse."

"Of course not. You have too much money. You'll go to the vicar's."

His brows snapped together. "That prosy old bore's? Impossible."

"No, it will be quite easy," she assured him, willfully misunderstanding. "He has a carriage with which to convey you. It's very well sprung. It will hardly bump your aching bones at all."

"I won't go."

"You won't?" She arched an eyebrow at him.

"I can't. I'm—I'm allergic to clergy. And windbags. And fruit bowls."

She laughed. "Nonsense."

"It's true," he said earnestly. "I come out in . . . hives . . . and . . . boils at the merest whiff of a sermon."

"But how can you possibly know that, Mr. Rider," she said sweetly, "when you don't even remember your name?"

He shrugged. "It's like Hadrian's Wall, one of those odd things I remember."

"Very odd. And quite irrelevant, I'm afraid. The minute you're able to move, I'm taking my bed back."

"You're more than welcome in it. Have I not made it clear?"

"On the contrary and that's the pr—" She stopped. She was not going to get into a debate with him.

"You're running scared." His gaze dropped briefly to her breasts and he smiled.

Aware that her nipples had hardened in the cold, she folded her arms over her chest. "Of what, pray, am I scared?"

He sat back against the pillows, folded his arms behind his head, and grinned. "You liked what's been happening in the bed and you're afraid that next time you won't have the strength of mind to stop."

Well, of course she was. She was only human, wasn't she? Her body, even now, was urging her to leap back into the bed and let him finish what they'd started, but she—thank God!—was in the grip of cold, hard reality.

"Nonsense," she said, and it sounded feeble, even to her own ears. "The moment you're well enough to be moved, you will go to the vicar's. My mind is made up. Now, I need to get the children ready for their lessons—"

"Ohhhh!" He groaned suddenly and doubled up.

"What?" She hurried closer to the bed. His face was screwed up with pain. "What's the matter?"

He opened one bright blue eye and said in a perfectly normal voice. "I'm having a relapse."

She fought a smile. "You're impossible. And you won't change my mind."

His eyes danced as he gave another artistic groan. "I'm

allergic to clergy. Vicars give me vertigo . . . priests give me palpitations . . . and bishops make me bilious." He added in an unconvincingly feeble voice, "I might be stuck here for weeks . . ."

"In that case, I'll call in the vicar for the laying on of hands." She pulled the bed curtains closed with a snap.

His voice followed her into the scullery. "He'd better not lay a hand on me! He poked a finger in my ribs yesterday in a thoroughly unfriendly manner! If he tries it again, I'll punch him, man of the cloth or not."

Maddy grinned. He was a devil, to be sure. She put the oatmeal on to cook, washed and dressed, and went upstairs to wake the children.

"Can I take Mr. Rider his breakfast?" Jane asked when the porridge was ready.

"You did it last time," Susan interrupted. "It's my turn."

"I'll take it," John offered. "I'm sure he'd rather have a man—"

"You can all take it," Maddy interrupted before the squabble could start. "Jane, take the tray with the porridge, Susan, take the honey, Henry carry the milk jug, and John give him his willow-bark tea. Tell Mr. Rider he can add more honey if it's too bitter."

"Amazingly enough, Mr. Rider can hear through the curtain," a deep voice said.

"I want to take something, too," Lucy spoke up.

"Yes, of course, you must take his napkin." Maddy handed it to the little girl, who marched importantly to the bed, stool for climbing on in one hand and napkin in the other.

Maddy waited for the children to stop fussing over him and return to the table. They were as fascinated with him as she was. He was so wretchedly charming. Quite impossible to resist.

But she had to.

Even when he was unconscious, she'd been drawn to him.

She hadn't known him at all, hadn't known that his eyes were bluer than a summer sky in the evening, that they could tease and dance with mischief, and suddenly turn somber as the night. Or that blue could burn with an intense light . . .

And yet she'd slept three nights with his body against hers, feeling—quite illogically—safe with a stranger in her bed.

Worse, she'd assumed it would continue to be safe once he came to his senses. Because he was a gentleman.

Madness! He was more dangerous than ever now. And in ways she would never have realized.

Who could see danger in watching him in serious conversation with two small boys, allowing them to tell him things about horses he'd probably known forever, not letting on for an instant that he was tired or bored or in pain?

But there was. There was danger in the way he smiled and thanked Jane or Susan for fetching him a cup or taking a plate, making little girls feel important and appreciated.

Lucy was quite possessive of him, certain it was her kiss that had awakened him. And though it was clear he'd had little to do with children, he hadn't dismissed her childish notions but responded with grave kindness that had the little girl glowing with pride.

He'd ignored his own injuries to protect them from an intruder. He must have known firing the gun would cause him pain, but he never hesitated.

Before, she didn't know the kind of man he was.

She didn't know it now, she reminded herself. She still knew nothing about him.

Only that he was kind to women and children. And chivalrous. And stubborn. A gentleman. And there was the rub. He was a gentleman, to his clean and well-tended fingertips.

But also a rake.

Even though she knew little about him, she could tell he didn't belong in her world. And she didn't fit in his and probably never had.

He had excellent manners. Was protective, gallant. Funny. Handsome.

Dangerous.

The lure, the lie of Prince Charming, she reminded herself. Women had a fatal tendency to see romance in men and situations where there was none. It was why Grand-mère had made Raoul wait for two years . . . Protecting herself from her own fatal tendencies.

Of course Mr. Rider was nice to her and the children—he had nothing else to do, nowhere to go. His very survival was dependent on their kindness.

He was just a man. But for her, dangerous.

She needed him gone. Her life would be drabber, less exciting, but her heart would be safer.

*T*he door flew open and Maddy put her head in. "Hide! Mr. Harris is coming."

Who the devil was Mr. Harris? He looked around for a place to hide. There was only the scullery and it was too cold to be cooling his heels out there for who knew how long. He climbed back into the bed and drew the curtains.

He watched through a gap in the fabric. Harris was about forty, solidly built, but his breeches were too tight, his coat too bright, and his thinning hair, once he carefully removed his hat, had been teased and pomaded and trained carefully over a bald patch.

A suitor? He was far too old for her, not to mention too damned ridiculous.

Harris entered the cottage and seated himself at the table without being invited. His confidence, almost an air of ownership, was annoying. He came straight to the point. "I've received instructions from the new owner—"

"I thought you said he was out of the country," she interrupted.

He gave her a tight look. "That's right, Russia. But he sent instructions to his brother, who has his power of attorney."

"His brother?"

"The Earl of Alverleigh." Harris turned his head. "What was that? Is there someone here?"

Behind the curtains, he stiffened. Damn. He must have made a sound. But the *Earl of Alverleigh*? The name meant something. But what?

"Who would there be?" she asked Harris. "Now about this letter—"

Harris didn't respond. He stared at the alcove, his brows knotted with suspicion. "Have you got someone in there?"

She made an impatient gesture. "The children sometimes play there. Perhaps Lucy is taking a nap. What does it matter? Did you inform the new owner about the promise Sir Jasper—"

"Five pounds by the end of the week."

Her jaw dropped in dismay. "Five pounds? But I don't have five pounds."

"Then you'll have to leave."

"Leave? But I can't poss—"

"Five pounds by the end of the week, or you're out. Mr. Renfrew's letter was adamant." The chair creaked as Harris leaned back, obviously savoring the moment.

"But that's tomorrow."

Harris shrugged.

"Who is this Mr. Renfrew? I need to speak with him."

"The Honorable Mr. Nash Renfrew is the new owner. He's Sir Jasper Brownrigg's nephew and brother to the Earl of Alverleigh," Harris said with ill-concealed satisfaction. He kept speaking, but his words seemed to fade away.

Renfrew? The Earl of Alverleigh? The little world of the bed in the alcove seemed to spin. *Renfrew . . .*

Nash Renfrew . . .

He'd seen an avalanche in Switzerland, once. First a tiny, almost invisible fracture, and a small piece of snow had slipped. An odd sort of ripple had followed and snow had started sliding, first in ribbons, then in ragged sheets, until suddenly an entire mountainside was falling, tumbling, the landscape shattering downward at a terrifying speed, taking everything with it.

And afterward a terrible, echoing silence.

His memory came back like that, a tiny fracture that started with his name, Nash Renfrew.

He was Nash Renfrew. And his brother was Marcus, Earl of Alverleigh.

And suddenly his brain was filled with ribbons, sheets of memory: names, faces, moments, smells, all reconnecting, swirling, crashing, falling into place like a mad puzzle that had been tormenting him elliptically for days, and now, finally, began to make sense.

He wasn't sure how much time had passed while it was happening; in some ways it felt like hours, yet it was over in a flash. A bit like the avalanche.

And afterward he was left almost as shattered, as he began to put it together, put himself together.

His name was Nash Renfrew and he was coming home

from . . . no, not coming home. He was going to see Uncle Jasper's estate. Someone had written—Marcus? No, some lawyer, he thought, to say that Uncle Jasper had died. Nash had known for several years that he was the heir. Whitethorn Manor was unentailed, Jasper had never married, and Nash being a younger son, had little property of his own.

So he was riding to Uncle Jasper's estate . . . no, that wasn't right. One didn't get off a ship and ride a horse right across the country. He'd just come back from . . . from Russia, from St. Petersburg. No, that was wrong, too. He'd gone to London first, and then visited Aunt Maude in Bath before he left, left . . . for . . .

The house party! He nearly spoke the words aloud. He'd almost forgotten he wasn't alone, that discretion was crucial. He was Nash Renfrew and discretion was his middle name.

He peered out between the curtains, but Harris was gone. Maddy was wrapping herself in a cloak, her face set and grim.

"Maddy," he said, "I must tell you—"

"Later," she said brusquely. "I have to go out."

"But I have my mem—"

The door closed behind her.

Nash didn't mind. He'd tell her when she returned. Power surged through him. He was himself again, in control, no longer a helpless creature with no idea of who he was. His physical injuries were irrelevant now. They would heal. He had himself back and that was what counted.

Bizarre how knowing one's identity mattered so very much.

Nine

He had his memory back. He was himself again. And to Nash's frustration, there was nobody here to tell.

He recalled Maddy's frequent questions about who would be worrying about his non-arrival. The answer was nobody.

From London, he'd called on Aunt Maude in Bath, and after her, his plan was to drop in on Harry and Nell at Firmin Court on his way to Whitethorn Manor. A rapid but thorough inspection of his inheritance, make any arrangements necessary, then back to London for the ball and the grand duchess.

And then . . . possibly . . . a wedding.

In Bath he'd run into an old acquaintance who'd invited him to a house party near Horningsham. But he soon realized the house party was simply an excuse for evening bed games and no place for any potential brides. Nash had no interest in random and indiscriminate coupling, and since Horningsham was only a day's ride across country from Whitethorn, he decided to ride ahead and arrive early at his new estate. He'd sent his valet on to Harry and Nell's. So nobody was expecting him anywhere until next week at least.

He wished Maddy hadn't run off; he wanted to tell her the

good news. Not just that he'd gotten his memory back, but that he was her new landlord and her worries were over. She could stay here rent-free for the rest of her life. It was the least he could do for the woman who'd saved his life.

If only she'd waited one minute . . .

What instructions?

Harris's exact words had been *I've received instructions from the new owner.*

Nash hadn't had any correspondence with Harris at all, least of all about raising rents. If Harris was lining his pockets with illegal rent increases, he was in for an unpleasant surprise.

Was Harris the "Bloody Abbot," and if so, why? Making money on the side, Nash could understand, but terrorizing a woman and children? And while Maddy and the children were in the slightest danger of being terrorized again, Nash couldn't leave them.

It was a problem. The moment he told Maddy he had his memory back, she'd insist he leave. Especially since, as it turned out, he had a large house down the road with a dozen beds or more. Why would she let him remain in her bed?

He liked being in her bed. He liked it more than he should. More than he had with any other woman.

In fact . . . it slowly dawned on him . . . he didn't want to leave her at all.

How the hell had that happened?

He'd always kept his dealings with women light—no strings, no commitment—choosing as his paramours ladies who wanted it that way as well. It was his rule: light, superficial fun, and nobody getting hurt.

This . . . this whatever-it-was with Maddy Woodford wasn't light or superficial at all. It was heading into seas he'd never navigated before, seas he'd managed to steer clear of his entire life, and he wasn't about to start now.

But if he realized the danger in time—and he had—he could act.

Thank God he'd gotten his memory back. Forgetting his own name wasn't nearly as bad as forgetting the danger Maddy Woodford posed to his peace of mind.

Thank God she'd had sense enough to stop him when he'd

tried to entice her into making love. A few kisses didn't matter, even if kissing her affected him like no other kisses had. It was probably a side effect of the amnesia.

He could still get out, save himself, save them both from an entanglement neither of them needed. He would. He'd go to Whitethorn this very afternoon.

But what if Maddy and the children faced another night of terror?

Dammit, he couldn't let that happen.

No choice, really. He had to stay on here. He'd set a trap, catch the bastard, and get him securely locked away, transported to the other side of the world. Then Maddy and the children would be safe and he could leave with a clear conscience.

He'd keep the recovery of his memory to himself a little longer. It wouldn't be a lie, exactly, just a withholding of the whole truth.

And in the meantime, he'd make sure he kept the luscious Maddy Woodford at a safe distance.

"Miss Woodford, this is for you," he said when Maddy returned to the cottage. He handed her a banknote.

She took it without thinking, but when she looked at what she had, her jaw dropped. "Ten pounds? What for?"

"Call it bed and board."

She stared at the crisp new banknote. "Ten pounds? But that's a ridiculous amount for a few days' accommodation and food—you've hardly eaten anything anyway."

Why was she arguing? He had money, and God knew she needed it. But ten pounds was a huge sum for three nights in a bed and a bit of soup and stew.

Ten pounds was more than the annual salary for a maidservant.

And he had a head injury. She didn't want to take advantage.

"Take it," he said, "and let there be no more talk of sending me to the vicar's." He saw her expression and added, "Just until I get my memory back, of course."

"I see—it's a bribe."

"Perish the thought!"

"But if the vicar asks me directly, you expect me to lie."

"Of *course* not," he said suavely. "I trust you will answer in your own, er, unique manner." His blue eyes danced.

He meant she lied by omission. She did. She wished she had some moral ground, high or otherwise, to stand on, but she didn't.

The banknote crackled appealingly between her fingers in a small papery siren song. She couldn't give it back, she just couldn't.

"Don't look at me like that," he said. "It won't be long before my memory returns, I'm sure. Already I've had a few small flashes—nothing important, but I'm sure it's just a matter of time."

"I will accept it, thank you. But you must ensure you aren't seen by any of the villagers." There would be scandal if anyone found out. An unconscious man was one thing: a handsome and obviously virile gentleman was quite another.

But homelessness was worse than any scandal.

Not that it would come to homelessness. She would return to Fyfield Place before she let the children starve or live on the streets. Since Mr. Harris's visit, the prospect of returning had hung over her like an ax waiting to fall.

With this ten pounds, she was safe, for a time. Just until he got his memory back.

She tucked the money away in the tin, adding it to the seven pence that until ten minutes earlier had been all that stood between her family and complete destitution.

Ten pounds would feed her and the children for months. It would pay for new shoes for children outgrowing theirs at a rate she couldn't keep up with.

But she could grow food, and the shoes would have to wait. This was rent, this would keep them safe. When Mr. Harris returned tomorrow, she'd be able to pay him.

Thank God.

In the meantime she'd write to the Earl of Alverleigh and put her case before him.

"Thank you," she said again to Mr. Rider. "The money will make all the difference in the world."

* * *

"What's worrying you?" Nash asked Maddy. She'd spent the last half hour sitting at the table composing a letter. Now it was sealed and she was pacing up and down, looking frustrated.

"I've written a letter to the Earl of Alverleigh, who's acting for my landlord while he's out of the country," she told him, "but now I don't know where to send it. I know it's Alverleigh House, but in what county? Near which town or village?"

"I see your point." Nash frowned, pretending to consider the problem. His first small, ironic hurdle. How to give her his brother's address without revealing his own identity?

"I told Mr. Harris I would write, and he said to give it to him and he would forward it, but I don't trust him."

"No, no, quite right. Would the vicar have a copy of Debrett's, perhaps?"

"Debrett's?" She glanced at him in surprise.

"Debrett's *Peerage*. It's a guide to all the best families in the kingdom—"

"Yes, I know what it is, but . . . you remembered it."

"Oh. So I did." He examined his fingernails. "Must be stored in the same part of the brain as Hadrian and his wall. I don't pretend to know how it works."

"Don't worry," she told him with warm sympathy. "I'm sure it will all come back to you soon."

She looked so beautiful, so concerned for him. Serpents of guilt coiled around Nash's conscience, squeezing it tight. He beat them off.

"I'm sure the vicar will have Debrett's. It's the kind of thing he's interested in—he's a bit of a snob. I'll call in on the way to the village. The children will be finishing their lessons, so it's perfect timing. I'll post the letter in the village and deliver Mrs. Richards's hat at the same time."

He had to get to that letter before she tucked it in her reticule. A small delay was called for . . . He peered at the window. "Looks like more rain on the way."

She looked out the window. "Do you think so?"

"Definitely. Those sort of clouds come up very quickly. But

if you don't mind your nice dry washing getting soaked . . ." He shrugged.

"You might be right. I'll bring it in." She put down the letter and hurried outside.

The moment she'd gone, he slid out of bed and, in two hops, reached the table. The letter was sealed with a simple blob of beeswax. He heated a knife in the fire and sliced the seal open. Around the neat margin she'd left, he scrawled a note to his brother.

Marcus, was injured but am recovering. Give Miss Wood-ford whatever she wants. Am at her cottage incognito. Funny business going on. Boots slashed, send new ones urgently. Nash.

He underlined "incognito" twice to emphasize the need for discretion, and "urgently" once to emphasize the need for boots. Then he blew on the letter to dry the ink, refolded it, and re-sealed the letter.

By the time she brought the washing in, he was back in bed looking innocent and bored.

"I won't be long," she told him. "If I can get this letter in the post today I'll be very pleased."

Without Maddy and the children, the cottage was very quiet. Nash should have welcomed the peace but he couldn't stay cooped up a moment longer. A jar would no longer do; he needed to visit the outhouse.

He swung his legs out of bed and cautiously put his foot to the floor. It hurt a bit, but if he didn't overdo it . . .

He took a few steps around the cottage, limping to favor his sore foot.

The stone floor of the cottage was icy. Lord knew why anyone wore a nightshirt, he decided: freezing draughts crept under the blasted thing, wrapping around his thighs and chilling more personal parts.

However did women stand it?

He found his clothes and dragged on a pair of drawers,

breeches, woolen stockings, and his one surviving boot. Better, but still very cold. Colder outside. He shrugged into his coat, then hopped to the back door.

There he found the ugly pair of working man's boots that Maddy wore for working outside. He shoved the toe of his injured foot into one, and limped out to the outhouse.

By the time he came inside he was shivering. He added a small log to the fire. A week ago he would have built a really good blaze. He loved a roaring fire, loved watching the flames dance and the sparks fly. There was a primitive satisfaction in making a fire roar.

But Maddy and the children had to gather the fuel themselves, wandering the forest in search of fallen timber, then dragging it home, chopping it as needed.

On that thought, he went back outside, found the ax she kept just inside the back door, chopped up the rest of her wood, and stacked it neatly by the back door. The combination of exercise and cold, fresh air got his blood moving again. He felt better than he had in days.

He prowled around the cottage in a kind of hop-limp, looking for something else to do. It was remarkably bare. Every item it contained had a utilitarian purpose, except for a handful of very amateurish and crudely framed watercolors that hung on the walls, signed Jane Woodford and Susan Woodford. Susan's were rather good.

He was about to return to the hearth when he noticed a small, brown leather case tucked away on a corner shelf. His curiosity was instantly roused. He hesitated. As a guest, he should respect his hostess's privacy. But he wanted to discover why she was being harassed by an imitation ghost and a bullying estate manager. The case could contain useful information.

Or so he told himself.

He brought it to the fireside to examine the contents. He found an unframed miniature carefully wrapped in a beautiful piece of antique brocade, a portrait of an enchantingly pretty girl in the costume of last century, with powdered hair piled high. Who was she? He rewrapped it carefully.

He found an old bible, in French, a battered tin containing

a sixpence and two ha'pennies, an old-fashioned doll, and something wrapped in the same antique brocade as the miniature: a hand-bound sketchbook.

The sketchbook was fascinating, dozens of drawings and watercolors executed with a skilled amateur hand. He turned the pages carefully, flicking over the landscapes, and stopped, riveted, when he came to one of an earnest young girl. Maddy as a child, a vivid little face, with that same expression of faint anxiety lurking in her eyes.

He found another sketch where she was sitting with a thin-faced old lady with a careworn expression and severe, upright bearing. Her grandmother?

There was a delicate drawing of a tiny babe with a wizened, ancient face and eyes he somehow knew had never opened on this world: a portrait of grief.

There was a story here . . .

He examined the landscapes with greater interest now; a crumbling ruin of a castle, lovingly detailed; the garden of a small, rural cottage, a laborer's cottage like this one and, in the foreground, the spare, upright figure of an old lady, veiled and gloved like a beekeeper; a few exquisitely rendered studies of wildlife—flowers, a fawn caught on the edge of a forest, a bee delving into a lavender flower. He rewrapped the sketchbook, his mind full of questions.

The last thing in the case was a cheaply bound, thick notebook tied with a faded ribbon. Curious, he untied it. Pages and pages of writing, French, in a round, girlish hand. A diary. The ink had started to fade at the edges but phrases jumped out at him.

He will be tall and handsome and very charming more charming even than Raoul and he will kiss my hand as if I am a princess and lead me onto the dance floor Grand-mère says he will come that I must be patient but nobody ever comes here and she says she read it in my tea-leaves but we never have tea anymore only tisanes and who ever heard of reading a fortune in a tisane?

He smiled at the rush and tumble of her thoughts, so young, so impatient, dreaming as he supposed all young girls did, of

Prince Charming. And who was this charming Raoul? He flipped a few pages.

> *. . . all this practicing. I grow so weary of it, as if there is*
> *any point to it. Papa said Grand-mère was cracked in the*
> *head and perhaps she is . . .*
> *. . . If I were a boy, Papa would love me, too, and I*
> *would not be here in a woodcutter's cottage, treading for-*
> *gotten measures in secret with no partner, to music I've*
> *never heard, hearing tales of people killed before I was*
> *born. I love Grand-mère but must I dwell with ghosts all my*
> *life? I want—*

Voices, Nash suddenly realized, outside. Dammit! Footsteps heading this way. No time to look out of the window. If she had visitors with her, he'd best be invisible.

He shoved her things back in the case, slammed it shut, and slid it across the floor to sit under the shelf he'd found it on. He dived into the bed, hitting his injured ankle on the wooden frame as he did so. It hurt like blazes.

His clothing! He pulled off his coat and started on his boot. It fitted so snugly it was a struggle, and when he heard the rattle of the latch he thrust his booted foot under the bedclothes, tugged the bed curtains closed, and lay back, just as the door opened. If it was that blasted vicar again . . .

But it was just Maddy and the children.

"You were right," Maddy said as she removed her hat. The children clattered past her and raced upstairs to change out of their good clothes. "The vicar did have a copy of Debrett's, so I addressed the letter and then, as luck would have it, the mail coach rolled into the village ten minutes after I posted the letter. So it's on its way to Hampshire. That's where Alverleigh House is."

She moved briskly around the cottage, straightening things. She suddenly paused and surveyed the room. "You've been up," she said, looking pleased. "Moving around. How wonderful. You must be feeling a lot better. How is your ank—" She broke off, noticing the small leather case out of place. One of the fastenings was undone. Her smile faded. "You've been looking at my things."

"I'm sorry, I was bored."

Her brandy eyes flashed. "Being bored is no excuse for snooping."

"I wasn't *snooping*," he said uncomfortably. "I was just . . . exploring."

"Exploring my private things!" She made it sound like he was going through her underwear.

"It wasn't like that at all. I was just . . ."

Maddy opened the case. There, on the top, was her girlhood journal, the ribbons that fastened it loose and untied. If he'd read her journal, full of her silly, precious, girlhood dreams, she would just die of mortification.

"Did you read my—can you read French?"

His eyes flickered guiltily. He had. He'd read her journal.

He said, as if it were an excuse, "I didn't mean to. I can read French—it's much used in dipl—" He caught himself in time. "A few phrases jumped out at me. I promise I read no more than that."

"Only because I came home." The look on his face told her she was right. How dare he go poking and prying in her private things. Was this how he repaid her for all her care of him? To violate her privacy? She wanted to cry. She wanted to hit him!

"It was wrong to open the case and I apologize. Unreservedly. I didn't read much of the journal but I did look through the sketch book. I wondered—"

She flung up a hand. "Not another word!" If he said one more thing she would hit him. How dare he wonder? He who had no history, no past. How could he know how painful some memories were?

She jammed the case into its little alcove. "I knew accepting money from you would complicate things. I suppose you think it gives you the right to—"

"It has *nothing* to do with the money. I wouldn't dream of holding it over your head in such away. That would be despicable."

"And looking through my belongings while my back is turned isn't?"

There was a small silence. "You're right, it is. I'm sorry."

He looked sorry, too, which mollified her somewhat. But not enough. He'd read her journal . . . She felt stripped bare.

He sat on the edge of the bed watching her as she began preparing the next meal. After about ten minutes she happened to glance at him.

"Forgive me?" he said instantly.

Maddy sniffed. Lying in wait for her, pouncing with a smile guaranteed to dissolve all remnants of anger, a smile too charming to resist. He knew it, the beast. "If those boots have torn my sheets, I'll have you out of here and up at the vicarage as quick as you can say Jack Robinson, ten pounds or no ten pounds."

"Boot," he corrected her. "You mangled the other one to death, remember. And the sheets aren't torn, so you needn't send for Rev. Prosy." His eyes danced; the wretch knew she was bluffing.

"You should be grateful I did ruin your boot. I could have left you to freeze in the mud."

"But you didn't," he said softly, "and I'm ever so grateful."

There should be a law against a voice like that. His coat lay on the bed beside him. She picked it up and hung it on a hook. It was bound to pull it out of shape, but did she care? Serve him right if he had to wear a shapeless rag when he finally left her house. She didn't own a wardrobe, a chest of drawers, or even a hanger. But the vicar did.

"It would do you a great deal of good to be prayed over. Ah, here are the children. If you need help getting that boot off, ask John or Henry to help you. I'm busy."

Ten

"Is there any hot water?" Nash asked before dinner. "I'd like a shave." She'd been perfectly polite to him all afternoon. So polite he was catching a chill.

He didn't enjoy Maddy keeping him at a distance, as if they were chance-met strangers—be damned to the fact that they were. They weren't strangers anymore. He'd tried several times to break through her courteous veneer. Without success.

"Yes, of course," she said pleasantly. She fetched his shaving kit and brought him hot water and towels.

"Thank you." With a smile, he held out the shaving brush. "Would you care to do the honors?" The ultimate gesture of appeasement, he thought, to trust her, in the mood she was in, with a razor at his throat.

"Your hands are no longer shaking; you don't need my help," she observed, and called John to come and hold the mirror for Mr. Rider.

Henry came, too, and what Nash had hoped would be a reconciliation turned into a shaving lesson for two young boys while Maddy bustled about getting dinner ready.

He didn't mind it, though. He hadn't had much to do with

young boys before, and initiating these two into the peculiarly masculine practice of shaving gave him a sense of . . . he wasn't sure what.

He'd never once watched his own father shaving. The man who'd taught him and Marcus to shave was the valet hired for them when they reached that age. Shaving should be, he decided as he showed the boys how to use the strop to sharpen the razor, something a man taught his sons. A small thing, but important.

He'd planned to join them at table for dinner, but almost immediately after they'd packed his shaving things away, the little girls arrived with his dinner on a tray.

He'd opened his mouth to suggest he might get up when he caught Maddy's eye.

"Is there something you wanted, Mr. Rider?" she asked so politely he decided it was better policy to stay in bed. Any more of her politeness and he'd end up with indigestion.

After dinner, when the table was cleared and the dishes done, she said to the children, "Mr. Rider has been very bored, stuck in bed with nothing to do. Why don't you show him some of your favorite card games?"

He sighed. Further punishment.

Within minutes all five children were on the bed and he was playing a game called Fish, which involved collecting pairs.

"Won't you join us?" he called to her at one stage.

"Thank you, Mr. Rider, but I have work to do." She Mr. Ridered him with every sentence now, treating him with pleasant indifference, as if he really were a lodger instead of . . . whatever he was.

"Mr. Rider, have you got a queen?" Jane said in the sort of voice that meant she'd said it before and that Nash wasn't paying attention. Nash meekly handed over his queen. Jane took it with a smug smile and Nash bent at least half his attention to the game. His pride had taken some beating in this cottage already, but he wasn't prepared to let himself be fleeced by small children—not without a battle.

While they played cards, Maddy brought out a large bucketful of straw and some coiled strips of some vine and sat herself on a low stool, a wicked-looking knife in her hands. He could smell damp straw and beeswax.

What the devil was she doing?

"Your turn, Mr. Rider!" Said with exaggerated patience.

Nash bent his mind to the game at hand. It was a simple game but surprisingly enjoyable. Nash didn't usually have much to do with children. He occasionally saw his brother Gabe's boys on visits to Zindaria, but they were mad about horses and most of their interaction had been on horseback or in the stables.

He'd never experienced anything like this noisy, happy informality. The children started off being carefully polite to him, but soon they were hooting with triumph as they sent him to fish, or squawking with glee as they relieved him of a card. They sprawled over him and his bed like a tumble of puppies.

Lucy, being too small to play, had, with a propriety air, claimed a place in Nash's lap. She watched each play with fierce concentration, crowing at each card he won and jealously guarding the pairs he—they—amassed, reluctant to give them up, even when the game was over.

From time to time he glanced at Maddy. She'd made some kind of disc from the straw and was coiling it round and round, first hammering it with a wooden mallet to flatten and shape it, then binding each coil with long springy strips of some vine that she'd dampened, and sewing it tight with a bodkin and twine.

It looked like difficult work, threading the strips through coiled bundles of straw and pulling the twine tight. From time to time she'd wince and suck her hand.

"That knife is dangerous," Nash said after the third time.

"It's not the knife," she told him. "It's the blackberry binding. I cut it into strips last summer and must have missed a few small thorns. They're just nicks, nothing serious."

"What on earth are you doing?"

"Making a skep."

"A what?"

The children stared at his ignorance. "A skep," Jane enunciated clearly, thinking he'd misheard. Then as he continued to look blank, she added, "For catching bees."

"Bees?" Nash exclaimed. "What, you catch real, live bees?"

"Yes, of course," Maddy said, laughing at his surprise. "How else would we get honey?" It was her first genuine response since the journal incident, and Nash wasn't going to let it go to waste. Besides he'd never met a lady who kept bees before.

"Don't you get stung?"

"Not very often. I wear a veil. And when I'm robbing the hives, I use smoke, or course."

"Smoke?"

"It calms them."

"You use smoke to catch them in that thing? How?"

John explained. "Every spring we go looking for swarms of bees in the forest, and when we find one, we tell Maddy. She brings a skep and knocks the bees into it—"

"But we don't use smoke in the forest," Jane corrected him.

"And then we bring the skep full of bees home," Henry said in a cutting-a-long-story-short kind of way. Henry wanted to get back to the card game.

"And then the bees make honey for us all summer long," Jane finished. "And wax."

Nash was astounded. "You catch wild bees? Bare-handed?"

They all laughed merrily at his expression. "A fresh swarm isn't usually aggressive," Maddy explained. "And, of course, I wear gloves, as well as a veil."

"Is it our turn yet?" Lucy asked with an impatient wriggle. Nash reluctantly returned to the game. Maddy caught and kept bees? He wanted to hear more.

From the corner of his eye he watched as the disc grew into a rounded basket shape and soon took on the familiar shape of a beehive. He'd seen them all his life and never once given a thought to how the honey was obtained: all he knew was that he liked to drizzle it on hot crumpets. He'd met a few beekeepers, too, but they'd been, without exception, grizzled men with large beards, not pretty, young women.

He watched her small, sturdy hands deftly shaping the hive. Damp straw, blackberry vines, and string. Maddy Woodford's specialty: wresting something productive out of nothing. She was an extraordinary girl.

Woman.

After a while Lucy grew tired. Slowly she slumped against his chest, then gave a large yawn and wriggled into the crook of his arm, where she simply went to sleep, her cheek against his chest. The other children quietened their noise when he asked them to, but it only lasted for about three minutes. Lucy slept on, regardless.

He'd never felt a child fall asleep in his lap before. It was an extraordinary sensation. Total trust.

He glanced at Maddy to see if she'd noticed, but her head was bent over her beehive as she tied off the final coil. She stood and stretched wearily, then tidied up the mess.

She swept up the straw remnants and shreds of blackberry binder and tossed them into the fire. Flames flared brightly and a few fiery twirls of blackberry danced up into the blackness of the chimney.

"When that game's ended it's time for bed," she told the children. She glanced at Lucy curled up asleep against Nash but said nothing. She collected the children's nightclothes and warmed them before the fire.

"I'll take Lucy." She scooped the little girl from his lap. He could smell Maddy's hair as she leaned across him.

The children washed, then changed into their nightclothes in front of the fire, the older ones helping the younger ones with buttons and buckles, while Maddy undressed the sleepy Lucy. It was cozy, domestic, and like nothing he'd ever experienced.

"Say good night to Mr. Rider," Maddy told them, and one by one they lined up beside the bed in their patched white nightclothes, faces scrubbed and shining, demon card players transformed into small angels.

"Thank you for the excellent card games, sir," John said. "You are a very sneaky player and I enjoyed it very much. Good night."

"Can we play again, sir?" Henry said. "Perhaps tomorrow?"

Nash laughed and ruffled the boy's hair. "Perhaps." Henry looked so pleased, Nash was absurdly flattered. Who would have dreamed that children could be good company?

"'Night, Mr. Rider," Susan said sleepily. "Sweet dreams."

"Is there anything I can do for you, Mr. Rider?" Jane asked.

"No, thank you, my dear. You're quite the demon card player, aren't you?"

She blinked and gave him an anxious look.

He smiled. "It's a compliment," he explained. "You're going to lead some man a merry dance when you're older."

She gave him a wondering look. "Me?"

"Yes, minx, you," he told her, and flicked her cheek gently with his finger. "'Night, Jane."

She blushed, mumbled something, got halfway to the stairs and came back to wish him, "A very good sleep and sweet dreams, Mr. Rider." Her eyes were shining.

Maddy stood at the foot of the steps, watching the exchange with Lucy draped over her shoulder, sound asleep. In the dim light, he couldn't read her expression. Jane ran up the stairs past her, but Maddy made no move to follow.

"What is it?" he asked quietly. The children had gone ahead of her. "Did I do something wrong?"

"No." She took two steps up the staircase, then turned back. "It was nice, what you said to Jane." Then she turned and carried Lucy upstairs. She would tuck them in, tell them a bedtime story, and kiss them good night. He already knew the routine.

Nash sat back, feeling strangely affected by the simple domestic routine. There had been nothing in his own experience like it.

When his father was in residence, Nash and Marcus would occasionally be brought down for half an hour's conversation in the drawing room. It was a nerve-wracking and humbling experience; their father was clearly bored by them.

He'd never played any sort of game with his sons. Not unless they happened to come across him at Whites, or some other club, as adults.

And Nash could no more imagine sitting on his father's bed than flying, let alone falling asleep in his lap.

As a child, Nash had been put to bed by servants, different servants each year. It wouldn't do for a son of the Earl of Alverleigh to get vulgarly attached to a servant.

The servants weren't interested, either. They were usually impatient, indifferent, not unkind—just in a hurry to get the boys off their hands.

Mama had never put them to bed. She occasionally burst into the nursery quarters like some kind of glamorous fairy princess in a cloud of perfume, glittering with jewels, her skirts rustling. She would swoop upon them, hugging and kissing them extravagantly, sprinkling questions over them but never waiting for the answers. And then she'd be gone, leaving two dazed sons behind, Marcus sneezing. Mama's perfume always made him sneeze.

Maddy wasn't even these children's mother . . .

Finally he heard her come down the stairs. He waited as she laid out the bedding in front of the fireplace, as usual, then—

"What are you doing?" he asked sharply.

Maddy gave him a cool glance. "What does it look like? I'm going to bed." She flipped back the covers and climbed in.

"Your bed is here."

Maddy shook her head. "You and I both know what will happen if we share a bed again." She'd tried all evening to hold on to her anger, to use it as a shield against his charm. But it was impossible to stay cross with him for long.

The way he'd played with the children, his patience, his sense of fun, his kindness . . . And then when Lucy fell asleep in his lap, his careful, cautious response, the look in his eyes . . .

She had to keep her distance. It would be too easy to fall in love with this man.

He swung his legs out of bed. "I gave you my word as a gentleman that no harm would come to you from sharing this bed."

"It depends on your definition of harm." She didn't trust herself with him one little bit. He was too appealing. Even in sleep her body sought to get closer to him, and it wasn't simply his body heat she wanted.

She'd never understood that part in the Bible where it said better to marry than burn. She didn't understand, then, what it meant to "burn." Now she did.

She burned, she yearned, she ached for him.

But it was impossible. She knew nothing about him. He knew nothing about himself. He could be married. She would not, could not seduce another woman's husband.

Did infidelity count if you did not know you were doing it?

Even if she gave herself to him, what then? Would the burning cease, or would it intensify? A craving: once tasted, never forgotten. He could get his memory back at any moment, and go on his merry way, leaving her behind . . . burning.

Maddy used to pride herself on her sound common sense. She was the practical, the realistic, the dependable one.

That Maddy was vanishing fast. A lifetime's common sense shattered by a pair of blue eyes that invited her to forget her worries and a smile that could melt her bones.

Five children depended on Maddy keeping her head. And her virtue.

A night on the cold hard floor would ensure that. And possibly bring her to her senses.

He frowned. "I'd never hurt you."

"I know." She believed him. He wouldn't harm her. Not deliberately. Not knowingly. But harm was not always physical. Or deliberate.

"Then get into this bed."

She shook her head and blew out the candle. "Good night, Mr. Rider." The cottage was lit by the gentle glow of the dying fire.

"Then if you must be so stubborn . . ." He hopped off the bed and limped across the room.

"What are you doing?" She sat up, defensively clutching the bedclothes to her.

He held out his hand to her. "Come on."

"No, I—"

"You're sleeping in the bed," he insisted. "I'll sleep here."

She didn't move.

He gave an exasperated sigh. "If you think I'm going to allow a woman to give up her bed and sleep on the floor while I sleep in hers in comfort—" He snorted and again, held out his hand. "I won't take no for an answer."

It was what he'd said the other night. She knew there was no point arguing. "Very well, but I warn you, if you get back into bed with me—"

"I won't." It was blunt and to the point, surprising her. Where had the flirtatious rogue gone? Or was this another of his tricks?

Cautiously she put her hand in his and he drew her to her feet. He led her back to her bed and courteously helped her into it as though he were helping a lady into a carriage.

"Lie down," he ordered, and when she did, he drew the covers up to her chin and tucked her in like a child. She didn't feel in the least childlike.

He limped across to the makeshift bed but didn't slide into it. Instead he poked a few more sticks into the fire, then straddled a chair and sat on it backward. With his elbows planted on the backrest and his chin resting on folded fists, he stared into the dancing flames.

"What are you doing?"

"Thinking. Go to sleep." Firelight limned the silhouette of his face and gilded the long, hard horseman's legs, inadequately covered by the vicar's nightshirt.

Maddy tried not to think about the body hidden beneath it. She closed her eyes, but knowing he was sitting there, awake, was too tempting. Was he brooding again about his memory loss? Staring into the coals, wondering who he was?

He looked . . . lonely.

It surprised her that he hadn't tried to talk her into sharing the bed. He seemed somehow different from the man of the previous night, the roguish flirt whose smile and laughing eyes were a constant threat to her sense of propriety. Tonight he was much more restrained, almost serious. As if he, too, wanted to put some a distance between them.

Because she'd lost her temper with him? She didn't think so. He wasn't sulking. It was as though he needed to be more—cautious? restrained? serious?—around her. Why?

As if he could read her mind, he turned and looked at her. "Why aren't you asleep?"

"I'm not sleepy," she admitted.

His face was hidden in shadows. "I can't help wondering about those sketches in the book. It's you, isn't it, the child in those pictures? Who was the artist?"

She hesitated. Part of her was still angry he'd pried into her past. "My mother."

"Would you let me look at the pictures again, and tell me about them?"

There was no reason to hide them, she supposed. He'd already seen what there was to see. And her memories had been stirred up; part of her wanted to share them with him. "If you like," she said, sitting up and tucking pillows behind her back.

He lit a candle and brought her Grand-mère's small valise, then sat on the bed beside her, on top of the bedclothes but close, so she had to scoot over to make room for him. The bed that had felt so spacious a moment before now felt small.

His big, warm body pressed against the full length of her, shoulder to calf. She tried not to let it affect her as she took out the sketchbook.

He turned to a drawing of Maddy as a child. "This is you, isn't it?"

Maddy was surprised he'd recognized her. "Yes."

His gaze passed over her face like a touch, sending a barely perceptible shiver through her. "This is in France, is it not? And you were how old?"

"About ten. And yes, it's France."

"Not for a holiday, I think."

"No, I lived there for ten years, with Grand-mère, until I was nineteen."

He turned another page. "The old lady . . . your grand-mother?"

She nodded. He placed a long finger on the picture of Grand-mère's cottage. "And this was her home?"

Again she nodded.

"And what of this castle?"

She hesitated. Better to keep it simple. "It was burned during the Terror. The revolution. It was not far from our cottage. We went there for picnics. It's beautiful, don't you think?" No need to tell him the castle had one belonged to Grand-mère's family. There was nothing worse than people who dwelt on past glories, lost possessions.

He gave her a searching look, as if he knew there was more to it than that, but all he said was, "So how did a young English girl come to be living in France for ten years?"

"It's a long story."

He smiled. "I'm not sleepy. Are you?"

She shivered. Far from it. With his big, warm, masculine body pressed against her, every bit of her was wide awake.

"My father met my mother in Paris just before his thirtieth birthday. She was seventeen and very beautiful and her family was rich." She'd often wondered what had attracted Papa most.

"Papa was a good-looking man, and had inherited a moderate fortune. But he was English. My grandfather despised the English. He told Papa he would horsewhip him if he tried to see Mama again." She sighed. "Papa was furious."

"Any man would be."

She nodded. "Papa was a man of great personal pride. It only made him more determined to have her."

"Perfectly understandable." He grinned. Clearly he saw it as a romance, and it was; at least it had started that way.

She went on, "This was at the beginning of the Terror—the revolution—and everything was in chaos. Mama's father and brother went out one morning and were torn apart by an angry mob. Grand-mère expected the mob to come for her any moment. Terrified for Mama, she summoned my father and said if he could get her safely out of France, he could marry her. Which he did." She should have finished the story there, with "and they lived happily ever after," but she couldn't bring herself to say it because they hadn't, they surely hadn't.

He frowned. "What about your grandmother? She didn't go with them?"

"No, she had a higher loyalty."

"Higher than to her own child?"

Maddy nodded. "Grand-mère served the queen, Marie Antoinette. Until she knew the fate of the queen, Grand-mère would not leave Paris."

"She did not share the fate of poor Marie Antoinette." His finger ran down the seam of the sketchbook. Her grandmother's face looked out at her.

"No, she lived. She felt guilty about it for the rest of her life, poor Grand-mère. They were the same age, born in the same month, Grand-mère and the queen, and so she'd always believed they would share the same fate, that it was written in the stars. Besides, she served the queen, it was her duty. Instead, her fate was to go on living when those she'd loved had died."

"You loved her," he said softly, his voice very deep and quiet.

"I did. I still miss her." Her voice cracked.

"She sounds like a remarkable woman."

"She was. She taught me how to keep bees." And so much

more. She'd always been proud of Grand-mère, even though she recognized her eccentricities. Grand-mère living like a peasant woman in a cottage, unembarrassed and with all her airs and graces intact . . .

Cracked in the head, Papa used to say, though not within Grand-mère's hearing.

If only Papa could see his own children now, dwelling in a run-down cottage, living off vegetables, chickens, honey, and their wits, just like Grand-mère. Would he perceive the irony? Probably not.

She opened it to another page at random. It was the portrait of baby Jean, the last of her poor little short-lived brothers . . . Her throat closed.

She took the sketchbook and closed it gently.

"You didn't answer my question."

With an effort she forced her mind back to the present. "What question?"

"How a gently born young English girl came to live like that"—he touched the sketchbook—"in France for ten years, while a war was raging."

Ah, that. "There was no war when we left England."

"No, but the wake of revolution is still a strange time for travel."

She bit her lip, trying to think of how to explain it. "Mama . . . Mama had had difficulty giving Papa the heir he so wanted." It was one way to describe endless miscarriages and stillbirths and misery.

"When I was nine, Mama decided to make a pilgrimage to Lourdes and pray for a boy. Papa agreed—he was desperate for a son—so we all went. They left me with Grand-mère while he and Mama went on to Lourdes, and when they returned, Mama was *enceinte* again." It was too soon, she'd known. The midwife had told Mama she should wait, heal, and get stronger before trying again, but Papa was too eager for a son.

"Travel would be dangerous for the child, so Papa left Mama and me with Grand-mère to await the birth."

"The baby in the picture."

She nodded. "He came too soon, and was small and sickly. He only lived a few weeks. And Mama . . ." Her voice cracked. "She just . . . faded away."

His arm slipped around her and he held her quietly against him. "I'm sorry."

She nodded unable to speak. Those endless months when Mama would barely speak or eat. Weep endlessly over the drawing of little Jean. He should have been named John, after Papa, but Mama always called him Jean.

She'd never told the children that. John would hate knowing there were others before him who'd died, all named John.

He held her, stroking the skin of her arm gently. "I presume the war prevented you from returning to England."

"No, it hadn't started then."

"Then why did you not return to England?"

She shook her head and shrugged awkwardly.

He frowned. "Your father wasn't able to get you out of France?"

"He didn't try."

"Not even after the war started?"

"No."

"Why not?"

How many times had she asked herself the same question? It had been a hollow, aching void inside her, all through her girlhood and beyond. "I don't know," she told him. "He never explained." And she'd never asked. She couldn't bear to hear the answer she knew he would give: that she was only a girl and he neither needed nor wanted a daughter. She'd heard him say it to her mother once.

Both arms tightened around her. She leaned into him, soaking up the care and the warmth and the . . . comfort.

"It's all right," she said. "I don't regret my years with Grand-mère, and I love the children and I love being part of a family again. I just wish . . ." That it had been different, that Papa had loved her, that she'd had her come-out . . . That he hadn't lost his fortune. Too many wishes. All pointless.

The candle guttered and went out in a smoky hiss. Taking it as a sign, she gently disengaged herself from his embrace. "Time for bed, I think—to sleep, I mean. I have a lot to do in the morning."

"You always have a lot to do."

She shrugged. "Being busy is better than being bored." Or starving. Being bored was a rich person's ailment.

He didn't move. She could just make out his silhouette in the dimness, could smell the clean freshness of his shaving soap and the deep masculine muskiness underneath.

He bent and kissed her lightly on the forehead, the way she kissed the children, a kind of blessing more than a kiss.

"Good night, Mr. Rider," she whispered in an echo of the children's good nights.

He cupped her cheek in his palm and stared down at her for the longest time, his expression lost in the darkness.

She waited, breathless.

The night smelled of beeswax and clean, damp straw, of soap and of man. One man. This man. The scent of his skin was part of her. Yes, she was playing with fire, but oh, how she wanted it, ached for it.

"I didn't intend this to happen," he murmured as if to himself and touched his lips to her mouth.

It was the lightest of caresses, a mere brush of skin across exquisitely sensitized skin. A prelude. It shivered softly through her like the sound of a violin on a still, dark night.

She was poised on a precipice of need. Wanting more.

His mouth brushed hers again, once, twice, teasing her lips apart, tasting her. Tantalizing. He nibbled on her upper lip, and it was heaven. He touched his tongue to hers and a thread of fire ran swiftly, delicately through her and she gasped, and breathed in his breath.

He kissed her again and ran the tip of his tongue over the roof of her mouth and a curl of hot pleasure tightened deep within her.

She speared her fingers into his hair and wriggled closer, moving against the hard warmth of his body, glorying in the hot, spice-salt taste of him, returning each caress instinctively, blindly, and wanting more . . . more.

"No." He broke the kiss and pushed her gently away. His breath was ragged, coming in great gasps, as if he'd been running.

She was mute, unable to think, dizzy with pleasure and need. And loss.

He slid from the bed, still panting. "Good night, Miss Woodford. Sweet dreams." And then he was nothing but a shadow lost in the darkness. She heard him climb into the bed on the floor.

The fire was almost dead now, nothing but ashes.

Sweet dreams?

Maddy curled into the warmth of her bed, aching, hollow. How did he expect her to sleep after that? She was wound up tight, like a spring.

What a time for him to decide to play the gentleman instead of the rake. She punched the pillow and willed her body to sleep.

Eleven

Someone was moving around outside the cottage. Maddy sat bolt upright in bed. The Bloody Abbot? She listened, straining to hear every sound, braced for moaning, banging, and scratching at the doors and windows.

Nothing. But someone, or something was definitely outside. An animal? A fox? The hens were making a noisy, but it wasn't the demented squawking that heralded a fox's arrival. A cow or sheep, perhaps, broken into her garden, intent on her sweet greens?

She slipped out of bed and hurried to the window.

"What's the matter?" He sat up.

"There's something outside." She peered through the thick distorted glass. It was hard to see much. The moon was out, but it was cloudy and the garden was dappled with shadows. Impossible to tell if something was moving or whether it was just the clouds.

He stood beside her, pistol in one hand, the other in the small of her back. Warm. Solid. Protective. "That swine again?"

"I don't think so. It might be an animal."

They listened. There was certainly something there. They could hear snapping noises as if twigs were being broken.

"I'll go out and see what it is," he said.

"I'll come, too," she told him and grabbed her cloak.

But just as they opened the door, there was a whooshing sound, then another, and suddenly a row of fires blazed up along the back wall of the garden.

For a moment Maddy couldn't think what was there to burn, but then—"My bee hives!" She ran toward them, then came to a shocked standstill. Her hives were all ablaze, the straw skeps a mass of flame, the beeswax inside fueling the fire to greater heights. Sparks and shreds of burning straw danced and twirled up into the darkness, carried on the brisk wind.

"My bees, oh, my bees!" But there was nothing she could do: the hives were already turning to glowing, charred lumps. White shreds of ash peeled off in the breeze. She shivered.

"What's that smell?" Nash sniffed the air. "Deliberately set," he said, lifting up a rag. "This is soaked in lamp oil."

What did she care how? Her bees were dead! Cruelly destroyed. Maddy felt sick. Her precious bees . . . They were part of the family, these bees. They knew her secrets, had been her confidantes and her comfort, her link with Grand-mère and her past.

"Who would do such a terrible thing? Murder bees? And why?" she asked.

Part of the answer was obvious. The robed silhouette stood on the crest of the hill, watching. Too far away to pursue.

"Why?" Maddy whispered again. "I've done nothing to him. And the bees harm no one—they only sting in self defense. They just work and give honey." Tears trickled down her cheeks unregarded.

Every hive was destroyed, every little worker, every martyred queen. All that honey, all that wax, all the work of weaving the skep . . . gone. The children running home in the summer, shrieking that they'd spotted a wild swarm in the forest, the adventure of catching the swarm and bringing home the bees, each new swarm another source of income . . . All the work of keeping the bees alive and fed through the coldest part of winter . . . ruined.

Maddy was ruined, too. The honey was a major source of income. All that stood now between her family and destitution were her chickens and the vegetable garden.

The chickens! She broke away from his comforting embrace and ran to the hen house. The door was open. The chickens were scattered throughout the garden and some in the field beyond the wall . . .

Her garden! The clouds parted, letting moonlight flood the garden . . . or what remained of it. Seedlings trampled into the ground, trellises knocked over and smashed.

The sound of breaking twigs.

Plants not simply uprooted, but broken and torn apart and ground beneath a hostile heel. Total, deliberate destruction.

She surveyed the devastation in silence, shivering. The wind sliced through her clothing, harsh and bitterly cold, chilling her to the bone.

All her work of the last year destroyed in one short night. To what purpose? So that children would starve? She felt sick.

His arm tightened around her. "Come inside, there's nothing you can do now."

She shook her head. "The chickens, I must get them back—"

"Leave the door open and they'll go back in soon enough. They don't like being out in the cold and dark, either."

"But a fox might—"

"Give Dorothy and Mabel and the girls a little time to return to their perches. I'll go out later and lock the hen house door. You're frozen and in shock. You need to get in to the warmth."

His words made sense. Her teeth were chattering and she felt sick to her stomach. Suddenly she wanted, more than anything, to return to the warmth and security of the cottage, to shut out the vileness that had happened.

She hated being out in the open with the beast, whoever he was, watching from up there, gloating over his wanton destruction. All her hard work. . . . her bees . . .

Tomorrow she'd be angry, but now she just felt ill. Devastated. Defeated. She allowed Nash to lead her back along the path that ran through neat beds of trampled vegetables, back to the cottage that she'd once thought a haven.

Nothing was a haven anymore. She might have the money for rent, and she could start a new garden, and establish new hives, but who was to say he wouldn't come back and destroy them again?

Who was this evil creature, and why did he bear her and her little family such hatred?

Nash led Maddy straight to the fire. She was half frozen, a product of shock as well as the cold night.

He glanced at the bed. He wanted to climb into it with her and hold her and drive the frozen look from her eyes, but he couldn't. Despite the events of the night, he couldn't trust himself to be in a bed with her.

He'd promised her she was safe with him. He'd failed to protect her garden and hives. He wasn't going to make things worse by taking her innocence.

He sat her in the chair nearest the fire and piled on wood until it was a solid blaze. He wedged a couple of bricks into the coals and swung the kettle over the fire. Maddy stared into the flames, brooding on the fate of her bees.

"It would have been fast," he told her. "They wouldn't have felt a thing." Did insects feel pain? He didn't know.

He found his flask and placed it against her lips. "Drink."

She obediently swallowed, then shuddered and gasped for breath. "What—" But she couldn't get a sentence out for coughing. She stared at him indignantly as she gasped and spluttered.

"It's only brandy, good quality French brandy." He rubbed her back soothingly. "It will do you good."

She finally stopped coughing. "It's horrid. It burns all the way down."

"And warms your blood. Don't you feel better for it?"

She gave him a withering look and didn't deign to respond, but her shivering had eased somewhat and that frozen look was gone from her eyes. A little bit of indignation was a fine, warming thing.

"I should go back out see if any of my plants can be saved—"

"You're not moving. We'll see what can be done in the morning," he told her firmly.

He spooned some honey into a cup, added more brandy, and

poured some hot water from the kettle. "Hot toddy," he said, pressing it into her hands, wrapping her chilly fingers around the warm cup. "Do you the power of good."

She accepted it gratefully and sipped its contents first with caution, then more happily. It was mostly honey, so the brandy slipped down easier this time.

Her fingers were icy to the touch. He glanced at her feet and swore silently. The hem of her nightgown and her flimsy little slippers were soaked and muddy. No wonder she was freezing.

He rummaged through the box where she kept her clothes and pulled out a clean nightgown and a woolen shawl. He shook the nightgown out and warmed it at the fire, grimly noting the number of places it had been patched. She'd finished the toddy and was sitting half curled in the chair, her eyes closed.

Swiftly he undid the fastenings of her cloak. No wonder she was cold, the damned thing was almost threadbare. He pushed the cloak off her shoulders, then began to undo the tiny buttons down the front of her nightgown.

Her eyes flew open. "Wha-what are you doing?"

"Your clothes are wet. You need to change."

"Don't." She pushed his hands away.

"Very well, you do it." He stood back and waited, telling himself it was better if she did it anyway. Her nipples were hard berries beneath the soft, well-worn fabric. Cold, not desire, he told himself savagely. He handed her the warm, dry nightgown and the shawl, stepped away, and turned his back.

Behind him, fabric rustled. He gritted his teeth, imagining her slipping the damp nightgown over her head, leaving her naked curves bathed in firelight. From the corner of his eye he saw the muddy-hemmed nightgown hit the floor. It took every shred of willpower he had not to turn around, not to take her in his arms, carry her to the bed, and warm her in the most elemental fashion of all.

What had possessed him to make that blasted promise?

It seemed an age before she said, "You can turn around now." He turned slowly, half hoping she'd decided to live up to his imaginary view of her and greet him wearing nothing but firelight, but she was buttoned to the chin and wrapped in the shawl.

"You're still wearing those slippers, dammit."

She frowned. "I forgot. I can hardly feel my feet, they're so cold."

Muttering under his breath, he grabbed a towel, knelt, pulled her slippers off, and dried her feet carefully. They were icy to the touch. He chafed them gently in his hands and she moaned, with pleasure or pain, he wasn't sure.

"The children slept right through it all," she said in a wondering voice. "So much destruction and they slept right through it. He was so quiet this time."

"That's something to be grateful for, then, isn't it?"

"Yes, it would have been dreadful if they'd seen the bees burning. So distressing . . . And Jane and Susan would fret about the hens and want to go out and make sure they were safe—you will check them later, won't you?" She didn't wait for him to reply. "The boys will be so upset, they've worked so hard in the garden. And Lucy—oh dear, Lucy loved the bees. She used to tell them s-stories." She bit her lip and fell silent. He could tell she was fighting tears.

He fought the urge to haul her into his arms and kiss the tears away.

He rubbed and kneaded her feet until they were warm and rosy and she was arching against his hands in pleasure—and this time he was sure.

"Bed." His voice came out hoarse.

She didn't move. He glanced at the expanse of stone flags between herself and the bed and didn't blame her; her feet would be cold again by the time she got there.

Unable to help himself, he bent and scooped her off the chair.

She started. "What are you doing? Your ankle!"

"Seems to have recovered." He was limping, but that was because of his ruined boot and the shuffling gait it required. His ankle ached, but not unbearably. "Must have been a sprain after all."

He carried her to the bed and slid her between the sheets. She pulled the bedcovers around her and curled up on her side like a little girl. "You've been very kind—" she began but he didn't wait to hear.

He stomped away, back to the hearth. Kind! He didn't want to be kind. He wanted to slide into that bed with her and take her, strip that blasted patched nightgown from her, and take possession of her, learning her inch by inch, driving every thought, every fear from her brain, drowning her in sensation. He wanted her arching against him, the way her feet had arched against his hands, moaning with pleasure. He wanted to taste her, to know her, to bury himself deep within her and to feel her shudder and cry out as he brought her to ecstasy. The gift of oblivion.

His body shuddered uncontrollably at the mere thought. He was rock hard and ready. And she was warm and pliant.

And vulnerable.

He grabbed the tongs and pulled the two hot bricks from the hearth. He wrapped them in rags until they were easy to handle, then brought them to the bed.

Her eyes were closed. She looked exhausted. He lifted the bedclothes and slid the hot bricks in, locating her feet and settling a brick at each foot. She sighed in contentment and her feet curled around them.

She didn't need him, he told himself savagely: a hot brick would do just as well.

As for himself, he had a cold, stone floor and that was all he needed. He dragged off his good boot and kicked off the other, removed his breeches, and climbed into the roll of bedding by the hearth. He tossed and turned. Could a floor be any colder or harder? At least the fire threw out some heat and he was marginally warmer on that side.

Jane and Susan would be fretting about the hens . . . You will check them later, won't you?

Cursing, he untangled himself from the bedclothes, pulled on his breeches and boots, and stomped outside to check on the blasted hens. Why did he make so many stupid, damned inconvenient promises?

It took Nash forever to get to sleep again. Never had he kissed a woman so briefly, not a woman he wanted. And he wanted Maddy Woodford; his body thrummed insistently, his blood singing and alive and wanting.

That moment when her lips had parted slightly, softly under his . . . The sweet, elusive taste of her, just like her scent. What he wouldn't give to taste her properly . . .

He groaned and turned over on the stone floor, wishing its coldness would pull the heat from him, but it was a different kind of heat keeping him awake.

Resolutely, he turned his mind to the problem at hand. Who was this evil bastard who came in the night? Who might have it in for Maddy and the children so badly he would destroy their livelihood? They wouldn't starve—Nash would see to that—but this swine wasn't to know that.

Somebody wanted her out of the cottage and was obviously prepared to commit wanton destruction to do it. And yet, there had been no attempt to hurt Maddy and the children.

Five "Bloody Abbot" visits in a few weeks and, apart from frightening a woman and children, burning beehives and destroying plants was the worst he'd done.

He fell asleep eventually, his mind full of questions, his body tense and edgy with desire.

*N*ash woke shortly after dawn to the click of a quietly closing door. He threw off the covers, grabbed his pistol, flung open the door, and nearly tripped over Maddy sitting on the front step, tying the laces on her big ugly work boots.

"What? What is it?" he demanded, scanning the horizon.

"Nothing." She stood, neatly dressed in her faded blue dress, her hair gleaming wine-bright in the morning sun and coiled into her usual neat knot. She looked lovelier than any woman should after a disturbed night and very little sleep.

Her gaze moved from his face to his hair, then down to his toes and back. "Good morning. I assume you slept poorly." Her eyes danced.

He stiffened, realizing he probably looked rather less dapper than he preferred to look in front of women he desired, in bare feet and wearing a nightshirt made for a short, rotund vicar. He raised a casual hand to his hair and found it standing in spikes. He tried to smooth it inconspicuously.

"What are you doing up at such an hour?" He sounded, even to his own ears, gruff and surly.

"I need to see to the hens."

"I shut them in after you went to bed."

"I know. I heard you go out again last night. Thank you." She started down the pathway.

"Wait," he said. "I'll dress and go with you."

"It's all right," she told him. "There's nothing you can do. I want to check on the damage before the children are up."

"I'm coming," he told her firmly, and went inside to pull on his breeches, boots, and coat. He made his ruined boot almost wearable by the simple expedient of tying it on with strips of rag. It looked utterly ridiculous, but he had no choice.

He found her on her knees in the vegetable garden, replanting any plants that hadn't been totally destroyed, and throwing the ruined ones into two piles: usable as food and only fit for the hens. She looked almost serene.

"I thought you'd still be upset after last night."

She sat back on her heels and wiped a strand of hair from her eyes with the back of her hand, leaving a stripe of dirt in its wake. "Upset? I'm more than upset, I'm furious. But I won't let that monster defeat me. It'll take a lot of work to get the garden back in shape, but at least this is the beginning of the growing season and not the end."

"Get the garden back in shape? You mean you're going to start again?" He looked at the mess that had been her garden. It was a huge amount of work.

She snorted. "What should I do? Give in, tuck my tail between my legs, and run back to Fyf—run away?" she amended. "No, no, and no! I will not be driven from my home by a coward who frightens children. Besides, I have the perfect solution to deal with him in future—geese."

"Geese?" How would more poultry solve her problem?

"Geese make excellent watchdogs. You should hear the fuss they make when any stranger is around—and they eat grass and grain, which is cheaper than feeding a dog," she finished triumphantly. "I cannot imagine why I didn't think of them sooner. Geese would honk a warning of any spineless creature creeping in the night to terrify children and burn innocent, hard-working little bees! That reminds me . . ." She glanced past him to where the bee hives had stood in their stone shelters. "I'd better clear the wreckage of the hives away. I want to clean up as much of the damage as I can before the children see it." Seizing a spade, she headed for the hives.

"I'll help, just tell me what to do." He'd never pulled a weed or tended a garden in his life but his muscles were at her disposal.

"Thank you." She gave him a dazzling smile that drove every thought from his mind. "Bring the wheelbarrow, please."

He fetched it, a big old clumsy thing that was hard to balance and harder to steer. As it wobbled toward the hives, she looked up and tossed him a quick grin. "That's what I used to bring you inside the house, after your accident."

"This?" He was shocked. "You carried me on this? How?"

She shrugged. "I didn't say it was easy. But needs must."

Needs must indeed. Nash was stunned, faced with the very physical evidence of what she must have done to save his life. Up until now it had been an academic exercise; he hadn't considered the logistics of how she'd managed to transfer his insensible body from the muddy ground, inside, and into her own bed.

He stared at the small, slender frame, currently scooping a mess of burned straw and honey into the barrow lined with fresh straw. How the hell had she managed to lift him?

"It wasn't easy," she admitted when he asked. She explained how she'd tied him to the wheelbarrow and he was dumbfounded.

She handed him a spade. "Can you dig a hole over there, please? I'm going to bury the hives."

Dig her a hole? He'd dig her a dozen.

*B*y the time the children woke and came looking for their breakfast, Maddy and Nash had cleared away most of the ruined plants. The stone alcoves where the hives had stood were cleaned out, stained with ash and still a bit sticky, but empty.

The blackened mess of hives had been tossed into a hole, but Maddy stopped Nash from covering it with soil. "We will have a ceremony," she told him. "The children will want to say good-bye."

The children wandered through the garden, exclaiming distressfully over the vandalism, but they took their cue from their older sister and started repairing trellises and replanting seedlings almost immediately. The girls counted the hens—all present and correct—and collected the eggs as usual, white-faced and shocked.

Maddy gave them time to absorb the destruction, then fed them a big breakfast of porridge with cream and honey, followed by a toast and honey for those who still had space.

After that they held a small simple ceremony for the bees. Nash had never attended a funeral for any animal, let alone bees.

Each child brought a flower of the sort that bees were known to like. They lined the grave. Maddy said a few words. "Dear bees, we're so sorry for the evil thing that was done to you. Thank you for the honey and wax you have given us, and for being part of our family, as always. We will bring your sisters from the forest here to make a new colony. Rest in peace."

Each of the children then said a few words and threw in their flower, even John, who told the bees he forgave whichever of them stung him that time and that even so, they made very nice honey.

Nash had no idea what to say. He couldn't quite believe their feelings for insects—stinging insects at that. He liked honey, but still . . .

He filled in the hole. Solemnly.

As they walked back to the house, he asked Maddy, "Why will you only bring the bees' sisters from the forest? Why not their brothers?"

Behind him the girls giggled. "Because it's the girl bees who do all the work," Jane told him. "The drones—that's what you call the boys—they don't work *at all*."

"Except for defending the hive," Nash said.

Jane made a scornful sound. "Drones don't fight, they can't even sting! The girls defend the hive, collect the honey, clean the hive, *everything*. All the drones do is *eat*."

Nash and the two boys exchanged glances. "They must be

good for something," he said, feeling the need to find and uphold some masculine virtue in the little creatures.

Maddy waved the children ahead, then turned and gave him a mischievous glance. "Reproduction. It's their sole purpose in life."

Nash kept a straight face. "Well, there you are then. Noble chaps, one and all. Doing their duty for king and country."

She shook her head. "For the queen," she said. "There's no king, it's all for the queen."

At lunch, which was the inevitable soup and cheese on toast, she said to Nash, "You think it's peculiar that we had a ceremony for the bees, don't you?"

"No, not at all," he lied.

"It's because of Grand-mère, you see. The bees saved her life."

His brows rose. "How so?"

Maddy's mood lifted. "By a very clever trick." The children exchanged knowing glances and settled down to listen to what was obviously a well-loved tale.

Nash knew his duty. "Tell me."

"You know how I told you that Papa had helped Mama escape from the Terror, while Grand-mère remained behind? Well, some days later Grand-mère heard people coming for her, just a handful, but nasty. They knew she'd been a beloved servant of the queen. So—"

"She hid herself among—" Lucy began.

"Hush, Lucy, let Maddy tell it," Jane said.

Maddy smiled and continued. "Grand-mère was at the queen's little farm, *le Hameau de la Reine*, at Versailles. The queen and her ladies like to play at being peasants, and they would dress as shepherdesses and milkmaids and milk the cows and so on. And Grand-mère kept the bees that made the queen's honey."

She lowered her voice to a thrilling pitch. "They were coming for her, screaming for blood! She had no horse or carriage to escape in, and she knew they would find her if she tried to hide inside. So what did she do?"

The children looked expectantly at Nash, their eyes alight with excitement.

"What?" There was no need to feign his fascination.

"She pulled all the beehives into a circle and sat in the middle of them, wearing her veil and gloves."

"Did they find her?"

Maddy nodded. "A few did but they were city people and they were afraid of the bees. When anyone came close, Grand-mère hit the hives with a stick and all the bees came boiling out, enraged, and buzzed furiously around, stinging whoever they came across."

She gave a short laugh. "If they'd known anything about bees they would have waited until dark when the bees retire for the night, but Grand-mère was lucky. The people went looking for easier prey and she managed to escape and make her way to a place she knew in the country."

The children chorused, "And there she lived happily for the rest of her days."

"And that, Mr. Rider, is why we in this family love and honor bees," Maddy finished.

"And we like the honey, too," Henry added.

*T*hey spent the rest of the day working in the garden. Nash was feeling weary, but when Maddy glanced at his face and suggested he stay inside and rest after the midday meal, he refused.

"Helping you with this is the least I can do," he told her.

"But it's your first day out of bed. You need to rest. You haven't finished healing yet."

But Nash worked doggedly on.

Around four o'clock Maddy called a halt. They'd done about as much as they could for the day, she said. Nash was secretly glad of it. He was exhausted.

"Scrambled eggs on toast for tea, and pancakes for supper," she declared. "And then we'll have a story."

They'd just finished their tea when Maddy, who was facing the window, said, "Mr. Harris! Quick, children, out the back way, please."

Their faces were alive with curiosity. "Oh, but Maddy . . ." John began.

Maddy held up a hand. "I don't want you in the cottage while he's here. Girls, lock up the hens for the night, then take half a dozen eggs to Lizzie's aunt and ask her for some cottage cheese. Wait there with Lizzie. John, Henry, have you checked Mr. Rider's horse this evening? No? Then off you go. And call past Lizzie's and collect the girls on the way home. Now go." The children ran off.

Twelve

"You, too," Maddy told Nash. "Outside please."

"I'll stay," Nash said grimly. Suddenly he was no longer tired.

She flung him an incredulous look. "Are you mad? I can't let him know I have a man staying here! Out, quickly! He's here!" A heavy knock sounded at the front door.

She was right, he knew, but he was damned if he'd leave her alone with that fellow. She'd sent the children away for a reason.

Besides, he wanted to hear what Harris had to say. Swearing under his breath Nash climbed into the bed and drew the curtains, leaving a small gap to watch through.

He was fed up with hiding. It went right against the grain, even though he knew there was a sound reason. But he was a man, dammit, not a mouse.

"Mr. Harris, how do you do? Please come in," he heard Maddy say.

Harris mumbled something and entered. He stood, his arms folded, legs braced apart, looking around the cottage with a proprietorial air. "So, you haven't packed yet?"

"As you see," Maddy said politely.

"I don't suppose it'll take you long," Harris said bluntly. "Not much to pack."

As before, Harris seated himself without being invited to. His breeches were even tighter, his waistcoat more garishly embroidered, and even from the bed, Nash could smell the man's scented pomade.

Maddy placed a pot of tea and some cups and saucers on the table. "Did you inform Mr. Renfrew or his brother, the earl, that Sir Jasper promised me we could stay here, in exchange for honey, until John turns twenty-one?" Her tone was mild, conversational.

"I told you, no record of that promise exists in the estate records." He leaned back, balanced on two legs of the chair, looking smug and totally in command.

Nash prayed for the chair to break.

Maddy said pleasantly, "I didn't ask if you'd found evidence of the promise, I asked whether you told Mr. Renfrew or his brother about it."

"Of course I didn't." Harris picked his nails in a show of supreme indifference. "The Honorable Mr. Renfrew has better things to do than worry about a claim that can't be proven. And he made it very clear that he wants you out of this cottage at once."

The devil he did, Nash thought. To his best recollection he'd never exchanged a word with this fellow. All immediate estate questions had been referred to Marcus.

Then again his memory hadn't been the most reliable lately. But it didn't make sense to be making decisions about an estate when he'd never inspected it. Neither he nor Marcus would do such a thing. Their father had drilled them both in the principles of estate management.

And to throw a woman and children out of their home? He didn't need a memory to tell him he'd never do such a thing, and nor would Marcus, so what the devil was Harris up to?

Maddy said, "I thought that might be the case, which is why I wrote to Lord Alverleigh himself and explained the whole situation. Tea?" She picked up the teapot and gave him a bright, false smile.

With a scowl, Harris pushed the cup aside. "Not for me."

He glanced around the room. "So where's the letter? I'll forward it for you."

Maddy poured herself a tea, added a little honey, and stirred it thoroughly before answering. "Oh, I posted it myself. Rev. Matheson had a copy of Debrett's *Peerage*, you know, the book that lists all the peers of the kingdom and—"

"I know what Debrett's is."

"Such an interesting volume, is it not? And so I found the address of the Earl of Alverleigh and sent the letter off myself."

Harris glared at her. Maddy sipped her tea, apparently oblivious of his annoyance.

He grunted. "Well, I'm not here to talk about letters. I'm here to collect the rent. Five pounds now, and no excuses."

"Of course." She fetched the tin.

Harris blinked in surprise. "You've got five pounds?"

"Not exactly." She struggled with the lid of the tin, which appeared stuck. "I still say it's an exorbitant rent and I intend to take it up with Mr. Renfrew when he gets here—"

"I'm warning you—"

She placed the ten pound banknote on the table between them. "I assume you can give me change?"

Harris stared at the banknote in disbelief, then picked it up and examined it carefully. He went to put it in his pocket but she twitched it nimbly from his fingers. "My change first, if you please," she said in a firm but pleasant voice.

Grudgingly Harris fished in his coat pocket and pulled out a fistful of change. "Where the hell did the likes of you get a sum like this?" he growled as he picked through the coins.

Her brows rose and she said crisply, "Where I got it is not your concern, Mr. Harris. All that should interest you is that I can pay."

With a bad grace, he tossed onto the table two sovereigns, three half sovereigns, a crown, six half crowns, and five florins. As Maddy counted up the coins, Harris reached for the ten-pound note.

In an instant, she slid it back across the table. "The receipt first, if you would be so good?" She stacked up the five pounds in coins he'd given her beside it.

"Receipt?" His face reddened. "*Receipt?*"

She kept her tone mild. "I believe it's standard business practice."

"Standard business practice!" He snorted. "What would you know of standard business practice? Or did Sir Jasper issue a receipt each time he dipped his wick in your honey pot?"

There was a sudden silence, then a loud slap echoed through the cottage.

Through the gap in the curtains, Nash could see Maddy leaning over the table, the picture of outraged female fury. He moved but she met his gaze squarely. *Get back,* her look said. *This is my battle.*

It took all of Nash's willpower to obey. If the bastard made one move toward her . . .

Harris jerked to his feet, knocking his chair backward, a hand to his cheek. "You little bitch!"

"How *dare* you!" Maddy blazed. "There was nothing, *nothing* improper in our friendship. Sir Jasper was a gallant old gentleman who knew my grandmother. And for her sake, he gave us this place and accepted honey as rent to save my pride!"

Harris sneered. "Save your pride? More like get his hands on your pretty hide, which is what I—" He lurched toward Maddy, his beefy hands reaching out.

Nash stepped from the alcove. "That's quite enough!" His voice was like a lash.

Harris swung around and stared, taking in Nash's stubbled chin, his riding breeches, the shirt open at the throat and with the arms rolled up, no coat, neckcloth, or waistcoat and, most damning of all, no shoes or stockings. "Who's this? Your fancy man, eh? Now I see how you got your ten-pound note, earned it on your ba—"

Nash punched Harris in the face.

Harris reeled and staggered back. "You bastard." He rallied and swung a blow at Nash, but beefy brute though he was, Nash was well skilled in the art of boxing. He blocked it easily.

"Watch your language. There's a lady present," Nash snapped.

Harris made a rude sound. "Lady? That little slu—"

Again Nash's fist smashed into Harris's face. "Apologize."

Harris grabbed a chair and swung it at Nash. He ducked but it caught him a glancing blow on the face. He wrenched it from Harris's grasp and tossed it aside.

"Apologize," Nash repeated.

"To her? You might take an old man's leavings but—"

This time Nash's blow sent Harris sprawling on the stone flags. He lay there, cowering, his nose bleeding profusely.

Nash stood over him, panting, his fists clenched. "I said, apologize to the lady."

Maddy tugged at his elbow. "He's had enough, Mr. Rider."

Nash didn't budge.

"Sorry, miss," Harris mumbled through his handkerchief. It was halfhearted at best.

Nash was tempted to thrash a proper apology out of the fellow, but Maddy clung to his arm so tightly he lowered his fists and stepped away.

Still on the floor, Harris snuffled noisily into his handkerchief. "I'll have the magistrate onto you," he mumbled in a very different tone from the way he'd apologized a moment earlier. "See if I don't. Onto the pair o' you."

"Do so with my goodwill," Nash said crisply. "And then you can explain to the magistrate why you've been threatening this lady—"

"Threatening? I never did." He heaved himself to his feet and gave Maddy a venomous glare. "Did she tell you that, the little—"

Nash took a step forward. Harris hastily scuttled sideways like a crab, putting the table between himself and Nash. He blotted blood from his nose. "You got no right—"

"Get out," Nash said coldly. "You're dismissed. Go and evict yourself from wherever you live, and if I catch you on my property again, I'll thrash you within an inch of your life."

Harris's brows gnashed together. "Evict myself? What the 'ell are you talking about? Your property?"

Nash gave a slight ironic bow. "Nash Renfrew, at your service. The *Honorable* Nash Renfrew."

There was a long silence. Over his bloodied handkerchief, Harris glanced from Nash to Maddy and then back to Nash. "That's a lie," he sneered, taking his cue from Maddy's surprised expression. "You heard me talking to her and—"

"I did," Nash agreed. "I heard you issue orders in my name that you never received from me and which I'll take my oath you never received from my brother. I heard you demand sums of money you had no right to demand, and"—his tone grew icy—"I heard you try to evict a young woman and five orphaned children, and when she demanded a fair hearing, you impugned her honor and the honor of my late uncle, Sir Jasper Brownrigg."

Harris mopped his bloodied face with a grubby handkerchief. His gaze darted back and forth between the two of them, gauging Maddy's bewilderment against Nash's icy poise.

"I don't believe you. She called you Rider before."

Nash shrugged. "A name from childhood." He could feel Maddy's gaze on him. She wasn't yet convinced it wasn't a clever bluff on his part.

Harris shook his head, unconvinced. "Nash Renfrew lives abroad."

"Usually I do, but at the moment, I'm home."

"Prove you're him," Harris said belligerently, clutching the edge of the table.

Nash shrugged. "I have no documents, if that's what you mean. But I have no need to prove myself to such as you."

Harris gave a triumphant smile. "Because it's all lies, and so I'll tell the magistrate."

Nash said coolly, "Go ahead."

Harris glared, hostile yet baffled.

Nash's energy was fading fast. His ankle and head were throbbing. He leaned inconspicuously on the edge of the bed and mused aloud, "Is Ferring still the butler at my uncle's house? I haven't been to Whitethorn since I was a child, but I don't imagine I've changed so much. And the housekeeper, what was her name? Terrifying woman—oh, yes, Mrs. Pickens. If you can produce them, they'll vouch for me."

A hunted expression crept over Harris's face. "Someone told you those names," he blustered. He jabbed an accusatory look at Maddy, but she was staring at Nash, looking just as puzzled.

Nash waved a hand. "By all means tell the magistrate so." He straightened, flexed his fingers, then formed two fists, and in a voice of steel said, "Now, I thought I told you to leave."

Harris eyed the ten-pound note still sitting on the table and reached for it.

"Leave it!" Nash ordered.

"What about my five quid in change?" Harris said belligerently.

"Compensation to the lady for the disturbance."

Harris scowled, wincing as he did from the cuts and bruises on his face. "I'll get you back, both of you," he swore as he stumbled from the cottage. "You see if I don't."

M addy plonked a bowl of hot salty water, some rags, and a salve for cuts on the table. The water sloshed over the rim; she didn't care. "Is it true?"

The hands washing the blood off them stilled. "That I'm Nash Renfrew? Yes, it's true." He dried his hands on a towel.

Maddy looked away, too upset to meet his gaze. So, he was Nash Renfrew—the *Honorable* Nash Renfrew—brother of an earl, no less. Her lodger. Her landlord.

And a big fat liar!

"How long have you known?"

He folded the towel carefully and put it on the table. As if tidiness would somehow appease her. "Since Harris's visit yesterday."

A tight, angry feeling lodged in her chest. He'd chosen to not to tell her.

"It was the most extraordinary thing," he explained, oblivious. "It was hearing Harris speak the names: mine, my brother Marcus's, and Uncle Jasper's. It shook something, some blockage, free and suddenly it all fell into place." He smiled at her, as if expecting her to celebrate with him.

She stared at the bowl of dirty water and thought about dumping it over his thick, handsome head. Did he have no idea of the position he'd put her in? And how stupid he'd made her feel?

And how hurt?

The intimacies they'd exchanged, those tender kisses . . . She'd shared her past with him, telling him about her life in France . . . They'd buried the bees together, worked in her ruined garden and all the time, all the time he *knew*.

"So, you got your memory back, just like that—how lovely!—but didn't think to mention it at the time?" Why wait so long to reveal it? And to Harris, of all people. Why not to her? Didn't he trust her? She'd saved his stupid life, risked her reputation to keep him safe.

"I started to, but—"

"But?"

"You left, and by the time you got back I'd decided it would be better if you didn't know who I really was."

"And. Why. Was. That. Pray?" Maddy sat on her hands to stop her fingers curling into fists. Did he have no idea of the damage he'd done her? Did he think nobody would find out that for all these days—and nights!—she'd had the lord of the manor in her bed?

"I wanted to find out what Harris was up to."

She snorted. "And I would have done everything I could to prevent you finding that out, of course."

"In a way. You'd have wanted me to leave."

"Hah! So I was right all along—it was a bribe—a bribe to let you stay on here!"

He looked puzzled. "You knew that."

"No! I thought it was because you didn't want to stay with the vicar—your oft-vaunted allergy to clergy and all. But that doesn't wash!" Too angry and hurt to stay in the same room with him, she got up and stalked to the door. "You didn't have to go to the vicar's; you could have gone to your own house, to Whitethorn Manor, not two miles away, with a dozen beds to choose from and a handful of servants to take care of you."

She wrenched open the door. "Instead you chose to hide your identity from me, bribe me, and then, after all our secrecy, you must reveal yourself to the one person in the village who wishes me ill!" She grabbed her cloak from the hook and left, slamming the door behind her.

She ran into the garden, battling tears of rage and frustration. And hurt.

He didn't need to give her that ten pounds. He'd let her sweat over that letter to his brother, when all the time he'd known there was no need. He could have solved all her problems with a wave of his hand.

And that ridiculous charade about his brother's address and

Debrett's—how he must have laughed up his sleeve at that one!

He'd even poked through her most private things and she'd forgiven him, eventually—the poor man who'd lost his memory!

What a fool she'd been, a stupid, trusting fool! It would be all over the village soon that he'd jumped from her bed, half dressed and without his boots! And in broad daylight! Defending her honor!

Her honor! That was rich! The Honorable Nash Blockhead had no idea of the fix he'd put her in.

Nobody would believe she was innocent, that nothing had happened between them. Except that foolish Maddy Woodford had gone and given her heart in exchange for a few tender kisses. Heartbreaking kisses!

Kisses for a foolish, gullible girl from a lying rake!

The villagers would think the worst. Everyone would believe she'd tried to trap the lord of the manor into marriage. And failed.

The man never suffered, was never blamed. It was always the woman.

She'd been walking—storming along—with no thought for where she was going. Now she came to a sudden, sickening standstill. Without thinking, she'd headed for her favorite place to take her troubles to—the beehives.

The empty hive spaces were still charred and sticky from the fire. A sick feeling welled up in her. There were no bees to tell her troubles to. Grand-mère was dead. She didn't even have a child to hug. And her life was in ruins.

She burst into tears.

She sat on the cold, stone seat, tears of anger and misery and betrayal pouring down her cheeks. How long since she'd cried, really cried? She couldn't remember. When she'd buried Grand-mère probably. Or when she'd closed up their cottage for the last time. Not for Papa. His death had been a blessed release.

She wept until she had no more tears.

She took a deep, shuddery breath and stood up, calm and weary. The storm of tears had done her good, like a rainstorm that washed away the detritus, leaving everything clear.

She scrubbed the tearstains from her cheeks and took the

path next to the forest. It was a favorite walk, the still, silent forest on one side, green rolling hills on the other, and it led to the top of the hill, where you could see for miles in several directions.

She loved that view, loved knowing herself a tiny creature in a huge landscape. It always put her problems into perspective, that view.

The trees were already budding with green tips. In the fields, snowdrops bloomed in drifts, their dainty heads nodding like shy maidens. Several fields over, a couple of lambs, bright white against the grass, stood on long, ungainly legs, drinking from their mothers, their tails wiggling in delight. Spring was all around her.

She'd never felt less renewed. She felt drained, empty.

She reached the top of the hill and breathed in the clean, cold, bracing air. Her options were spread out before her. In one direction was the village, in the other Whitethorn Manor, and far away, to the northeast, lay Fyfield Place . . . Fyfield Place and Mr. Hulme.

Oh, Grand-mère, I've made such a mess of everything.

She would have to leave the village. Perhaps it was weak of her, but she couldn't bear to be scorned and whispered about, to have her new-found friends turn their backs on her. She'd never had friends before, not like this. In France they'd kept their distance.

The children, too, would suffer from her ruined reputation. She couldn't stay.

She had fifteen pounds. Not enough to start again. The only reason they'd survived before was Sir Jasper's peppercorn rent on the cottage. And while she had no doubt Nash would honor the agreement, she couldn't stay on. A token rent would only fuel the rumor mill.

Sick at heart, she contemplated the view and shivered. There was only one option . . .

Nash cursed himself. His blasted temper. After all they'd done to avoid compromising her . . . And with Harris of all people. Worse was the look in her eyes when she realized he'd regained his memory and not told her. He hadn't even considered her feelings. All he'd thought about was how to remain here, in the cottage, how to protect her from the Bloody Abbot. He'd hurt her. Badly, from the look of it. Damn and blast! And by protecting her from Harris, he'd got her into a worse pickle. What the hell was he going to do?

He'd caused the scandal, he would fix it. But how?

The usual solution to compromised virtue was marriage. His body hummed approval. Nash's gaze drifted to the line of worn, faded dresses on the hooks in the alcove, to the little collection of homemade books, to the pot of soup, simmering gently over the fire . . .

Maddy was an unsophisticated little soul. A keeper of bees and chickens and children. Beauty, but no training and a basic education. Apart from a short period in her gentleman father's home, she'd spent most of her life in cottages growing vegetables.

Could Maddy live the life he lived, mixing with la crème de la crème of international society? The men would appreciate her beauty, but the women . . . They'd have her for breakfast, he thought. They'd sniff out her background—they always did—and peck her to pieces.

No, it would be selfish and cruel of him to drag Maddy into that world. She might leap at the idea, but she wouldn't know the implications. And he would have to watch as the people of his world crushed her bright spirit. And that he couldn't bear.

He hadn't taken her virginity, only compromised her reputation, and to a man who bore them both a grudge.

All she really needed was new place to live, to escape the gossip, and an income, he reminded himself. And protection.

A cottage on his brother's estate would do perfectly. Nash would settle an income on her and the children, and Marcus would ensure they didn't come to any harm.

It was an adequate solution. But the guilt remained.

"*I* want you to leave." Maddy hung her cloak on the hook. The children would be back soon. She needed to make supper.

He gave her a startled look. "What? Now?"

"As soon as possible." She was pleased he'd recovered his

memory, she really was, but right now she just felt . . . beaten. Trying to muster the courage to do what she knew she would have to do. Marry Mr. Hulme.

The only way to cope, when your life was turned upside down, was to put one step in front of the other and do whatever came next. Which was making the pancakes she'd promised the children for supper.

The ten-pound note still sat on the table where she'd left it, the five pounds in change piled neatly on top of it. She put it in the tin. At least they could afford to take the stagecoach back to Leicestershire. She knotted a cloth high around her middle to protect her from splatters and fetched a basket of eggs, a basin, and a fork.

He watched her somberly. "I didn't—" he began, then stopped. He could see how serious she was. "Very well, I'll leave, but I'll wait until the children return. I'd want to say good-bye."

She nodded. The children would be upset. They liked him. So did she, for that matter, and if she liked him too much for her own peace of mind, it was her secret. But they all knew he would leave one day. And today was the day.

She cracked eggs into the basin and whisked them briskly with a fork. Unanswered questions flew round and round in her head. Why had he really kept it a secret? She didn't believe his excuse about catching Harris. That didn't require him sleeping on her floor. Did he think she couldn't be trusted? Or worse, did he fear she'd try to—to encroach . . .

It was the last thing she'd do.

She'd always known there could be nothing between them. Once it might have been possible, if only Nash was not the heir to an earldom . . . if only Papa had not lost all his money . . . if only she'd had a normal upbringing and an education to equip her for her station in life and she'd made her come-out like other girls of her station. If she didn't have five little brothers and sisters to bring up, if she wasn't his tenant, living on his uncle's charity.

If only . . .

But if onlys buttered no parsnips, as Lizzie often said, and there was no use in trying to cling to past glories. Maddy had learned that from Grand-mère.

As she'd aged and become forgetful, Grand-mère had clung more and more to her airs and graces, refusing to admit what she'd lost. Most of the locals laughed at her, albeit behind her back. She had too much innate dignity for them to do it to her face, but Maddy knew.

Maddy had too much pride to leave herself open to that kind of mockery. One needed money to keep up appearances and she had none. No money and no illusions.

She stopped beating the eggs and put the fork down. "Why didn't you tell me you'd recovered your memory? Why keep it a secret?"

"I told you before. I wanted to catch Harris in the act, and you would have booted me out. As today has proved." He linked his hands behind his head, as if pleased with his answer and rocked back on two legs of the chair.

"When Mr. Harris was doing that I was hoping the chair would break," she observed, and sloshed some buttermilk into the mix.

He grinned. "Me, too."

She eyed the chair. "He certainly weakened it."

All four chair legs instantly resumed their place on the floor.

That wiped the smile off his face, she thought. "So it was all about catching Harris?"

"Yes."

She didn't believe a word of it. She sifted flour into the basin. "You could have slept comfortably at Whitethorn, then come back here in the morning."

She put a knob of butter in a pan and put it by the fire to melt. "There was no reason for anyone to connect the Honorable Nash Renfrew to me." She added the melted butter to the pancake mix and beat it vigorously.

"Hang it all," he said irritably. "If you must know, it was vanity, pure and simple. I couldn't arrive at Whitethorn in only one boot, not on my first night as the new master. I'd look ridiculous. One needs to make an entrance for that kind of thing, you know—make an impression, begin as you mean to go on."

"Fustian!" She covered the bowl of pancake batter with a clean cloth, and as she placed the bowl on a shelf to sit, the answer came to her. She knew why he'd stayed on in her cottage. The mystery was why he didn't want to admit it. The last of her anger drained away.

"Fustian?" he repeated when she returned to the table.

"You're a fraud, Nash Renfrew," she said softly. "You stayed here, you slept on that cold, hard floor for one reason only: to protect me and the children from the Bloody Abbot."

"Well, of course I did," he said, looking embarrassed. "What sort of fellow would I be to leave you in a fix like that, to go on my merry way after all you'd done for me?"

So, she thought. It was gratitude, pure and simple. And gallantry. Repayment in kind. So much for morning dreams and foolish hopes.

And if he'd left her in a worse mess when he left than she'd been in when he arrived, it was nobody's fault. Not his, not hers. One of life's accidents.

Thirteen

"So who are you, Mr. Nash Renfrew?" Maddy asked. She'd made them both a cup of rose hip and mint tea and sat down at the table to drink it. "I know you're the brother of the Earl of Alverleigh, and Sir Jasper's nephew—and please accept my condolences on the death of your uncle."

He nodded in acknowledgment, and she continued. "But apart from the fact that you've been living abroad, I know nothing else about you."

"I'm a diplomat," he told her. "I've been posted to Russia for the last few years, living in St. Petersburg and Moscow."

"St. Petersburg," she exclaimed. "I've heard it's very beautiful."

"It's the most beautiful city I've ever been to, with the possible exception of Venice. They call St. Petersburg the Venice of the north." It felt so peculiar, sitting here, exchanging polite chitchat like strangers over a table, when he'd slept with her in his arms. Nash sipped his tea. He was even used to the taste of her strange brews.

"And do you like being a diplomat?"

"I love it," he said simply. "I can't imagine doing anything else. Travel, intrigue, glittering palaces, and political fencing in the dark, and all the while, I'm serving my country."

"So you're not planning to become a squire on the land."

He laughed and shook his head. "Far from it. I've been granted leave of absence to untangle the affairs of Uncle Jasper, among other things. I gather he grew rather muddled toward the end."

She shook her head. "Not muddled so much as very frail. He couldn't leave his bed, but I used to visit him often, and his mind was quite clear until the last few weeks, when the laudanum the doctor prescribed made him very groggy."

"I see." So the financial discrepancies he'd discovered were not the result of an old man's forgetfulness. Marcus had written to him in Russia, saying he sensed something was amiss. Marcus had a nose for that sort of thing.

"I don't have long to sort it out. I'm expected back in St. Petersburg in June."

She refilled his cup and her own. "You have much to do then, in such a short time. The estate will need a lot of work, I fear."

He pulled a face. "As bad as that, is it? Oh well, I'll get it started and my brother will help—he loves that kind of thing. I'm not completely off the hook as far as work is concerned. The czar's aunt, the Grand Duchess Anna Petrovna Romanova, is making her first visit to London, and since she knows me well, I must go to London and dance attendance on her. She's an old lady and very difficult to please."

She gave him a dry look. "I gather you please her."

He was startled.

Her eyes danced. "My grandmother was the same—very crotchety and picky in general, but in the company of a handsome young man, she blossomed. You'd think her nothing but milk and honey." She began to clear away the cups and saucers. "So, no other close relatives who might be worrying? Parents? A wife? Should you write to your brother and tell him you are all right?"

"No, I've al—" He broke off, recalling how he'd broken into her letter to Marcus. "No one will be worried. My parents are dead and I have no wife." He took a breath and added,

"Though my aunt is even now making arrangements for my wedding."

"You're betrothed?" Was there a constraint in her voice? Her back was turned so he couldn't read her expression. Surely she didn't think . . . didn't expect . . .

His chest felt suddenly tight.

She turned with a brilliant smile. "How exciting. Tell me about your fiancée. Is she pretty? Is the wedding to be soon? You must tell the girls, they love to hear about weddings."

No, she didn't expect . . .

On balance, he was relieved, he thought. She was a lovely girl, but life didn't work like that. Marriages were like treaties between countries, made for practical reasons, not emotional ones. He knew it and Maddy, being of French descent, would know it, too. The French, even after their revolution, remained hardheaded and practical in separating marriage from matters of the heart.

Besides, who knew what Aunt Maude had already arranged? He'd given her more than three weeks. Aunt Maude could settle the affairs of a small country in three weeks. She'd probably picked out the perfect bride for him already. And booked the church.

The tightness in his chest didn't ease.

"I'm not yet betrothed," he said. "My aunt has guaranteed to find me a suitable bride."

"Suitable?" Her eyes widened. "You're leaving it to your aunt?"

He shrugged. "It's the most practical solution."

"You don't plan to marry for love, then?" She sounded amazed.

There was a short silence, then, "I've always believed an arranged marriage is the most prudent approach."

"Prudent, yes, but a little . . . cold-blooded, don't you think? Especially when you have a choice," said the girl who had none.

He hesitated. If she was harboring any female dreams of hearts and flowers, it was best to put her straight now. "My parents made a love match. From the point of view of a child of that marriage, it was a living hell. My opinion hasn't altered since." His opinion had, in fact, hardened. The more bored and restless wives invited him for dalliance, the more he realized that marriage and love was the worst possible combination.

He pretended not to notice her troubled expression and added in a light voice, "Besides, I don't have time to go a'courting. I'm only in England for a short time. The Foreign Office frowns on English diplomats marrying foreigners, and my aunt can be trusted to find the right sort of girl."

"I'm fascinated by this glimpse into another world," she said. "What is 'the right sort of girl'?"

He ran a finger around his collar. Even though he wasn't wearing a neckcloth, it felt quite tight. "Oh, you know, a girl with the right sort of upbringing, the right sort of connections for a life in diplomatic circl—"

"Maddy, Maddy, we're home." The children burst into the cottage. Nash was never so glad to see a bunch of muddy children in his life. The conversation had strayed into sticky areas.

They both knew anything more between them was impossible, but still . . .

"We saw Mr. Harris going into the village," John told them. "He looked like someone had punched him in the nose." He scrutinized Nash's face, glanced at his knuckles, and exchanged a satisfied look with Henry.

"Lizzie's aunt gave us a quart of fresh milk," Jane said, shutting the door behind them.

"And some cream to have with our pancakes, as well as the cottage cheese," Susan added. "Lucy's got the cheese."

"Your horse is in splendid fettle, sir," Henry told Nash, inspecting the signs of battle. "Needs to be ridden, we think," he added hopefully.

Nash thanked the boys. His horse would be ridden soon enough.

Jane plonked the heavy quart jug on the table. "I carried it all the way."

Maddy raised one eyebrow at the boys. "I did offer," John said in an aggrieved tone, "but she said we were too clumsy and would spill it."

"You did last time," Jane retorted.

"Enough!" Maddy clapped her hands. "Off, all of you, and wash your hands for supper. We have some news for you."

The children raced off, squabbling lightheartedly.

"So the murder is out," he said quietly.

She gave him a quizzical look.

"My fight with Harris."

"Oh, that." She placed the griddle pan over the fire and began to set the table. "I don't mind. Mr. Harris is a bully, and what he said about your uncle and me was horrid. I was only upset because of—" She broke off. "Well, you know."

"I know." He still couldn't quite believe she was booting him out. "I'm glad it wasn't the fighting that upset you. Most ladies abhor such scenes."

"Far from it, I have a deplorable bloodthirsty streak," she admitted as she dropped a small knob of butter onto the pan. It sizzled as she angled the pan to allow the butter to cover the base. A delicious smell filled the room.

She poured batter into the foaming butter. "I've never had a white knight come to my rescue before."

From what he could work out, she'd never had anyone look out for her at all. Bubbles rose to the surface of the batter.

She flipped the pancakes and called toward the scullery, where the sounds of splashing and childish laughter was getting louder, "Hurry along, children. Pancakes in two minutes."

She slid the first batch onto a tin plate and set them near the fire to keep warm. She dropped in another small knob of butter. He watched it sizzle and foam. His stomach rumbled.

"You're welcome to stay for supper, Mr. Renfrew," she said as if he were a stranger, a chance visitor, not someone who'd lived here for the past however many days. Drawing the line in the sand. Putting him at a distance, where he belonged.

"A last supper?" he said with irony.

She met his gaze somberly. "Exactly."

A heavy weight settled in his chest. He wished it hadn't ended like this, but though he regretted the final result, and upsetting her, he couldn't regret his actions.

Leave her to face that night-creeping bastard alone? Never. And no self-respecting man could stand by, hiding behind bed curtains, while Harris threatened and bullied her.

He glanced at the bed. If he had any regrets, they were ones he couldn't admit to, not to her . . .

N ash had never dined with children before. They arrived at the table in an exuberant tumble, yet once seated, were quite composed and relatively well behaved.

"I hope your face is not too sore, Mr. Rider?" Jane enquired once she'd helped Lucy into the chair beside Nash. "John says you were in a fight with Mr. Harris."

"Did you win?" Henry asked.

"Of course he won," John declared stoutly.

Maddy placed a pot of honey, some cut lemons, a large jug of milk, and a bowl of cream on the table. "Don't pester Mr. Rider at supper, boys."

"I wish I'd seen it," Henry said.

"Me, too," John said. "I've never seen a proper fight."

"It was hardly a proper fight," Nash said with an apologetic glance at Maddy. "Three punches only—and no, I didn't knock him out."

"And it was only because Mr. Harris was nasty to me," added Maddy.

"If he was nasty to Maddy, I would have punched him, too," John said darkly.

"Me, too," Henry agreed.

"And me," Lucy said.

"Young ladies do not punch people," Jane told her.

Lucy pondered this. "Then I would have kicked him."

Nash tried not to smile as her sisters tried to explain to the little girl the error of her ways. None of their explanations pleased her.

"But if I must not punch or kick or bite, what can I do when someone is mean to me?" she asked, frustrated. "Maddy?"

They all looked at Maddy.

"It's most unjust, I agree," she said. "My grandmother used to carry a stick and if anyone was nasty to her she would hit them with it, but I would not recommend you do that, Lucy. It's something only for older ladies, not young girls."

"Did you hit Mr. Harris with a stick?" Lucy persisted.

She hesitated, clearly debating the wisdom of telling them the truth. Nash waited, curious to see how she would handle the question. The question of women defending themselves was a thorny one; theoretically women—ladies, at least—were never supposed to find themselves in such a position. It was up to the men of her family to protect her. But when you had no man to defend you . . .

What would she have done if he hadn't been there? It did not bear thinking about. She had courage enough for two, but Harris was a big, strong man with an ugly temper.

"No, I slapped him, hard across the face," she told them. "But that was my bad temper showing. I should not have done it. Most of the time the best defense a lady has is her tongue. No, not poking it out, Lucy, I mean using words."

"Like when Maddy's cross with us for being naughty," Jane said.

"Something like that, yes," Maddy agreed. "Though if you are ever in real danger from some bad person, Lucy, you may punch and kick *and* bite. Now, that's enough talk about fighting. Suppertime is for eating and conversation. Jane, will you pour everyone a cup of milk, please?"

The table fell silent as the children drank their milk.

Checking to see that Maddy was occupied flipping pancakes, John leaned over and whispered, "Will you teach Henry and me to fight? We need to learn. Some of the village boys—" He broke off as Maddy turned around.

Nash knew what it meant. They were being bullied and keeping it from Maddy. Nash, to his shame, knew all about boys and bullying. "I'll teach you."

At that, Maddy shot him a hard glance over the children's heads. "Mr. Rider will be leaving shortly, John, so you mustn't expect too much from his promises." She hadn't missed the exchange at all.

"Leaving?" The children turned to him in dismay. "When, sir? Where are you going?"

Nash found it surprisingly difficult to tell them. "I've recovered from my injuries," he said apologetically, "and must be on my way."

"But what of your memory, sir?" Jane asked.

"It's returned."

"What, all of it?" Henry clearly hoped the answer would be no.

Nash ruffled the boy's hair. "Yes, every bit. My name is Nash Renfrew and I was coming here to visit my new home, Whitethorn Manor."

"Sir Jasper's house?"

"Yes, I'm his nephew. He left it to me in his will."

The children brightened visibly. "Then we'll be neighbors, sir."

"Enough questions, children," Maddy interrupted. She placed a platter of pancakes in the middle of the table. "Careful, the plate is hot." She stripped off her apron and went to take her place at the head of the table.

Nash rose, but John was there before him, holding Maddy's chair to seat her. It was part of the boy's training, he saw. Henry, too, stood by his chair, waiting for Maddy to be seated before sitting down.

She smiled at both boys and caressed John's hair briefly as she sat and began serving out the pancakes.

A small gesture of approval and affection, and so everyday neither of them even seemed aware of it, but it struck Nash that he had no memory of either his father or his mother doing such a thing to him or Marcus.

His father would have scorned it. Children were born as savages and weren't to be coddled: they needed harsh discipline and rigid training to turn them into civilized beings.

His mother used or withheld her affection as a reward or punishment, to her sons and her husband, and there was never any predicting which it would be. Mama like to keep men on their toes, and that meant keeping them guessing. Even her sons.

Maddy kept these children on the lightest of reins without any of the intimidation or discipline Nash had experienced. She assumed they'd behave well and most of the time they did. When any correction was needed, she did it with the raising of a brow or a quiet word. And still with affection.

Extraordinary.

These children were less perfectly behaved than he or Marcus had been, but there was a relaxed, pleasant charm about them. If anyone had informed him a week ago that he would be dining at table with a bunch of lively young children, he would have been appalled. It would be an event to be endured.

Now . . .

"Mr. Rid—er, Mr. Renfrew," John asked, cutting into Nash's reverie. "Will you be bringing more horses like Pepper to Whitethorn?"

"Pepper is actually my brother's horse," Nash explained. "I generally use his horses when I'm in England."

John wrinkled his brow. "When you're in England, sir?"

Maddy said, "Mr. Renfrew has just returned from St. Petersburg. That's in Russia."

"Why were you in Russia, Mr. Renfrew?" Jane asked.

"I'm a diplomat," Nash explained. "That means I do a lot of traveling in different countries. I'm hardly ever in England."

"Don't you keep any horses in England?" John asked in dismay.

"No, I'm not here long enough."

"But now you'll be living at Whitethorn Manor, that will change, won't it?"

"I'll certainly be seeing to the running of the estate and making a few changes," Nash agreed. "But I doubt I'll be purchasing any horses. I'll be returning to St. Petersburg in June."

"But that's just over a month away."

All talk and clattering of cutlery ceased. John said, "You're not going to live at Whitethorn?"

"You won't be our neighbor?" Jane said.

Lucy clutched his sleeve with a small hand. "You're not going to leave us, Mr. Rider, are you?" she said in a tragic little voice. "But you're s'posed to be the prince."

Nash looked at the sad little faces ranged around the table. Good God, he hadn't even known them a week, and for most of that he'd been unconscious. He liked them, too, but surely they could see . . .

No, they were just children . . .

"I must," he explained gently. "It's my profession. It's how I serve my country. I only came to England to settle my uncle's estate and to—" He broke off. He didn't suppose they'd be any more amenable to the idea of him finding a bride. Lucy had said it all: Maddy was Cinderella and he was supposed to be the prince.

He and Maddy knew better.

*R*ain set in during supper, cold and steady. Maddy glanced outside. There was no sign of it letting up. She wouldn't send a dog out in this weather, let alone a man who'd been sick so recently. She glanced at Nash. He knew it, too.

"With your permission I'll stay one last night," he said in a low voice.

Maddy gave him a doubtful look.

"I promise I'll leave first thing in the morning."

She nodded. He'd misunderstood. She didn't doubt his sincerity. She had every faith he'd leave in the morning. He had the look of a man who was ready to get on with his life. To sort out his new estate and get back to St. Petersburg. Marrying the "right sort of girl" along the way.

"Are you expecting the Bloody Abbot to come again?" she asked quietly. She didn't want the children to hear.

He shrugged. "I dare not risk it."

"It's my home," she reminded him. "You don't have to stay and protect me. I'll manage. I always do."

"I'm your landlord," he countered. "Your safety is my responsibility."

It wasn't true, but if he wanted to pretend, Maddy didn't mind. Truth to tell, she was glad he was staying another night. There was so much more she wanted to know about him before he left forever. She was under no illusions about neighborly popping in and such in the future.

Even if he did come to Whitethorn Manor, she wouldn't be living here. She'd be at Fyfield Hall.

"You don't mind another night on the floor?" She needed to make it clear that was all she was offering.

She might wonder, and wish, and maybe even dream about having a last night together in her bed, but she couldn't bring herself to offer.

If he tried to seduce her . . . well, she'd face that then, see if there was any resistance in her. She doubted it. What virtue mattered now?

Maddy had promised the children a story before bed, but instead, Mr. Renfrew ended up telling them about some of the places he'd visited: St. Petersburg, Venice, Zindaria, Vienna, where the waltz had been invented.

He told them of traveling in a coach without wheels, zig-zagging across great, frozen lakes, feeling the ice shift beneath them. He told a story about a journey through a still, dark, snow-covered forest, with a pack of wolves baying at their heels, of wild Cossacks who rode like the veriest daredevils and danced squatting down and leaping up with whoops and shouts, of peasant women who wore as many as sixteen skirts, one on top of another—Maddy wondered dryly how he'd learned that last little fact.

They were all enthralled; it was like another world.

It *was* another world. His world.

At bedtime the children said their good nights with somber little faces. They knew he was leaving. Lucy, of course, wanted Mr. Rider—she refused to use his real name—to carry her up to bed, but Maddy vetoed it, saying his leg was too sore, but really, she knew it would just stretch things out.

She stayed with the children until they drifted off to sleep.

By the time she came down, he'd banked the fire for the night, placed the screen in front of it, and was stretched out in the makeshift bed in front of the hearth.

That was one question answered. There'd be no need to battle with her conscience and resist seduction tonight. It was probably just as well.

Probably.

She bathed quickly in the scullery, changed into her night-gown, and wrapped a warm shawl around her. She set her candle on the table and blew it out. The wick was still smoking by the time she was in bed.

She lay on her side with the curtains open, watching the glow of the fire and the silhouette of the man who lay before it. Despite the long day and the disturbed previous night, she wasn't the slightest bit sleepy.

Outside the wind soughed through the branches of the trees,

reminding her of when she was a little girl listening to the wind, imagining she was on a boat at sea.

"Will you sail from England direct to St. Petersburg?" She spoke softly in case he was asleep.

"Yes. It'll be summer when I return. In winter it's a different story. The Baltic Sea is often locked with ice."

Some coals fell in the fire, sending a twirl of sparks up the chimney. The rain beat steadily down.

"I've been thinking about the rent," she said after a while.

He shifted, turning on his side to face her. "I suspect Harris has been fiddling the books for some time. I'll wager he planned to grab what he could and disappear before anyone found him out. He didn't expect me until the summer."

Maddy pondered that. There was more to it, she was sure. "He was quite taken aback when I produced the note you gave me. He didn't expect me to pay. I think that's what made him so angry."

"That you paid?"

"Yes. He was in quite a good mood until I produced the money. And then suddenly he began to insult me. He never has before. He's been arrogant, but not insulting."

"He dresses very fine for an estate manager," Nash observed after a moment. "Bit of a ladies' man, is he?"

"Perhaps, but he's never shown any interest of that sort in me. He must know I'd never consider such a thing. Though if he thought I had such an arrangement with your uncle . . ."

Nash raised himself on his elbow. "But his original plan was to evict you. That's what I don't understand. If he was charging extra rent and pocketing the difference, why evict you?"

"A lesson to others?"

"Possibly, but Harris wasn't the only one trying to drive you away."

Maddy sat up in bed, pulling the bedclothes around her. "You think Harris is the Bloody Abbot?" It made sense, and yet . . . "How would he benefit from a vacant cottage?"

She could almost feel his shrug as he said, "It's a mystery. How long have you lived here?"

"Not quite eighteen months. It was vacant and quite tumble-down. The children and I had to clean it up and whitewash it."

"You didn't find any secret hidey holes or hidden trap-doors?"

"Nothing. Not even a loose floorboard. I assure you, if there was any hidden treasure here we would have found it."

They lay staring at each other across the darkened room, pondering the problem. The darkness seemed to thicken.

Their last night together and they lay on opposite sides of the room discussing a crooked estate manager and hidden trap-doors.

Maddy sat with the bedclothes huddled around her, willing him to rise from his bed and come to her.

Nash shifted. She tensed.

He lay back down and said, "Well, whatever it is, we can investigate further in the morning. I'll get the story out of him one way or another."

Maddy reluctantly slid back down in her bed. It wasn't Harris she was worrying about.

She lay listening to the wind in the trees. Sleep was still no closer. She was too aware of the man at the hearth.

Maddy's dream, back when she was a girl, was to fall deeply, madly, wholly in love. To be swept off her feet, and to walk down the aisle toward a man who waited with love shining from his eyes.

She gazed at Nash's silhouette, limned by the glow of the fire. Had he ever dreamed of love? Why make a practical arrangement when you didn't have to? The Honorable Nash Renfrew had all the choices in the world. Even as plain Mr. Rider of just around the corner, he'd have no trouble finding a wife, no trouble finding love.

He wouldn't have to look very far, either.

But he was not plain Mr. Rider and he never would be. A marriage between them was out of the question. She'd spend the rest of her life in the bed of an old man . . . and here was the man of her dreams, lying uncomfortably on her cold, hard floor.

But she could love him, just once, for one night. Couldn't she? Her reputation was already ruined.

What did she have to lose? Only her virginity. Her heart was already lost to him. She stared across the room at Nash's profile. His last night here. Her last chance.

Might as well be hanged for a sheep as a lamb.

"Are you cold?" she whispered into the darkness.

"A bit, why?" The question hung in the air.

"You can sleep here if you like. With me." There, she'd said it.

There was a long pause. She wondered if he'd heard. Then the deep voice came out of the darkness. "If I sleep there with you, I won't be able to resist."

Maddy swallowed. "I don't want you to resist."

Fourteen

❧

*H*e was silent. Rain hammered on the windows in a steady drumming. His silhouette against the dancing flames of the fire was motionless. Tension thickened in the air.

"I know nothing can come of it," Maddy said. "I know you're leaving in the morning. I want nothing from you . . . nothing but this one night."

"And afterward?"

"I will return with the children to Leicestershire."

"But—"

"This isn't a *discussion*!" She was unable to stand the suspense, unwilling to think about the future. "If you don't want me, then—"

"I want you." His deep voice cut her off, sure and strong, leaving her breathless. "I want you," he repeated. "So are you sure about this? Because once I'm in your bed, there's no going back."

"I'm sure," she half whispered, and she was, despite her doubts and fears. The fear that she would live the rest of her life in regret for not making love with Nash banished all lesser anxieties.

She heard the rustle of fabric as he pushed aside the bed-clothes on the makeshift bed and braced herself for his arrival in her bed. He surprised her.

"I'll build up the fire. You won't go short—I'll send a man over with a load of firewood in a few days."

It was an unconscious reminder of his new lord of the manor status. Such a gesture, well meant as it was, would only confirm her status as his mistress. "That would be lovely," she told him. He could burn all her wood—she didn't care. She would be leaving soon.

Burning her wood, burning her bridges, it was all the same.

This one night was hers, her own private, particular blaze of glory to keep her warm throughout the long, lonely nights ahead.

She lay quietly, almost breathlessly, watching him move around her cottage, his limp only slightly in evidence. The vicar's nightshirt was too tight across his shoulders, too loose in the middle, and too short for his long, rangy body. The hem ended at midthigh.

A coil of excitement unraveled deep within her at the thought of running her hands over his body—and not because of fever. Well, it was, but a different kind of fever.

He built the fire to a bright blaze, dousing the shadows of the night, burning away her anxieties. Next, he lit a handful of candles, stuffed them, manlike, into various incongruous containers and placed them around the bed.

"Do you mind?" he asked, pausing in the act of lighting a candle. "If this is our one night together, I want to remember everything, including how beautiful you look as God made you."

"No, it's lovely." She wanted to remember the sight of him, too, golden skinned, very male, and . . . utterly irresistible.

As God made you. That meant naked. Her nightgown was old and patched. She wished she had something pretty to wear for him. Should she remove her nightgown now?

But she was too shy to take it off while he was still wearing his.

He hurried to the bed, his limp still in evidence. "Brrr, that stone floor is freezing. We must get you some rugs."

She could see how his mind was working, providing her

with all the comforts, assuming he would have the right to take care of her.

It wasn't going to happen. She would not live like that, as his dependent, with the whole village knowing. Watching. Whispering. And taking it out on the children.

Still, it was a kind thought.

A draft of cool air driftered over her skin as he lifted the bedclothes and slid in beside her. She jumped as his large, cold feet brushed against her calves. "Your turn to warm my feet, I think," he murmured. He lay on his side beside her and smoothed a strand of hair back from her face. "You have the most beautiful eyes."

She gazed back in silence, unable to think of a thing to say. She just wanted to kiss him and get started. She wasn't quite sure what to do, but she'd invited him to her bed, so she should take the initiative . . .

She leaned forward and kissed him. It was a bit rushed and clumsy—their teeth clunked—but he steadied her with one hand on her shoulder. His other hand cupped the nape of her neck and his lips closed over hers as he took control, and her nerves—and bones—dissolved.

Maddy ran her hands over his shoulders, over the clean linen of his nightshirt that smelled of sunshine and soap, and freshly shaven man. Beneath the fabric, his shoulders were warm and hard, and he smiled lazily, like a big tawny cat, enjoying her appreciation as she smoothed her hands over him.

She dipped her fingers into the half-unbuttoned neckline of his nightshirt, caressing the strong column of his throat, slipping lightly over the upper planes of his chest.

He made a low sound deep in his throat, caught her hand, and kissed her palm. It sent tingles right to the core of her and her fingers curled around his jaw. "Shall I remove the nightshirt now?"

Her mouth dried. "Yes," she croaked.

In one swift movement, he sat up, yanked it over his head, and tossed it aside. He was naked. As naked as he'd been that first night in her bed. But this time, for this one, precious night, he was hers to caress, absorb, love.

Firelight danced over the golden expanse of his long, hard body. Maddy stroked her palms slowly, luxuriously over him, loving the strength of his shoulders and the hard, elegant muscularity of his arms, the solid planes of his chest.

"You're beautiful," she whispered.

"No, that's my line." He pulled the thick plaits of her hair forward and unraveled them slowly, loosening one at the time, trailing his fingers through the thick locks, murmuring things about corn silk and fire as he rubbed it against his face and between his fingers and arranged it over her shoulders. When he finished, his fingers rested lightly just above her breasts.

"Do you want me to—" she began, reaching for the buttons at the front of her nightgown.

"No." He pressed his hand over hers, stilling the movement. He smiled at her surprise. "Not yet."

Before she could ask why, he bent and kissed her lightly on the mouth, once, twice, and then he was raining kisses on her face, on her eyelids, on her cheeks, soft and sweet, like summer rain.

Like a cat, she rubbed against him, running her hands over his chest and shoulders, loving the spare, hard feel of him.

His skin was cool but it warmed under her touch, and the intense heat at the core of him seeped into her as it had on the nights they'd slept together.

He planted kisses from the corner of her mouth along her jawline in a slow, sensual exploration down the column of her neck.

Her lips felt swollen, ultrasensitive, even though he'd barely skimmed over them. She ached for the deeper kisses he'd given her before, and moistened her lips, enjoying the delicious hunger of anticipation. All she had was this night with him. She would not waste a moment of it by hurrying.

But she was hungry . . . and he was a feast.

Her fingers moved of their own accord, stroking lightly over the small hard nubs. Were his nipples as sensitive as hers? She circled them with her nails, scratching them lightly, like a cat. He made a soft growling noise deep in his throat and moved against her hands, pushing against her, demanding more.

Her beautiful . . . lion? No, he was a cougar, elegant and powerful and tawny.

Catlike, she licked his skin, tasting salt and spice and essence of Nash. He tensed. Did he not like it?

She glanced up and caught the glint of his smile. "Again," he murmured.

This time she bit him very gently, scraping her teeth over the hard little raised nubs and he arched and shuddered beneath her touch. She smiled, filled with female power, then gasped as he brushed her breast though the fabric of her nightgown.

He stroked over the fabric so lightly, so delicately she should not even feel it. Instead she quivered uncontrollably at the lightest touch. Her breasts were achingly sensitive, their hardened tips thrusting against the fabric, craving his touch. He caressed her again and again and she shuddered and arched and pressed herself against him.

"And now . . ." he said and reached for the buttons on her nightgown. She moved to help him, eager for the sensation of lying skin to skin with him, but again he stopped her with his hands, saying, "These are *my* buttons."

She waited breathlessly.

He undid one small bone button, then kissed her slowly, sumptuously. Delicious, but she wanted more.

Instead he undid another button, clumsily, with shaking hands.

She groaned silently. Why had she worn a nightgown with so many buttons? "I bet you were the kind of little boy who unwrapped his presents very slowly."

"I was." He took the next tiny bone button between long, strong fingers and gave her a slow smile. "I still am. Anticipation builds hunger."

It certainly did. How many buttons were there? She tried to remember and failed. All she knew was that if he continued unfastening buttons at this torturous rate, she'd melt, or explode, or something.

"I'm not a parcel." In one movement she pulled the nightgown over her head and tossed it aside. It floated to the floor and settled gently over his.

And she was naked in front of a man, for the first time in her life. Cool night air whispered against her skin.

"No," he breathed. "You're a gift."

Under the scorching heat of his gaze, the last of her shyness melted. He'd called her beautiful and now, as he gazed, she felt beautiful, bathed in soft candlelight. The scent of burning apple wood and wax candles filled the air; her beeswax, from her own bees. Her world contracted to this place, this bed, this man. No yesterdays, no tomorrows. Only now.

"Cream and silk, honey and fire," he murmured. He trailed the back of his finger lightly down her cheek, then leaned slowly forward until his mouth was a hairsbreadth from hers.

She forgot to breathe. Her heart was pounding in her breast.

And then he captured her mouth, claiming possession with a hungry tenderness that unraveled her.

He stroked the inside of her mouth with his tongue, running his hands over her, warming, heating, melting her, demanding responses she hadn't known were in her. Long shudders rippled down her spine in an insistent, rhythmic pull and flow.

With mouth, tongue, and hands he explored her, tasting, stroking, knowing her with a sureness that made her melt with pleasure, even as she arched against him. Every touch sent luscious ripples through her, curling her toes and causing aching quivers deep inside her. She was melting under his heat, spinning, holding him as if she were falling instead of lying safely in her own bed, in his arms.

She moved against him restlessly, clutching his shoulders as if riding out a storm at sea. She didn't know exactly what she wanted, only that he, and only he, could give it.

His hand was between her thighs, stroking, caressing, parting her and ohh . . . ohhh. She gasped, her body lost to her control, arching and shivering deep into her very core, and the world dissolved and there was only him.

Nash clung to the last desperate shreds of control. He wanted to savor every movement, every sensation, each gasp and moan and tremulous sigh. Her golden brandy eyes widened, piercing him, lancing him, and then she closed them, shutting him out, pale crescents fringed in dark lashes, gilded in fire as she shuddered and thrashed under him in climax.

He groaned, desperate to bury himself deeply in the slender, golden, willing body, sweet as new hay, hot as brandy. He held back with every shred of self-command he could muster. Her first time. He was determined to make it the best it could be.

But she was so damned responsive. And he was so damned hungry for her. It felt like years that he'd been waiting to do this with her, not days. His body ached and throbbed with unfulfilled agony, a starving beast clawing to be fed.

Slowly the shudders passed from her and she lay in his arms, gasping for breath. He planted slow kisses in a glorious exploration down the creamy length of her body. His silken-skinned beauty. He could taste the salt-sweet dampness of her skin, the scent of her soap, made of beeswax and flowers, and the most addictive taste of all, the scent of Maddy.

He rubbed his cheek lightly over her breasts and took one rosy nipple in his mouth, teasing lightly at first, then becoming more demanding. Lavishing her with desire, loving the small soft cries of pleasure she made.

Her hands ran over his body feverishly, sending his inner beast into a silent screaming frenzy. Not yet, not yet.

He trailed kisses over her soft belly and buried his face in the dark nest of curls at the apex of her silky thighs. She made a small sound of surprise but her limbs fell apart in helpless desire and he tasted her, salt-sweet, elixir of Maddy, more potent than anything he'd ever tasted.

Her breath hitched in a series of little gasps and she began to moan and twist beneath him, urging him on with fluttering, distracted caresses as he devoured her.

He was hard as the rocks of hell and burning with desperate desire, and the taste and scent and feel of her ate at his control. He continued caressing her with his hand as he nibbled his way back up her body, leashing every bit of self-control.

He raised himself to possess her and she ran her fingers lightly over his cock in curious exploration. God, but it nearly unmanned him. He bucked under the featherlight touch, wanting so much more.

A long racking shudder consumed him. He couldn't hold back much longer. But she was ready, more than ready, and when he positioned himself at her entrance, she pushed eagerly against him.

He entered her in a long, slow movement, feeling the frail barrier of her innocence shred, catching her gasp of pain in a kiss. Her legs came up and closed tightly around him and she rained blind, clumsy, feverish kisses on his chest and chin and arms, anywhere she could reach as her body struggled to adjust to his. His heart tightened in his chest, like a fist in a glove.

He clung to the last shred of his control and soothed her with his fingers, arousing her anew, and was soon rewarded with the tight rolling clench of her acceptance. One deep female quiver was all it took to send his body leaping for release, spinning out of his control, and he was rolling with her, thrusting deep, claiming her inexorably in that most ancient and eternal of rhythms. Soaring. Diving into fire and ecstasy . . . and darkness.

When next he was aware of anything, the fire had died to a dull glow of coals, and the candles were burning low. Maddy lay curled against him, watching him with soft eyes. Damp eyes. He moved to let the candlelight illuminate her face and saw tear tracks.

He rubbed them gently with a thumb. "I'm sorr—" he began but she didn't let him finish.

"I'm not," she said and kissed him softly, sweetly, and sighed. It was the sigh of a woman well satisfied. But the tears worried him.

"You've been crying." Never, ever had his lovemaking ended in tears. Women's tears unsettled him, unmanned him.

She shook her head and gave him a curious little half smile, the smile of Mona Lisa, hinting at things no man could hope to understand. She snuggled her head in the hollow between his jaw and his shoulder, settled her palm on his chest, closed her eyes, and went to sleep.

Tired as he was, it took Nash some time to follow her into sleep. It wasn't just her tears that kept him awake. The whole thing was . . . disturbing.

He'd made love to a number of women in his life. He'd always looked on the act of lovemaking as an agreeable exchange of pleasure. Nothing more, nothing less.

But this . . . this was nothing like that. Yes there had been pleasure, but pleasure was too small a word. Too ordinary, too . . . tame.

Making love with Maddy Woodford had been nothing less than . . . shattering. No, it was more, it was . . .

He fell asleep searching for a word . . .

* * *

They made love once more in the stillness of the night, a short, intense, desperate coupling that left him sweating, exhausted, sated, and yet unsatisfied.

This time she fell asleep on top of him, her arms and legs still wrapped around him, and his arms locked around her, unwilling to let go.

The cold fingers of dawn were stealing into the cottage when she woke him a third time, running her hands over him so softly he woke gradually, as if floating to the surface of a very deep lake.

He was still only half awake when he entered her, every movement slow, as if in a dream, but the chill morning air licked at his flanks like a hungry wolf He would never forget the expression on her face as she loved him quietly, tenderly, with hands and mouth and body. Asking for nothing, giving all.

They came together in a shattering climax, the like of which he'd never experienced, the aftermath a piercing bittersweetness, like sweet wine cut with salt.

Nash held her against him as the sweat dried on him, unwilling to move. Still joined in the most elemental way, their limbs tangled, their breathing now quiet, seemingly at peace. But something niggled at him, an expression he'd glimpsed in her eyes in the cool dawn light. Familiar, but elusive.

He worried at it, as a tongue worries at a sore tooth, repeatedly, but to no effect.

Eventually she straightened and disentangled herself from him. "Time to go," she whispered. "The children will be waking in an hour or so. They've already said their good-byes. It would be best if you were gone before they come down for breakfast." She kissed him to soften the implacability in her words and in her eyes, and gave him a little push.

She reached down and grabbed her nightgown from the floor and pulled it over her head with a shiver and said, "Do you want breakfast?"

"No." He was ravenous, but the expression in her eyes, the brightness in her voice disturbed him.

He rose and dressed swiftly, aware all the time of the way she watched his every movement. She helped him tie his ruined boot on with black ribbons, a leftover from her days in mourning, she said, and though he knew it must look ridiculous, he didn't give it more than a passing thought.

She was all he could think of, too quiet for comfort, her glorious brandy eyes avoiding his for the most part. Once he'd caught a glimpse of, what . . . grief? Anger? Regret? Just a brief flicker that passed too quickly for him to interpret.

But it niggled at him, too.

For two pins, he'd climb back into bed with her and kiss every look from her eyes except ecstasy, but when he took a step toward her, she flung up a hand as if to ward him off.

Was it because he'd taken her virginity? Was she worried about pregnancy? "If you find you are with child—"

"Don't worry." She hurried to the door, opened it, and smiled, a wide smile that was meant to reassure, but unsettled him even more, and said, "You must go now."

He hesitated, portmanteau in hand. "I'm only going up the road."

"I know."

"Whitethorn is maybe an hour's walk or fifteen minutes on horseback from here."

"I know."

"So this is not good-bye, just . . . good morning." The first in what he hoped would be many such good mornings. "I'll be there for several weeks at least," he told her.

She nodded, biting her lip, her eyes luminous.

"And even though I must return to Russia next month . . ." Suddenly he didn't know what to say. "It's not good-bye," he repeated firmly.

"I know." Her voice hitched. She gave a quick smile—he was sure it wobbled—raised herself on tiptoes, and kissed him again, a slow, lingering caress. A definite blasted good-bye, Nash thought.

He responded by ravishing her mouth possessively, almost savagely, determined to show her he had no intention of abandoning her.

What the hell was she thinking?

He was usually quite good at reading people's expressions, divining their thoughts and feelings—it was an asset in his work—but apart from a brief, blind look in her eyes as he released her, he could read nothing in her face as she stepped back. "God keep you safe, Nash Renfrew," she whispered and pushed him gently out the door.

She closed it behind him and he heard the bolt's slow slide.

He tramped along the frosty path toward the vicarage where his horse was stabled. What the devil had got into her?

The answer came to him. He had.

She'd been a virgin. That was why she was so emotional this morning. It should have been her bridal morning. Guilt poked at Nash's conscience with long, spiny fingers as he stamped on his way.

She *knew* there was no question of marriage. And, dammit, he *wasn't* abandoning her. How could he? She was . . . She was the most important thing that had ever happened to him.

Did she think he could just walk away?

He was, in fact, walking away at this very minute. Brooding over what couldn't be helped. Over the look in a woman's eyes. Maddy's eyes.

Damn and blast! He kicked a pebble viciously, and nearly lost his tied-on boot.

What a bloody mess. He should never have stayed the night, never have accepted her invitation to come to her bed. But the deed was done. And done well. So . . . glorious he couldn't regret it.

But did she?

He stopped, encountering a herd of sheep, and waited as they flowed around him in the narrow lane. The shepherd gave him a laconic nod and touched his cap. Nash returned the greeting absently.

Did she imagine he would abandon her and the children? Dammit, he was fond of those brats. Very fond. The very first thing he would do when he got to his house would be to summon his man of business—not Harris—Marcus's man of business, and set up a trust for Maddy and the children, so that they need never live on honey and eggs and weed blasted soup again.

How much farther to this damned vicarage? His feet hurt. His boots were made for riding, not for walking miles over frozen ground.

She'd be safe on one of Marcus's estates. She couldn't stay here, facing down the gossip she didn't deserve, but she'd be all right.

So why did the thought make him feel so empty?

The vicarage stood still and silent. At this ungodly hour, nobody was awake. Nash found his horse, saddled it, and left a note thanking the vicar, saying he'd call at a more civil hour to give his thanks in person. He left a bright, new-minted sovereign for the groom.

Then he headed for Whitethorn at a fast gallop. Cold air lanced through him, scouring his lungs as he bent over the horse's neck, urging him faster and faster, enjoying the speed, seeking some kind of release—from what, he didn't know. He'd had more releases last night than any man had a right to. He ought to be relaxed and on top of the world. Instead he was a bunch of angry knots.

There were more people out and about now, farm workers who lifted a hand in greeting, as if they knew him. His tenants perhaps. Thank God they were too far away to engage him in conversation.

They galloped until horse and master were breathless, blood singing, cold air stinging, Nash's brain going over that last little scene in the cottage over and over.

Damn it all, he wasn't ready to end it yet. Whatever "it" was.

Whitethorn Manor came into view in the valley between the trees, floating in wisps of fog in the bowl of a valley. He pulled his horse to a halt and stared blankly in front of him.

How did he want it to end?

He could have—he *should* have—made it all neat and tidy. He hadn't even told her of his plan to secure her future. And if she was too stubborn and prideful to accept his help, he'd find her a position where she could earn a good living. He'd pay for the boys' education, of course, and the girls would have a generous dowry—he'd find some way that little Miss Stuffrump would accept.

He clenched his jaw, frustrated. The trouble was, such plans were all well and good for some other woman, but she was Maddy. She wasn't like other women.

The more he thought about it, the more that elusive expression of hers, that last time they'd made love, worried him. A kind of quiet, resigned acceptance.

Of what, dammit? He'd made it as clear as a man could that he wasn't abandoning her!

If abandonment worried her, God knew she hadn't clung. He knew about clingy women. Maddy had all but thrust him out the door. And bolted it after him.

As he stared down through the trees, a memory tugged at him. He'd seen that expression before. But when?

And then it hit him. It was with just that resigned tenderness that she'd rewrapped her grandmother's portrait, that sketchbook, and her girlhood journal.

Dammit, she was mentally wrapping him in faded silk brocade, getting ready to put him away with all her other treasured memories. He stared blindly down at the mellow gold stone of his inheritance, then wrenched his horse around and galloped back the way he came.

Fifteen

❦

"It's all over the village, miss," Lizzie panted. She'd run all the way from the farm and knocked on the cottage door just after the children had left for the vicarage.

For a mad, delirious moment, Maddy had thought Nash had come back. But it was just Lizzie, racing to warn her. Maddy put aside the letters she'd been writing—trying to write. Trying to make herself write. She couldn't seem to find the words.

"What is, Lizzie?" Though she knew full well.

"My uncle was having a drink in the inn yesterday and Mr. Harris was tellin' anyone who'd listen that he caught you with a fancy man in your bed. And plenty did listen and believe him, miss, including Uncle Bill." She gave Maddy a shamefaced look. "He didn't at first. He's never liked that Mr. Harris and so, when he came home last night from the pub, he asked me straight out, did you have a man living with you."

She flushed. "It kind of took me by surprise, miss, and I told him no, but I'm no good at tellin' fibs and he knew there was something. And so I explained that your gentleman was an 'elpless invalid, but Uncle Bill didn't believe that. 'No helpless invalid gave Harris that there broken nose,' he said, and that was that."

"I see." Maddy sighed. The scandal had spread faster than she'd thought.

"It's true, isn't it, miss? I can see you've been crying."

Maddy shook her head. "Mr. Renfrew did nothing wrong, Lizzie, and so you must tell your uncle and everyone else." Not for her sake—she would be gone and what the villagers thought of her wouldn't matter once she'd left, but Nash would be the main landowner in the district, and it wasn't fair that he would be blamed for something that was her fault. Her choice.

Lizzie eyed her shrewdly. "If he done nothing wrong, then why were you crying?"

"He's gone." Maddy bit off the words and tried to look unconcerned. It was a miserable failure.

Lizzie's face fell. "Oh, miss, you've gone and fallen in love with him, haven't you?" she whispered. "Oh, miss." Lizzie pulled her into a warm hug and the unexpected comfort of it set off Maddy's tears again.

Stupid to be crying, she berated herself silently, when it was all of her own doing. It was just that she hadn't known how it would feel, to feel so much . . . and then watch him ride away, knowing it was over . . .

After a moment she pulled back. "Don't mind me," she muttered, groping for a handkerchief. "I'm just a fool who fell for a handsome face." And let herself dream secret, impossible dreams.

Lizzie wiped Maddy's cheeks with a corner of her apron. "You and me both, miss," she said. "That's the trouble with bein' a woman—we're built to give our hearts away. I even married my handsome face and it still done me no good. Heartbreak on two legs, that's what my Reuben and your Mr. Renfrew are."

Maddy gave a shaky laugh. Lizzie's practical acceptance of her fate was heartening. She supposed all women did go through it. Mama had and so had Grand-mère.

"Uncle Bill don't blame you, miss—he says it's what all them fine gentleman are like: 'Rakes one and all, and built to take advantage.' But he says . . ." Lizzie screwed up her face in frustration. "He says I'm not to go and be a maidservant now, that if a fine gentleman can ruin a nice lady like you, then a girl like me, with a weakness for a fine-lookin' man, hasn't a hope of stayin' virtuous." Lizzie pulled a face. "But there's no danger of that. My Reuben cured me of fallin' for a handsome charmer. Plenty of lads have tried to have their way with me, thinkin' me lonely, now that I've tasted the pleasures of the marriage bed— and that's true enough . . ." Lizzie's expression grew soft and distant, remembering.

Maddy tried not to think about the lonely nights that lay in her future. Her feelings were too raw and tender to express, but she knew exactly how Lizzie felt. *The pleasures of the marriage bed . . .*

How long had Reuben been gone? Nearly two years? He was never coming back, that was clear to Maddy. Yet all this time later Lizzie could still look like this at the mention of his name . . .

Oh God.

Lizzie continued, "But if I can't have Reuben, I don't want nobody." She winked at Maddy. "Especially not some village bumpkin with sweaty great clumsy hands."

Maddy managed a smile, but a sick feeling settled in the pit of her stomach. Not a village bumpkin, but a fastidious old man with soft, white, powdery skin and perfectly manicured hands . . . She repressed a shudder.

How could she bear Mr. Hulme to touch her after Nash? But she must, she must. If Lizzie's Uncle Bill, who had always been an ally, could think the worst of her . . .

She abruptly became aware of what Lizzie was saying. "He says I'm not to come here for lessons anymore, miss, that if your good name has been tainted . . ." She took Maddy's hands in her own work-roughened grip. "Don't look like that, miss. I'll come anyway, you see if I don't. And I don't care what Uncle Bill says, I will too become a maidservant. I'm not going to live with cows the rest of my life. Or if I must, I'm determined they'll be the two-legged sort with fancy clothes and airs and graces." She winked.

Maddy gave a choked laugh. It simply wasn't possible to stay gloomy with Lizzie around. "You don't need any more lessons. And I've written you a character reference." She took it from the mantelpiece and handed it to Lizzie. "Besides, I'm leaving the village."

Lizzie tucked the precious document in her apron pocket, unread. "Thanks, miss. Leaving the village? Where for?"

"I'm going back to Leicestershire. To where the children used to live."

"But I thought—" Lizzie stopped.

"Thought what?"

"I always had the feeling you never liked it there."

Maddy made a rueful gesture. "I didn't. But I've no choice now. I can't stay here. Mr. Harris has seen to that."

"The old baskit!" Lizzie muttered, but she made no attempt to argue. Her ready acceptance of Maddy's leaving only confirmed Maddy's decision to leave. "When do you go?"

"Tomorrow morning. We'll take the coach to Salisbury and then change."

"What did the little 'uns say when you told them?"

"I haven't told them yet." She'd sent them off for their lessons, as usual, unable to face their questions so soon after Nash leaving.

Lizzie grimaced in wordless sympathy. "So what'll you do in Leicestershire, miss?"

Maddy hesitated, but there was no point in keeping it a secret. "I've had an offer of marriage." The fact that it was years old made no difference. Mr. Hulme had waited years for her — the offer would still be open.

"From—" Lizzie exclaimed, but her excitement deflated when she saw Maddy's face. "Not Mr. Renfrew, then?"

Maddy shook her head. "A friend of my father's."

Lizzie screwed up her nose. "Old?"

Maddy nodded.

"Rich?"

Again, Maddy nodded. "I'm tired of battling for every mouthful, and the children are growing out of their clothes so fast."

"Ah, well, if he's rich I suppose it's not so bad. Better than staying here and havin' all the old biddies whisperin' and turning their backs on you," Lizzie said bluntly. She glanced at the window where the sun was burning off the morning mist. "I'd better go, miss. I had to stay and get the milking done with, but there's butter to be churned, and if I don't go now I'll be in even more hot water than I am already."

Maddy saw her to the door and the two girls embraced. "Oh, miss, I'm going to miss you that much," Lizzie said tearfully.

She would miss Lizzie, too, Maddy thought, hugging her tight. She was going to be so lonely without—

"Lizzie!" She clutched Lizzie's shoulders tightly. "Come with me.

Lizzie's eyes widened. "Where? To Leicestershire?"

Maddy nodded. "As my maid. Mr.—the man I'm marrying can easily afford an extra maid, and it would mean so much to me to have a friend with me."

A grin almost split Lizzie's face. "I'll come," she said. "In a heartbeat, I will, miss. You really mean it?"

"I really do."

"Well, then, I will," Lizzie declared. "Whether Uncle Bill says I can go or not." They hugged each other again, then Lizzie glanced at the sky. "I'll get hopping now. I'll churn a mountain of butter first and see if I can turn him up sweet before I break the news."

She started running toward the farm, then stopped, and tuned back with a grin. "No more of them bloody cows! Hooray!" And in a series of joyful little skips, she sped off.

Maddy watched her go, but slowly her smile faded. If the villagers were reacting as Lizzie said, she'd better go and face the vicar. She needed to explain, and to say good-bye to him and Mrs. Matheson. And a few other friends.

She put on her cloak and set off for the vicarage.

Nash dismounted, tied his horse to Maddy's gate, and knocked. No answer. He tried the door and found it latched, but unlocked. "Maddy?" he called, but there was no answer. She'd probably taken the children to their lessons.

He stepped inside. And came to a surprised halt. The normally neat cottage was cluttered. On the table, in the center of the neatly made bed, and on the floor, were piles of clothing and other items. Small piles—the sum total of what they owned

was pathetically meager, but it was clear to Nash that everything Maddy and the children owned was assembled here.

Two large, shabby leather portmanteaux sat beside the bed.
She was packing to leave.

She wasn't worried about being abandoned—she was abandoning him!

When had she planned to tell him? he wondered savagely.
She'd worked bloody fast! He'd left only an hour or two ago.

He prowled around the room, glaring at the neat little piles.
Two piles for each person, things to take on the bed, and on the
floor the things they would leave behind. Clothes—a pitiful
pile—and a few treasures of childhood; Susan's sketchbook,
their handmade books, the Luciella book on top, and the kind
of treasures Nash remembered from his boyhood: a bird's
skull, a curious stone, a horse shoe, a cricket bat and ball.
Maddy's pile contained a few threadbare dresses, a couple of
battered books, and the small leather case containing her treasured memories. Wrapped in faded blasted brocade.

Dammit! How could she plan to leave just like that without
telling him? And where the hell was she going?

Writing materials were scattered on the table. One letter,
addressed to him but only just begun; she'd got as far as *Dear
Nash, I was not able to say this when you left, but . . .*

Say what? His mind was a boiling stew of questions, but no
matter how many times he read it, he was just as much in the
dark.

He picked up the other letter, lying open on the table, a
draft, with many scratchings out.

> *Dear Mr. Hulme, I hope you are in good health. I am writing
> to ask if your offer is still . . . I am writing to inform you that
> I am now willing . . . The children and I need to leave the
> place where we have been living, and . . . I will accept the
> conditions you laid before me last time . . .*

Offer? Conditions? Not so willing, if the scratched-out
lines were any indication. He turned the letter over.

It was addressed to someone called Mr. Geo. Hulme, Esq.
of Fyfield Place, in Gilmorton, Leicestershire.

Who the devil was Mr. George Hulme, Esquire? And what

was he to Maddy? Whatever offer he'd made before, she'd obviously refused it. Was she now reconsidering? Because of Nash?

"Did you forget something?" Maddy's voice came from the open doorway.

He swung around. "Who's George Hulme?"

Her eyes were immediately shuttered. She closed the door behind her before saying, "My father's neighbor." Her gaze dropped to the letter in his hand. She swung her cloak off and plonked it roughly on its hook. "I cannot bear it when people read other people's letters," she told him roundly. "It is the most dishonorable, most intrusive, despicable—"

"George Hulme. What sort of neighbor?"

Her eyes snapped with irritation. "Not that it's any of your concern, but he was a good friend of my father's. He is executor of Papa's will and co-trustee of the estate Papa left, such as it is."

"Co-trustee?"

"He is responsible for the purely financial matters—Papa's debts, in other words. I have complete control of the children."

"This"—he brandished the incomplete letter—"this mentions he made you an offer. What sort of offer?"

"Have you no shame, to quote my private correspondence?"

"It was open on the table. What offer?"

She did not respond. Instead she began to gather up the clothing discarded on the floor. The prosaic action infuriated him. He caught her by the wrist. "What offer?"

She pulled away. "A very respectable one."

"*Marriage?*" He blinked. "How old is this Hulme fellow?"

She shrugged. "I don't know. A couple of years older than Papa, I think. Past sixty?"

"*Past sixty?* The lecherous old goat! You will refuse him, of course. You did in the past, I collect."

She gave him an opaque look. "When a man takes good care of himself—and Mr. Hulme is very well preserved—sixty is not that old."

Nash snorted. "It is when you're offering marriage to a young woman of twenty."

"Two and twenty." She'd harnessed her temper and presented an irritatingly calm appearance.

Superficial, Nash knew; nevertheless, his own temper mounted. "What did his own children think of this outrageous offer?"

"He has no children."

"Widowed long?"

"No." Her gaze slid away. She was hiding something.

"What do you mean, no? When was he widowed?"

"He's not a widower. He's never been married."

"Never been married? And yet now, in his sixth decade, he decides to take a wife young enough to be his granddaughter?" Nash shook his head. "There's something wrong there. A man of that age, a bachelor of long standing—more than sixty years!—suddenly decides to change his life? I don't believe it. What does he have to gain?"

She bared her teeth in imitation of a smile. "Me."

He snorted again. It was outrageous. The very thought of her, and some old man . . . any man . . . He jammed tightly clenched fists into his pockets, out of sight.

"It's true," she insisted. "He told me when I was a little girl that he would marry me one day."

He rolled his eyes. "That's just something you say to a child."

The anger sighed out of her. "I know," she said more quietly. "But he maintained that position ever since. I thought his references to it were mere pleasantries. But when Papa died Mr. Hulme insisted that that Papa had approved the match." She grimaced. "I think the real attraction is that he admired the way I looked after Papa when he was dying."

Nash was revolted. "You mean he wants to tie a lovely young woman to him so he'll be well looked after in his old age? I've never heard of anything so . . . so . . ."

"Selfish?"

"Wasteful," he snapped. "Wasteful of you, your life, and all its wonderful possibilities."

She gave a mirthless laugh and looked around her. "Yes, indeed, why would anyone give up all these wonderful possibilities"—she indicated the small cottage, barren now of its warmth—"to marry a wealthy old man? Why give up the constant and unrelenting struggle to feed and clothe five children when by marrying you could give them everything they need and want?"

"And what about what you want?"

She gave him a long look, then shrugged enigmatically.

"You refused him before," Nash persisted. The very idea of her marrying this unknown old man appalled him. She couldn't be allowed to sacrifice herself so cold-bloodedly. She deserved something better, much better.

She turned away from him and started briskly folding clothing. "Yes, well, I'm older now, and wiser."

Guilt lashed Nash's anger and frustration to breaking point. She hadn't spoken of becoming an old man's darling two days ago, when her garden was destroyed and her hives burned. She hadn't talked about marrying Hulme then. On the contrary, she'd been determined to fight back.

Now, all the fight was gone from her and he hated it, hating seeing resignation and acceptance in her eyes, knowing that he was the cause of it.

"If it's money you need, I said before I could—"

She turned on him, enraged. "Do not dare offer me money!"

Dammit, had all his diplomatic skills deserted him? Nash took a calming breath and rephrased it. "I didn't mean it like that, you know I don't. But naturally you want security for the children. I thought you understood that I would look after them, as well as you. I mustn't have made it clear."

"You made it quite clear and you have nothing to reproach yourself about. But I cannot accept that kind of support. You may not know what it's like in a small village, where everyone knows everyone's business, but if you sent men along with firewood, the village would know, if you gave me a rug for the floor, they would know. And they would whisper and talk. And the good, respectable women who have been my friends up to now will sh—speculate. And no longer commission bonnets. And everyone would gossip. And the children would suffer for it."

She'd been going to say something else, he thought. Sh—

Shun? Her friends would shun her? "I will buy you a house somewhere else—on one of my brother's—"

"Thank you, but no," she cut him off firmly. "You mean I would live as your mistress I suppose."

She paused and, horrified, he realized he had no answer. He hadn't thought about anything, except that he was going to lose her just when he'd found her.

She read an answer in his frozen face and shook her head. "Living as your mistress, seeing you only when you returned to England, when you could spare the time?" She made a decisive gesture. "I refuse to live on crumbs of attention and spend my life waiting. I will make my own choices."

Her cold-blooded assessment of the situation lashed at his guilt. A fine fellow he was indeed, to bring a girl to this when all she'd done was save his life. "I'm sorry. I know it's my fault, that my being here—and what happened between us last night—"

"Do *not* apologize for last night!" Her eyes flashed, her honey-smoke voice vibrated with emotion. "Last night has nothing to do with this—nothing! It was between you and me alone, and if there's anything I regret, it's not that we made love."

She passed a hand wearily over her face, gathering her composure. Her fingers trembled and pain twisted in him.

In a quieter voice she said, "Your offer is very generous, Nash, but you don't need to take care of me or give me money or cottages or rugs or firewood to assuage any guilt you think you have. You have nothing to reproach yourself for. Everything that happened in this cottage was my choice—*mine*! And I regret none of it." She paused. "Except perhaps for Mr. Harris discovering you here. But again, that was my responsibility—I knew the risk and accepted it—"

She was being far too generous, Nash thought. He'd provoked Harris's vindictiveness and caused the scandal that would force her to leave, to marry an old man.

"—and if I return to Leicestershire and marry Mr. Hulme, it will also be my choice. So please, put aside any misplaced guilt you have, set your new estate to rights, return to Russia and your life as a diplomat, and let me get on with my life."

He grabbed her arm and swung her around to face him.

"You can't bloody well marry a man old enough to be your grandfather! It's obscene."

She pulled herself out of his grip with an irritable movement. "Kindly do not swear at me. It's not your business what I do, Nash Renfrew. It's my life, my choice."

"And your body that will have an old man slavering incompetently over it!"

She turned, trying to hide the involuntary shudder that passed through her at his words, but Nash saw it, saw and pounced on it with triumph. "Admit it, you don't want to marry him."

"I admit nothing!" she flashed. "It's my decision. Now please—" She broke off and flung away to another part of the small room. She stood, her back to him, breathing deeply, almost visibly reassembling her composure. When she turned back, her face was smooth and clear of all visible signs of emotion.

She walked up to Nash and in a calm, pleasant voice said, "Good-bye, Mr. Renfrew. I wish you all the best in your life." She held out her hand.

He stared at it as if at a live snake. If he took it, it meant he accepted her dismissal. Damned if he would. Let her go and marry some disgusting old goat, just because Nash Renfrew had ruined her life?

"All right then, I'll marry you," he heard himself say.

Sixteen

*I*t was like cold water dashed in her face. *All right then, I'll marry you?* Flung at her in anger, resentfully, as if she'd been begging him to marry her.

All right then, I'll marry you. And then he'd looked vaguely alarmed, as if he'd shocked himself as well as her. He hadn't meant to say it.

He'd schooled his face into an expression of polite anticipation, all his anger and jealousy—for that's what it was, she knew—belatedly muzzled and packed away out of sight, presenting her with his diplomat's face. Waiting for her response to his ill-considered, obviously unplanned, and apparently instantly regretted marriage proposal.

She wanted to slap him, to burst into tears—no, slap him! Impossible man!

Serve him right if she accepted him.

He waited, his eyes unreadable, all signs of emotion subdued. A diplomat's job was to lie for his country. He would be a wonderful diplomat, she was sure.

He might have made love to her with a tenderness and passion that had stolen away the last piece of her hopelessly ill-guarded heart, but in one unguarded flash she'd seen what he really thought.

It sliced deep into her heart.

Want him as she might—and, oh, she did—she had too much pride to accept what was clearly a unintended proposal of marriage. Especially knowing the kind of bride he wanted—a girl with the right sort of upbringing, the right sort of connections. Of which she had none.

She might be desperate enough to marry Mr. Hulme, but with him, she was only laying her body on the line. With Nash, it would be everything, body, heart, and soul.

He waited, watching her with that horrid, blank, *diploma-tish* expression.

If she did accept him, took advantage of his momentary guilt and jealousy to trap him into marriage, this would be the face she'd see for the rest of her life, all politeness and diplomacy and blank, unreadable eyes. It wouldn't just break her heart, it would grind it to dust.

She gave him a proud look. "Do you think I would accept such a proposal as that? Uttered in begrudging resentment and flung down in the dust for me to pick up?"

His clenched jaw dropped.

"Thank you, Mr. Renfrew, but no thank you. I have made my decision. Good-bye. It's been a pleasure knowing you. You may see yourself out." She turned her back so that he wouldn't see that she was fighting tears.

"Very well, madam," he said in a tight clipped voice and stormed from the cottage.

She'd refused him. Nash stalked to where he'd tied his horse. She'd *refused* him. Sent him away with a flea in his ear in a dismissal worthy of a duchess.

He was relieved; that went without saying. He hadn't meant to make her an offer. He had no idea what possessed him.

He wanted to gallop away, to leave the whole mortifying mess behind him, but his horse was tired. Two wild rides were enough for a morning.

Leaving at a sedate trot was . . . frustrating.

He tried to block out the memory of her stricken expression.

He reminded himself that, it wouldn't have worked, that Maddy was too unsophisticated, too innocent for the life he led. The frozen feeling lodged at his core had everything to do with being appalled at his lapse in judgment, and nothing to do with her refusal.

Her refusal stung.

What had she said? *A proposal as that? Uttered in begrudging resentment*—begrudging resentment?—*and flung down in the dust.*

What nonsense. He hadn't flung any damn thing in the dust. There was no dust in that cottage; she kept it clean and neat as a new pin. And as for begrudging resentment . . .

A middle-aged woman came toward him in a dogcart, a basket of flowers sitting beside her on the seat. Smiling at him with pleased expectation, she stopped with the clear intent of engaging him in conversation. Another blasted tenant?

"How do you do, madam?" Nash snapped and trotted on.

Rather than marry Nash, Maddy had chosen a lecherous old goat three times her age!

It more than stung. It cut deep. And festered.

A scraggly dog raced out from a farmhouse, yapping fiercely.

All right then, I'll marry you.

Good God, had he really said that? In that tone of voice? To the woman he'd made love to all night, who'd shattered him with her warmth and generosity. Who'd made no effort to trap him into marriage, who'd only saved his life, tended his injuries, and given him more care than anyone in his life.

Oaf! Where was the silver-tongued diplomat famed for his smooth address?

The trouble was, he was used to dealing with men, negotiating with men. He understood men. Men were logical, or if not precisely logical, easy enough to read, driven by passions he could understand: greed, self-interest, power.

Women now . . . He'd never understood women. He kept them at a distance, flirting, deflecting any with serious intent, indulging in the occasional lighthearted affair with a like-minded female. Never, ever anything remotely emotional. He always made that clear, right from the start.

He'd let Maddy Woodford get closer to him than any woman in his life.

Yet Maddy Woodford hadn't waxed emotional over him. She hadn't wept or stormed or railed at him; she hadn't clung, she hadn't begged. She'd asked nothing of him at all, only his body. She'd loved him so sweetly and generously through the night, shattering all his self-control, then sent him on her way with a smile, albeit wobbly, and a firm good-bye.

He was the one who'd become emotional. For the first time in his life. The very idea of her marrying that ghastly old goat, lying in a bed while an old man pawed over her, dribbling, slavering his vile, old-man drool over her pure, silken skin . . . It drove him to the brink of insanity.

He closed his eyes, recognizing the emotion roiling through him.

Jealousy.

His father and mother all over again.

Put her out of your mind, man! Forget her. You offered, and she refused.

Dammit, life had been so much simpler before he met Maddy Woodford: calm, pleasant, relatively ordered. He'd known exactly who he was and what he wanted.

Now he had a mass of conflicting desires clawing at his insides like wild beasts, tearing him apart.

He wanted to ride out a storm, to curse the wind and howl at the moon. Instead he was forced to trot sedately through sunshine and spring flowers and twittering blasted birds.

He wanted to punch someone, shoot something, strangle someone. Dammit, he had to do *something*!

*F*oolish, foolish creature! Maddy upbraided herself silently as she moved about the cottage, packing and sorting clothes. *After everything you've always said about seizing a chance when it came. So he might have come to resent you for taking advantage of his momentary jealousy. At least you'd have the husband your heart desires.*

Not just her heart. As she moved about the cottage, she felt twinges and tenderness in unexpected places, and echoes of the night's loving rippled gently through her.

Each time it happened, she closed her eyes, luxuriating in every tiny sensation, memorizing, hoarding it for the long, lonely future she'd so foolishly embraced.

She blamed all those songs and poems and stories of giving it all up for love. For the sake of her beloved.

Her beloved, who'd shocked himself with an accidental proposal, and was even now riding away, heading for his glittering future, no doubt congratulating himself about his lucky escape from a most unsuitable woman.

Her beloved, who kissed like a dream, and made love like . . .

A hot, luscious shiver rippled through her, pooling at her center, clenching like a velvet fist deep inside her. She closed her eyes to savor it.

"Wrapping me in faded silk brocade, are you?" said a deep voice from the doorway.

She whirled. *Faded silk brocade?*

"I won't have it." He strode into the cottage. "I'm a living, breathing man. With needs." He closed the door behind him and turned, his blue eyes boring into her in a way that set her heart fluttering. "And I'm not ready to be put away in a box."

"What—"

"Sit. Down." It was not a request.

Maddy blinked. And sat. And watched wide-eyed as he took a couple of paces about the cottage, as if coming to a decision, and then came to stand in front of her.

And then knelt on one knee.

Maddy stopped breathing. Her heart thudded in her chest like a fist pounding on a door.

His eyes were dark blue and somber. He took her left hand in his and said, "Madeleine Woodford, would you do me the honor of giving me your hand in marriage?"

For a moment she was too stunned to answer.

He gave a rueful smile. "Every man is entitled to make a mull of his first marriage proposal. You must acknowledge this one is neither flung down in the dust, nor uttered in begrudging resentment."

She'd flicked him on the raw with those comments, she saw. Offended his sense of himself.

He waited for her response.

"Why do you want to marry me?" she asked, then silently

cursed herself for doing so. It was a miracle he'd come back, asked her again. Few people were given a second chance in life. But she wanted to know—*had* to know why.

Ached for the words . . .

He smiled. "Having jeopardized your good name, I can do no less than retrieve you from the consequences of my imprudence."

Oh, that. Maddy swallowed her disappointment. It shouldn't matter why—it didn't, really. She would still accept his offer. Gallantry was a fine reason to marry.

No point crying for the moon.

"The offer, of course, includes the children," he said. "I know you want to keep everyone together. I'm a wealthy man. None of you will lack for anything."

She bit her lip and managed a nod.

He misinterpreted the reason for her silence and squeezed her hand. "Believe me, if I didn't think this was the best thing to do I'd find another solution to the problem."

The problem. That would be her.

Oh, why couldn't she just say yes and get it over with? What was the matter with her? She tried to swallow again, but there was a large lump in her throat.

A slight crease formed between his brows. "I suppose you think it's too soon, that you've only known me a short time. But it's essential we scotch the gossip."

The gossip, yes.

He gave her a shrewd look. "You're worried, perhaps, because you know I'd planned on a . . . a different sort of bride."

Maddy gave a sort of a shrug. She knew.

He must have seen something in her expression, for his frown deepened. "You have other desirable qualities."

Maddy was suddenly breathless again. "Really?"

"Yes, indeed. The ability to cope with difficult and unexpected circumstances is important for a diplomat's wife. In the last week we two have managed to rub along in a cramped cottage under stressful conditions. You keep a cool head and respond practically, rather than with a high degree of sensibility, as most ladies of my acquaintance do."

Oh. He meant she didn't scream or become hysterical in a crisis. True enough. She was boringly practical.

A high degree of sensibility was something only a pampered lady could afford. As a tactic, it was wholly dependent on having someone ready and waiting to come to your rescue. Nobody ever rescued Maddy; she'd always had to rescue herself.

Until Nash Renfrew came into her life, she reminded herself. And now he was offering to take all her troubles away and marry her.

Marry her. Marry *her*. The reasons didn't matter, Maddy told herself. The words didn't matter. Only the fact.

Nash took her hand. "I believe we will deal well together."

Deal well together? Maddy tried to reconcile the man who'd made shiveringly hot, luscious love to her through the night with this cool-voiced stranger who proposed marriage with a recitation of her deficiencies and her qualities.

"It's not a love match, Maddy," he said gently. "Don't mistake what passed between us last night for, for love. It's . . . it's just how it is between a man and a woman. Sometimes. If they're lucky. It's a healthy expression of desire, that's all."

Perhaps, Maddy thought. She couldn't speak for his feelings, only hers.

He tucked a curl behind her ear and even such a light brush of skin against skin left her melting inside. He said, "You have romantic notions, I suspect, but believe me, this practical arrangement is far better than a love match."

At her doubtful look, he explained further. "I told you that my parents made a love match. The love of a lifetime, they called it. Every interaction was overly passionate and rife with . . . *emotion.*" His eyes were somber. "It tore our family apart. Such a liaison would be anathema to me."

Anathema? It was Maddy's turn to stare. He couldn't possibly mean it.

This, from the man who had caressed her breasts when he was barely conscious? Who, even when he didn't know his own name, curled his big warm body around hers, protective and loving, even in sleep. Who slept with his hand cupping her breast? Who could make her weep in the night with the beauty and the power of his lovemaking? And who made her insides melt with pleasure even when he was absent.

He wanted a passionless, emotionless marriage?

She would promise nothing of the sort. But now was not the time to confess it. She folded her hands and tried to look demure. And suitably emotionless. Her heart was pounding.

"So, what do you say, Maddy Woodford? Will you marry me?"

A better person would refuse him. It wasn't fair to reward his gallantry knowing, despite his reassurance, that his world would see marriage to her as a *mésalliance*.

But life wasn't fair.

It hadn't been fair to Grand-mère, it hadn't been fair to Mama, and it hadn't been fair to Maddy or the children.

Nash had had his chance. Of his own free will, he'd asked her a second time. That was his folly, to live with or regret.

She would seize this opportunity—and this man—with both hands.

Grand-mère, are you watching? Maddy took a deep breath and uttered the fateful words, "Thank you, Mr. Renfrew. I would be honored to accept your proposal of marriage."

"Excellent," he said and kissed her hand.

He kissed the back of her hand slowly, and with a burning look from those intense, blue eyes. And it sent a hot shiver through her, collecting in the pit of her stomach.

She wanted him to kiss her mouth and leaned forward, inviting it.

He rose to his feet and took a small notebook and pencil from his pocket, saying, "I'll make all the arrangements."

Perhaps proper kissing was to be restricted to the bedchamber. It didn't matter, Maddy decided, as long as there was kissing.

She was going to marry Nash Renfrew.

Grand-mère would be delighted: the marriage would return Maddy to the status her ancestry and birth, if not her upbringing, entitled her to.

Grand-mère would also approve of the way the man filled a tight coat and a pair of buckskin breeches, not to mention his pretty blue eyes. Grand-mère had ever an eye for a handsome young man and a particular soft spot for a blue-eyed man. She'd passed both on to Maddy. Her French side . . .

Nash Renfrew in a tight coat and a pair of buckskin breeches was a fine, handsome man. Naked in a bed he was downright beautiful.

Would she marry him? Try and stop her.

Would their marriage be the cold-blooded arrangement he said he wanted? Not if she could help it.

Would they be happy? She hoped so. She would certainly try.

Would he ever love her? Ah, that was the question . . .

"Now," Nash said, pencil and notebook at the ready, "Who should I notify of our betrothal?"

Maddy thought. "Nobody," she said finally. The few scattered relatives who remained had been uninterested in Maddy and the children when they needed help; she wanted nothing to do with them now her luck had changed. And her only friends were in the village, and she didn't know yet how they'd respond to the gossip about her.

He frowned and glanced at the unfinished letter to Mr. Hulme on the table. "Not even that fellow?"

Especially not that fellow, Maddy thought. "No. He doesn't know where I am, and I'd rather he didn't know I was getting married."

Nash frowned. "But weren't you engaged to him?"

Maddy shook her head. "No, never. He asked me to marry him two years ago, but I refused. But he said at the time the offer would remain open indefinitely, so when I was . . . was . . ."

"Desperate, you decided to change your mind," he said softly.

"Yes."

He hesitated, as if about to say something, then changed his mind. He said briskly, "Very well. So, a small, quiet wedding, yes?"

She nodded.

"And would you prefer to be married in the church here, or somewhere else? The alternatives are the family chapel at Alverleigh, St. George's, Hanover Square in London, or another place of your preference."

"In the village church, I think, with Rev. Matheson." At least then there would be some people she knew at the wedding, even if they were just Lizzie, Mrs. Matheson, and a few curious villagers come to gawk and whisper.

"Good, then I'll arrange it for as soon as possible. I'll go and see him now." He picked up his gloves.

"I'll need a new dress," she blurted. "I had to receive a marriage proposal in my old blue dress but I refuse to be married in it."

He waved a careless hand. "Of course. All that will be taken care of.

"And new slippers. These have a hole and when I kneel at the altar rail in the church, everyone will see—"

He glanced at her slippers and frowned. "Good God, I wouldn't dream of letting you be married in those old things. You'll need a whole new wardrobe, of course."

Illogically, his condemnation of her attire annoyed her. She'd tried so hard to maintain a respectable outward appearance and—suddenly she realized what he'd said. "A whole new wardrobe?"

He looked up from his list. "Naturally. After the wedding, we will travel to London where a mantua maker will fit you with everything you need."

A whole new wardrobe? She swallowed. For a girl who'd been fretting about how to pay for a new pair of children's shoes, it was all moving so fast. But a whole new wardrobe. She could adapt to that. Clothes. Beautiful, new clothes. How long since she'd had new clothes?

He added in a reassuring voice, as if shopping for a whole new wardrobe would be difficult, "My aunt will help you with that aspect of things. She has excellent taste and she adores shopping."

His aunt. "Would that be the aunt who's been searching for a suitable bride for you?"

He nodded. "Yes, my aunt Gosforth, Maude, Lady Gosforth. Our father's sister, she's been widowed these many years, and was childless. She is excellent *ton*, knows everyone, and is completely *à la mode*. She'll be delighted to show you the ropes."

"I see," Maddy said cautiously. "You don't think she might resent me?"

He looked at her in surprise. "Resent you? Why should she?"

"Perhaps because after all her work in searching for an eligible bride you went ahead and chose me."

He shrugged it off. "Any coals of blame she'll heap on me, not you. Aunt Maude never holds a grudge. She's very fond of me—of all her nephews—and can never stay cross for long."

Maddy gave him a doubtful look. She wasn't so sure.

"Besides," he added, "even if she were furious, she couldn't resist the prospect of outfitting you and the children."

"The children?" Well, of course he'd want the children to be properly dressed, too, she chided herself. It was all so sudden; she hadn't quite taken in the magnitude of change in her life yet.

He misunderstood her. "Aunt Maude is very fond of children, so don't worry about a thing—I'll arrange everything. You just finish the packing and get ready. We leave this afternoon, as soon after luncheon as I can manage."

"Leave this afternoon? Why? And where—"

At that moment someone knocked at the door. She hesitated.

"Get the door," he told her. "I'll explain after that."

But it was Lizzie, big with news.

"Oh, Lizzie," Maddy exclaimed. "Could you wait a mom—"

"Nonsense," Nash interrupted. He nodded to Lizzie and gestured her to come in. "I'll be off now. Don't worry about the whys or wheres, just get ready." He glanced at Lizzie and added in an undertone, "And not a word to anyone about leaving, not even Lizzie, understand?" He picked up his portmanteau and hat.

"But—"

"Trust me." He left, closing the door behind him.

She turned to find Lizzie eyeing her quizzically. "What's going on Miss Maddy?"

"Make us a cup of tea, will you Lizzie, and I'll tell you all about it. It's been an eventful morning."

"*Y*ou!" the vicar exclaimed with loathing when he opened the door to Nash. His thick eyebrows gnashed together, like angry gray caterpillars. "You dare to show your face here when you've caused that poor girl—"

"I'm here to arrange a wedding," Nash said crisply.

"Ah. Indeed? Harrumph. I suppose you'd better come in

then." The vicar ushered Nash into a small, cozy study. Books and writing paper were spread over a small side table, and from somewhere outside, the sounds of children's voices floated. Presumably they were taking a break from their studies.

"Is it true?" the vicar demanded.

"Is what true?"

"That you're the brother of the Earl of Alverleigh. And the heir to Sir Jasper Brownrigg's estate. Sit down, sit down," the vicar added testily, waving Nash to a worn but comfortable-looking chair.

"It's true." Nash sat in the seat indicated and crossed his legs.

The vicar eyed Nash's boot with the black ribbons tied around it and snorted. "I suppose that's all the rage among London dandies."

Nash smiled. "No, it's a fashion all of my own."

The vicar snorted again. "But you're going to make an honest woman of that poor girl?"

"She was never anything else," Nash said silkily. "Never."

The vicar's thick brows beetled upward. "I see." He scrutinized Nash's face for a long time. "She's ruined as far as the village is concerned. Don't take a fire to make smoke. Reputation is all in the imagination, never mind about facts."

"Indeed," Nash countered smoothly. "Which is why I'm here. A wedding, as soon as can be arranged."

The vicar gave a curt nod. "As it happens the bishop is coming this afternoon for a short stay. He can issue you with a license. Save you a trip into Salisbury." He opened his diary and perused the entries. "You cannot marry until ten days after the license has been issued. That brings us to Friday week. If you want to marry any sooner, you'll need a special license, which will involve a trip to London."

"No, Friday week will be soon enough." Nash paused. "How long does the bishop plan to stay?"

"A week. Why?"

"Could he be persuaded to stay on for the wedding?" A bishop's presence would be to Maddy's advantage, make the marriage look less hasty.

The vicar gave him a shrewd look. "Will any of your relatives be attending? Your brother, the earl, for instance?"

Nash nodded. "My brother, the earl; my aunt, Lady Gosforth; my half brother and his wife, Lady Helen; and some others. And a small reception afterward at Whitethorn Manor, to which the bishop, yourself, and Mrs. Matheson would be invited, of course."

The Reverend Matheson nodded. "Then I believe the bishop would indeed be interested." He slanted Nash a speculative look. "A wedding conducted by the bishop and attended by such exalted guests would also have the village ladies in a tizz of excitement."

Nash smiled. "One hopes it will turn their minds to more . . . pleasant topics."

The vicar said frankly, "Nothing more vicious than a clutch of genteel tabbies turning on one of their own."

"Quite. And, of course, Miss Woodford would invite those she considers her friends."

The Reverend Matheson smiled for the first time. "Oh, that would change their tune, indeed it would. Very well, I'll relay your request to the bishop." He glanced at Nash and gave a small nod, as if confirming something to himself. "My wife and I will do what we can to persuade him to stay. Hasty it may be, but that little gel deserves as fine a wedding as we can give her."

"Excellent, we understand one another then." Nash stood. "I'll be taking Maddy and the children on a visit to meet my family later today, but I'd appreciate it if you kept that to yourself. We'll be back in a week, but in the meantime, I want people to think Maddy is at home as usual."

Rev. Matheson agreed, and looked intrigued, but Nash didn't explain.

The vicar led him toward the front door. "My wife will be thrilled to hear about the wedding. She's very fond of that gel and the children. Anything we can do to help, just you ask." He held out his hand to Nash.

Nash shook it firmly. He'd misread this man in so many ways. "There's just one small misapprehension: the bishop can say a prayer or perform a blessing or some such, but we want you to perform the actual ceremony."

The vicar's eyes almost popped from their sockets. "Me? Instead of the bishop? Bless my soul, why?"

"You've been a staunch friend to Maddy and it will mean

more to her to have you marry us than a dozen bishops or even an archbishop."

The vicar stared for a moment and his face slowly flushed. He pulled out a large white handkerchief and blew fiercely into it. "I'd be delighted, my boy, delighted," he said in a thick voice.

*M*aking his third journey that day to his new home, Nash stopped in the village, famished, and ate two meat pies washed down with an ale at the village inn. To the girl who brought the pies and the man who drew the ale, he casually dropped the information that he'd be back next week to attend his wedding. Yes, to Miss Woodford. A secret, long-standing engagement. These last two years she'd been waiting for his return from Russia. Yes, she was very patient, he was indeed a lucky man. And yes, Russia was a long way from here. Foreign parts indeed.

And that, he thought as he rode toward Whitethorn, should deflect the gossip nicely.

Next, to take control of his inheritance.

Seventeen

∽

Word had obviously reached Whitethorn Manor that Nash was in the district, for by the time he rode down the long drive that led to the house, a handful of staff had lined up at the front door to meet him.

He recognized Ferring, the butler and Mrs. Pickens, the housekeeper. They looked so much smaller and older than he remembered. Ferring had to be in his seventies, and Mrs. Pickens perhaps sixty. With them stood a stocky, middle-aged woman and a young girl of about sixteen. As he dismounted, a wiry, gray-haired groom appeared from around the side of the house.

"Grainger, isn't it?" Nash dragged the name out of his memory and handed the groom the reins. On his rare childhood visits to Uncle Jasper's, he'd haunted the stables.

The man gave a quick smile and bobbed his head in a kind of bow. "Aye, sir. I'm surprised you remember; it must be twenty years or more since you was here last."

Nash smiled back. "I was nine. But how could I forget your patience with a pestilential brat?"

"You was never a brat, sir, just a lad with a passion for

horses and a knack for mischief." The groom slapped the horse's neck. "I see you've grown into a fine judge of horse-flesh."

"Alas, this fine fellow belongs to my brother. Take good care of him, won't you? I'll need him later on. And have my baggage brought into the house—yes, the cloth bundle as well as the portmanteau."

The elderly butler had been waiting stiffly at the top of the steps during this exchange, a worried look on his face that intensified as Nash drew closer. "Welcome to Whitethorn Manor, Mr. Renfrew. I'm sorry—if we'd had a little more warning—"

Nash shook the old man's hand. "How do you do, Ferring? You look the same as ever. The lack of advance warning is deliberate. The estate is just as I want to see it—unprepared. Mrs. Pickens, good to see a familiar face."

The butler looked even more unhappy and introduced him to Mrs. Goode, the cook, and her niece, Emily, some sort of housemaid or kitchen maid, Nash presumed.

"There is a great deal to be done," Nash told Ferring. "But first I must write some letters. I'll require four grooms to deliver them on horseback: one to ride to Bath, another to London, one to Alverleigh, my brother's house, and the fourth to Firmin Court, which is near Ferne, in the next county."

Ferring and Mrs. Pickens exchanged glances. Perhaps they were out of the habit of grooms delivering notes, but Nash had no time to waste. "In addition I'll need my uncle's carriage—I presume he has something better than the antiquated vehicle he had last time I was here."

"I'm afraid not, sir."

"Good God. What did he use?"

"Nothing, sir. Sir Jasper rarely left the estate."

"Oh, well, you'll have to send someone to hire one—"

"I'm sorry, sir," Ferring quavered. "But I don't see how I could manage it."

"Why not?" Nash suddenly realized the problem. The old man probably should have been pensioned off years ago. "Very well," he said in a gentler voice. "Assemble all the staff in the library in fifteen minutes and I will find someone to run the errands myself."

"But, sir, the staff is already assembled," Ferring told him.

"Where?" Nash looked down the hallway.

"Here, sir." Ferring gestured with a sweep of his arm.

With a sinking feeling, Nash stared at his staff. All four of them. Not counting the groom who'd taken his horse. "I suppose Grainger is the only groom left?"

"I'm afraid so, sir."

"Any horses?"

"Just the one that pulls the gig, sir, for shopping and to take us to church on Sundays."

Nash ran his fingers through his hair. No doubt the horse was as slow and elderly as the retainers. A skeleton staff was one thing—that was normal when the family was not in residence—but he suspected he was about to discover years of neglect.

"Ferring, I'll speak to you and Mrs. Pickens in the library in fifteen minutes, and then I want to speak to you all twenty minutes after that—that includes Grainger and the gardener, if there is one. Anyone who currently works on the estate."

"The estate manager, Mr. Harris?"

"Not Harris. I've already met him. And Ferring, bring down all my uncle's boots." Catching Ferring's expression, Nash added, "I hope to find boots to fit me; you can see the state of mine."

Ferring glanced at the ribbon-wrapped boot and his face resumed its human expression.

In the next fifteen minutes, Nash dashed off two identical letters to Aunt Maude—two because he wasn't sure whether she was in Bath or London—a hasty note to Marcus, and a fourth letter to accompany the items he extracted from the cloth bundle that Grainger had brought in. He wrapped them in brown paper and tied it up with string.

He started a fifth letter to Harry and Nell at Firmin Court, but recalling the difficulty in finding delivery boys, decided they could do without. He hoped they liked surprises.

Ferring coughed at the door, his arms full of boots. Nash tried several pairs on, but the boots were too small.

"Pity." He set them aside. "Now, a tour of the house, if you please."

Fifteen minutes later he'd inspected most of the house. Its condition wasn't as bad as he'd imagined. It was old and shabby and worn at the edges, but that was no surprise in the home of an elderly bachelor. With a little spit and polish, it would do, at a pinch.

He returned to the library, seated himself at the large carved oak desk, and called in the rest of the staff. They filed in, their faces glum.

"I'm about to be married," he told them. "The wedding will be on Friday week, which gives you just over a week to prepare for guests."

Their jaws collectively dropped. "How many guests do you expect, sir?" Mrs. Pickens asked hesitantly.

"Not many, just my aunt, Lady Gosforth; my brother, the Earl of Alverleigh; my half brother, Mr. Morant; and his wife, Lady Helen Morant; and possibly some others. And, of course, their servants—my aunt will bring her dresser, her coachman, and several grooms. Oh, and of course the bride, Miss Madeleine Woodford, and her siblings—five children under the age of twelve, so the nursery will need to be opened."

"Five children?" Ferring quavered.

Nash frowned. "Is that a problem?"

The old man looked about to burst into tears. "Oh no, sir, it's just that, that . . ."

Mrs. Pickens stepped forward. "It's just that the last child that was in this house was yourself, sir. And may I say"—she glanced at the butler—"and I speak for us all, sir, that it's been too long since this old place had children running about in it."

Ferring pulled out a handkerchief and blew on it loudly, nodding vigorously to show his agreement with the sentiments expressed. "Whitethorn will be a family home again, as it was when I was a boy."

"Only for a week I'm afraid, and then I'm closing it down—"

"Closing it down?"

"For repairs and refurbishment. I'll be returning to Russia shortly, but this will be our country home. I will, of course, keep you all on here. Those who wish to retire will receive a pension."

There was an almost audible exhaling of breath.

Nash continued. "First things first. I want the house thoroughly cleaned, the rooms opened up, the bedrooms scrubbed, the sheets and bedding aired, and . . ." He made a vague gesture. "You will know better than I what needs to be done." He turned to Grainger. "I haven't inspected the stables yet—"

"All tidy and shipshape, sir," Grainger said.

Nash wasn't surprised. "Good man. You'll be busy, too. Most of the visitors will bring their own grooms and drivers, but you'll need to get in supplies and manage the whole."

Grainger's eyes gleamed. "Like the old days, it'll be, sir. Be good to see the stables busy again."

Nash looked at the cook. "Mrs. Goode, can you cook for that number of guests? And for a small reception for the wedding guests, after the ceremony?"

"I can, as long as they don't mind good country cooking—there'll be none of your fancy French dishes, sir."

"Excellent. Now, Ferring—"

But the cook wasn't finished with him. "And *if* you give me a proper budget, freedom to order what I want, and *if* you give me the help I require." She tilted her jaw pugnaciously.

Mrs. Pickens and Ferring whispered in an agitated manner to her, but she only set her jaw more firmly and said, "*And* I want my wages. And Emily's." At which Ferring and Mrs. Pickens fluttered in visible distress. Grainger stared at a spot on the carpet, plainly wishing himself elsewhere.

Nash raised a brow. "Your wages?"

"She didn't mean anything by it—" Mrs. Pickens began, but Nash held up his hand.

"What do you mean, you want your wages, Mrs. Goode?"

"I'm owed nearly six months," she told him with nervous belligerence. She jerked her head toward the other servants. "And they're owed more, though they won't say how much. I've gotten some money out of him but only when I've threatened him with the law."

"You're speaking of Harris, I presume?"

"I am."

"He's in arrears with your wages?" Why was Nash not surprised? "How long?" he asked each of them, and when they told him, he was shocked.

Except for the cook, who was obviously a woman to be reckoned with, the others hadn't been paid in more than a year—since before Sir Jasper had died. Harris had claimed he had no authority to pay wages. The heir's instructions, he said;

he was only following orders. It would all be sorted out when the heir took over. All Harris did was pay for their food, and even that, according to Mrs. Goode, was a niggardly amount.

"But why have you all stayed so long?" Nash asked, appalled, and found they couldn't afford to leave. They had nowhere else to go.

"I will sort everything out," he promised them. "I sacked Harris yesterday."

"Sacked him?" All the servants brightened.

"Yes, he had no authority to handle matters the way he has. I apologize most profoundly for the situation you've been in. Naturally I'll make up the deficit in your wages."

"Would it be you, sir, who gave Harris the black eye and the bruises he was sporting at the inn last night?" Grainger enquired laconically.

"I don't tolerate incivility to women," was all Nash said. He pulled out his roll of banknotes—thank goodness he'd come well provided—and peeled off a number of notes. "Ferring, here is five pounds for each of you owed wages. The rest is to be used for immediate needs. Present me with a list of what is owed and I will make up the balance. You and Mrs. Pickens have carte blanche to take on temporary staff; do not stint, I want this place to be sparkling clean, the garden to be tidied, and the grass to be cut.

"Grainger, hire some likely lads from the village to help you out in the stables, and also to deliver my letters."

He turned to the cook. "Mrs. Goode, draw up an estimate of your requirements for the week to come—food and staff— and present it to Mrs. Pickens for approval. Again, do not stint. I want my guests to be as comfortable and well fed as we can make them. I'm leaving almost immediately but will return in a day or so. Questions?"

They were too shocked to say a word.

Nash stood. "Grainger, come with me to Harris's house. I told him to be quit of it immediately, but I must warn you, if he's there, it's bound to get ugly."

"In that case, it'll be a pleasure, sir," Grainger said with a grin.

"Good man."

Nash took his pistol from the portmanteau that Grainger

had brought in, checked it, then placed it in the pocket of his coat. "I intend to have him arrested. I'll need to examine the estate records, but there's no doubt in my mind there are criminal charges to answer. The man's no fool, however, so I expect he is long gone."

"Not so sure of that, sir," Grainger said. "Harris was dead drunk in the inn by closing time last night. Couldn't hardly sit his horse, so I reckon he'll wake late. And in an ugly mood."

Nash wished now he had knocked the man cold and conveyed him to a magistrate then and there, but it was too late for such regrets.

"*T*hat's the house." Grainger pointed to a solid-looking gray stone house on the edge of the estate. Smoke curled from one of the chimneys. Someone was home.

"Go around the back," Nash told Grainger. He knocked on the front door. No answer. He knocked again. Silence.

He peered in at the windows but could see no sign of anyone. After a few minutes, Grainger came back.

"He's gone, sir. His horse isn't in the stable. He hasn't been gone long, though; there are warm horse droppings near the back door. And he don't keep any servants. Can't, I should say. Can't get nobody to live in. Only dailies."

Nash picked up a stone, intending to break in, but Grainger stopped him. "Back door's only on the latch, sir."

Inside, they smelled a strong stench of burning. They found the estate office fireplace gushing smoke and a fire smoldering, half smothered under a pile of papers and heavy, bound books.

"The estate accounts!" Nash dived toward the fireplace and dragged the smoldering pile onto the hearth, ruining his gloves in the process. Most of the papers were unreadable, but books didn't burn so easily. The edges were charred but they were still usable.

"Good thing he was so mashed last night," Grainger commented. "In no fit state to destroy the evidence."

Nash went through the office, making a pile of whatever he thought was relevant. He wrapped them in an oil-proof cloth and tucked the bundle under his arm.

"I'll take these away with me," he said as Grainger locked up behind them. "Find me a couple of trustworthy men to stay here. If Harris comes back, they're to arrest him and take him to the local magistrate on my authority."

Grainger grinned. "I know just the men. Be a pleasure for them to deal with Mr. Harris, I reckon."

As they passed the stables, Nash was reminded of the need for transport. "Where can I hire a carriage to transport six people as far as the next county?"

"Have to ride into Salisbury, I reckon. Unless the vicar will lend you his traveling chaise," he added as an afterthought. "It's a fine vehicle."

"Excellent," Nash said. "I'll speak to him this afternoon."

It occurred to Nash suddenly that he was expecting rather a lot from a small group of servants getting on in years and possibly set in their ways. "I'm not asking too much of you all, am I, Grainger? Expecting you to perform a small miracle in such a short time? Be honest now, I won't hold it against you."

Grainger laughed. "Mr. Renfrew, sir, I'm going to be the most popular man in the village, I reckon, handing out jobs, right, left, and center. Same goes for Ferring and Mrs. Pickens. And Mrs. Goode. Don't you worry about us, sir. We know how the old house ought to be, and it'll be our pleasure as much as yours to see it brought back to rights."

Nash gave a satisfied nod. "Excellent. Then if you could bring my horse around, I'll be off to see a vicar about a chaise."

As Nash crested the hill that led down to the vicarage, he couldn't help but glance across at Maddy's cottage. What the devil? A smart traveling chaise and four matched bays waited on the road outside her cottage. A coachman sat on top, and a groom in plain gray livery walked the horses back and forth so they wouldn't take a chill in the cold breeze.

Who was bothering her now? He left the road and galloped toward the cottage.

He approached from the back so he wouldn't be seen and quietly entered by the back door. Voices were raised in argument, two female and one male, voices he recognized. The male was his brother, Marcus.

Nash leaned against the doorway, just out of sight, and unashamedly eavesdropped.

"He said there was funny business going on here and I don't doubt it!" Marcus at his most cold and menacing.

"Oh, sir, Miss Maddy would never—" Lizzie began.

Maddy cut her off. "What sort of funny business, pray?" Her tone of voice would be a warning to any other man. A man who understood anything about women, that was. Not his brother.

Nash folded his arms and settled back to enjoy the exchange. Flame meeting ice. There was no doubt in his mind who would win.

"He said I should meet all of your demands but—"

"Demands?" Maddy was outraged. "I never made *any* demands of him *or* his brother. I wrote a perfectly civil—"

"I have written evidence, madam," Marcus's voice was an icy whiplash. "In which my client begged me to give you whatever you asked for, and that, I tell you, is not at all like—"

His *client*? What the devil was Marcus playing at? He didn't have any clients.

"I don't believe you! There was no reason for him to—"

"Enough! If you don't produce him this instant, I'll have my man fetch the local magistrate."

"Oh, your honor, sir, Miss Maddy never done nothing wro—"

"Be quiet, Lizzie, I have no need to defend myself." Maddy's voice sharpened. "I tell you he left here this morning, perfectly unharmed—"

Marcus snorted. "Without his boots? I think not!"

"Of course he wore his boots."

"He told me they'd been slashed. And to bring these." Nash peeped around the corner and saw his brother brandish a pair of boots. Excellent.

Marcus continued, "How could he go out without boots? Now, enough of these evasions, madam: produce your prisoner, or I shall send for the magistrate."

"How many times do I have to tell you, he's *not* my prisoner, he never *was* my prisoner, and he left here of his own volition!" Maddy said through audibly gritted teeth. "And his boots *were* ruined, at least one was, but he tied it on with black ribbons."

"*With black ribbons?*" Marcus said in frigid disbelief. "You show your ignorance, madam. Na—my client is always immaculately dressed and complete to a shade: he would *never* tie his boots on with black ribbons. He wouldn't be seen *dead* in boots tied with—"

"Ah, but as you see, my standards have slipped sadly." Nash sauntered in.

"Nash!" Marcus exclaimed. "You're all right?"

"In the pink, as you see." Nash smiled and spread his hands. "Afternoon, Marcus. Miss Woodford, Lizzie, I see you've met my brother, Marcus, the Earl of Alverleigh."

Marcus's gaze ran over him quickly, freezing on Nash's left boot. His brow arched, seeing the black ribbons tied in neat bows.

"Oh my Lord," Lizzie moaned.

"What?" Marcus glanced at her.

"Oh, no, I meant . . ." Lizzie sheepishly pointed to the heavens. Marcus's eyes glazed.

"Your brother?" Maddy gasped. "The Earl of Alverleigh? I thought he was some kind of lawyer. He said as much—"

"Implied," Marcus corrected her frostily. "I simply referred to 'my client' and you jumped to the conclusion."

"No, you deliberately misled me," Maddy began. She was practically toe-to-toe with his brother.

"And you defied me, madam."

"Children, children, stop this unseemly brangling," Nash said soothingly, though truth to tell he was enjoying the sight of his fiery little fiancée ripping into his normally cool, contained brother.

They both ignored him. "Why did you not simply tell me who you were? Why stalk in here under false pretenses and start throwing threats around?" Maddy demanded.

Nash would wager nobody had ever spoken to Marcus like that in his life. He had their father's knack of silent intimidation.

It obviously didn't work on Maddy.

Marcus stared down his long nose at her. "Because I was

under the impression that Nash was injured and being held prisoner by you, possibly to prevent him leaving, or possibly in exchange for a pair of new boots. That part was not clear."

"Held in exchange for a pair of boots?" Maddy scoffed. "That's ridiculous! Why on earth would I want a pair of man's riding boots?"

"I have no idea," he said coldly. "For all I knew you were a madwoman." His tone implied the suspicion still lingered.

"Why did you not tell me who you were? Why pretend to be a lawyer?"

"Nash told me he was traveling incognito. Naturally, after such a request, I would not reveal his identity or mine."

They both turned to Nash for an explanation. "Well?"

Nash stared at his brother. "Traveling incognito? Held prisoner by Miss Woodford in exchange for a pair of boots? What the devil are you talking about, Marcus?"

For answer, his brother pulled out a letter and handed it to him. Nash read over his hastily scrawled message and began to laugh. "I see the problem. I was writing in haste, you see."

Marcus, was injured but am recovering. Give Miss Woodford whatever she wants. Am at her cottage incognito. Funny business going on. Boots slashed, send new ones urgently. Nash.

"Let me see that." Maddy twitched the letter from his fingers and glanced at it. She saw his scrawl in the margins of her letter, and her jaw dropped. "But this is my letter. I sealed it myself. How did you manage to write this message in a sealed letter?"

"Ah," Nash began. "It was when I'd got my memory back but before I told you who I—"

"You opened my letter," she said fiercely. "You know how I feel about people who read other people's letters!"

"But there was nothing personal in th—"

Her eyes flashed. "It doesn't matter what the contents are! The very act is—"

"No, no, you are very right and I promise I will never do it to you again," he said, holding up his hands in surrender.

Her amber eyes glittered. She took several deep, steadying breaths, trying to harness her ire. Her breasts rose and fell delectably.

Nash wished his brother and Lizzie would just go away. She was adorable like this, with her temper up, all rosy and flushed and lovely. Ripe for a tumbling.

"Oh, I see," Marcus said suddenly.

They both looked at him.

"She's your mistress. It all makes sense now."

"I am not his mistress!" Maddy snapped. And then flushed, recalling that by the usual definitions, she, in fact, was.

"She's not my mistress; she's my affianced bride," Nash told his brother.

"What?" Marcus's normally flinty eyes nearly fell out of their sockets. "You are betrothed to this, this . . ."

"Lovely lady, yes," Nash said smoothly, his own eyes gimlet hard and delivering a silent message to his brother.

"I knew you were in trouble," said Marcus in a grim voice. "So she's trapped you into—"

Nash grabbed his brother's arm and pushed him toward the door. "I'll just explain to my brother what's going on," he told Maddy. "Talk among yourselves." He winked at Lizzie. "Cup of tea, Lizzie?" He thrust his brother outside and took him into the garden.

"What on earth do you think you're doing?" he said. He took the boots from his brother's grasp, sat on a bench, and began undoing the mourning ribbons from his ruined boot.

Marcus said stiffly, "You were in trouble."

"I was, in a way—" He saw his brother staring at the sliced-open boot and explained, "She had to cut it off. My ankle was swollen and she thought it might be broken."

"I will buy the jade off."

"Jad—Oh, you mean Maddy, Miss Woodford? She's no jade. I intend to marry her." He pulled on the new boot and held his foot up for his brother to yank off the other one.

"There's no need to. I'll pay her off." Marcus removed the boot and stood it neatly beside its ruined twin.

Nash stood up and stamped a few paces back and forth in the new boots. "Excellent, they fit perfectly. Thank you for bringing them. I don't want you to buy her off."

Marcus gave him a searching look. "But she has trapped you into marriage?"

"No."

Marcus's flinty gray eyes narrowed. "You can't possibly be in love with her."

"Of course not. Nevertheless, I will marry her."

"Why?"

Nash hesitated, but there was no way around it. "I have compromised her so—"

"So she did entrap you."

"She did not. It was wholly my own doing. There is no point arguing, Marcus, my mind is made up. I will marry Miss Woodford on Friday week. The arrangements are already in place." Almost. A small matter of a license.

"The injury to your head must be worse than you think. Have you forgotten Aunt Maude is searching the length and breadth of three kingdoms—"

"Only three? Not Wales, then? Or is she avoiding Ireland?"

"Don't be flippant. She's been scouring the country, sifting through every blue-blooded family in search of a bride for you—at your instigation—and now you say you are going to marry this, this—"

"Lady," said Nash in a hard voice.

Marcus stiffened. "You are in love with her," he said in a shocked voice.

"Nonsense! But she is in my care and will become my wife." He locked eyes with his brother, and after a moment, Marcus gave a noncommittal half shrug.

"You'd better tell me all about it, then. Aunt Maude will not be happy."

Nash glanced at the sky. "I don't have time. I have to get Maddy to Harry and Nell's before dark." He nodded toward Marcus's chaise. "When I saw that chaise, I had no idea it was yours. New is it?"

"Yes, it's the latest desi—"

"Why isn't your crest on it? And why the plain livery?"

"I like to travel incognito myself, from time to time."

"Those bays look magnificent. Fast, are they?"

"Yes, they're splendid goers and on an open road—No. You can't have them, Nash."

"I need them, Marcus," Nash said coaxingly. "Just for one night."

"I am not lending you my new chaise and the bays so you can take this woman—"

"She saved my life, Marcus."

"So it's gratitude?"

"No, it's—" He didn't know what it was. "I'm not going to discuss it. She's in danger and I need to get her out of the area tonight, to keep her safe."

Marcus frowned. "Danger? What danger?"

"She's been harassed by a man dressing up as a ghost to frighten her. On several occasions, her cottage has been attacked and two nights ago her beehives were burned and her vegetable garden destroyed." He gestured to the ruined garden with its wilted, newly replanted plants. "My actions may have made it worse, so I need to get her to safety."

Marcus eyed him enigmatically. Nash stared him down. Marcus could be annoyingly stubborn. "It touches on my honor, Marcus."

"Mmm." Marcus pursed his lips.

"Will you help me, dammit, or must I beg the local vicar to lend me his carriage?"

Marcus gave a cool nod. "Very well, I have a fancy to visit Nell and Harry myself, see how my horses are doing—"

"No, sorry," Nash interrupted. "I need you to stay here."

"Here? You mean at Whitethorn Manor?"

"I mean here, in the cottage. I need someone here for when this villain attacks. Keep your groom with you just in case. I want to get to the bottom of this, catch the bastard and find out why he's doing it."

Marcus's brow rose. "I see, you want me to lend you my new chaise and my favorite team, while you take that red-headed termagant—"

"She's very sweet when you get to know her."

"—termagant to Harry and Nell's and in the meantime I'm to wait in this poky little cottage and expect to be attacked by person or persons unknown. Is that it?"

"In a nutshell." Nash grinned. "You're quite astute, you know, brother. So that's a yes, then?"

His older brother gave him a long-suffering look. "And

what am I to do while I'm waiting to be attacked? I can't imagine this cottage stretches to a library."

"I have just the thing." From his saddlebag, Nash pulled out the bundle containing the charred estate books and handed it to Marcus. "The Whitethorn estate manager has been cooking the books—literally and metaphorically. The evidence will be in there. You know how much you enjoy accounts and puzzles."

Marcus peered disdainfully into the bundle, sighed, and rewrapped it. "I don't understand why anyone thinks you have talent at diplomacy. As far as I can see it's nothing but sheer, unmitigated cheek. At least the cottage is warm." He tucked the bundle under his arm.

"Ah," Nash said in a tone that made Marcus look at him with foreboding. "Maddy keeps early hours so after about nine you must let the fire go out. And no candles or lanterns, either. I want the Bloody Abbot to think them all asleep—that's when he usually strikes."

"The bloody who?"

"It's a disguise the swine wears, pretending to be the ghost of some long-dead murdered abbot who's famous hereabouts."

"I see, so I am to sit in a poky little cottage in the cold and dark, waiting to be attacked by a desperate criminal dressed up as a ghostly monk, while you ride in the comfort of my chaise, accompanying Miss Woodford to Nell and Harry's. How delightful. I don't suppose I could convey her there in my own carriage while you sit in the dark. No? I didn't think so."

"The mood she's in at the moment, I doubt she'd go to the end of the lane with you. I'll ride back here after I've dropped Maddy and the children at Harry and Nell's."

"Children? What children? You're marrying a woman with children? Who by? And how many?"

"It's not what you think, they're her orphaned half-siblings. Five of them, aged between four and twelve."

Marcus's brows shot up. "Five?"

Nash nodded.

Marcus's eyes narrowed. "Machiavelli had nothing on you, little brother. Don't think I haven't noticed you didn't mention this little detail until after I'd given you my word, so I'm warning you now: if one of those brats throws up in my chaise, you will buy me a new one. And it won't be cheap—I had it specially built to my specifications."

Nash laughed. "Done."

Eighteen

"Are you packed?" Nash asked Maddy as he reentered the cottage with his brother. His brother indeed. Maddy was still annoyed with the earl, though much of her annoyance was now directed at herself.

She should have known. Seeing them standing side by side, the family resemblance was obvious. She shouldn't have lost her temper so easily, should have asked more questions at the beginning.

But he'd swept in like a lord and spoken to her with such icy disdain, making threats in the same breath before he'd even introduced himself—he hadn't introduced himself at all, just demanded to see his client and, in the same breath, threatened her with the magistrate. And all the while clutching those boots in his fist as if he might hit her with them.

She caught his eye. He gave her a curt nod, and a stiff, "I apologize for the misunderstanding, Miss Woodford." His gray eyes were as cold as ever. Maddy was not deceived into thinking the apology was anything more than a polite form.

She inclined her head. At least he'd apologized. Many men

could not, would not bring themselves to ever admit they were wrong.

Nash was wearing the boots the earl had brought.

Her lips twitched. Had the earl really believed she'd held his brother to ransom in exchange for *boots*? It was ridiculous. She felt a bubble of laughter rising and tried to squash it.

"What?" Nash asked.

"J-Just thinking that your ransom looks very s-smart. I must say, you're a very cheap hostage." A giggle escaped her.

The earl stiffened. Nash glanced down at his boots and gave a crack of laughter. "You must have thought you were rescuing me from a lunatic, Marcus."

"Nothing new in that. You've spent your whole life falling into scrapes and usually talking your way out of them. I believe I am to wish you joy, Miss Woodford." The coldness with which he said it contradicted his words. He was not reconciled to their marriage in the slightest. He thought her a scrape from which Nash hadn't been able to talk his way out of.

Too bad, Maddy thought. Nash had made the offer of his own free will. She wasn't going to renege on her promise simply because his brother thought she wasn't good enough.

She'd show him.

Nash glanced at the bed. "I thought you would have finished packing by now."

"Why? There's no need for us to leave now."

"But I told you to pack."

"You told me to trust you, but you didn't explain why, or where we're going, or for how long. If you think I'm moving to Whitethorn Manor—"

"I want to get you and the children away from here, to safety. Tonight."

"Why? We're perfectly safe here."

"That swine might come back—"

"I told you, he's done nothing against the children or me. I'm certain his aim is to frighten us away, and I don't intend to give him the satisfaction."

"When he burned your beehives, he went a step further than merely frightening, so I want you out of here."

"No." Maddy folded her arms. "I won't be frightened out of

my home by a coward who dresses up in silly costumes and wails around the house to scare children at night."

Nash gave her a frustrated look. "It is not a matter of running away. If it's Harris, he's my responsibility. I want to catch the fellow and find out what he's up to."

"Good, then you can catch him with me here."

"And endanger the children?"

"If you and your brother are here, they won't be in danger. And the children will learn to stand up for themselves and not be intimidated by cowardly bullies."

The earl seated himself at the table. "I can see this is going to take some time," he said to nobody in particular. "Is that pot of tea still hot, by any chance?"

"I'll fetch you a cup, my lord." Lizzie jumped to it.

Nash and Maddy both glared at the earl, annoyed by the interruption.

"Don't mind me," he said, waving them on with a lordly air. "It's quite entertaining."

"In any case, it's nothing to do with running away," Nash told Maddy. "I've arranged for you to meet my family before the wedding. And since the wedding is on Friday week, it doesn't give us much time."

"Meet your family?" Maddy couldn't believe her ears.

"Yes, you've met Marcus. My half brother, Harry Morant, and his wife, Nell—Lady Helen—are expecting us tonight, and since their home, Firmin Court, is at least twenty miles from here, we'll be traveling in the dark unless you get a move on with the packing."

"What? They're expecting us tonight? Why didn't you tell me?"

Nash made an apologetic gesture. "So much to do, it must have slipped my mind. If we don't arrive at a reasonable hour, Nell will worry. But if you don't want to go . . ."

"No," Maddy said. "Of course, we must go, if she's expecting us. I just wish you'd discussed it with me before you wrote to her." She narrowed her eyes at Nash, who wore a suspiciously innocent look. "You did it deliberately, didn't you? Arranged the visit to Firmin Court because you knew I'd want to stay here and confront the Bloody Abbot. And now I have no choice."

"It's a habit of his, to arrange things to his liking," Marcus said dryly. "Annoying isn't it?"

"Very," Maddy agreed. But she wasn't going to side with his brother against Nash. "But this time it can't be helped. I wouldn't want to cause Lady Helen needless anxiety." She hoped Nash noted the "this time."

"Can I come with you, Miss Maddy?" Lizzie blurted as she plonked a cup of tea in front of the earl.

"What?" Nash looked at Lizzie in surprise. "Why should you—"

"Lizzie has agreed to become my maid, so if I'm going to Firmin Court, of course she will come with us," Maddy declared. If she was going to be pitchforked with no warning into the bosom of his family—a family who she was sure would receive her with the same cozy warmth the earl was showing—she wanted an ally with her. Particularly one who could do her hair.

Nash made an indifferent gesture. "If you want Lizzie, of course she can come, though the chaise will be rather crowded. Still, the more the merrier." He smiled. "Now, get packing."

"I'll run and get me bundle, miss," Lizzie said. "Me uncle won't mind me going off without any warning, not if you're going to be married to Mr. Renfrew here. I'll be back in a wink, see if I'm not."

"Lizzie, tell your uncle not to tell anyone Maddy's going away. I'm setting a trap for the Bloody Abbot."

"Right you are, Mr. Renfrew, sir." A sudden grin split Lizzie's face. "I'll have to miss the evening milking. That means I've milked me last-ever cow—Lord be praised!" She rushed off.

"I'll fetch the children from the vicarage, shall I?" Nash suggested and strolled toward the door.

Nash's brother, who had taken one sip of Maddy's home-grown tea and put it down with a shudder, pushed back his chair and stood. "I'll accompany you."

"Oh, but I should tell the Mathesons—" Maddy began.

"I've told them. And you'll be back before the wedding, in just over a week's time. You can see them then."

Maddy made a distracted gesture. "Oh, very well. Please convey my apologies to Mrs. Matheson. I really don't know why it all has to be such a rush . . ."

"We don't want to travel in the dark," Nash said. Marcus gave him a sidelong look.

Maddy, her mind awhirl, nodded vaguely. "Go ahead. I'll be ready when you return. Oh, I wish you'd told me about this earlier." It went against the grain to flee from their mysterious persecutor, but her hand had been forced.

Besides, it could be days before he made another appearance, and she had a wedding to prepare for. A new life beckoned; she would put it behind her.

She regarded the various piles of clothes with a sinking stomach. She had nothing suitable to wear to visit someone called Lady Helen—presumably the daughter of an earl—and neither did the children. They were going to look like the veriest beggars.

It couldn't be helped. She gritted her teeth and started packing again.

"Neat maneuver," Marcus commented as they drove toward the vicarage. "Do Nell and Harry expect you, by the way?"

"No," Nash said. "But there was no other way to shift her. She's a stubborn little creature, my Maddy, and prideful." And with too much courage for her own good.

He glanced up and found Marcus watching him with an odd expression. "What?"

"You're sure you're not in love with her?"

"No, of course not. Good God, Marcus, you grew up in the same house I did. Do you think I'd commit the folly of marrying for love?"

Marcus gave him a thoughtful look, then transferred his gaze to the scenery passing by. "I didn't think it, no."

Just over an hour later, Nash, Maddy, Lizzie, and the children set off for Firmin Court, leaving Marcus and his groom behind. It was rather a squash, three adults and five children in a chaise built for four, but it was also built for luxury, so was roomier than usual.

Nash would have ridden, but Marcus had put his foot down

there, refusing to be marooned without transport. Nash could borrow one of Harry's horses if he needed one, Marcus pointed out. Besides, Nash needed to watch out for Marcus's new upholstery.

To Nash's dismay, Mrs. Matheson had given the children a large midday meal and, with Marcus's dire threats in his ears, Nash watched as Henry grew progressively quieter and paler with every bounce and jolt of the carriage. It was an extremely well-sprung carriage, but the road was rough and rutted.

Just as Nash was about to say something, Maddy said, "Are you feeling unwell, Henry?"

"I'm all right," Henry mumbled. Nash wasn't convinced.

"Henry always gets ill in carriages," Jane told Nash.

"And on boats," John added. "They'll never let him in the navy if he gets seasick all the time."

"I will too join the nav—" Henry turned almost green and clapped his hand over his mouth.

"Stop the carriage!" Nash roared and lifted the boy out of the carriage and onto the side of the road.

"Don't worry," he told Henry after the lad had rid himself of his meal. "Many quite distinguished naval officers suffer from *mal de mer*." He gave Henry a handkerchief to wipe his mouth.

"Who?" Henry muttered skeptically. He was mortified.

"Admiral Lord Nelson, the late Hero of Trafalgar," Nash told him. "Suffered from terrible seasickness his entire life."

"Truly, sir?" Henry made to return the handkerchief. It was revolting.

"Throw it in the ditch," Nash told him and, with an air of great daring, Henry did. "Admiral Nelson had a foolproof cure for seasickness, too."

"What was it?"

Nash winked. "He used to tell people, 'You'll feel better if you sit under a tree.' "

It took Henry a moment to work it out, then he gave a wobbly grin. "It's a very good joke, sir."

"Good lad," Nash said. "Now, I think you'll find the movement easier if you're up on the box with the driver. John, too," he added, noticing John hanging out of the carriage window. "And perhaps, if you ask him nicely, Hawkins might show you how to hold the ribbons." He glanced at the coachman who nodded.

"Happy to take the lads, sir," Hawkins said. "Like old times with you and his lordship, it'll be."

"Hawkins taught me how to drive when I was a boy," Nash explained to the boys as he helped them up.

"They're in very reliable hands," he told Maddy as he climbed into the carriage again. "It's a fine day, and they're well rugged up."

"Thank you, it's the perfect solution," she agreed. "Henry is so ashamed of his weak stomach. Now he'll be so excited about riding with the coachman, he won't give it a thought."

"What about the rest of the children? Do they suffer like Henry?" he asked. How many he could fit on the roof?

"No, only Henry. You're very kind to be so concerned."

Nash inclined his head modestly. He was more worried about Marcus's upholstery but she didn't need to know that. "Excellent." He rapped on the roof for the carriage to continue and relaxed back against the very comfortable squabs.

With the crowding of the carriage ameliorated, the girls and Lizzie spread out and snuggled into the luxurious fur rugs provided. Soon their excitement wore off and they slept, lulled by the rocking of the carriage and the steady rhythm of the horses' hooves. Lizzie slept, too. She'd been up before dawn, milking.

Maddy was tired, but she knew she'd never sleep. Not with Nash sitting opposite her, looking handsomer than any man had a right to be. His gaze passed over her from time to time like a featherlight caress.

Of course she couldn't sleep. What if her mouth fell open? Or she snored? Besides, Lucy had fallen asleep in her lap and Maddy's arm was aching. She shifted uncomfortably.

"What is it?" Nash leaned forward.

"Nothing. Just pins and needles."

"I'll take her." Nash lifted the little girl out of her arms. Lucy stirred but didn't wake.

"Thank you." Maddy stretched and massaged her arm. She sat back and gazed out of the window, pretending to look at the scenery, but secretly watching his face in the reflection of the glass.

He was a constant surprise, this man she was going to marry. In the last few days she'd seen sides of him she hadn't imagined. And today seeing him with his brother showed her yet another aspect of him.

What had Nash said about his family? That they'd been torn apart? She'd seen no sign of that with Marcus. The two men were obviously close, despite their different natures.

And soon she would meet his half brother, Harry, and his wife.

She nudged his leg with her foot. "Tell me about Harry. Is he like you?"

He gave a muffled snort of laughter. "Like me? In looks, perhaps, but not in other ways. I've probably talked more to you in the last week than Harry has talked to anyone in his whole lifetime. The strong, silent type, my half brother, Harry."

"Half brother?"

He glanced at the sleeping children and shrugged. "It's no secret, but it's not a pretty story. Harry's mother was a maidservant who fell pregnant to my father during a brief period when he and my mother were estranged. When the pregnancy started to show, Father had her married off to the local blacksmith, one Mr. Morant. She died and the smith mistreated Harry, so my great-aunt Gert, no respecter of convention, took him in, along with Gabe."

Maddy hesitated, trying to tread delicately. "So Gabe is also a half brother?"

"No, he's the true, legitimate son of both my mother and father. The resemblance to my father is unmistakable, though we both have our mother's blue eyes."

Maddy turned the information over in her mind. It didn't make sense. Why had his great-aunt taken Gabe in? Why wasn't he reared with Nash and Marcus? "I'm a little confused."

Over Lucy's tumbled curls he gave her a rueful sigh. "I'm not surprised. It was the result of my parents' tumultuous marriage. I told you before that they were madly in love. Their life together consisted of a series of passionate quarrels and even more passionate reconciliations. To Mama, it was the breath of life."

"And your father?" She was beginning to understand why Nash rejected the very notion of a love match. Or what he thought was one.

"Father adored my mother, loathed the fuss. Marcus takes after him rather a lot, only he's more . . . contained. Quieter."

Maddy wasn't interested in Marcus. She wanted to hear about the little boy who was brought up away from his siblings . . . as she had been.

"But why did Gabe live with your great-aunt? Surely the children weren't involved with the quarrels?"

Nash stared out of the carriage window for a long time, watching the scenery slip by. His eyes were bleak.

"I told you once how my parent's passionate emotionalism tore the family apart. Gabe was the real victim."

She waited.

"During one quarrel, Mama, who was *enceinte* at the time, told Father the baby was another man's—it wasn't, of course, but she wanted to provoke his jealousy." He grimaced. "It did. He threw her out and took Harry's mother as his mistress. Mama gave birth to Gabe in London, and though they made it up later, Father would never allow Gabe to be brought home to Alverleigh. Mama left him in the care of servants in London for the first seven years of his life, only seeing him when she came to London. He'd probably still be there had it not been for Greataunt Gert."

He moved, adjusting Lucy's position, and shook his head when Maddy made a gesture to take the little girl. "She was a character, Great-aunt Gert. Extraordinary old woman. We boys were in tremendous awe of her because of the way she ordered Father around—and as far as we knew, only God could tell Father what to do." He chuckled. "Even my aunt Gosforth claims she was terrified of her, and once you meet Aunt Gosforth you'll know she's not lightly intimidated."

"What did your great-aunt do?"

"As the story goes, she marched into the London house and confiscated Gabe from my mother, tucked him under her arm like a brown paper parcel, and whisked him off to Dorset, where she brought him and Harry up as gentlemen and brothers, Renfrew blood counting for more, with Great-aunt Gert, than any nonsense about legitimacy. Legitimacy, she used to say, was nothing but man's vanity, but children came from God."

"Oh, I *like* Great-aunt Gert."

He chuckled. "She'd have terrified even you."

"I wouldn't mind, as long as she rescued children. So when did you and Marcus meet Gabe? Did you come together for Christmas?"

"No, he never saw us, nor we him, until we all met at school when I was about fifteen. And we called Gabe 'the bastard,' as Father always did, and Harry 'the other bastard.' And we made trouble for him and Harry until they were both expelled."

"You? You did that to your own brothers?" Maddy could barely believe it. "But why?"

He sighed and made a rueful grimace. "It's the kind of thing that comes easily to boys of that age. Father egged us on, of course. He was furious that Great-aunt Gert had dared to send his bastard spawn—his words not mine—to his old, very exclusive school."

He touched the tiny scar on his mouth. "Harry gave me this, in one of our fights." He gave a mirthless laugh. "We've made it up since, of course. Marcus and I have long regretted our behavior. Once you become a man, your father becomes less godlike, more fallible, and we understood more about the world. Besides, it was as plain as the nose on my face that Gabe was our father's son, just as much as we were. And that it was all the result of our parents' grand passion." He stared out of the window with a grim expression, lost in the past.

Maddy leaned back against the cushions and watched his face in the glass. It was a very enlightening tale . . .

At Donhead St. Andrew, the chaise pulled up at an inn to spell and water the horses before the last leg of the journey. Everyone got out to stretch their legs, make use of the inn's facilities, and take some refreshment.

John and Henry came flying down from the driver's box, not the least bit chilled, and bursting with tales about how Mr. Hawkins, the coachman, had shown them how to hold the ribbons and even let them drive for a bit—didn't they notice?—and he'd explained to them how to point their leaders, and had promised to show them how to use the whip when they got to Firmin Court and—and—and—Interrupting and talking over the top of each other, they told Maddy and Lizzie and their sisters all about it, while they wolfed down Eccles cakes and sandwiches and mugs of milk.

Nash nudged Maddy. "I think we've found the cure for Henry's delicate stomach."

She laughed. "It seems so, indeed."

She watched the children and wondered at a mother and father who could let a lovers' quarrel destroy their own child's life. If it hadn't been for Great-aunt Gert . . .

Refreshed, they returned to the carriage and continued on their way. Maddy watched Nash's reflection in the glass and ruminated on the story he'd told.

She understood now why he didn't trust love.

She sat rocking with the movement of the carriage. Grandmère used to say people were endlessly greedy, that no matter what you gave them, they would always want more. It was true, Maddy realized. Nash Renfrew had given her his body and promised her his fortune and his name.

Maddy was greedy. She wanted more. She wanted his heart.

Nineteen

$\mathcal{T}$he entrance to Firmin Court was through impressive, old wrought iron gates set into a high stone wall. Each gate featured a central design of a horse's head.

"The estate has been in Nell's family for generations. Horse breeding is in her blood as well as Harry's," Nash commented, nodding at the gates. "They're carrying on the tradition."

The driver blew a horn, and a man from the gatehouse ran out. After a brief exchange, he opened the gates and they drove down the curving driveway in the hazy lilac twilight. The sound of the horses' hooves on the hard-packed drive echoed in the stillness. Shreds of mist drifted low to the ground.

Maddy knotted her hands tightly under the rug. She would not be nervous, she would not, she told herself.

The carriage stopped at a shallow flight of stone steps leading up to the front door and they all alighted. Maddy busied herself tidying herself and the children.

"Lordy, Miss Maddy, I dunno if I'm ready for this," Lizzie whispered nervously. "This place is a lot grander than I expected."

Maddy squeezed her hand. Somehow Lizzie's anxiety

calmed her own. "Head up, Lizzie. My grandmother used to tell me, never display your nerves to strangers."

Nash mounted the stairs and tugged on the bellpull. Somewhere deep inside the house the bell jangled.

The door was opened by a tough-looking butler with a twisted scar that ran from one ear down to his chin. Nash nodded to him. "Bronson. I've brought guests. Miss Woodford, this is Bronson."

Bronson bowed. "How do you do, miss? Mr. Renfrew, sir, come in, come in. I'll let Lady Helen know." Bronson snapped his fingers and a footman came forward to collect their coats and hats, while Bronson headed briskly down the corridor.

Maddy hadn't had a lot of experience with butlers, but those she'd met seemed to glide. Bronson marched with a crisp tread, his back ramrod straight.

"Many of Harry's employees fought with him and Gabe in the war," Nash explained, noticing her expression. "Bronson was a sergeant, assistant to the regimental quartermaster, and somewhat of a legend, I'm told. Can organize or obtain anything. In peacetime, however, that disfiguring scar of his made people uncomfortable, and he wasn't able to get work. Ethan Delaney, Harry's partner, ran into him, half-starved on the waterfront, and brought him home."

"How nice," she murmured, not really paying attention.

He glanced at her and grinned. "Don't look so nervous; Nell won't eat you."

"I'm not nervous," she lied.

A door opened and a gust of masculine laughter escaped. It seemed Lady Helen was entertaining guests. More strangers, and no doubt all in their best clothes. Maddy swallowed and lifted her chin.

A small woman came hurrying toward them. "Nash, what a delightful surprise. We weren't expecting you until next week at least."

Next week? Maddy shot Nash a look, but he was already embracing Lady Helen and kissing her cheek. "Nell, my dear, you look lovelier than ever. Come, let me introduce you to everyone."

Lady Helen was a small, thin-faced woman with light brown hair, simply dressed, and with beautiful eyes. At first glance,

Maddy thought her plain, but when she smiled, there was such warmth in her expression you forgot about her looks.

"What a lovely surprise—I do like unexpected guests."

"Unexpected?" Maddy repeated. She gave Nash a hard look.

Nash made a helpless gesture. "Letters so oft go astray . . ." His eyes twinkled.

Astray, my foot, Maddy thought. He'd dragged her from her cottage at a moment's notice, and dumped six unexpected guests on his sister-in-law—seven if you counted Lizzie. Men! They were so inconsiderate.

"Lady Helen, I'm so sorry to arrive on you without warning. I—"

"Nonsense. I'm delighted to meet you, Miss Woodford. Any friend of Nash's is welcome here. You're just in time for dinner—"

"Thank you, but if you have guests, I'd rather not intrude." Especially not travel worn and in a shabby gown.

"Not guests, just my husband, his partner, Ethan Delaney, and our friend, Luke, Lord Ripton, who's visiting. They were all in the army together and are more like brothers than guests—and now here is Nash—so if you don't take pity on me, I'll be the only lady at the dinner table." She smiled mischievously at Maddy. "Not that I'm complaining, mind you. What woman wouldn't want to dine with four of the handsomest men in England."

"Four?" Nash interjected with a grin. "Not if Ethan is one of the four."

"Ethan may not be conventionally handsome, but to many women, his kind of rugged, rough-hewn looks are very attractive," Lady Helen informed him loftily. "Being a male, you do not see it."

"I certainly don't. Big ugly brute, that's what Ethan is. Has Tibby abandoned him, then, if you've been left on your own with all of us handsome fellows?"

"No, she couldn't join us tonight. Poor little Patrick has a touch of the colic tonight and of course she had to stay with him."

Lady Helen turned and gave the butler some rapid instructions.

"Tibby is Mrs. Delaney," Nash explained. "Patrick is her infant son."

"Six months old and such a bonny boy," said Lady Helen overhearing. "You'll meet him and my own little Torie tomorrow." She smiled at the children. "Now, who are all these lovely children? Nash, introduce us, if you please."

Jane and Susan made beautiful curtsies. Maddy felt so proud of them. Then Lucy tried to curtsy, got stuck, and almost fell over. Before Maddy could move, Nash quietly caught her and helped the little girl to rise with a minimum of fuss. Maddy noticed Lady Helen observe him thoughtfully. She glanced at Maddy, a speculative look in her eyes, but said nothing.

When John and Henry made their bows, she commented on their bright rosy cheeks. "Have you been out in the cold air, boys?"

Henry burst out excitedly, "Yes, we sat up with the driver all the way, and helped drive the carriage. He let us hold the reins and everything."

"Did you indeed?" she said warmly. "It is a very exciting thing to do, is it not? I remember when I first learned to handle the ribbons, I was only a little older than you."

"You, ma'am?" Jane said in surprise.

Lady Helen laughed. "Yes, I was a terrible hoyden and utterly horse mad." She winked. "I still am. Do you like dogs? I hope you do because I can hear one coming now."

The clacking of claws sounded on the well-polished parquetry floor and an amiable-looking brown-spotted white springer spaniel came trotting up, wagging her tail and wiggling with joy at the sight of the visitors.

"This is my dog, Freckles," Lady Helen told them. "I hope you will all be great friends."

The children clustered around the dog, letting themselves be sniffed, patting her, and making friends.

"They've always wanted a dog," Maddy told Lady Helen. "But we could never afford to feed one." She wasn't going to pretend she was anything other than she was.

Lady Helen touched Maddy's arm sympathetically. "Oh, my dear, I understand. There was a time when all I had in the world was Freckles and she was such a comfort."

Maddy looked at her in surprise. All she had in the world?

But Nash had said this house had been in her family for generations.

Lady Helen continued, "Let me show you to your room. Nash will have his usual bedchamber, but I think we'll put you near the children, yes? You won't mind an extra flight of stairs? They'll be a little nervous in a new place, I'm sure, and you'll want to be on hand for them."

Maddy nodded. "That would be very kind, thank you. The children are used to sharing a bed . . ."

"Of course, so much more cozy." She turned to a gray-haired motherly looking woman standing quietly in the background. "Aggie, will you take the children to the nursery and help them wash their hands and faces? I think an early night is warranted, so supper on trays upstairs and then bed?" She glanced at Maddy for confirmation and added, "Aggie—Mrs. Deane—is my old nurse so they couldn't be in better hands."

Maddy nodded. "That would be perfect, thank you. Go with Mrs. Deane, children, and I'll be up to tuck you into bed, as usual."

"Can Freckles come with us, please?" Lucy asked. The little girl had her arms around the dog's neck, hugging her. Freckles thumped her tail, not seeming to mind being hugged in the least.

Lady Helen laughed. "Of course. Freckles goes everywhere." The children went off with Aggie Deane and Freckles.

Lady Helen linked her arm through Maddy's. "Now, Miss Woodford—and Lizzie, is it?" She smiled at Lizzie, who had been hanging back shyly. "I'll send my own maid, Cooper, to show you around, Lizzie, after you and your mistress have had time to wash and tidy up after your journey. Miss Woodford, you mustn't mind my nonsense about balancing numbers at dinner. If you're too tired to join us, you're very welcome to have supper on a tray in your room, or with the children if you prefer."

For one cowardly moment, Maddy thought about eating with the children. It was tempting, but she really shouldn't put off the moment.

"She'll dine with us," Nash said before Maddy could answer. "I should perhaps have mentioned this at the outset— Miss Woodford is my betrothed."

"Betrothed?" Lady Helen gasped.

Nash grinned. "We're to be married on Friday week in Maddy's parish church."

"Nash, you rascal, why did you not say so in the first place? Here I am treating the poor girl like a stranger."

"But I am a str—"

"Nonsense, you're to be my sister." Lady Helen hugged her. "Congratulations, Miss Woodf—what is your first name? I cannot call you Miss Woodford if you're to be my sister. And you must call me Nell. Oh, I'm so pleased. I liked you from the moment we met."

Maddy blinked and hugged her back, a little overwhelmed by the warmth of her reception. And immensely relieved. She'd also liked Lady Helen—Nell—from the beginning.

"I am Maddy, short for Madeleine."

"Oh, what a pretty name. I am so glad I married a man with plenty of brothers, for I grew up as an only child and I always longed for sisters. I would have married my darling Harry if he'd been a lone orphan, of course, but it is nice to become part of a big family."

Nash gave a crack of laughter. "Lord, Nell, if you think we're a family—"

"We are becoming one," Nell said airily. "The rifts are healing. All we need now is for you and Marcus to be married and—"

"Better to find Luke a wife. You'll have no luck with Marcus."

Nell frowned. "Well, we have been, but Luke is . . . slippery." She explained to Maddy, "Luke is the handsomest of all of them—he has the face of a fallen angel, you will see. Ladies fall at his feet in droves, but will he give the least bit of encouragement to anyone? His mother and sisters are almost in despair, for he is the only son, and though he has recently come into a title, he shows no interest in marriage." She glanced at Nash and added in a lowered tone, "And it's not that he isn't interested in *women*, for I wormed it out of Harry that he *is*."

She took a deep breath and smiled at Nash. "Still, I thought you might never marry, too, and here you are betrothed to this beautiful girl, so there's hope for Luke and Marcus yet. However, I've given up matchmaking—Luke told Harry this is one of the few places left where he can relax in the surety that we will not fling eligible young women at his head, poor boy, so I'll leave him in peace. Now, I'd better stop gossiping and give you time to get ready, for dinner will be served in half an hour."

C andlelight was kind to women and faded dresses, Maddy told herself as she took one last, critical glance in the looking glass. She wasn't sure if they'd dressed for dinner, but she'd put on her best gown, regardless. Not that it would measure up. "The hair, at least, is wonderful, thank you, Lizzie."

There was a knock on the door. Lizzie answered it, and after a quiet exchange, came back with a shawl draped over her hands. "Lady Helen's maid brought this for you to wear, Miss Maddy. She said it can get cold in this house, but oh, I've never seen anything so beautiful in me life. I think it might be silk or summat like that."

The shawl was exquisite, a soft, creamy fabric with a wide, silk-embroidered border of red, blue, and green. "It's a cashmere shawl," Maddy said, examining it. "They cost a fortune." Mama had owned one once. Maddy had sold it long ago.

Lizzie draped it around Maddy's shoulders. It fell in soft folds around her, reaching almost to her knees. Swathed in the beautiful, luxurious garment, the faded fabric of her gown wouldn't be so noticeable. And Maddy wouldn't feel so much like the beggar at the feast.

Maybe Lady Helen did understand what it was like to have nothing.

Nash arrived to escort her downstairs. His eyes ran over her and warmed with approval. "You look beautiful," he said softly. "Like a glowing candle."

She felt herself blushing. He'd never said anything like that to her before. He was looking very nice himself, and had changed his clothes, but . . . "Why are you wearing riding dress? Is it some custom here?"

He laughed. "No, but it's very informal tonight."

"So am I overdressed?"

"Not in the least."

"Then why did you change into riding breeches?"

"Because I'm leaving after dinner to rejoin Marcus."

She stopped halfway down the stairs and stared at him. "You mean you're riding back to my cottage tonight?"

"That's right. Come on, they've already set dinner back half an hour for us." He tugged her gently.

She withdrew her arm from his grasp. "You've brought me here to a houseful of strangers—in a rush and under the pretense we were expected, I might add—and now you're going to abandon me?"

He frowned. "I can't very well leave Marcus there on his own, can I? Don't you want to catch the Bloody Abbot?"

"Of course I do." She took a few breaths, trying to marshal her thoughts. "It's the lack of consultation I'm not happy about. And being lied to," she told him. "The Bloody Abbot is my problem, but you've allowed me no say in this."

"But I'm only trying to protect—"

"I know, and I know I ought to be grateful, but I don't *feel* grateful. Well, I do a bit," she admitted. "But I have a score to settle with him, and I hate being made to feel redundant and helpless. And I don't want to be abandoned here in a place where I know nobody—and, yes, Lady Helen has been more than kind and I'm sure your brother and his friends will be just as welcoming, but that's not the point."

Actually, she wasn't at all sure of his brother's welcome. Nash's older brother had already made his disapproval of her more than clear. No doubt the rest of Nash's family would agree with the earl, that Nash was making a *mésalliance*. She was going to do her damnedest to prove them wrong, but at the moment, she would much rather face the Bloody Abbot barehanded than spend a week alone with his family and friends.

"I am not a—a *parcel* to be moved about the country at your whim and dumped on people's doorsteps. I have opinions and ideas, and this is about *me*, so I *will* be listened to, Nash, do you understand?"

"I am listening," he said stiffly.

She sighed. He was offended. "The thing is," she explained in a softer voice, "I'm not like the young, sheltered, biddable girls your aunt would have found for you. I'm not used to having a man take over and make decisions for me. Papa left me and Mama in France with Grand-mère when I was nine, and he didn't send for me until I was nineteen. All that time I lived with Grand-mère, and she was . . . not always able to grasp how the world had changed, so I made most of the decisions. And then, not long after I returned to England, Papa had his accident, and there I was, in charge of him and the children. So I am used to deciding for myself, and not having things decided for me."

"Most women like it."

"I like it about as much as you would if I decided what was best for you all the time."

He stared at her for a long time, his eyes unreadable. "Have you changed your mind about this marriage?"

Maddy bit her lip and looked away. Oh, God, was he asking to be released from the promise? Having second thoughts now he'd learned what a hurly-burly, argumentative female she really was? "No."

He let out his breath in a rush, as if he'd been holding it. "Good." He took her arm again. "Now come on, dinner will be getting cold."

He hadn't conceded a thing, but Maddy took his arm and continued down the stairs. She would have preferred to finish the argument but she didn't want to keep everyone waiting. It would keep.

He would learn to listen to her, she was determined on it.

*T*hree men rose to their feet when she entered the dining room on Nash's arm. They almost took her breath away. As Lady Helen had said, they were all extraordinarily attractive.

She knew at once who each man was, even before Nash introduced them: the Renfrew family resemblance was very strong. Harry looked tough and hard—his years as a soldier, she supposed. His hair was much the same color as Nash's, but his eyes were lighter, gray, like Marcus's, as cold looking as Marcus was.

He glanced at his wife. Ah, but the coldness softened then, Maddy saw, as they exchanged a swift, light glance that warmed the room. He loved her.

Harry came forward and bowed over her hand. He murmured a greeting but said nothing else. Reserving judgment? Or the habitual taciturnity Nash had mentioned?

Next was Lord Ripton. If ever a man could be called beautiful, it was he, she thought. A fallen angel, with brooding dark eyes, cheekbones molded by a master sculptor, and thick, tumbled black hair.

She had no trouble imagining ladies following him about . . . Perhaps he was simply spoilt for choice.

Ethan Delaney kissed her hand with a flourish. Built like a bruiser, tall, and with a deep barrel chest, he could not be called handsome with his scarred and battered face, crooked nose, and an ear that looked . . . chewed? But when he smiled at her, a brilliant, lopsided slash of white in his tanned face, and greeted her in a soft Irish brogue, she instantly felt the appeal Lady Helen had mentioned. A ladies' man. She wondered what his wife was like.

Conversation over the soup course was general—about horses, mainly, and the exchange of news. Apart from answering the few polite questions directed at her, Maddy didn't say much.

She was too interested in watching Nash with his brother. The family resemblance was very obvious, but Harry was more strongly built than Nash and a shade shorter, with wider shoulders. Nash was the taller, loose-limbed and elegant, and in her eyes, the handsomest of the three brothers she'd met.

It was a hearty country-style meal; after the soup came steak and kidney pie, baked ham, creamed potatoes, and mushrooms.

Maddy hadn't seen so much food on a table in years.

"So, Nash, lost your luggage, eh?" Luke asked.

Nash looked up from the pie, which he was enjoying as much as Maddy. "No, I sent it ahead with Phelps when I left Bath nearly a fortnight ago. Why?"

Luke raised his brows. "Riding clothes? At dinner? Not like you."

Nash glanced at Maddy before he responded. "I'd planned to ride back to Maddy's cottage tonight."

"Good Lord, why?"

Nash explained the problems Maddy had experienced with

the man who dressed up as the Bloody Abbot. "And two nights ago, he destroyed her vegetable garden and burned all her bee-hives. Marcus is there now, with a groom, ready to waylay the ruffian if he comes back."

Harry gave a sharp laugh. "Marcus? Lurking in a cottage? I wish I might see it!"

"How did you arrange that?" Luke asked.

Nash gave a wry grin. "I, er, talked him into it."

The others laughed. "Talked him into it? Press-ganged him, I'll wager," Harry said.

Ethan shook his head. "I've said it before, the lad's part Irish, there's no other accounting for it. He can talk anyone into anything."

Nash glanced at Maddy with a rueful smile. "Not quite. Anyway, I've changed my mind, I'm not going. Marcus will have to manage on his own."

He wasn't going? He'd listened to her after all? Maddy was shocked. She'd spent half the dinner silently marshaling arguments to convince him. She caught his eye, and he winked, and a small bubble of happiness rose in her.

He'd listened. He cared about her opinions.

"Well, of course, you're not going," Lady Helen spoke up. "You can't just abandon Miss Woodford like that and ride off on some adventure."

To Maddy's amazement, the other men agreed. "I'd be in it like a shot," Ethan admitted, "but with young Patrick fretful with the colic, I'll not leave Tibby."

"Don't look at me," was all Harry said, but the look he gave to Nell almost took Maddy's breath away. The gray eyes she'd first thought so cold and hard blazed with love and pride.

Nell hid a smile but her face glowed, too, with secret pride, and suddenly Maddy knew what they weren't saying—Nell was increasing. That's why Harry wouldn't leave her.

Oh, to be on the receiving end of a look like that . . .

"Well, I'm free to go, and I wouldn't mind a bit of adventure," Luke declared. "Life's wretchedly tame at the moment, and it's worse now, since all you fellows have turned into staid married men. But if you give me the directions, I'll happily join Marcus and catch this villain for Miss Woodford."

"Excellent," Nash said. "Thanks, Luke, much appreciated."

The evening broke up soon afterward as Nash and Harry went off to see Luke on his way, Ethan returned to Tibby and the baby, and Maddy and Nell went upstairs to check on the children.

"Torie's been asleep for hours," Nell told Maddy as they reached the nursery level. "Still, I always check on her before I go to bed. Would you like to come in and see her?"

Maddy nodded. The nursery area took up almost half of the top floor of the house and was one big room, with a number of smaller rooms, presumably bedchambers, coming off it. Clearly at one stage this house had been filled with children.

Like many of the rooms in the house, it was spotlessly clean and well cared for, but well worn and comfortably shabby. "We're slowly fixing up the house," Nell explained. "But we're very busy with the horses."

"It's a wonderful place," Maddy assured her. "The children will love it." And they would, she knew. There were shelves and shelves of books and toys, an old dollhouse, a battered rocking horse, even a scarred old pianoforte—everything to delight a child. The floors were polished wood, scattered with old Turkish rugs. Along one side were dozens of windows and a long window seat, padded with squashy-looking, faded crimson cushions.

"On wet days I used to love to curl up there and read," Nell said, noticing her look.

The room where baby Torie was asleep in her cot was, by contrast, freshly wallpapered in yellow and white, with everything gleaming new.

"Harry did it all himself," Nell told her with a little smile. "For himself, he could happily sleep in a barn, but when it comes to Torie, he's very particular."

Maddy smiled and squeezed her arm. She'd noticed at dinner that the taciturn Harry Morant was equally particular about his wife's comfort and well-being. The love between these two was almost palpable.

Would Nash ever feel that way about her? She ached for it to be so.

If wishes were horses, beggars would ride . . .

A nursery maid sleeping in a bed in the corner of the room stirred and sat up. "It's just me, Mary," Nell whispered, and the girl lay down again.

They tiptoed to the baby's high-railed cot and looked down. Torie slept on her side, curled up like a sweet little caterpillar. In the light of Nell's candle, Maddy saw a tumble of brown curls, the rich curve of a baby's cheek, a sweep of long lashes, and a tiny thumb wedged firmly in the baby's rosy little mouth.

"She's beautiful," she whispered.

Nell nodded. "My precious." She blinked fiercely and Maddy realized her hostess was fighting tears.

"Oh, how silly, please forgive me," Nell muttered. "I have nothing at all to be weeping about. I just . . . get emotional for no reason at the moment."

Maddy touched her arm gently. "My mother was like that whenever she was increasing."

Nell gave her a searching look and then a watery smile. "It's early days. We haven't told anyone yet."

Maddy assured her she would say nothing. She wished Nell good night and went to tuck her own brood into bed.

Henry and John, worn out from all the excitement of driving the carriage, fell asleep almost as soon as Maddy kissed them good night. She tiptoed into the girls' room and found Lucy so heavy-eyed that in minutes, the little girl was also sound asleep. Jane and Susan, however, were wide awake.

"Maddy," Jane asked her, "when you marry Mr. Renfrew, where will we live?"

"With us both, of course," she assured them, and saw from the easing of tension that the girls had been worried. "Silly, of course I wouldn't leave you behind. We're a family and we stick together, no matter what."

She hugged Jane. Of all the children, Jane felt any disruption to their life most keenly. It was only natural; she had the strongest memories of losing both her parents. "You don't just lose people from a family, my darlings, you gain them, too."

"Like we gained you?" Jane said.

"Yes, and I gained you," she said, hugging them both. "And now Mr. Renfrew joins our family. You're still happy about that, aren't you?" The girls assured her they were.

"But where will we live?" Jane asked. "Will we be going to Russia, with Mr. Renfrew?"

"Yes, of course. A family sticks together, remember? And since Mr. Renfrew's work takes him to Russia, to Russia we will go."

"Will we see bears and have sleigh rides over frozen lakes and be chased by bloodthirsty wolves?" Susan said, her eyes wide.

"I don't know, but I'm sure it will all be a splendid adventure," Maddy told her. She was excited by the prospect, too.

"To Russia we will go, to Russia we will go, hi-ho the derry-o, to Russia we will go," Jane sang.

Maddy laughed and tucked her in tightly. "Now, go to sleep and dream of Cossacks and onion-domed towers . . ."

"And sleigh rides through the snow pulled by horses with bells on their harnesses . . ." murmured Jane.

"And ladies wearing dozens and dozens of petticoats . . ." Susan drifted off.

Twenty

$\mathcal{M}$addy closed the nursery door quietly behind her, turned, and almost dropped the candle holder as a shadowy figure loomed out of the gloom. "Oh, it's you," she gasped. "You gave me such a fright."

"Sorry, I just came to check that all was well with the children," Nash said quietly. "Strange house and all that."

"They're all asleep." She was touched at his concern.

"Good, and how about you?" The light from the single candle caught the facets of two crystal wineglasses dangling from his fingers. In his other hand he held a crystal decanter containing some dark liquid. "I thought you might like a small composer before bed. A glass of Harry's best Madeira, to help you sleep."

Maddy was so tired she didn't need anything to help her sleep, but she wasn't going to turn down a moment alone with Nash. Besides, she was so full of questions. "Madeira? All right." She looked around. "Where shall we go to drink it?"

"Here, on the stairs? Or I suppose we could return to the drawing room downstairs."

"I've always thought stairs were a cozy place to sit and talk," she said and caught a flash of gleaming white as he smiled.

They sat, side by side, though he sat one step lower to bring their faces level. The stairs were narrower than she thought, and their bodies touched. Echoes of the previous night shimmered through her.

Nash put the glasses and decanter between them, took the candleholder from her, and set it on the steps behind them, so it cast their faces half in shadow, half in a soft golden glow.

"Your hair was made for candlelight."

"Because it dulls the red?" Grand-mère thought her hair too bright and frequently regretted the passing of the fashion for hair powder, which would have disguised it.

"Perish the thought. One of the things I love about your hair is the way it's different in different light, and beautiful in all of them, but in candlelight, it gleams like fire. Try this, I think you'll like it."

She took the glass he handed her with a murmur of thanks, a warm glow inside her from the unexpected compliment.

She'd never tasted Madeira before. She swished the heavy, silky-looking liquid around in the glass and inhaled the aroma. Slightly smoky with a tang of sweet almonds. She held it to the light. It glowed a beautiful dark gold.

"The exact color of your eyes."

She looked at him, startled. His eyes were in shadow but she could feel the intensity of his gaze and the warmth of his body beside her. Was he going to make love to her here on his sister-in-law's steps? She took a large gulp of Madeira, and immediately choked.

"Madeira is not meant to be gulped," he said, taking the glass from her hand and patting her back soothingly. "You should sip it."

"It went down the wrong way," she muttered.

His hand didn't stop moving, up and down her back, soothingly. She didn't feel the least bit soothed. Every stroke sent warm, delicious shivers through her.

"It's meant to be sipped slowly, and savored. Like this." He put her glass to her lips, and feeling a little foolish, she sipped. The sweet, spicy wine slid down her throat like warm, honeyed silk. His hand moved up and down her spine, slowly, sensuously.

"It's delicious," she whispered, not entirely sure whether she was talking about the wine or his touch.

"So are you." His breath was warm on her cheek. His hand slid around her waist and drew her closer.

"The girls are so excited about going to Russia." She snatched the topic from the air.

"Were they?" He drew back with a frown. "It might be better not to discuss it with them just yet," he said after a moment.

"But why? If they're going to—"

"I haven't sorted everything out yet," he said.

"Sorted what? I don't—"

"Let's not discuss this now." His lips brushed her cheek, a featherlight brush of skin against skin, barely discernible, but she lost all track of what she was saying.

"But I want to kn—"

"You want what?" he murmured against her skin. The deep timbre of his voice vibrated through flesh made suddenly more sensitive. "This?" His lips touched hers lightly, once, twice.

"Or this?" He trailed his knuckles slowly across her aching breasts and a hot shiver of anticipation thrilled through her.

"Or this?" He made a low sound deep in his throat, his arm tightened around her, and he licked at her lips like a big hot cat, teasing at the seam until she parted for him. He entered and tasted her slowly, deliberately, languorously but with a sharp intensity that thrilled her to the marrow.

"Delicious," he murmured, and kissed her again, and she grasped his shoulders and kissed him back, tasting the sweetness of Madeira and the hot dark salt intensity of the man.

"Nash . . ."

He kissed her then with a delicate ferocity that thrilled her to the marrow, nipping, tasting, possessing. His mouth was his instrument and she unraveled beneath it, joyously.

She ran her palms along the harsh, pure line of his jaw, reveling in the abrasion of the masculine bristles; she speared her fingers through his thick, soft hair, and wriggled closer and closer, until she was plastered against his hard, masculine body, squirming against him; and all the time kissing, kissing, kissing him as he devoured her in return.

His big warm hands ran over her, feverishly, and she wished they weren't on the stairs, were in her lovely bed back home, in her own red-curtained alcove, cut off from the world. But the guest room she'd been given had a large and comfortable bed . . .

"My bedchamber is just past the landing," she murmured.

He hesitated, then kissed her with renewed passion, then gave a groan and lifted her from his lap back onto the stairs. "No," he said in a harsh voice.

She blinked at him, dazed, dizzy with passion, barely able to sit straight. "But it's just down there." She pointed. Her hand was shaking.

He groaned again, groped for the glass of Madeira, and gulped it down in one mouthful. He was breathing heavily. She was panting, too, she realized, as if she'd run up all the stairs and down again. "No," he repeated. "Not tonight."

"Why not?" They were going to be married, after all. She wanted him, and now, suddenly, with no warning, he seemed to want her at last, and she wanted to seize the opportunity while it presented itself.

But Nash Renfrew, it slowly dawned on her, was not presenting himself. He drew back, and when his hand encountered her glass that he'd put down, he drained it, too, putting his mouth deliberately over the smudge left by her own mouth and putting it down again without looking, his eyes never leaving hers. He stood slowly and held his hand out to assist her to rise.

Her heart leapt with hope. Her body throbbed, tense with longing, aching with need. And he—she glanced at him with a knowing eye—his long, lean body was tense, hard, visibly aroused. There was no reason to wait.

Nash waited, his face in shadow, his hand outstretched. She allowed him to help her stand and was glad of the leashed strength in the light clasp, for her legs trembled beneath her, all their strength drained.

He led her to her bedchamber door, opened it, handed her the candle. "Come in with me," she whispered.

He shook his head and kissed her lightly on the mouth, a firm, possessive promise of a kiss, tasting of Madeira and Nash, and tinged, she fancied, with regret.

"Sleep well, Maddy," he said softly and strode away down the dark corridor, leaving her clutching the door, staring after him.

*I*t was the very definition of control, Nash told himself. To send her to bed—alone—with nothing but a chaste—chaste-ish kiss and then walk away. To his own bed. His own, empty bed.

It was the civilized thing to do.

Nash let himself into his bedchamber. A cozy sight greeted him. His valet, Phelps, was waiting, a fire crackled merrily in the grate, a glass of brandy sat on the bedside table, and the bedclothes were turned down, ready for him to slide into bed. Perfect, Nash told himself. Everything he could possibly want. Except one.

Desire gnawed at his vitals.

Leaving her to sleep alone was the wise thing to do, he told himself. He wasn't besotted by lust. He was not his father. He would not be ruled by passion.

He could wait for the wedding before bedding her again. He wasn't an animal, governed by primitive instincts. He was a gentleman. A gentleman in complete control of himself.

"Evening, Phelps."

"Good evening, sir." Phelps helped Nash out of his coat and waistcoat and hung them up. "I trust Lord Ripton made his departure in good time."

"He has, yes." Nash didn't bother to ask how Phelps knew Luke was taking his place. Phelps always knew everything. Nash yanked the arrangement of his neckcloth apart and tossed it on the bed, then dragged his shirt off over his head.

Phelps stood by with Nash's dressing gown ready. "Shall you require this, sir?"

"Mmm, yes. I might read for a bit by the fire." Nash shrugged on the dressing gown, then sat for Phelps to assist him in the removal of his boots. Nash pulled off his stockings, then dragged off his breeches and kicked them aside. "That'll be all, Phelps."

"Very good, sir," Phelps brought the brandy glass and a bottle to the table beside the fireside chair. "The cognac you enjoyed so much last time we were here," he murmured. "Mr. Bronson sent up a bottle." He picked up Nash's discarded clothing. "Good night, sir, sleep well."

"'Night, Phelps." Nash picked up the crystal glass and swirled the cognac around, watching the fire through it. The rich aroma of the cognac teased his senses, reminding him of the way her kisses had tasted. Madeira and Maddy, a headier combination by far than the finest French cognac.

Come in with me.

He glanced at the bedclothes, turned back so invitingly on his bed. Damn it all, why should he wait?

She'd invited him in.

It wasn't gentlemanly to turn down a lady's invitation.

And Nash was a gentleman to his fingertips. A gentleman under perfect control. Making a rational, logical, polite decision not to disappoint a lady.

He put down the brandy glass and let himself quietly out into the dark corridor.

*H*e eased open her door in case she was already asleep, but she was kneeling by the fire in her night rail, her head bent over, vigorously brushing her hair.

Her spine formed a graceful arch. The thin, worn fabric of the nightgown pulled tight over the sweet curve of her hips and bottom. The undersides of her small pink toes peeked from under her buttocks. Her body moved gently with each movement of the brush, her breasts swaying gently as, like a living thing, her hair lifted and crackled with each stroke, gleaming in the firelight.

His mouth dried. His body hardened in a rush of hot blood. God, but she was beautiful. His bride-to-be.

He must have made a noise, for she looked up. And waited for him to speak.

His throat was tight, too tight to speak.

"What is it?" she asked.

"Are you sure you want me to stay with you tonight?" he croaked.

She set down the brush and gave him a slow smile. "Of course I'm sure." She rose to her feet in one graceful movement, running her fingers through her hair to tame its wildness. It crackled and clung to her skin. He knew just how it felt.

"Don't." His voice sounded hoarse.

A pucker formed between her brows. "Don't what?" she murmured, moving toward him. Her hair was damp, curling in tendrils around her neck and ears.

She placed her hands on his chest—he wondered if she could feel the pounding of his heart—and raised her face for his kiss. The fragrance of new-washed hair and warm, clean woman enveloped him. His body throbbed, hard and wanting. Demanding.

"You smell so good," muttered the man of words. But he could barely string two thoughts together, let alone a sentence.

With Maddy like this, so warm and close and beautiful and welcoming, his brain was empty of all except desire. Thick, pulsing desire, hot and heavy, urging him to just toss her on the bed and take her, possess her, bury himself deep. Mindless, savage, desire.

He fought for every shred of control. Tonight, since his ability to resist her had proven so weak, he was going to make it good for her, to take her slowly, gently. Even if it killed him.

He trailed his fingers through the thick silky mass. "Don't ever cut this."

"I won't." Her lashes lowered demurely and she brushed her body lightly against him, moving in a slow tantalizing dance. Innocent eroticism, he told himself. Unbearably delicate friction.

His pulse pounded through his body, his body racked with agony, craving possession, demanding release. He groaned and she smiled a small, feminine smile.

"Shall we move to the bed?" she murmured.

Without a word, he swung her into his arms and in two long strides reached the bed. But he couldn't seem to let her go. Her arms twined around his neck and she pressed kisses on his jaw, his neck, the opening of his dressing gown.

Nash closed his eyes, savagely leashing his rampant desire into something resembling control. Like a tiger held by a ribbon. At this rate, he was going to fall on her and ravish her like a mindless beast. He forced himself to set her gently on the bed and stood back, breathing heavily.

She leaned back on her elbows and regarded him thought-fully, her glorious hair spread out in a wild, beautiful mass, her thin cotton night rail rucked up, revealing the pale, sweet slen-derness of her thighs. Parted slightly in unknowing invitation.

He forced his eyes away from the velvet shadow between her thighs and gave her a searching look. "Are you sure you're not too sore from . . . the other night?"

Again, that small, female smile. Mona Lisa in a worn cot-ton nightgown. "I ache," she told him, and his heart sank. It was as he thought. It was too soon.

"I ache for you," she said. "And if you walk out of here now, after leading me on and getting me all hot and bothered—for the second time tonight—I—I'll strangle you."

It took a moment for the meaning of her words to sink in, and in that moment, she'd unfastened his dressing gown and was pushing it off his shoulders. "It seems my French blood, once aroused, demands satisfaction," she murmured in dulcet apology. "I do hope it won't be a problem."

"It . . . won't," he managed to say, and then he was naked and she was kissing him, and he was kissing her and pushing up the hem of her nightgown with one hand, smoothing up those long, slender silken thighs toward the hot, moist wel-come of her center.

"My nightgown," she muttered feverishly and struggled to pull it off, but it was buttoned to the neck.

He cursed silently, caressing her intimately with one hand while he tried to undo dozens of stupid little buttons with the other hand. It was going to take forever to get the blasted thing off her and he couldn't wait that long. With a muttered curse and a "sorry about this," he grabbed the neckline of her night-gown in both hands and in one movement ripped it open from neck to hem. And stared, struck afresh by the naked, creamy beauty of her.

Seeing his expression, her eyes grew darker, half closed and sultry like a sleepy cat. She stroked his body in slow, sensual appreciation, rubbing herself against him, openly glorying in the sensation of touching him. He felt like a king, a god, all powerful and . . . about to explode.

He lowered his face to her breasts and caressed them with lips, tongue, and jaw, all the while stroking her between the legs, feeling her readiness, her eagerness. She arched and writhed beneath him. He couldn't wait much longer. He positioned himself between her thighs and she responded by wrapping her legs around him tightly, urging him on.

He entered her in one slow, smooth stroke, once . . . twice . . . and the rhythm took him, driving all thought from his brain. He battled to delay his climax as long as possible, but it was too late, too late . . . until she arched and screamed and shuddered uncontrollably, shattering around him as he shattered within her . . .

*W*hen Maddy woke, the sun was up and Nash was gone. The only evidence of his visit in the night was the tenderness between her legs and the ruined night gown. And the dent on the pillow beside her.

She turned over, snuggled her cheek into it, and relived their lovemaking from the night before. It was better than a morning dream, any day.

She stretched luxuriously and tried to tamp down the happy, fizzing feeling in her blood.

Don't mistake what passed between us for love . . . It's just how it is between a man and a woman . . . A healthy expression of desire.

Perhaps it was. She was new to lovemaking and the effects of desire, but one thing was very clear in her mind: she loved Nash Renfrew with all her heart. And if desire was all he could offer her, then she would take it gladly, for to be the object of his desire was . . . utterly splendiferous . . .

"*H*ow are you finding life as a maid, Lizzie?" Maddy asked as Lizzie brushed out the tangles in her hair later that morning.

"A bit different from what I expected, miss, but still better'n milking cows any day."

"In what way different?"

Lizzie pulled a face and began to braid Maddy's hair in a coronet around her head. "Belowstairs they're that starchy and hoity-toity, you wouldn't believe, miss. I sat in the cook's chair yesterday—just for a minute, I mean she wasn't using it or anything—but you would've thought I'd spat on the floor, the way everyone reacted." She put on a starchy voice, "'Maidservants sit at that end of the table, Brown; this end is reserved for the more important members of the household.'" Lizzie pulled a face and winked. "Cows, wherever I go."

"They're not unkind, are they?"

"Oh, no, miss, don't you worry. Old Mrs. Deane, she's a darlin'. And Cooper, that's Lady Nell's maid, she reckons it's worse in other big houses, believe it or not."

Cooper had been the maid who'd brought Maddy the beautiful cashmere shawl on the first night. "I thought she looked nice," Maddy said.

"She is. She's been showin' me the ropes. Said Lady Nell took a chance on her like you're takin' on me. And Mr. Benson, the butler, is a good sort. He likes everything just so and is a demon for hard work and treats us all like we're in the army, but for all that, he ain't no snob and he don't mind a joke. It's the ones who've been in service all their lives I can't stand. They act as though they've swallowed a poker and look at me like I'm something they stepped in."

Maddy laughed. Lizzie was far too outspoken and down-to-earth for a maidservant, but Maddy loved her for it. She could understand, however, that the girl would raise some hackles in the formally trained ranks belowstairs. "I'm so glad you came with me, Lizzie. But if anyone does mistreat you, you must come to me at once."

Lizzie snorted. "Nah, I can handle meself, miss." She frowned critically in the mirror. "Hair's always difficult after it's washed, ain't it?" She used a hot iron carefully and turned a few escaping wisps into tiny ringlets. "There, that's better. Suits you lovely, it does, miss. Mr. Renfrew will be dazzled all over again."

"Dazzled?" It was a lovely thought. Unlikely, but lovely.

Lizzie laughed. "Haven't you noticed, miss? Whenever he claps eyes on you, he can't seem to look at anything else. The poor man doesn't know whether he's comin' or goin'. Just like my Reuben was." She turned away and added in a slightly husky voice, "So keep on dazzlin' him, miss, and don't let him run off on you."

She would try, Maddy thought, but as poor Lizzie had learned the hard way, you couldn't make someone love you. It happened or it didn't.

Briskly Lizzie began to tidy the room. "Now, you'd better get on, else there'll be nothing left for breakfast. I could smell bacon cooking when I went past the kitchen. Lovely, it was. Oh, and Lady Nell said to tell you someone's coming at ten to measure up the children for new clothes."

"*T*hat's a sight I haven't seen before," Nash commented from the library door. "You sitting down, peacefully reading."

Maddy jumped and put down her book. It was their second day at Firmin Court and the children had settled in well, so well in fact that Maddy had some time to herself for a change. "I did offer to help—I'm sure there is any amount of work to be done, but Nell told me I was a guest and should do whatever I pleased." She sounded a bit guilty.

"Quite right," he said approvingly. "I haven't seen you take time for your own pleasure in all the time I've known you. What's the book?" He picked it up and frowned. "Russia?"

"It's a little out of date, but very interesting. Did you know that—"

"Don't bother with it." He closed it with a snap and put it aside.

"But I'm interested—"

"Other possibilities have arisen."

She looked up at him, puzzled. "What possibilities? Do you mean we're not going to Russia in June?"

"I don't know, yet. It doesn't matter." Nash made an impatient gesture. He really didn't want to discuss this now. "I bring a message from Jane and Nell that you're to come at once."

She rose, anxiously. "Is something wrong?"

"No, but you must come. Now." He caught her by the hand and led her from the house.

"But this is the way to the stables," she said after a moment. "I thought you said Jane wanted me."

"She does. We're going behind the stables. The boys are in

the stables, mucking out stalls, filling water troughs, cleaning tack, and working like navvies. Apparently they consider this seventh heaven."

She laughed and gave a little skip. "That's because Harry exchanges work for riding lessons."

Nash nodded. He knew all about it. He was the one giving the lessons. "I'm surprised they haven't learned to ride before this."

"John had a few lessons, but after Papa fell from one and broke his back while hunting, there was no question of any of us riding—all the horses were sold."

He squeezed her hand. "For someone who's seen so much death, you're a cheerful soul, aren't you?"

She gave a philosophical smile. "Grand-mère lost almost everyone she ever loved in the Terror, but she taught me to make the most of life while I can. Papa died two years ago, and I did mourn him for a year, but out of respect more than anything. We were never close. Besides, you can't stay gloomy when there are young children to take care of."

"I suppose not, especially with your lively five."

"And, of course, finding Papa had left only debts was another distraction."

He gave a snort of laughter. "I suppose you could call it a distraction." Survival was what she meant. He glanced down at her with a smile. A living example of everyday courage, his bride.

"I looked your father up in an old copy of Debrett's," he told her. "Sir John Woodford?" She nodded. He continued, "It listed an estate. I gather it was sold."

She shook her head. "It's entailed—the estate goes to John when he turns one and twenty. Mr. Hulme has rented it out to tenants for a very good sum."

"Hulme? The old goat you were going to marry?"

She nodded. "He's John's trustee. He was Papa's lifelong friend and neighbor and undertook to restore the estate to profitability by the time of John's majority. Finance is his passion."

It wasn't his only passion, Nash thought darkly. "Why didn't your father leave the children in his charge, rather than burden a young, single woman?"

"I suppose Papa thought the children were better off with a woman, and finances were more suited to a man. Besides, Papa wanted me to marry Mr. Hulme, too."

Nash stopped dead. "So when you refused, this Hulme fellow turned you out of the family home and didn't even provide you with a house?"

She avoided his gaze. "I know some would say it was selfish of me, to put my own desires before the welfare of the children—"

"Nonsense! You did the right thing."

"Well, I think so, too," she said frankly. "Mr. Hulme wanted to send the boys and Jane away to school and once I married him I'd have no say in the matter. But they'd just lost their parents and their home. They didn't need to be sent away to live with strangers. So I wrote to a friend of Grand-mère's— your uncle—and he offered me the cottage." She tugged on his arm. "Come on, I don't want to keep Nell waiting. I think I can guess what I'm going to see," she told him.

"Oh?" He glanced down at her.

"It appears Jane has always had a burning, though secret ambition to be a horsewoman." She slanted a mischievous look up at him. "Am I close?"

"My lips are sealed."

"I thought so. I'm very glad. Papa didn't approve of ladies riding: he said it was unfeminine and dangerous. But I saw Jane watching Lady Nell ride yesterday—she's a very accomplished horsewoman, isn't she?"

"Best seat in the county," Nash confirmed.

"And this morning Jane found one of Nell's girlhood riding habits in an old trunk in the nursery. It had a couple of rips in it but Jane—my Jane, who has to be forced to take up a needle— happily sewed them up without a word of complaint! And all day she's been whispering to Nell in corners and disappearing on mysterious errands. She's determined to outdo the boys, of course."

He laughed. "My money's on Jane."

They turned down the pathway that skirted the stables. Early roses were coming into bloom all along the south-facing wall, soaking up the warmth of the sun. The rich rose scent surrounded them and she hugged his arm unselfconsciously. There was a spring in her step he'd never seen before.

She was born for this life, he thought suddenly. A country house filled with children. How could he drag her off to foreign lands and a life of careful diplomacy?

"You like it here, don't you?"

She glanced up with a smile, her eyes shining. "It's wonderful. Everyone is so kind and the children are happy and excited and busy and . . ." She let go his arm, plucked a rose, and twirled around. "I feel suddenly free . . . and young and alive."

"You *are* young and alive." And sweet and lissome and utterly irresistible. He caught her twirling body in his arms and swung her off her feet. They twirled together, until, dizzy, he staggered sideways and collapsed against the wall, Maddy clasped to his chest, laughing and breathless.

"But you're not—" He broke off, shocked by what he'd been about to say.

"Not what?" She laughed up at him. "A fool in—"

He stopped whatever it was she'd been about to say by covering her mouth with his in a swift, firm kiss. Then he set her abruptly on her feet, suddenly chastened, almost serious.

In silence they walked on. Nash couldn't believe what he'd been about to say to her. *But you're not free—you're mine.* Claiming her. Claiming her, what's more, on a surge of possessive lust. Jealously.

He stared blindly ahead as he strode along the path, seeing in his head his mother twirling coquettishly, laughing, teasing, tormenting . . .

It was in the rose garden at Alverleigh. Nash was . . . eight? Nine? Children weren't allowed in the rose garden, but he'd hit a cricket ball over the hedge and had sneaked in to fetch it. He'd found his parents strolling among the roses. Fearful of being caught there, he'd hidden. And watched.

Father was picking roses and giving them to Mama, who pulled them slowly to pieces, one by one, tossing the petals at Father's head, and laughing as he brushed them from his hair.

Father picked off the thorns, but he must have missed one, because Mama's hand got scratched and she exclaimed, and held it out reproachfully to Father. Nash could see the thin line of blood on her palm.

Father had taken her hand and licked off the blood, carefully, licking up her arm. Then he'd growled like an animal and snatched her up against his chest—just as Nash had done with Maddy—and carried Mama into the house. They were laughing and murmuring and left a trail of rose petals behind them.

But later that day Mama's bags stood in the hall and they were screaming at each other, Mama white and tense and brittle, and Father so enraged his face was dark red and mottled and terrifying.

Nash and Marcus had watched from behind the rails of the staircase, quiet as mice, knowing they'd be beaten if they were caught eavesdropping. Nash wanted to do something to make them stop. Marcus said no, nothing could. It was always like this when Mama came home. She hated the country.

But Nash wouldn't listen. He knew how to make Mama happy again, make them both happy, and stop the terrible screaming. Taking the hidden servants' stairs, he ran out to the rose garden and plucked a dozen roses.

He even picked off all the thorns, like Father had, so Mama wouldn't scratch her fingers. His hands got all scratched and bloody himself but he didn't care. As long as Mama stayed . . .

He still remembered how hard his little heart beat as he stood in the hallway, holding out the roses to his mother, so determined to make her happy again.

He'd never forget the silence as the yelling suddenly stopped, the shocking silence that somehow pressed on him like a physical weight.

And the terror as his father turned on him with a hiss of rage.

He wanted to run, but he couldn't move, couldn't speak. He just squeezed his eyes shut and held out the roses to Mama. His hands shook. And Mama laughed.

Father dashed the flowers from his hands and flung him from the room, halfway across the hall . . .

Mama left for London shortly afterward.

Father stayed long enough to give Nash a severe beating for interrupting his parents' conversation and for stealing the roses. And then he'd beaten Marcus for not stopping Nash—he was the eldest, Nash's behavior was his responsibility.

And then Father had left to follow Mama back to London. He couldn't live without her; they loved each other too much, the servants murmured when they thought the boys weren't listening.

Nash learned that day: this was what happened if you loved someone too much.

As an adult he'd seen it ruin other people's lives: marriages and families torn apart for what they called love, for a passion that could not be denied.

There was no longer a rose garden at Alverleigh. When Mama had died, Father had ordered all the roses ripped out of the earth and burned, the bowers and archways torn down, the garden put to the plough. Now only a sward of smooth green lawn remained where roses had once bloomed.

Nash glanced sideways at the lovely young woman hurrying along beside him, her hand tucked into the crook of his arm, skipping every second or third step, as carefree as a young girl.

She would stay that way, he vowed.

Nash would not be jealous and possessive and tormented by love. He would have a civilized marriage, one where nobody got hurt and where children would not have to watch, agonized and helpless, consumed by fear.

A marriage of mutual respect and esteem, not passion.

All that was required was the necessary self-control.

Twenty-one

On their third afternoon at Firmin Court, the peace of Maddy's existence was shattered by the arrival of three more guests. First the Earl of Alverleigh and Lord Ripton arrived, riding neck and neck down the driveway, scattering gravel as they thundered toward the front steps. Maddy thought the horses would leap up the steps, but at the last second, they drew up, Luke announcing that he'd won by a nose.

"Dashed fine bit of blood, that, Marcus," he commented as he tossed the reins to a waiting groom. "Didn't know earls could ride."

"Didn't know barons were lunatics," Marcus retorted coolly. He glanced at Harry and Nash, who'd come out to welcome the new arrivals. "He's quite insane."

They both nodded. "Yes, but only when it comes to racing," Harry said. "He and Rafe egg each other on. I'm surprised you did, though." He eyed his half brother narrowly.

"He's almost as good a rider as Rafe," Luke admitted reluctantly.

"I'm better than Rafe," Marcus said coolly.

Luke snorted. "I'll lay you a monkey you're not."

"Did you see the Bloody Abbot?" Maddy burst out, fearing the manly horse talk would never end.

"He came last night," Luke said, shrugging off his great-coat. "The swine destroyed the rest of your garden, I'm afraid, and then he started banging on the windows and doing the moaning wailing thing you told us about—creepy stuff, I must say—for a woman and children, that is."

"Yes, but did you catch him?"

Luke shook his head. "Sorry. I tackled him—got in a few punches—he's got a black eye at the very least, but we lost him in the blasted fog." Luke handed his hat and coat to Bronson. "Wretched stuff was so thick you could only see a few feet in front of you. The villain disappeared into it before Marcus could shoot him again."

"You shot him?" Nash asked his brother.

"Winged him in the shoulder, I think," Marcus said. "He let out a yelp, at any rate, and clutched his shoulder."

"And this morning we found blood on the path and the garden gate," added Luke.

"But since Luke was swirling around in the fog with him, I didn't dare risk a second shot." Marcus tossed his greatcoat and hat to a footman.

"You lost him, Luke?" Harry said incredulously. "Slipping in your old age?"

Luke snorted. "You'd have lost him, too, if you'd been belted over the head with a blasted lump of wood. Look." He bent and showed them a large lump on his head. "You never told us he had an accomplice."

"He never has before," Maddy said, surprised. "It's always been just one man."

"So what now? You've left the cottage to him?" Nash asked.

"Of course not, my footman's still there, guarding it, and he's got my pistols," Marcus told him. "But we don't think there will be any more trouble. When I was grappling with him, he called out to his mate, 'The pigeon's flown the coop,' Miss Woodford being, presumably, the pigeon in question."

Maddy and Nash exchanged glances. Did that mean it was about her, and not the cottage?

Luke continued, "Now he knows there are three men in the

cottage and not a lone young woman and a handful of children, we doubt the bast—er, swine'll return. So we came back here."

"Why? Why not stay and be sure?" Nash asked, squeezing Maddy's hand. He knew she wanted the man caught so they'd discover the reason behind the trouble.

"His lordship here," Luke jerked his head at Marcus, "isn't used to cramped conditions."

"You kicked me, twice in one night," Marcus retorted. "Stormy dreams, this fellow has. Might as well share a bed with a wild beast."

"Better than an earl who's never had to share a thing in his life."

Nash's lips twitched. "You two were sharing a bed?"

His brother shrugged. "Nobody mentioned the extreme shortness of the beds upstairs. And since Luke and I are both around the six-foot mark . . ."

"I'm bored with talking about beds. Isn't anyone going to offer us a drink?" Luke interrupted.

"In a minute." Harry peered past him through the door that Bronson was just closing. "Unless I'm mistaken, that's Aunt Maude's carriage bowling down the drive."

"Good, she must have received my letter," Nash said.

His aunt? Maddy's stomach turned into a bottomless pit.

Harry swung around and gave him a long look. "Rather free with the invitations to my home, aren't you, brother?"

Nash smiled sweetly. "She's your aunt, too."

"This is the aunt who's spent the last few weeks scouring the country to find you a suitable bride, is it not?" Maddy said to Nash. "Does she know about me?"

At her words, there was a sudden silence in the hall.

"Not . . . exactly," Nash said. "Some things are better done face-to-face. Leave it to me."

Harry laughed. "History repeats itself," he said obscurely. "Aunt Maude's going to love this."

"I can manage Aunt Maude," Nash said with confidence.

"He's a diplomat," Harry said dryly to Maddy. There was an unholy twinkle in his eye. It didn't reassure her in the least.

The sight of Maude, Lady Gosforth, striding up the front

stairs, dripping furs and complaining bitterly of the state of the road from Bath, was no less reassuring. A tall Roman-nosed matron, she swept into the house and shrugged her furs into the waiting hands of the butler and footmen as if they didn't exist.

Dressed in the first stare of elegance she exuded the kind of self-confidence that came of a lifetime of telling people what to do, and a set of ancestors who'd done the same.

She paused a moment and regarded the spectacle of the four tall young men standing in the hall with open appreciation. "I don't know why you're all standing around in the entrance hall at this time of day, but I can't fault the picture you make. Harry, my boy"—she presented a lightly rouged cheek to be kissed—"you look splendid but you smell of horse—quite pleasant but I trust you will have bathed and shaved before dinner.

"Marcus, good God, what brings you here? Some crisis prized you away from your beloved Alverleigh, has it?" She didn't give the earl a chance to respond but continued almost in the same breath, "Luke, my dear boy, what a delightful surprise. Just arrived? And how is your dear mother? It's been an age since we had a comfortable coze." She gave her hand to Luke to kiss, then patted him on the cheek as if he were a boy of twelve.

She glanced at Maddy, lifted her lorgnette briefly, then passed her over, no doubt taking her for a maid in her faded and outmoded dress, Maddy thought.

She turned to Nash and presented her cheek for kissing. "Nash, dear boy, why on earth have you summoned me here so urgently? Your letter was remarkable for its lack of information, a dubious skill that I suppose you diplomatic fellows pride yourself on, government being all about the appearance of doing something while doing quite another. And why here? I thought you would have been at Whitethorn Manor putting Jasper's estate to rights—he got quite reclusive and peculiar toward the end, you know. So why am I here, instead of putting the finishing touches to the ball in London? It's all arranged, naturally, but I will explain—" She broke off with a frown. "Why, for that matter, are you all here?" She turned to Harry in sudden anxiety. "It's not Nell, is it? Or the child?"

"No, no, Nell and Torie are both blooming," Harry said. "Nell was just putting Torie down for her nap."

Nash drew Maddy forward. "Marcus and Luke arrived minutes before you, so Nell will be down in a moment and will no doubt arrange refreshments, but before you go upstairs to compose yourself, dear Aunt Maude, I would like to present to you Miss Madeleine Woodford—"

Lady Gosforth raised the lorgnette while he was speaking and examined Maddy with unnerving concentration. It took in everything about her, from the auburn tendrils escaping untidily from the knot that had looked so elegant this morning to her shabby clothing and down to her well-worn slippers.

Maddy stiffened her spine.

"—my betrothed," Nash finished.

The lorgnette froze. Nash's aunt stared over it, down her long, Roman nose with all the disapproval of a dozen generations of unamused ancestors.

But Maddy had her own ancestors and they were French, and they scorned Lady Gosforth's English disapproval. "How do you do, Lady Gosforth?" she said calmly and made a curtsy finely calculated to show respect to an older lady, but not intimidation. It was a you-may-not-approve-of-me-but-I'm-going-to-be-polite-anyway kind of curtsy.

Merci, *Grand-mère for your instruction in the polite arts.* She'd thought all those hours of learning various kinds of curtsies for various ranks and situations were a waste of time. This one gesture made it all worthwhile.

Lady Gosforth's brows rose. "Charmed," she said in a voice that was anything but. "Nash, I will speak to you in private in forty minutes. You, butler, conduct me to my bedchamber." She stalked upstairs, Bronson in attendance.

"*H*ave you taken leave of your senses, boy?" Aunt Maude groped for her lorgnette and stared through it in a way that reminded Nash of an incident when he was fourteen, involving a cricket ball and an ornately framed looking glass.

She had not taken the news well. But he was not fourteen any longer. "Not at all," he began in a contrite but firm voice. "Dear Aunt, I'm very sorry to have caused you inconvenience—"

"Don't 'dear aunt' me! Inconvenience? Do you realize I've invited the daughters of three dukes, two marquesses, a dozen earls, several ambassador's daughters—"

"Yes, and I'm very sorry to have wasted your time," he said, cutting off what promised to be a very long list. "But there was no way to inform you of my change of plans. I was injured and insensible for several days, and when I awoke I had no idea who I was. I've only had my memory back for a few days."

"Presumably your common sense will return in another week," she said acidly. "I'm out of sherry." She held out her glass.

He refilled it. The sherry might have been a mistake. He'd sent it up ahead of him, thinking it would mellow her mood; instead, it had sharpened her tongue.

He cursed the chance that had them all gathered at the door when she arrived. He knew better than to spring an unwelcome surprise on an elderly lady after a long and uncomfortable journey and had planned to break the news of his betrothal gently, after she was rested and relaxed from her journey.

Then, when she was reconciled to his news, he'd tell her Maddy's story and finally he'd introduce her to Maddy. Aunt Maude would love Maddy, he was certain.

Instead he'd had to present his betrothed then and there, and she'd lifted that damned lorgnette and stared at Maddy as if she were an insect.

Maddy hadn't liked that one bit and her temper showed. She wouldn't realize it, but the way she'd curtsied almost looked like a challenge. And now Aunt Maude's back was up, too.

It had been a mistake, too, to allow Aunt Maude forty minutes to compose herself. Two minutes into the interview he realized the wily old woman had used the time to advantage and sent her dresser down to the servants' hall to gather information about Maddy.

And they'd got their information from her milkmaid-turned-maidservant.

Aunt Maude was not impressed.

"I sift through every eligible lady in the kingdom—"

"Not Wales and Scotland, then?" he interjected irrepressibly.

"Do not," she ordered with a gimlet look, "be flippant."

"No, Aunt," he said, looking humble. He knew how to coax her out of the sullens.

"And don't think I don't know what you're trying to do. I've known you since you were an infant, boy, and you cannot charm me."

"No, Aunt."

She took a deep sip of the sherry. "Never thought I'd see you, of all my nephews, making a *mésalliance*."

"It is not a *mésalliance*. Miss Woodford's father was a baronet—"

"An obscure baronet of obscure family. A dull little man who I gather died in debt."

"Birth is not everything," he said stiffly. How the devil did she know that? Did she know everyone in England? Probably.

"You wanted a bride with connections in the diplomatic field. Has this girl such connections?"

"No."

"Has she had a fine education, perhaps, or experience in running a great house that would make up for her deficiencies in other areas? Is she a skilled hostess, who can organize a ball, a Venetian breakfast, or a dinner for fifty at a moment's notice?"

He gritted his teeth. "You know she has not. But most new brides are unskilled in this area, too, and yet—"

"The difference is that most of them—and *all* the gels on my list—have grown up assisting their mothers in the conducting of such events. They, at least, know how it *should* be done."

He set his jaw. "It doesn't matter. Miss Woodford and I have—"

"This girl has *no* idea how to further your career. She will be *completely* out of her depth. For heaven's sake, Nash, it will be a disaster for your career."

Nash set his jaw. "It doesn't matter."

His aunt's eyes almost threw sparks, they snapped so angrily. "Doesn't *matter*? Have you taken leave of your senses?"

He hadn't planned to tell her so soon, had planned to let her learn it gradually, but there was no way around it now. He said with a casual air, "I may not remain in the diplomatic service."

"What the devil do you mean?"

"I might take up, er, animal husbandry."

"Animal husbandry?" she echoed with loathing.

"Yes, now I have an estate, there is no need for me to keep traveling. It's very tedious moving from place to place all the time—"

"Tedious? You love it."

"—so I'm considering settling down to run Uncle Jasper's— that is, my estate. Breeding animals and . . . er, growing things."

The lorgnette dropped. "You? A farmer? Pigs might fly!" She stared beadily at him. "So, it's come to that, has it? In that case, there's no alternative: you'll have to buy the gel off."

Nash stiffened. "I beg your pardon?"

"You heard me, buy her off. It's the only thing to do— unless you've tumbled her already. In which case you might have to find her a husband." She raised the lorgnette again. "Have you?"

"None of your damned business, Aunt. And I'll be damned if I buy her off." He thought about it and if he hadn't been so angry, he might have smiled at the thought of how Maddy would react. "If I tried, she'd fling it back in my face."

She snorted. "Because you're worth more to her in marriage."

"She's not after my money."

"Nonsense, of course she is—not that I blame her for that. According to that maid of hers, she was about to be tossed into the streets."

Nash said nothing. He wasn't about to confirm or deny it. Not that his aunt cared.

"And up you rode like a character out of a fairy tale, fell off your horse, scrambled your brains so you didn't know whether you were Arthur or Martha, and before you know it, little Miss Woodford had her hooks in you. I wouldn't be surprised if she caused the accident in the first place."

Nash clenched his fists. "That's not how it was."

"Faugh!" she exclaimed. "Men are so blind. Made you think yourself a hero, did she?"

Nash clenched his fists. If his aunt were a man, he'd hit her.

"My mind is made up. I will marry Miss Woodford. You may say what you will to me in private, but I insist you treat her with respect. If not . . ." He gave her a hard look.

His aunt raised her well-plucked brows so high they almost disappeared into her coiffure. "Like that, is it?"

"It is."

She drank the last of her sherry and set down the glass with a sniff. "Even Harry, with all the disadvantages of his birth, managed to get himself an earl's daughter."

"Harry didn't 'get himself an earl's daughter.' He fell in love with a woman who happened to be one. There's a difference."

She eyed him shrewdly. "Is that it? Have you fallen in love with this gel?"

"No," he said shortly. "But it is a matter of honor." And besides, he liked her. And desired her. But he wasn't going to justify his feelings to his aunt. She could accept his decision—and Maddy—or she could take herself off.

"Honor!" She snorted. "Foolish male notion. You've let a doe-eyed schemer—"

"Aunt," he said in a warning voice.

She gave him a long look, then shrugged. "Very well, if that's how you want it . . ."

"I do."

"What do we do about the ball? Everyone has been invited—*la crème de la crème*—and everyone has accepted, even your Russian grand duchess."

Nash smiled with confidence he did not feel. "It goes ahead, of course. Only it will be a wedding ball."

"Then you'd better get her a dress. A whole wardrobe, in fact. The dress she's wearing now I wouldn't give a housemaid to dust with."

"I have that in hand."

She gave him a skeptical glance. "What arrangements have you made? The season starts in a few weeks and every dressmaker of note will be working around the clock as it is. It will hardly add to her consequence if she's dressed by some provincial dressmaker."

"I have obtained the services of the finest mantua maker in London."

"The finest mantua maker in London is a Frenchwoman and very exclusive—my own mantua maker, Giselle."

Nash bowed. "Precisely."

Aunt Maude gaped. "You've got Giselle to agree to leave London on the eve of the season? I don't believe it!"

"Not quite. Giselle has Miss Woodford's measurements and coloring and is making up several dresses, including a wedding dress. Any day now I expect her assistant to arrive for final fittings before the wedding and to finish off the garments. Then she will return to London, and when we arrive, Giselle will be ready with the rest."

His aunt regarded him with something akin to awe. "How on earth did you manage that? Giselle is notoriously difficult."

Nash merely smiled and said, "I have my ways, Aunt." His ways including a hefty wad of cash and a lot of fast talking from one of his most skilled and charming colleagues in the diplomatic service. He now owed a lot of favors, but it was worth it, if only for the look on his aunt's face.

She stared at him a long time, then shook her head. "It will be a criminal waste if you molder on Jasper's estate instead of putting those skills to use in the service of your country, but if that's what you want . . ." She waved a dismissive hand. "Now take yourself off and tell Nell I'll be down for a cup of tea in ten minutes."

"Yes, Aunt."

"And I'll be polite to that young woman but I won't promise to like her." She held out her hand in clear dismissal.

Nash kissed it. "You will once you get to know her, I'm sure. Thank you for all your help, dear Aunt Maude, and for arranging the ball. I know you are troubled about this wedding, but I assure you it will all work out."

As he closed the door behind him, his aunt's voice followed. "I just hope the chit can dance."

*O*f course she can dance, Nash thought. All girls learned to dance, didn't they? All the girls he knew did. They all played the pianoforte, too, and painted insipid watercolors. But she might need to polish her skills. It would be wise to check. He hastened to find Maddy.

He found her supervising a fitting of clothes for the girls. The three little girls and Lizzie stood on chairs, standing like slowly rotating statues while the village dressmaker and her assistants pinned up the hems of their new dresses.

Lucy squirmed, trying to see herself in the looking glass.

"Hold still, Lucy, unless you want to be pricked by pins," Maddy told her.

The little girl saw Nash standing in the doorway. "I'm wearing a new dress. Don't I look beautiful, Mr. Rider?"

"You do indeed, Lucy," he assured her. "A very fetching picture you all make. Susan, I like that pink dress, and Jane, that blue matches your eyes perfectly." He winked at Lizzie who was wearing checks. "Very smart, Lizzie."

"But Maddy hasn't got any new dresses," Susan told him worriedly. "Only us. She should look pretty, too."

"She does look pretty, and she'll get new clothes soon," Nash assured her. "Maddy's dresses are coming from London."

"London? But how will they know to make them the right size?" Jane asked.

Nash smiled. "I sent one of Maddy's old dresses to London so they could get the measurements. And her old slippers, so the shoemaker could do the same."

Maddy, who had half a dozen pins held between her lips, nearly spat them out. "You sent them one of my dresses? Without telling me? How? And which one?" She didn't seem very pleased by his ingenuity.

"From that bundle of old clothes you left on the door. Remember, you were sorting out what to pack?"

Her eyes widened. "You sent a fancy London mantua maker my oldest rag of a dress?"

He frowned. "You didn't want it, did you?"

She closed her eyes for a moment. "No, of course I didn't want it, it's a rag!" She groaned. "Oh, how could you, Nash?"

How could he? He explained, "It's actually rather a coup to have got her to take you on at all, especially at this time of the year, before the season. She's the most fashionable mantua maker in London." Aunt Maude would kill him when she learned that Nash had used her name in his armory to convince Giselle.

Maddy groaned. "So you sent the most fashionable dressmaker in London the tattiest old rag I owned and told her it was mine."

Her attitude confused him. Perhaps she didn't understand the full genius of his plan. "But it was the perfect solution. Giselle can copy all the measurements from the old dress and whip up a new one for you in no time. Well, in time for the wedding, actually. Only a week to go."

"Yes, but now she will know that I wore old rags."

"What does that matter?"

"She'll think I'm the veriest pauper, some kind of desperate fortune hunter."

Nash stared at her. "What do you care what she thinks? She's only a dressmaker. And you're buying a lot of new dresses and they won't be cheap, so she'd better keep her tongue between her teeth if she wants any more of your custom."

"Cinderella wore old rags," Lucy said into the silence that followed.

Maddy laughed and hugged the little girl. "Yes, she did, darling, and her fairy godmother gave her a new dress. And I'm sorry I was cross with Mr. Renfrew for doing the same, no matter what his methods were, his intentions were the best."

Lucy frowned. "He's not the fairy godmother, he's the prince."

The talk of Cinderella reminded Nash why he'd sought Maddy in the first place. "Can you dance?" he asked her.

"I beg your pardon?"

"Can you dance?" Nash repeated. "You know, country dances, cotillions, waltzes, quadrilles, that sort of thing. You can, can't you?"

She bit her lip. "I know some country dances, and I've learned the steps of the cotillion, and a quadrille is a variation on that, is it not?" He nodded. "So I can probably manage that, but I've never learned to waltz, never even seen it danced."

"Never seen it danced?" he repeated. "You must have attended some very dowdy balls then."

"I've never attended any sort of ball at all."

Nash was shocked. He knew she hadn't made her come out, but . . . "Not even a local assembly?"

"Not one."

"An impromptu dance at a party?"

She shook her head. "I've never been to a party, and never actually danced with anyone, except for a couple of country dances at the village fair last year. Strip the Willow, and the Scotch Reel, that sort of thing. Oh, and we danced around a maypole, didn't we girls?"

Nash did his best to mask his shock, but his heart sank. She'd never even been to a party? Her sole experience of dancing in public was at a village fete with some drunken rural clodhopper? And dancing around a maypole, for pity's sake! It was worse than he thought.

He thought of the hundreds of glittering balls he'd attended in palaces and ballrooms all over Europe, where men and women flirted, plotted, and made scintillating conversation as they danced, each step and complicated sequence as familiar as walking. And she'd never even been to a party.

The gulf between his diplomatic life and her knowledge and experience widened by the minute. His future as a country squire seemed inevitable.

Aunt Maude must never find out how socially inexperienced Maddy was.

"Very well then," he said. "We'll commence dancing lessons this afternoon. Three o'clock in the green saloon." At his words, the little girls squealed with excitement, and he kicked himself for mentioning it in front of them. "Oh, but—" he began, but then it occurred to him it was as good an excuse as any. If Aunt Maude enquired, he and Maddy were teaching the children how to dance.

Maddy's eyes shone. "I look forward to it," she said quietly. "I've heard the waltz is a very romantic dance."

Nash nodded brusquely. It was a romantic dance, but not when his whole future was riding on it.

Twenty-two

❧

Maddy was running late for her waltzing lesson. The modiste from London had arrived at noon, and most of the afternoon had been taken up with fittings and adjustments.

To Maddy's relief, the modiste was not the famous Giselle, but her assistant, Claudine, another Frenchwoman, and though Claudine initially eyed Maddy's shabby clothing with ill-disguised distaste, from the moment Maddy addressed her in French, Claudine softened.

Maddy wasn't able to get away until well after three, but she left Claudine and her two assistants enthusiastically planning a range of stunning dresses for her.

Maddy hurried down the stairs and along the corridor. The green saloon was in the far wing of the building. She slowed to walk more softly past the pink drawing room. Lady Gosforth had established it as her own special territory, and Maddy had no desire to attract the woman's attention.

The door was ajar. As Maddy tiptoed past, a voice floated out. "That chit has caught him in her toils somehow."

Maddy froze. It was Lady Gosforth, Nash's aunt.

Lady Gosforth continued, "I wouldn't have thought it of

your brother to be caught by a brazen little fortune hunter with big brown eyes. Of all you boys, I always thought Nash the most level headed."

They were discussing her. She ought to do the polite thing and tiptoe away. Outraged curiosity glued her to the spot. Brazen little fortune hunter indeed!

"To be fair, Nash was seriously injured. His brains were quite addled," said Maddy's future brother-in-law, the earl. "She took advantage of that to entrap him."

Entrap? Maddy bristled. How dare he suggest such a thing! Nash wasn't addled in the least when he asked her. And she'd done everything she could *not* to entrap him—and at considerable risk to her own reputation. If anything, he had entrapped her!

"You know the gel better than I, Marcus. What do you make of her?"

"She's interesting," Marcus began.

His aunt cut him off. "I meant, can you suggest a way out of this pickle?"

Maddy clenched her fists. Her marriage to Nash might not be what his family expected, but it was *not* a pickle.

"She's as poor as a church mouse, so I doubt it." The earl snorted. "There's no shifting Nash when he's in one of his gallant moods—you know how stubborn he can be."

"Pish, tush! All you Renfrew men are as stubborn as blocks," his aunt said caustically. "That simply means we can't expect him to act on his own advantage. Doesn't mean we can't act for him. Good God, boy, have I searched the length and breadth of the kingdom for the finest available brides, only to have him trapped into marriage by some scheming little nobody who for all I know caused the accident deliberately?"

"How dare you!" Maddy stepped into the room. She was shaking with anger. "I did *not* cause Nash's accident. All I did was to try to save a stranger's life, and if you must know, it put me to a great deal of trouble and inconvenience!"

Lady Gosforth peered disdainfully at Maddy through her lorgnette, then sniffed, and turned her attention back to her knitting.

Maddy's temper rose. "Don't sniff at me, you obnoxious old woman! I would scorn to entrap any man. You may call me a nobody, and it's true that my father's family was undistinguished, though it was genteel, but my mother's family was noble and well connected—"

Lady Gosforth's finely plucked eyebrows rose.

"—even though most of them died during the Terror—"

"Oh, French," the old woman said with a dismissive wave.

"Yes, French, and very proud of it I am, too!" Maddy snapped, almost dancing with rage. "I know the marriage is not the grand one you'd hoped for, and no doubt I should have refused your nephew when he made his offer, but I could not! I simply could not—and don't curl your lip at me like that—my reasons are my own, of concern only to Nash and myself, and if he is happy with the situation, then you should respect his choice. He's a man, not a foolish boy suffering from a fit of gallantry."

She glared at his brother. "And, yes, he is gallant, but you should be proud of that and not dismiss it with a sneer. If there were more gallant men in the world, it would be a better place."

She took a couple of deep breaths and when she spoke again, it was in a calmer voice. "You may call me a fortune hunter, and I admit, I do want the security and the position—and the pretty dresses and jewels that come with it."

Lady Gosforth made a rude sound.

"Snort all you want, I won't deny they appeal," Maddy told her. "I'm as human as the next girl. But if you think that's the only appeal, or even the main appeal, you couldn't be more wrong." She glared at the old lady. "Have you *looked* at your nephew, really looked? Have you spoken to him? Do you even *know* him? Because if you did, you couldn't possibly think any woman would marry him for his fortune."

Lady Gosforth stared down her long arrogant nose, as if Maddy were an insect, and in the most skeptical of tones drawled, "You would have me believe you desire my nephew for himself alone?"

"I don't give a fig for what you believe!" Maddy snapped her fingers. "But I will make him a better wife than any of those blue-blooded girls on your precious list."

"Pshaw! You haven't the first idea how to support his career."

"No, I don't," Maddy admitted. "Yet. But I will learn, just see if I don't. I might not have lived in my father's house for most of my life, but it was a gentleman's establishment, and I ran it for the last year of his life. My mother and grandmother also trained me in some of the accomplishments of a lady—"

"Some?"

"I may not play the pianoforte or paint in watercolors, but my Italian is excellent," Maddy responded coolly. She scorned to hide the deficiencies of her education to this vile old busybody.

"Your manners, however"—Lady Gosforth started a new row of knitting; it seemed such an incongruous occupation for such an elegant woman—"leave a great deal to be desired."

"My manners are appropriate to the company in which I find myself," Maddy flashed.

The finely plucked brows rose in faint incredulity at her blunt speaking. Maddy felt a spurt of satisfaction. She would not be cowed by this arrogant old woman.

She took a deep breath and continued, "I am not like the girls on your list, I know. I am not beautiful or rich, I haven't received a fine education, and I no longer have any family, let alone one with influence. But unlike your girls, I'm not spoiled and I've never been indulged. I know that nothing worthwhile comes without hard work, I have courage and brains and determination. You think I'm greedy, and perhaps I am, but I'm not selfish. And I *will* be a good wife to Nash."

Lady Gosforth stopped knitting and gave Maddy a hard look. "Such a good wife, in fact, that he is talking about giving up his career as a diplomat and becoming a country squire."

Maddy blanched. "That's not true." It couldn't be.

"It is," Lady Gosforth said. "He told me so this very day. Said he'd developed an interest in agricultural endeavors."

"Nash?" Marcus exclaimed in incredulity. "Interested in agriculture? What rot."

"Precisely, Marcus. It's as plain as the nose on your face that Nash is contemplating giving up the career he has worked so hard for and excels at, simply because he's been forced into a *mésalliance* with a chit who is no more suited to be a diplomat's wife than her maid." She turned to Maddy and added, "He knows that you will drag him down."

Maddy swallowed, her throat dry. "I *won't* drag him down,"

she said in a low, fierce voice. "I *won't* let him resign from his job and I *will* make him a good wife. I don't expect you to believe it or to take my word for it; time will prove me right."

She took a few steps toward the door, then stopped. She wanted to get everything off her chest while her temper was up. She might not have the courage later. Or the opportunity. "I *will* marry Nash, and nothing you can say or do will change my mind. And I mean to make a success of the marriage. But you"—her glance took in both Lady Gosforth and Lord Alverleigh—"you still have a choice."

Lady Gosforth exchanged an opaque look with Marcus. "We have a choice, do we? And what might that be?"

Maddy straightened her back. "You can continue to undermine me, whispering in corners and sniping behind my back, or you can help me make a success of my marriage to Nash, help me learn the things I must learn to help him with his career. And help me make him happy."

She looked at Marcus, so like Nash, but with none of the warmth, and his aunt, who stared back with narrowed, gimlet eyes. "So which is it to be?" Maddy finished.

There was a long silence. Lady Gosforth examined the rings on her elegantly manicured, gnarled hands. Lord Alverleigh picked an invisible piece of fluff off his sleeve. Closing ranks.

Maddy had expected indifference; nevertheless, a ball of disappointment settled in her stomach.

"Then," she said with resolution, "I will manage it on my own." She turned to leave.

Lady Gosforth's voice stopped her. "I was not whispering."

"My apologies, Lady Gosforth, you are quite correct. You have a very carrying voice and your words were audible halfway down the corridor." Maddy inclined her head in ironic concession.

"Young woman!" Lady Gosforth rapped, interrupting Maddy's attempt to make a dignified exit yet again.

She swung around. "What?"

"Do you love my nephew?"

"That," Maddy said, "is none of your business." And finally she stalked from the room.

* * *

"*H*as she gone?" Lady Gosforth asked Marcus.

Marcus looked out into the corridor and nodded.

Lady Gosforth sat back in her chair and gave a large sigh. "What do you make of that?"

Marcus gave her an enigmatic look. "Nash won't thank you for interfering, you know."

"Pshaw! Interfering? I never interfere." Lady Gosforth twirled her lorgnette on its ribbon. "I like the gel! She has the kind of spirit you don't see in the mealy mouthed chits of today."

"She certainly has spirit," Marcus agreed.

"And breeding."

"Breeding? How do you surmise that?"

"Of course there's breeding. Did she once treat you or me as anything but an equal? Was there even a sniff of toadyism? The slightest attempt to ingratiate? No, she slapped me down, stood there in that atrocious rag of a dress, flung my accusations in my teeth, took me to task, and even had the face to call me an obnoxious woman."

"An obnoxious *old* woman," Marcus corrected her, earning himself a sharp rap over the knuckles with a fan.

"You completely misled me about the gel."

"Me? I never said a—"

"She'll lead that boy a merry dance, and she'll make him a splendid wife. She's in love with him, of course."

"In love? How can you possibly know that?"

"Dolt!" She smacked him again with her fan. "To anyone but a thick-headed Renfrew, it's obvious. The real question is, does Nash love her?"

"It's my opinion he's besotted," Marcus said. "But that could be the result of his accident."

His aunt made a rude noise. "Accident! An accidental wedding, to be sure." She gave a spurt of caustic laughter. "What fun! I'm so glad that I let myself be dragged to the wilds of Wiltshire. Now don't lollygag around, boy, help me to my feet. I have a wedding to organize." She bounced up with no help from anyone.

"Nash has already made the wedding arrangements," Marcus said.

"Pshaw!" His aunt dismissed Nash's abilities with a scornful wave. "Arrangements? He's marrying the gel in some hasty, hole-in-the-corner fashion in some poky and obscure village church."

"He has arranged a bishop to be present."

Lady Gosforth sniffed. "Only one? I suppose that will have to do. But what has he done about her dress? And clothing for those children? And what about afterward?"

Marcus gave her a blank look.

"Exactly! That child has no family to support her—and don't look at me like that, I know she has a gaggle of siblings, but pray, what use are children? It's a mature and knowledgeable woman the gel needs, and as usual, it falls to me to do what must be done."

O dious, arrogant old woman.

Maddy was still shaking with anger . . . or reaction . . . or something. She should have walked on, pretended not to hear. What was that saying about eavesdroppers never hearing any good?

Part of her was glad she'd given the old harridan a piece of her mind. It was immensely satisfying. If only she didn't feel the slightest bit sick about it.

She hated fights. Her wretched, wretched temper.

And now she was so late for her waltzing lesson Nash had probably given up on her and gone riding. She wouldn't blame him if he had.

She would, however, blame him for thinking about resigning his job—if it was true, of course, and she was by no means convinced it was. Though Lady Gosforth had seemed quite sure.

How could he even consider such a thing? He loved his work.

She reached the green saloon just as someone played the opening chords of a waltz on the pianoforte. Maddy eased open the door and peeped in. And watched transfixed.

The carpet had been rolled back to make a dance floor. Tibby, Mrs. Delaney, was at the pianoforte.

Two couples stood on the floor, ready to commence. Jane

and Susan were partners. Jane bowed and Susan curtsied—both very nicely, Maddy thought proudly. She'd taught them, as Grand-mère had taught her. The girls wore their pretty new dresses. Their faces were bright with concentration and excitement. Maddy smiled mistily. Her little sisters, growing up before her eyes, preparing for their new life.

Oh, yes, indeed, she would marry Nash Renfrew. To secure this future for her little brothers and sisters she would probably have married a gargoyle.

But Nash Renfrew was no gargoyle. She watched him now, tall and elegant and as handsome a man as she'd ever dreamed of. He bowed gracefully to his very diminutive partner.

Lucy made a deep, wobbly curtsy, then bounced up in triumph. She gripped his hands and carefully climbed onto his feet, standing with one small foot on each large boot. Maddy swallowed.

"Ready?" Nash asked the little girl.

Lucy nodded. Tibby played the opening bars and off they danced, tall man and tiny girl standing on his feet, her little hands clinging to his in an excited death grip.

They circled, first in a very slow *clump-clump-clump, clump-clump-clump*, then faster and faster as Lucy became used to the rhythm and the movement. Soon they were stepping to the music, then twirling around the room.

Maddy's eyes misted up. Lucy was so proud, so thrilled. Once, Nash swept her up in an arc through the air and she squealed with delight, then he settled her deftly back on his boots and they continued as before.

"Maddy, Maddy, look at me, I'm dancing!" Lucy caught sight of her and shrieked gleefully. "Me and Mr. Rider are dancing a waltz!"

Maddy laughed and clapped and nodded, halfway to tears.

Even if she hadn't already fallen head over heels in love with Nash Renfrew, watching him now with her little sisters, she fell in love with him again.

Do you love my nephew? Of course she loved him. How could she not?

The music finished, and again, Nash made an elegant bow. Lucy, a little dizzy from the dance and also from the excitement, began a curtsy, wobbled, then landed with a bump on her bottom.

She looked up, dismayed. Her lower lip quivered, but before she could burst into mortified tears, Nash bent and swept her up in a dizzying arc, whooshing her high above his head, and twirling her around until she screamed with delight again.

He deposited her on chair saying, "Thank you for the dance, Miss Lucy. Miss Jane and Miss Susan, well done, you were grace personified and a credit to your teacher, who is clearly brilliant." They giggled, as he'd intended.

"And now," he turned to Maddy with a gleam in his eye, "for your older sister."

"I'm sorry, Mr. Renfrew," Tibby interrupted, "but we must finish now." She blushed slightly. "I need to feed my son."

"Yes, of course," Nash said. "Thank you, Tibby, for playing so beautifully for us." The girls, to Maddy's pride, chimed in with their thanks.

"I'm sorry. It's my fault for coming so late," Maddy said. "Girls, it's nearly four o'clock, and Mrs. Deane and Lizzie will be expecting you in the nursery for the final fitting of your dresses for the wedding. I'll be up later."

Tibby and the girls left and suddenly the room was too quiet, too empty. Maddy wiped her palms nervously on her dress, hoping the trepidation she felt didn't show. But if his aunt was right and he was considering resigning his job, she had to talk to him about it at once.

"I can manage without music." Nash held out his hands to her, his blue, blue eyes smiling. "It won't hurt a bit, I promise."

She swallowed. Maybe she should get the lesson over with first. And then talk. "All right."

"You put this hand here." Nash placed her hand on his shoulder. "And I place my hand here." Just above the curve of her waist. His fingers were inches from her breast.

She pulled back, frowning. "Ladies and gentlemen don't touch when they're dancing, except for their hands."

"That's why the waltz caused such a scandal when it first appeared in ballrooms. Now it's so widely accepted only the dowdiest prudes refuse to dance it."

She would not be a dowdy prude. She gave a curt little nod and moved back into position.

Nash said, "It's a one-two-three step, and all you need to do is to relax and trust me. On the first step, I will move forward with my left foot, and you will move backward with your right. After that just follow my moves. Now, on the count of three: one, two, three."

They moved off and almost immediately she tried to steer him in the direction she wanted. He stopped. "The man is supposed to lead," he told her. "The woman follows."

"Lead then," she said.

Again they stepped off in perfect harmony, but half a dozen steps later, she was trying to steer him to the left while he wanted her to go right. The trouble was she needed to have it out with him, and while her emotions were in such a turmoil, she couldn't concentrate on the wretched dance.

"It's a matter of trust," he murmured in her ear. "The children did it instinctively."

"They're children, they trust easily."

"The trouble is, you've been running your life for so long by yourself that you're used to being in control. But it's like marriage. I lead, you follow, and we move forward together as a team."

It was the perfect opening. She dropped his hand and stepped back. "But you don't think that about marriage, do you? You don't expect us to move forward, you think I'll drag you down." Her voice shook on the last part of the sentence.

"What?"

"That's what your aunt said." She bit her lips to stop them trembling.

"Well, she's wrong. I don't think anything of the sort." Nash was outraged. "I'd never say such a thing. Or even think it," he added angrily, seeing the doubt in her eyes. And the hurt. He reached to take her hands but she snatched them away. He swore under his breath.

She folded her arms in what he recognized was a defensive position and said, "Then why did you tell her you're considering resigning your position in the diplomatic service and becoming a country squire?"

"Blast Aunt Maude for an interfering old woman!"

"I quite agree, but is it true?" She waited.

Nash forced himself to calm. "I am considering it," he said coolly, "though nothing is decided."

"Why?"

He cast around for the most convincing way to put it. "I've never had the opportunity to run my own estate before. It interests me. And I find I enjoy country life. I could breed horses, like Harry, and—"

"Fustian!"

"Fustian?" He wasn't used to people, especially women contradicting him. Apart from Aunt Maude.

"Complete and utter fustian," she said composedly. "You're afraid I'll be a disaster in diplomatic circles."

"I am not!" He denied it indignantly. He hadn't though any such thing. Out of her depth, perhaps, but not a disaster.

"You are. You haven't said it, and perhaps you haven't thought it in so many words, but that's what's behind this. And I won't have it." She lifted her chin in a challenge.

God, but she was adorable when her temper was up. He raised an eyebrow. "You won't?"

"No, I won't. Have a little faith in me, Nash Renfrew. I might not have been raised in government circles, but I will learn. And manage. And have a little faith in yourself. A few mistakes on my part will not reflect on you and the years of excellent service you have given your country."

He blinked at the confidence she had in him. The pride. And felt ashamed that he'd doubted her, even for a minute.

"Don't listen to that horrid old aunt of yours."

"She's not so bad when you get to—"

"You and I will make an excellent team. And we're going to be very happy."

He knew that. He was already very happy. Frighteningly happy. She wasn't going to call off the marriage. For a second he'd feared she might.

Maddy swept on. "I won't be hidden away at Whitethorn simply because I might fail. All my life I've been stuck in the country, dreaming dreams of how life could be, of travel, adventures, and lo—" She broke off. "And now I have the chance to make those dreams come true," she amended.

Nash swore silently and tried not to wonder about the word she'd bitten off so abruptly.

She opened her mouth, closed it, drew a deep breath, and said quietly, "You are the man of my dreams, Nash Renfrew, and if it is truly your heart's desire to live the rest of your life at Whitethorn, then I'll live there with you gladly."

He opened his mouth to respond, but she held up her hand to stop him, and continued, "But I think you want a brilliant diplomatic career, and I would love to be a part of it. Not just for you, but for myself, to travel and meet people and serve my country, too, as your wife. If you could bring yourself to trust me, we could have a glorious life together. But if I do fail—"

"You won't," he said and took her in his arms. "I never for a minute thought you might fail. I did wonder if I was asking too much of you," he admitted, "but if you are sure . . ."

"I'm very sure." She slipped her arms around him, her eyes shining with faith and . . . and something else.

A fist closed around Nash's heart. He swallowed, unable to think of a thing to say in the face of such a gift.

So he kissed her. Long, hard, and possessively.

And then they danced. And this time they moved as one, locked together in a slow-moving embrace, their bodies touching from chest to thigh.

At one point he murmured, "There's supposed to be several inches between our bodies."

"I'll try to remember," she said.

"Good." He pulled her closer.

*M*r. Benson has sent a message up to say you're wanted— we're both wanted—in the front anteroom at your earliest convenience, miss," Lizzie said from the door as Maddy finished dressing for dinner.

"Me? Why would he want me?"

"No idea, Lizzie, so let's find out." Benson, the butler, must think Maddy would need her maid with her, which meant it was serious. They hurried downstairs toward the anteroom nearest the front door. A rumble of male voices came from within.

When Maddy entered she found Nash and Benson with a big, brawny man of about thirty with dark, curly hair and very tanned skin. Dressed in a smart blue coat with large brass buttons, tight, dark breeches, and shiny black boots, he had a tough, vaguely nautical air. Maddy had never seen him before in her life.

Behind her Lizzie gasped. Maddy turned in time to see Lizzie blanch and take two uncertain steps. Slowly Lizzie's knees buckled.

Nash and Benson leapt forward to catch her, but the big, tough seaman was faster than all of them. He caught Lizzie before she hit the floor and swept her into his arms, cradling her against his chest. "Lizzie? Lizzie, love, it's Reuben." He stroked her cheek, his big, work-roughened hands.

"Smelling salts, ma'am?" Benson proffered a small bottle. Maddy took it and waved it under Lizzie's nose. She sneezed, screwed up her nose, and opened her eyes. She stared at the man who held her so tightly.

"Reuben?" Lizzie whispered.

"Aye, Lizzie, love, I've come back to you," he said softly. "Come a long way, I have. Your Uncle Bill told me I'd find you here. He said you'd become a lady's maid. Had enough of cows, love?"

"Put me down," Lizzie said.

Reuben carefully placed her back on her feet. "All right now, love?"

"Just perfect," Lizzie said and smacked him hard across the face. "Where have you been all this time?"

"I—" Reuben began.

"No, don't tell me, I don't want to know. Had your fun with whoever it was, and now she's kicked you out and you've come crawling back."

"No, I—"

"Well, just you think again, Reuben Brown! I wouldn't have you back if—mmph!" Her tirade came to an abrupt end as Reuben lifted her off her feet and kissed her. Lizzie struggled, kicking and punching.

Nash stepped forward to intervene but Maddy stopped him with a hand on his arm. A moment later Lizzie's struggles faded, and she was returning the big man's kisses, her arms twined around his neck and her legs lifting—quite scandalously—to wrap around his middle.

"Now, lass, you'll shock the good folk here." Reuben eased

Lizzie back to her feet. Lizzie glanced at Maddy and gave her a sheepish grin. Then she remembered her grievances and gave her errant husband an unconvincing glare. "You'd better explain yourself to my satisfaction, Reuben Brown, or that's the last one of those you'll get from me!"

Reuben winked at Maddy, then straightened Lizzie's cap, which had almost fallen off, and kissed her on the nose, ignoring the irritated swat she gave him in return. "No need to take on," he told her. "There was never anyone but you, lass, and you should know that."

"Then where have you been all this time?"

"I was press-ganged," Reuben said simply. "Went to town to buy the black bull, and before the sale, had an ale with some lads celebrating a wedding. They must've slipped sommat into the drink. Next thing I knew my wits were addled and I was on a cart bound to Bristol—a member of the Royal Navy."

"Press-ganged?"

Reuben nodded. "I've spent the last couple of years sailing the seven seas in the service of Mad King George. India, the Americas, Tahiti—you name it, I've been there."

"Why didn't you let me know?"

"How? No post offices in foreign parts. Besides, I couldn't write and you can't read."

"I can now," Lizzie told him with pride.

"Me, too." Reuben grinned with a flash of white teeth. "A shipmate taught me to read and write. I'm an educated man now. And"—he took out a leather pouch and jangled it—"I've still got the money for the breeding bull and a bit of extra besides."

Lizzie's jaw dropped. "You didn't spend it?"

He grinned. "No black bulls at sea."

"Oh, Reuben," Lizzie breathed.

Reuben's face softened. "I missed you mortal bad, Lizzie."

Nash nudged Maddy and jerked his head. Reluctantly she agreed. She was dying of curiosity, but Lizzie and her long-lost husband needed to be alone. "Lizzie, take Reuben away where you two can be private. Give him something to eat and spend as long as you need catching up and sorting out your plans. I won't need you until tomorrow."

"Lizzie will be giving her notice, ma'am," Reuben said quickly.

Lizzie thumped him on the arm. "I speak for meself, Reuben Brown. I haven't decided whether to take you back, yet."

"Have you not?" Reuben said with an unworried grin.

Lizzie tried to look severe and failed. "Can this big lummox stay here with me tonight, Miss Maddy?" she asked, blushing.

"Yes, of course," Maddy said and hugged her. "I'm so glad for you, Lizzie." She gave Reuben a clear, direct look. "Lizzie is my friend, Mr. Brown, and she'll always have a place with me if she needs it."

"And for that I thank you, ma'am," Reuben said easily. "She won't be needin' it, but I'm grateful she's had a friend like you while I was gone. Her Uncle Bill told me what you done for Lizzie and I'm in your debt."

"Thank you ever so much, Miss Maddy. I'll stay with you until the wedding. Give this man time to find us somewhere to live." Lizzie glanced up at her husband with a glowing expression, turned, and dragged Reuben toward the stairs.

Nash laughed softly and wrapped his arm around Maddy's waist. "Couldn't we take a leaf out of their book and just disappear upstairs for the rest of the day? And night," he murmured.

She sighed longingly. "I wish we could. Propriety is such a burden at times, is it not?"

Nash came to her room that night, as he had every other night, but he didn't bring her a drink, or compliment her hair, or make light conversation about the day, as he usually did.

He simply strode into the room, and without a word, swept her into his arms and kissed her, deeply, passionately, so that by the time he finished, she was on her bed, her senses spinning, her nightgown up around her neck, and her legs locked ecstatically around him.

She wasn't sure if he'd been inspired by the romance of Lizzie and Reuben's reunion, or whether it was a result of their argument about his plans to give up diplomacy. Either way, she didn't care.

But he lifted himself a little away from her, cupped her face between his hands, and fixed her with an intent gaze. "I do have faith in you," he told her. His blue eyes glittered in the candlelight. "More than faith."

And then he proceeded to make love to her with a bone-melting combination of tenderness and intensity, and as the candles guttered in their sockets, she shattered in his arms, tears pouring down her cheeks.

Shattered. And was made whole.

He hadn't said the words she ached to hear, but he'd shown her, in more than words. Nash Renfrew had given himself to her, as much as he was able. It was enough.

It would have to be.

Twenty-three

The day of the wedding dawned clear and bright, a perfect spring day. Maddy woke alone. Since they'd arrived at Whitethorn Manor two days before, she'd slept alone. Nash's decision. Some peculiar masculine form of honor, she supposed. She didn't care what the servants thought, she missed him.

Amazing how she could sleep alone for years, then in a matter of a few weeks find that a lanky masculine body curled around her had become essential to a good night's sleep.

Lizzie brought her a hearty breakfast on a tray, but Maddy's stomach was too full of butterflies to eat. She forced herself to nibble on a warm roll and drink some hot chocolate. Lizzie ate the bacon and eggs, saying, "A shame to waste it, miss."

After a long, hot bath, using some delicious-smelling French soap delivered by Nell's dresser, Maddy dressed for her wedding.

Her dress was the most beautiful she'd ever seen, let alone worn. Giselle and Claudine had outdone themselves. Made of heavy white satin, the bodice was covered in fine, handmade

Brussels lace to just below the waist. The same lace rose from the hem to midthigh, like foam rising up the dress.

Lizzie and Cooper, Lady Nell's maid, lifted the dress carefully over Maddy's head, careful not to disturb her hair. Lizzie had outdone herself, twirling Maddy's hair into a knot high on the crown and letting it fall in a tumble of artless curls. The hairstyle looked soft and pretty but was designed to bear the weight of a long lace train held in place by a slender tiara.

Maddy owned no jewelry, only Grand-mère's locket, which Grand-mère had worn as a bride, one of the few things she'd saved from the Terror that Maddy hadn't sold.

But how to wear it? She'd long ago sold the gold chain that held it. Maddy didn't want to pin it onto the dress and risk tearing the fine satin, but she wasn't going to be married without it.

"Perhaps you could string it on a white satin ribbon, miss," Cooper suggested. "Tie it around your neck."

They were searching for a suitable ribbon when a knock sounded at the door. Lizzie went to answer it. She returned with an air of suppressed excitement. "Mr. Nash said to give you this, with his compliments, miss." She handed Maddy an oblong box covered in creamy velvet.

"Oh," Maddy whispered as she opened it. Inside was a pearl necklace, along with a pair of diamond and pearl earrings, the most beautiful she'd ever seen.

She took out the necklace and held it against her neck. There was a small clasp at the center. Suddenly breathless, she opened the clasp and hooked on her grandmother's locket. The clasp snapped shut and she stared at it in amazement. It was as if the necklace had been designed solely to hold her grandmother's locket. "It's perfect. But how . . . ?"

"Mr. Nash asked me about jewelry, miss, and I told him you only had this," Lizzie confided. "You showed it to me once, and told me it was your gran's."

"And he had a necklace especially made to fit it." Maddy's eyes swam. How could he have known how much it meant to her?

She tried to put the necklace and earrings on, but her hands were shaking so much she had to let Lizzie and Cooper do it for her.

She stared at her reflection in the looking glass, at the beloved locket gleaming at her neck in its frame of pearls, at the diamonds and pearls dangling from her ears.

Grand-mère, see what he did for me? So I can wear your locket for my wedding.

"*A*re you ready, Maddy?" John asked. Dressed in his new, smart, formal suit, her little brother was taking his role as head of the family very seriously. Had he grown taller in the last few weeks? she wondered. Or was it simply that he'd been modeling himself on Nash and his brothers and held himself taller?

The boys hero-worshipped all the men, Nash and Harry in particular, and Nash's care for them all, and Harry's attitude to Nell and Torie, had certainly rubbed off on John and Henry. Several times Maddy had been caught between laughter and tears, realizing that some strange action by John or Henry was actually a small-boy attempt to be protective of her. It was very, very sweet.

"I'm ready," she told him. They stepped into the church and paused to let their eyes to adjust to the dimmer light. It smelt of beeswax, brass cleaner, and flowers—flowers brought by the ladies of the parish: graceful sheaves of foxglove, chrysanthemum, and delphinium; branches of lilac, lilies, daffodils, and sweet-scented stocks.

To Maddy's surprise every pew was filled and people stood around the walls. Lavishly dressed, elegant strangers, as well as the new friends who'd drawn Maddy into their close-knit circle. Harry and Nell had driven down two days before with Ethan and Tibby. Luke had come with his mother and sister, who loved weddings, and brought his friend, Rafe Ramsey, and Rafe's lovely dark-haired wife, Ayisha.

Most of the villagers had crammed into the church as well, all dressed in their Sunday best. Maddy looked out over the sea of hats and her eyes blurred. Every village woman who'd ever had a hat refurbished by Maddy was wearing it now, at her wedding.

Maddy started trembling. So much love and goodwill was gathered here . . . for her. It was overwhelming. She'd felt so alone for so long.

The music started and John and Maddy walked slowly
down the aisle, followed by Jane, Henry, Susan, and Lucy.
Maddy was vaguely aware of Nash's brothers standing beside
him at the altar, of the bishop, gorgeous in his robes, of Mr.
Matheson beaming, and Mrs. Matheson at the organ, of a sea
of faces, some beloved, some strange, most smiling, Lady
Gosforth dabbing lace to her eyes and Lizzie smiling wistfully,
but Maddy's gaze never wavered from Nash, who waited, tall
and handsome, his blue eyes fixed on her, blazing . . .

He held out his hand to her and she took it, glad of the
strong, male warmth of him. Rev. Matheson glanced at Nash,
gave a little nod, and began, *Dearly beloved . . .*

The words passed in a blur . . . *ordained for the procreation
of children* . . . A child of her own, hers and Nash's. Perhaps in
Russia . . . *any just cause why they may not lawfully be joined
together, let him now speak* . . . She would to have to speak
soon, make her vows. Would her voice even work?

"Stop the wedding," a voice thundered through the church.
"That woman is legally promised to me."

There was a sudden silence, then a buzz of speculation. As
if in a dream, Maddy turned. "Mr. Hulme," she whispered. Her
knees buckled under her, but Nash caught her and held her
against him, his arm like a band of steel around her, holding
her up, claiming her.

"What is the meaning of this, sir?" the bishop boomed.

Mr. Hulme strode down the aisle waving a document.
"Madeleine Woodford is promised to me and I have the paper
to prove it."

"Hulme? The old goat?" Nash's eyes blazed with a martial
light. "He dares to interrupt my wedding? Look after Maddy,"
he said and passed her to Marcus, then stepped out into the
aisle to face Mr. Hulme.

"Hulme?" Marcus asked Maddy. "George Hulme?"

She nodded, her eyes glued to the drama taking place before her.

Daunted by the expression on Nash's face, Mr. Hulme
stopped dead in midmarch. He snapped his fingers and a liver-
ied servant stepped forward. A second servant stood behind,
his collar turned up high.

As one, Harry, Luke, Ethan, and Rafe stepped forward to flank Nash.

"Magnificent collection of masculinity, don't you think?" Lady Gosforth's comment was audible. A few titters sounded in the nearby pews.

"This is a house of God!" Rev. Matheson and the bishop boomed almost in unison.

Mrs. Matheson appeared at Maddy's side. "Come, my dear, wait in the vestry. The gentlemen will sort everything out."

But Maddy could see how the gentlemen were planning to sort it out. With fists. She shook off the restraining hands and pushed between Nash's friends. "I won't have my wedding turned into a brawl. I can deal with this."

Nash took her hand and said firmly, "*We* will deal with it."

The bishop and Rev. Matheson made their way to the no man's land between Mr. Hulme and the wedding party. "Show me this document," the bishop demanded.

Mr. Hulme handed over the paper, saying loudly, "Sir John Woodford promised me his daughter, Madeleine, in marriage, in exchange for debts incurred by him. This is a legal document properly signed, sealed, and witnessed."

A horrified buzz rippled through the church, followed almost immediately by a sea of shushing from people who wanted to hear.

"I am not a piece of property," Maddy snapped. "I told you before, I don't care how many seals it has or what my father promised you, I repudiate that document. And I'm marrying Nash Renfrew, so go away."

"Good gel!" Lady Gosforth said, and there was a murmur of agreement from the congregation.

The bishop finished scanning the document. "As I understand it, Miss Woodford is over the age of consent, and I can see no reason why she should be bound by such a document. Slavery is illegal in England and women cannot be sold for debts." He handed it back to Mr. Hulme. "Take yourself off, sirrah, and let the wedding service resume."

The congregation burst into spontaneous applause, and Marcus, Harry, Luke, Ethan, and Rafe seized Mr. Hulme and his servants by the collar and began to march them out. There was a loud yelp and a scuffle, then Luke dragged one of the servants forward.

"Miss Woodford, meet the Bloody Abbot," Luke said, shaking the man like a dog shakes a rat. "He's wearing the black eye I gave him, among other bruises. No wonder he was skulking in the background."

The congregation buzzed and shushed furiously.

"The villain whose shoulder I winged the other night?" Marcus leaned forward and poked the man just below the shoulder and the man yelped again. "So he is," Marcus agreed. "Well spotted, Ripton."

"Terrorize my woman and children will you, you filthy cur!" Nash strode toward the cringing man, a murderous light in his eye.

"Not in the house of God," the bishop shrieked. Maddy grabbed Nash's arm and hung on with all her strength. Mr. Hulme and the Bloody Abbot had done enough to spoil her life; they were *not* going to ruin her wedding.

"It weren't my fault," the man whined. "Mr. 'Ulme, 'e made me do it, said to drive the girl out of 'er cottage, starve her out, or burn her out so she 'ad no choice but come back to 'im."

A loud buzz of outrage rose at his words and the man hastily added, "But I never 'urt nobody, I swear."

"That's not all Hulme's done," Marcus said when there was a slight lull.

"What?" Nash demanded savagely.

"In my investigations into the illegal depredations of your man Harris," Marcus began.

"Harris? Harris?" The whisper went through the church. Then instant, hushed silence.

Marcus continued, "Among Harris's papers I found a promissory note. One hundred pounds to be paid to Harris when a certain woman is evicted from her home, hounded out of the district, and forced to return to Leicestershire. Signed by one George Hulme."

Five large menacing men turned toward Hulme, who turned gray and backed toward the exit, his lips writhing with fear, babbling, "Lies, all lies . . ." But nobody believed him.

"Hold him!" Nash snapped and a dozen men responded. Nash took a step forward. Maddy clung to his arm and he glanced down at her tense, white face. Slowly the ugly light died from his eyes.

"Would someone ensure these . . . men are delivered to the authorities?" Nash said without taking his eyes off Maddy. "There's a brave and beautiful bride here who's suffered quite enough at the hands of this scum, and I won't allow her wedding to be ruined. This is neither the time nor the place for anger or retribution—only joy. And beauty." He lifted Maddy's hand and kissed it.

Maddy's eyes misted up. She managed a tremulous smile.

"We'll take 'em, Mr. Renfrew, sir." It was Grainger, the groom from Whitethorn Manor, flanked by half a dozen burly fellows. "We'll haul 'em off to the magistrate, our pleasure, sir, ma'am."

"Thank you, Grainger," Nash said.

Grainger nodded to Maddy. "Beautiful, you look, miss. Bonniest bride this church has ever seen." There was a murmur of agreement from the congregation, and in seconds, Mr. Hulme and his two servants were bundled out of the church.

There was an audible sigh of relief in the church, then everyone began talking.

Nash slipped his arm around her. "Are you all right, sweetheart?"

"A bit shaky," Maddy admitted, "but very glad it's all over."

"Do you need some time to compose yourself, my dear?" Rev. Matheson asked anxiously. "Smelling salts? A brandy?"

Maddy took a deep breath. "No," she said. "I'd like to get on with my wedding, please." Nash's hand tightened around hers.

Rev. Matheson cleared his throat loudly, once, twice, but everyone was too excited to listen. The bishop joined him in a clerical throat-clearing duet and eventually the congregation settled down.

"Now, where were we?" the vicar said. "Oh, yes. If any man can show any just cause why they may not lawfully be joined together, let him now speak, or else hereafter forever hold his peace." He paused and there was not a breath, not a rustle in the church. "Nobody? Excellent, then let us continue . . ."

* * *

"Good-bye, good-bye." The carriage pulled away from Whitethorn Manor to the sounds of well wishes and laughter. The reception was over and the honeymoon begun.

Nash and Maddy settled back against the comfortably padded leather seats of Marcus's carriage. "Might as well take it as a wedding present," Marcus had grumbled, but Nash only wanted it for a few hours.

"The reception, at least, went well," Nash found himself saying. "Everyone seemed to have a good time."

The servants at Whitethorn had performed a miracle with the old house. No longer dusty and neglected, the old house now gleamed with polish and pride. Vases were bursting with greenery and flowers, the carpets, thoroughly beaten, glowed with ancient glory, the curtains were freshly washed and ironed, and the best linens, silverware, crockery, and crystal had been brought out of retirement and presented in pristine order. And the food was delicious—the cook had excelled herself.

"Yes, it was wonderful."

"The wedding less so," he added. "I expect people around here will be talking about it for many years to come." Ye gods, making small talk to his bride. He was absurdly nervous.

"Yes, but I don't mind. Even Mr. Hulme's interruption couldn't spoil it for me," Maddy told him. "And it's wonderful to start married life with all that behind us—Mr. Hulme, the Bloody Abbot. I was so shocked to discover it. I never once thought Mr. Hulme might be behind the Bloody Abbot."

"Me, neither. I was certain it was Harris. And that it was about the cottage, not the inhabitants." Nash stretched out his legs, crossing them at the ankle. Looking relaxed and in control. "Bow Street will hunt Harris down soon enough."

"I wonder how Mr. Hulme found me?" She slipped her arm through his and rested her cheek against his shoulder. "We ran away from him, you know, one day when he was away on business overnight. His housekeeper helped us. She knew how uncomfortable I felt. She had a cousin who was a carter and arranged for us to get a lift with him. Mr. Hulme never suspected we would ride in a slow-moving wagon. He actually passed us on the road, in pursuit of the stage coach, but we hid under a canvas cover."

Nash slid his arm around her. He hated to think of her being driven to such straits. "Why couldn't you leave openly?"

"He'd become very possessive. Even when I was a child, I felt uncomfortable around him. But his strangeness was growing. One day I saw him staring at Jane in the strangest way, as if he'd take her if he couldn't have me. I panicked." She sighed. "Later, after we'd settled in at the cottage, I wondered if I'd overreacted, exaggerated his strangeness."

"Which is why, when you were desperate, you were prepared to return." Nash put his arm around her. He'd come so close to losing her that day. He couldn't imagine how his life would be if he'd lost her. His arm tightened.

"Yes, but seeing him today, I know I did the right thing."

"In marrying me? Definitely."

She laughed. "You know I didn't mean that. Of course marrying you was the right thing to do. I meant I did the right thing in running away from Mr. Hulme. He's not . . . normal, is he?"

"No, he's not. But he's safely locked away now, and he'll never bother you or anyone again. So let us forget unpleasant matters and contemplate the prospect of our honeymoon." Nash leaned forward and pulled the blinds of the carriage down.

Maddy laughed. "This looks exciting."

"You are my prisoner, and if you don't behave, you will suffer a terrible punishment," he growled.

"Oh, I'm terrified. What's the punishment?"

"This." He kissed her.

"How very dreadful. Do it again."

"Baggage!" And he did it again.

A short time later the carriage drew to a halt.

"Why are we stopping?" Maddy asked. "Where are we?"

"No questions, prisoner," he told her. "Just close your eyes." He waited for Hawkins, the coachman, to carry out the instructions Nash had given him earlier. After a few minutes, Hawkins opened the carriage door. Nash got out of the carriage, and under the guise of lifting Maddy down, swept her into his arms.

"Thank you, Hawkins, that will be all," Nash said, stepping over the threshold through the open door, and kicking it shut behind him. He kissed Maddy and lowered her to the floor. "You may open them now."

"Ohh," she said on a long note of wonder as she looked around the cottage. "How . . . who?"

"Nell and Tibby and Ayisha and Lizzie and Aunt Maude—"

"Your *aunt*?" Maddy's jaw dropped. "I can't work her out. One minute she despises me, and the next thing . . ." She shook her head.

He laughed. "That's Aunt Maude. Loves to keep us all guessing. She masterminded this. Demanded to know where I was taking you for your wedding night and when I told her here, she was appalled. Ayisha suggested the changes—she and Rafe have a cottage retreat, apparently—but Nell and Aunt Maude ran the operation. And this is the result."

"I can barely recognize the place," Maddy breathed. "Look at these beautiful rugs. You always said it needed rugs." She kicked off her slippers, peeled off her stockings, and walked on the thick, deep, exotic Turkish rugs that covered the entire floor. "So soft . . ." She wiggled her toes in the deep pile.

Nash eyed her small pink toes and suppressed a harsh groan. He wanted her spread out bare on those thick, soft rugs. He wanted to taste those toes, and then work his way up, till his mouth found the core of salt-dark honey at her center . . . Heat slammed through him at the thought. He rammed it under control. Civilized, he told himself. On one's wedding night, one should approach one's bride with care and circumspection. And a certain degree of *politesse*.

A fire burned brightly, and freshly lit candles were scattered around the room, bathing everything in a soft light. Like the night they'd first made love, when she'd bared her silken beauty to his gaze and taken him into herself . . .

The worn, scrubbed table was covered with a richly embroidered tablecloth and was laid for two. An enormous hamper of food stood on a bench nearby, along with a crate of champagne and a pitcher of milk . . .

"Anything and everything one could desire," Maddy exclaimed, peeping into the hamper. "We could be here for days and not go hungry."

Nash nodded. He was starved, aching and ravenous, but not for anything in the hamper.

"And look at the bed." Maddy hurried over to it. "What a beautiful cover."

Only the faded red curtains were the same. Nash was fond of those curtains and had told his aunt not to touch them. But everything else was new. Fine white cotton sheets had replaced the threadbare old ones, and soft wool blankets and an eiderdown quilt lay on top.

Maddy ran her hands over the quilt and picked up a pillow, plumped it, and pressed her cheek against it. "Goose feather, Nash, come and feel," she invited. She sat on the bed and gasped. "They've replaced my straw mattress with a feather one. Nash you must feel this."

Her eyes met his. Her gaze slowly raked him from head to toe, lingering on the area that ached and throbbed in torment. Her eyes darkened and a smile as old as Eve teased her lips. "Yes, Nash, come and feel," she murmured. She wriggled back in sensuous pleasure and patted the bed invitingly.

Watching the feather-soft quilt slide beneath her bare calves, Nash cast any notions of control to the wind. In two strides, he crossed the room and launched himself onto the bed beside her.

With a low growl, he pushed her skirts up past her hips in a foam of lace and petticoats. And stared. She was bare to the waist, no drawers, just long, slender legs ending in a wine-colored triangle of soft curls.

His manhood surged, rock hard. Her thighs parted and she reached eagerly for him, fumbling at the fall of his breeches to release him, and then he was braced between her thighs, parting her gently and finding her ready, more than ready. He sank into her heated depths with a groan of satisfaction. She arched beneath him, urging him on with little cries and moans, and he plunged again and again, faster and faster, until with a roar of satisfaction, he climaxed.

Afterward, lightheaded and loose, he held her as his breathing slowly returned to normal. The sweat dried on his skin and the bliss evaporated with it.

Shame prickled his conscience. He'd just taken his new bride with all the greedy lack of finesse of a boy with his first woman, not even taking the time to undress or caress her, just dragging her skirts up and burying himself in her without a care for her pleasure or dignity. As if she were a prostitute.

Beside him, Maddy sat up and began straightening her clothes.

"I'm sorr—" he began.

"That," she said, "was a lovely appetizer." She grinned and kissed him. "I'm looking forward to the main course—and pudding—but first you must help me out of this dress. It's too pretty to have you ruin it the way you've ruined so many of my old nightgowns." She gave him a mischievous glance. "That's why I didn't wear any drawers, either. You should see my new underclothes, they're so beautiful I don't dare wear them for fear of what you might do to them."

Nash blinked. "You mean you didn't mind what I just did?"

She laughed. "I love what you just did, Nash, and I love you."

He froze. "What did you say."

She bit her lip as she realized what she'd just said. "I'm sorry, I didn't mean—it just slipped out. It's just that I'm so happy, and—"

"You didn't mean it?"

"Oh, I meant it." She gave him a clear look. "I just didn't mean it to slip out. I know you don't want our marriage to be complicated by things such as love and passion, and I did try, really I did. But I do love you. With all my heart"—she kissed him—"and body"—she kissed him again—"and soul." She kissed him for the third time, like a holy vow.

He lay still, staring up at her, frozen.

She sighed. "You'll just have to get used to it. It's going to keep slipping out, because I'm so full of love for you it keeps bubbling up like a spring."

He stared at her, agonized, his throat too thick to speak, unable to think of a thing to say. *She loved him.*

She smoothed his hair back from his forehead and added, "Don't look so appalled; you don't need to say anything. I know how you feel. I don't expect anything else from you. As long as you're faithful, and desire my body, I'll be happy." But the glow in her clear topaz eyes had dulled, and the smile wore an edge of wistfulness.

She slipped off the bed and padded across the floor, barefoot, her hair messy and falling down her back in tumbled curls, her bridal dress crushed. In a bright voice she said, "Now, come and open one of these bottles for me. I want some champagne. I was too nervous to eat or drink anything before the wedding, and now I find I'm ravenous."

So beautiful and generous, giving him everything, asking for nothing. She shamed him with her courage.

"No," he croaked.

She turned, puzzled. "You won't open the champagne for me?"

"No," he croaked again. It wasn't what he meant but his throat seemed clogged.

She shrugged. "Then I'll open it myself." She picked up a bottle and began to wrestle with the cork.

"No, you don't know how I feel." Nash forced out the words.

Holding the bottle against her, she swiveled slowly to face him. And waited, saying nothing.

"I was wrong," he said. "I didn't . . . understand." He stared at her, willing her to understand what he was trying to tell her. But she waited, frozen and silent, clutching the champagne bottle against her like a baby.

He cleared his throat, closed his eyes, took a deep breath, looked her in the eye, and said, "I love you, Maddy."

For an endless moment all he could hear was the sound of the fire crackling and hissing in the grate. An owl hooted on the wind, and then she whispered, "You love me?"

He nodded. "I love you." It was getting easier to say it now it was out. "I love you, Madeleine Renfrew, wholly and completely. With all my heart. And body. And probably soul, though I don't know so much about that."

With shaking hands, she put the champagne bottle down on the table. "You really love me?"

"I do. I have for the longest time. I was just too much of a coward to say it." He opened his arms and she flew into them.

"*I*t's why I wanted to spend our wedding night here," he told her after they'd made love for a second time, again with her dress rucked up around her waist. "I fell in love with you in this cottage, in this bed. And that day I left you, I hadn't gone more than a few miles when I knew I couldn't leave you. I thought I could marry you and still keep it to myself . . ."

"And not risk exposing yourself to what your father suffered?" she said.

He nodded, amazed and grateful for her understanding. "The risk is worth it—"

"There is no risk," she corrected him. "We're not like your parents. Just have faith." She kissed him. "And open the champagne."

He laughed. "Better than champagne, I have a pot of your honey here."

"Honey? But—"

"I've had plans for this honey for the longest time. Only first, you really do need to take off that dress . . ."

Twenty-four

❦

Make an entrance, Grand-mère always said. In the hall-way that led to the stairs, Maddy took a deep breath. Her first public test as Nash's wife.

The ball at Alverleigh House, the earl's residence in May-fair, had not yet commenced, but already it was the talk of the season. The cream of London society would be here tonight— European society if you counted the ambassdors—every one of them curious to meet—and judge—the nobody that Nash Renfrew had unaccountably married. And, of course, to meet the Grand Duchess Anna Petrovna—sister, daughter, and aunt of Czars.

Maddy didn't just have butterflies in her stomach, they were dragonflies . . . An entire flock, dipping and buzzing.

Lady Gosforth appeared at her elbow, superbly gowned in a ball gown of puce and gold lace. "Nervous?"

Maddy swallowed. "A little."

Lady Gosforth raised her lorgnette and gave Maddy a sweeping examination. The effect was enhanced by the enor-mous, magnificently embroidered turban from which sprouted

at least a dozen puce and gold plumes. She had the height—
and the nose—to carry it off.

Maddy waited calmly for the scrutiny to end. She knew
now that much of Lady Gosforth's imperious manner was
bluff. Still, in the old woman's eyes Maddy was yet to prove
herself a worthy wife for Nash.

Lady Gosforth gave a brisk nod. "Very nice, my dear. That
old gold color is perfect on you. And that topaz set both com-
plements it and matches your eyes." She peered through her
lorgnette at Maddy's necklace and frowned. "Most unusual.
Those gold designs look like some kind of insect."

Maddy touched her necklace and smiled. "Yes, they're
bees. I'm very fond of bees." Nash had given Maddy the topaz
necklace, earrings, and bracelet set that morning. He'd had it
especially made for her.

Lady Gosforth blinked. "Good God, are you? How very
odd. Never mind, it looks quite pretty anyway. And setting
your own style is to be admired."

Downstairs, people were beginning to gather. Maddy's
palms felt damp. She smoothed her long white gloves over
them. So far there were just the close friends and relatives
who'd dined with them before the ball, Nash's friends. Her
friends, too, now.

"There will be quite a few noses out of joint tonight, so be
on your guard."

Maddy nodded. She knew. All the girls Lady Gosforth had
picked out for Nash, for a start. And all those who resented an
outsider.

"Don't look so worried; it's a game," Lady Gosforth told
her. "One with serious consequences, but a game, nevertheless." She rapped Maddy's arm with her fan. "Parry, thrust, and
smile. Win and win gracefully, but if you can't, don't let them
draw blood."

Maddy grimaced. "Easier said than done."

"Most things worth doing are," said the elderly lady loftily.
"Not for nothing is it called polite society. But it's like the old
maps: *here be dragons*."

They reached the landing at the top of the grand staircase.
From here, Maddy would descend the stairs alone, all eyes on
her. She paused, willing the dragonflies to settle.

"Screw your courage to the sticking place and you'll not fail," Lady Gosforth told her.

"You're quoting *Macbeth* at me? *Lady* Macbeth?" Maddy asked with a choked laugh. "Are you perhaps suggesting I follow her example and murder my husband's more . . . inconvenient guests?"

Lady Gosforth gave a crack of laughter. "That's the ticket, show a bit of pepper! You'll do, my dear, you'll do." She gave her a little push. "Down you go. And don't let 'em see your nerves."

It might have been her grandmother speaking. Maddy took a deep breath and began the long descent down the staircase, trying to appear unaware of the many eyes on her.

This is it, Grand-mère. Wish me luck.

An hour later, the dragonflies had settled. Somewhat. Maddy stood with Nash, Marcus, and Aunt Maude at the entrance to the ballroom, greeting each guest as they arrived, being introduced as Nash's bride.

Lady Gosforth had given Maddy a guest list several days before, saying Maddy should commit to memory some of the more exalted names. She'd had made some notes against a few of them. Maddy was very grateful for it.

Better still, Nash murmured wicked little snippets about each couple as they arrived, with the result that Maddy forgot to be nervous and was able to curtsy and greet the guests in a more natural manner.

Everyone smiled, everyone was gracious. Still, you never knew when the sting was going to come. *Here be dragons.*

"Mrs. Renfrew, you are originally from Leicestershire, I'm told." A thin, elegant blonde in bronze silk and diamonds smiled warmly at her.

Maddy smiled warmly back. "That's correct, Lady Mannering."

"And yet nobody in Leicestershire has ever heard of you," the woman said, her smile thinning to a faint sneer. "Nobody. At. All." Her friends tittered, exchanging sly glances as they waited for Maddy's defense.

But Maddy had grown up in a country where the English and aristocrats were universally despised. If she could survive

the open hostility of French peasants, she could survive the
silken insults of an inadequately dressed skinny blonde. *Parry,
thrust, and smile.*

"No doubt because when I was a child, my mother and I
moved to France," Maddy responded with a smooth smile.
"I only recently returned to England, and my father had a serious hunting accident shortly afterward, so of course we did no
entertaining and attended none of the local gatherings. And
then we were in mourning . . . Have you been to France, Lady
Mannering?"

"No." Lady Mannering bared her teeth and moved sinu-
ously off.

"Nicely handled," Lady Gosforth murmured in her ear. "A
nasty piece of work, that one. Widow. Had her eye on Nash.
You're doing very well."

But Lady Mannering was only the first of many.

"One hears Woodford House has been let to tenants," the
Honorable Mrs. Lethbridge said, with a cold smile that told
Maddy she'd also heard about Papa's debts.

"Indeed it has," Maddy responded affably. "One would not
wish to leave the house uncared for and unoccupied while the
family is in Russia, would one? And one is so glad to have
found such excellent tenants."

It was a game. And she was far from alone. Nash never moved
far from her side, trusting her to manage, yet there, she knew, to
step in, if necessary. He had the knack of making the kind of
light, charming comment that defused tension. She resolved to
acquire it.

On Maddy's other side stood Lady Gosforth, declaring her
acceptance of Maddy by her manner and stance, if not the actual words. Even the earl, who never said much, showed his
support of her in small, significant ways.

The message was clear: Nash's family and friends supported this marriage. And his wife.

Many people were genuinely welcoming. Maddy curtsied
to an elderly duke and duchess, who nodded graciously at
Maddy, congratulated Nash on his marriage, invited Lady Gosforth to call with her niece next week, and tottered away.

Already the ball was declared a sad crush, by which Maddy
gathered it was a huge success.

Maddy had shown she could cope with the cut and thrust of sophisticated conversation. There was only one more hurdle: the Russian grand duchess. Once she'd arrived and Maddy was introduced, Maddy could leave her post and dance. She was looking forward to it so much. She and Nash had practiced every day, and for dancing she was ready, more than ready.

"Her Imperial Highness, the Grand Duchess Anna Petrovna Romanova, Grand Duchess of Russia." The name boomed out over the crowded ballroom

A hush fell over the room. Everyone turned toward the entrance. A tiny, magnificently robed old lady moved slowly forward, leaning on an ivory cane. She was flanked by half a dozen handsome escorts in glittering military uniforms and followed a small bevy of Russian ladies, clutching shawls and other necessities.

Nash, smiling, bowed deeply and said formally in English, "Welcome, Your Highness, to England." He added in French, "I hope your voyage from St. Petersburg was swift, smooth, and pleasant."

Everyone craned forward to hear.

The grand duchess gave a rusty laugh. "It was atrocious, dear boy. Luckily I am never seasick."

Returning to English, Nash introduced his brother and his aunt, and the grand old lady greeted them, then switched to French to comment on the brothers' likeness, the general handsomeness of the earl, and the elegance of his aunt.

The crowd pressed closer, the people in front whispering to those behind, reporting what the grand duchess said. Clearly English was not a language she used easily.

Then Nash drew Maddy forward. "May I present my bride, Mrs. Madeleine Renfrew."

Maddy sank into a slow, deep curtsy, suitable only for the highest rank of royalty. In the cottage in the woods, Grand-mère had made her practice it hundreds of times until she had it perfect, even though Maddy was certain she would never meet any kind of royalty.

Lady Gosforth gasped. Maddy froze for a second. Had she made a mistake? But Grand-mère's training held firm. She rose smoothly from the curtsy, and for the first time, met the grand duchess's gaze.

The old lady was smiling. "I didn't think any young girls knew how to do that anymore," she said to Nash in French. "So French, so graceful. It took me right back to my days in Versailles. Do you speak French, child? I find the English tongue barbarous."

"Yes, Your Highness, I am half French," Maddy responded in that language.

"Not just French, but the French of the Royal Court of Versailles," the grand duchess declared delightedly. "I spent some years there when I, too, was a young bride. They were the happiest days of my life. Who was your mother, child? Perhaps I knew her."

"My mother was Louise, the only daughter of Marianne de Rohan, Comtesse de Bellegarde."

A ripple of whispers spread through the room.

The grand duchess's brow furrowed. "De Rohan, de Rohan . . ." She shook her head. "There is something, but I cannot recall. She was at the court at Versailles, yes?"

"Yes, Your Highness, my grandmother was one of the queen's ladies."

"I knew all the queen's ladies—poor Marie Antoinette, such a terrible fate. She was a sweet lady. Your grandmother, was she . . . ?" She faded off delicately.

"No, Your Highness, Grand-mère escaped the Terror, though she lost her husband and son and most of her relatives. Maman escaped by marrying an Englishman."

The grand duchess tutted sympathetically. "Dreadful, the things people were driven to. It could never happen in Russia, thank God." She crossed herself.

"Maddy's grandmother survived by hiding among the beehives," Nash told her.

"The beehives?" The grand duchess stared. "She was Marie Antoinette's lady of the bees? But I remember her! She gave me honey. And it was delicious." She tilted her head like a little bird, examining Maddy, then nodded. "You have, I think, the same hair, now I come to recall her."

Maddy touched her hair wonderingly. "Do I, your Highness? Grand-mère's hair was white, as long as I knew her." It had turned white after her husband and son had been torn apart by the mob, she knew, but she'd never thought to wonder about the original color.

"That lovely dark auburn. I admired it greatly as a girl." The grand duchess beamed at Maddy. "And so, Marianne de Rohan's granddaughter has married my dear Mr. Renfrew. How delightful. You must visit me often in St. Petersburg. Give me your arm, child, and find me a chair. I would talk further with the granddaughter of my friend from Versailles." And she led Maddy across the room, followed by a buzz of conversation.

"A triumph!" Aunt Maude said in Nash's ear. "A complete triumph! I couldn't have planned it better if I'd tried."

Nash stared after his wife, dazed. "She's . . . amazing." He caught his breath. "I never knew. Why did she never tell me her grandmother was a countess?"

"Would it have made any difference?"

"No, of course not."

Lady Gosforth smiled. "She told me something of the sort when I first met her, but I dismissed it as empty boasting. So many people claim noble French relatives, knowing they're conveniently dead. "

"And what an extraordinary coincidence, Maddy's grandmother being an old friend of the grand duchess."

Lady Gosforth gave a genteel snort. "I very much doubt she was."

Nash gave her a sharp glance. "What do you mean? Why should the grand duchess make it up?"

"I don't mean she's lying. It's my belief that your wife reminded an old lady of her girlhood, and she has seized on the memory. She wants to remember a friendship with Maddy's grandmother and so she does. And why not? In a strange country, at the end of her life, when so many of her friends are dead . . ." She shrugged.

"Frankly, I don't care one way or the other," Nash said, gazing across the room to where his wife was getting the grand duchess settled. "That wonderful old lady has set my Maddy on the road to success."

Lady Gosforth nodded and took a deep, satisfied breath. "You can thank me later."

Nash gave her a stunned look. "Thank *you*? Even you could

not have planned this amazing coup. For arranging the ball, yes, of course I thank—"

"No, foolish boy. You told me you wanted an excellent marriage, *et voila!*" Lady Gosforth gestured, suddenly Gallic. "You have one. And after tonight, the whole world will know it. That curtsy! I couldn't have taught the dear child better myself! And she even has connections, even though they're all dead. It doesn't seem to matter. With your grand duchess eating out of her hand, my niece will become all the rage in the Russian court, just mark my words."

"I didn't marry her for her curtsy or her connections," Nash said. "And you had nothing to do with it."

"Of course not, dear boy. You fell off your horse—"

"I did not fall, the horse slipped."

"—and gave that stubborn Renfrew head the crack it needed to let you tumble into love. A perfect outcome for all concerned. And a personal triumph for me!" His aunt patted him on the cheek and sailed off to circulate and gloat.

The orchestra struck up a waltz. Nash cleaved a determined path through the crowded ballroom where a crowd had gathered around the grand duchess and her new *protégée*.

Her Imperial Highness, Grand Duchess Anna Petrovna Romanova, could find someone else to talk to. Nash wanted to dance with his wife.

Epilogue

Two nights before they departed for St. Petersburg, Lady Gosforth held a farewell party for Nash and Maddy at her London house. "Just a small, intimate affair," she'd told Maddy. "Quite paltry, really. A few friends, nothing more."

When Maddy informed Nash of this, he snorted with laughter but wouldn't explain why.

It was a wonderful night, a crowded, glittering reception, but for Maddy, the real farewell took place the next afternoon, when just the family and close friends gathered for tea.

It was an occasion of laughter and tears. Everyone brought presents.

Lady Gosforth gave gloves and warm fur-lined hats to the boys and white fur muffs and fur-lined bonnets for the girls. And for Maddy, a blue velvet cloak, fully lined with soft, luxurious fur, and a matching fur muff. "Gets cold in Russia, I'm told," she said gruffly, twitching it into place as Maddy tried it on.

"I used to think you detested me," Maddy admitted.

"No, my dear, I was simply testing you. And you passed with flying colors. The moment you told me to mind my own business, I knew you loved that boy of mine."

"How could you know from that?"

"If you'd been any sort of a schemer you'd have assured me you loved him more than life itself." Lady Gosforth smiled. "Instead you told me it was none of my business. And I knew then that it was love—new, tender, private, and precious. Too precious to be shared with a meddling, obnoxious old woman." She blinked away a tear. "Dratted piece of dirt in my eye."

Maddy, her own eyes misty with emotion, hugged her again. "I do love him, with all my heart. And I love you, too, Lady Gosforth. And you're not meddling, obnoxious, or old."

"Lady Gosforth? Lady Gosforth?" the old woman said crossly, scrubbing at her eyes with a wisp of lace. "Aunt Maude, if you please, young woman. You're family now."

Maddy smiled mistily. "I'll take good care of him, I promise."

"Pish, tush, foolish gel. It's his job to take care of you."

For the children, there were all sorts of things to help pass the time on the journey: knitting needles and wool, a chess set, a set of drafts, playing cards and books, none of which were of the improving sort, and blank journals, writing paper, and ink. "To write about your adventures in Russia," Tibby told them and, glancing at Jane, added, "and any stories you might dream up, as well."

Jane received a pair of red riding boots, John, a whip and a book about horses. Henry was delighted to receive a magnetic compass and a book of star constellations, and Susan was thrilled with a beautiful painting set and a pad of fine art paper.

"And this is for you," Nell said to Lucy, who'd been hopping up and down in excitement, watching everyone else unwrap their presents.

Lucy unwrapped it and stared. "It's a doll," she said. "And she's got red hair." She frowned. "And she's wearing my old blue dress." She gave Nell an odd look, clearly not as impressed with her present as she'd hoped.

Nell smiled. "Turn her upside down."

Bemused, Lucy turned the doll upside down and gasped as the old blue skirts fell down to reveal a head. "It's another doll," she exclaimed, and then, "She looks like a princess." The doll was dressed in a sparkly white dress with blue satin bows, and she wore a glittery tiara in her elegant, red wool hair.

Suddenly Lucy's eyes opened wide. "It's Cinderella!" she almost shouted. "Look, here she's Cinders, and here"—she turned the doll upside down—"she's the princess, going to the ball!"

"Yes, but she's not Cinderella," Nell corrected her.

Lucy turned, quite prepared to argue her case.

"She's Luciella," Nell said with a smile.

"Luciella?" Lucy whispered. She turned the doll back and forward, marveling over the transformation. Then she clasped the doll tightly to her chest and turned to Nell. "Is there a prince?"

Everyone laughed.

"Not yet, darling," Maddy told her. "You'll have to wait a while yet for your prince." She leaned contentedly back against hers.

Lucy nodded, content, and turned her gaze to Nash. "Isn't there a present for Mr. Rider?"

He laughed and slipped his arm around Maddy. "I have the best present of all, Lucy—a new family."

"And we've got a new family, too," Jane said with quiet satisfaction.

Now, in the cold gray light of dawn, they stood on the deck of the ship, about to sail with the morning tide.

On the docks below, Harry and Nell waved, Torie sitting on Harry's shoulders, one fist knotted in his hair, the other hand waving vaguely. Marcus stood aloof and grave beside Lady Gosforth, who was swathed in furs and dabbing a lace handkerchief to her eyes. Rafe, Ayisha, and Luke had come to wave them off, too, Ayisha with her little spotted cat on a leash, like a dog. Only Lizzie was absent. Maddy had said good-bye to her at Whitethorn. Nash had given Reuben the position of estate manager, and Lizzie was as proud as punch. She'd wept, though, promising to write.

Maddy stood with Nash and the children at the rail, waving, smiling, and teary-eyed. Nash slipped his arms around her. "You're not sorry to be leaving England?"

She shook her head. "Not as long as I have you. I'll miss everyone, of course, but we can write, and we'll be back from time to time, won't we? So go ahead, Nash Renfrew; waltz me away. Wherever you lead, I'll follow."

"To the world and beyond," Nash told her. "A team."

Historical Note

The Grand Duchess Anna Petrovna Romanova in fact died as a baby. In this story she didn't die, but had a long and happy life.

Marie Antoinette really did have a farm at *le Hameau de la Reine,* near Versailles, where the queen and her ladies liked to play at milkmaids. There was not, as far as I know, a beekeeper among them.